SENSELESS

Damien Galeone lives in Prague, where he teaches English at a small university, eats sandwiches and writes a blog. He is unable to smell stuff and plays roulette once a month.

He invites readers to email him at dg@damiengaleone.com

SENSELESS

DAMIEN GALEONE

ISBN-10 1463701756
ISBN-13 978-1463701758

To E.G.

1

He was hearing the story for the seventh time.

He was almost certain, anyway. Once every October since 1999 and twice on request—he vaguely recalled a persistent customer and a persuasion tip. So, yes, this was the seventh time.

He was standing behind the bar regarding the funny bald man with the pink face standing on the rungs of a barstool. It was a creation myth, he thought, the creation of Larry's Pub and Grub, growing and changing with each retelling. This time, as far as he could remember the seventh, three edits had been made.

This time, the man's winnings had risen by $430, the suicide got messier and the phone call to the police got wittier.

The bar at Larry's Pub and Grub in Oakland, Pittsburgh, resembled most other bars in Pittsburgh. A long, red-topped bar that ran along the wall, a rectangular mirror behind it, dozens of bottles and four taps. From a nail above the mirror hung a purple thong with a white stain, pressed into the frame on the side of the mirror were a picture of someone's impressive cleavage, and postcards of both a naked fat woman and an elephant, neither of which discernable from the other without squinting. Four lanterns hung above the bar, one cracked. The stools had cushioned backs.

The man behind the bar was in a state of constant, aware motion. There was an ease to it, careful not to draw attention away from drinks or the pursuit of leisure. Drafts to customers, whiskeys on ice, cocktails to the waitresses, pick up the drinks, wipe the bar – nobody likes a sticky bar. His perpetual activity was incongruous to the inaction of his customers, most of whom were gathered around the bald man telling the story a perch the stool.

The barman's hair was slick with sweat on the sides and frizzy on top, he listened to the story, noting the changes, admiring the caesura. It was a legend. As the ending drew near, he poured the shots that always came,

7

and went, along with it. He dropped a splash of peppermint schnapps into his blue coffee mug and waited for the ending.

When it came, the bald man stood a hair higher on the metal rung and raised his shot glass, "To Louis becoming a silent partner."

Everyone laughed, cheered and drank. The barman downed the schnapps and opened his mouth, the fresh, intoxicating spring of peppermint dancing on his tongue, and then he cleared the empty shot glasses.

It was the eighth time, the barman thought, as he realized that he had somehow forgotten the first time.

The barman was Phineas Troy, the bald man Larry Joycowski, usually called Larry Joy, the bar was Larry's Pub and Grub and the date, October 4, 2004. And for Phineas, this was his eighth hearing of the story that always changed.

His part in the story began five years earlier.

In the exaggerated manner of every bar room tale, Phineas' story too would become legend. His story would be told and retold; the imaginary parlayed with the truth, until it, like all others, ended, and in doing so became the beginning of another story.

In any case, his part in the story began five years earlier.

2

In 1999, at the age of twenty four, Phineas Troy was the poster boy for collegiate post graduates in the United States. He was $14,000 in debt, holder of a somewhat useless degree in journalism and a painfully underpaid intern at *The Rock Courier*. He covered concerts, wrote book, album and movie reviews and interviewed local musicians. He also worked part-time at the university library and wrote freelance articles for the city's two free papers to make ends meet.

One afternoon in December, Phineas stood at the Giant Eagle supermarket with coupons he had been clipping to stock up on groceries for the weekend. He liked shopping for food; he would stroll along with his cart, prod the vegetables like his grandmother had shown him, press the packaged meat with his index finger (to measure rebound) and scoff at the dented cans and two for one sales. Sometimes he played make-believe and collected all the food he wanted, piling them in his cart with promises of nourishment, then he'd sigh and return 98% of the items to the shelves before wandering to the six items or less line.

On this Friday he pushed the cart, leaning over it with his elbows, and swayed his hips to the piped elevator-rock medley that was constantly being interrupted by calls for price check and notifications of employee phone calls. He chose his groceries with care, a 3 lb. portion of ground beef for $2.99, 32oz. can of Aunt Susie's Corn Chowder for 99 cents (with coupon), four russet potatoes for 32 cents, a carrot and a pound of Giant Eagle brand American cheese for $1.99 (for Giant Eagle value card holders, which Phineas had been for years).

The line at check out stretched into ladies' needs, the seed of which was an ancient woman arguing over the price of eggs. She explained to red-faced employees that the price was too high as she had paid 65 cents less the week before. They, in turn, explained that it hadn't been the week before, but 1982 and the price was nonnegotiable. Phineas flapped his lips with a long breath, seeing no end in sight and no other line opening, and searched for reading material. A Penny Saver stuffed between the front gates of his cart suited his immediate need and he pulled it out, tearing the bottom. He flipped through the advertisements, stopping at anything interesting or unusual (Desk for sale. Dog for sale. Who needs an old person? Do you desire sex and have a stump?). Tapping his foot at the octogenarian in the front of the line, something caught his eye. BARTENDER WANTED, CALL 412-363-1208, ASK FOR GIZMO.

Later that evening, after the giggling had finally stopped, Phineas asked again. "May I please speak to Gizmo, please?"

He sat in the drafty, yet relative warmth of his third floor Squirrel Hill apartment wearing a sweater, pajama bottoms, socks and slippers. A dark blue winter cap sat on his coffee table in case of temperate emergency. The comforting aroma of cooked-just-soon-enough ground beef and hearty corn chowder thickened the air around him. The windows had iced over and fogged from the cold air. A made for TV Christmas movie played on the muted television featuring a young boy in hysterics over the tortuous hijinks of a coonskin-cap-donning bully.

"Hold on," the older woman said in a gravelly voice, then she coughed into the receiver and plopped it down with a thud. Phineas felt the blood beat in his cheeks as the thought of being played a dunce rolled through his mind. People laughed in the background and Phineas heard the woman's voice murmur over the tinkling of glasses and a sports commentator on television. Someone barked an order for a beer. The receiver fumbled against the hard surface.

"Gizmo here," the man coughed and there was more laughing. Phineas imagined him winking to people and suppressing a guffaw.

"Uh hi, I'm calling about the bartending job." Phineas spoke tentatively but was getting annoyed. He slapped his hand onto the coffee table and his spoon jumped with a rattle.

"Yeah, you got any experience?"

"Not really," he winced, keeping his mouth frozen in an expectant grin that bore his teeth.

"Hm, you know Larry's Pub and Grub daan Oakland?"

"Yeah, I know it." Phineas released his cheeks from the grin and squinted as his memory leaped into action.

"Can you be there, I don't know, Sunday noon?"

"Yeah sure, um, ask for Gizmo?"

"No, ask for Larry. See you Sunday."

"My name's Phineas, by the way."

"Good, see you Sunday."

"Bye," Phineas hung up the phone and turned up the volume on the television. He slid onto his lower back and popped his slippered feet onto the coffee table. It started to snow as Phineas fitted the unfinished Pittsburgh Post Gazette crossword puzzle next to his soup bowl. He tapped his pen on the neatly-folded paper, then he doodled a large dog and contemplated a cheese sandwich.

Phineas' hands covered his eyes as he peered through the '*&*' and the '*Grub*' on the glass-front door into the dark restaurant. He checked his watch: 12:06 p.m. He looked through again and saw the long bar backed by shelves of high-priced alcohol standing at attention. Phineas stepped back for a moment and read the hours of operation: 11-2 a.m. Mon-Sat, 12-1 a.m. Sun. He jammed his hands into his jeans and tried to stomp the cold from his feet. The collar of his dark navy pea-coat was turned up around his neck and the edge of his wool cap covered his ears.

Some movement deep inside the room caught his eye and Phineas leaned against the door to get a clearer look. Two large men wearing Carhartt work suits carried a long pipe through the room. A cigarette bounced on the lip of the man in front and the man bringing up the rear was wearing a Pittsburgh Steelers' winter cap. A fluffy, white ball rode on top of his head.

"Phineas, I'm guessing?"

Phineas turned his head to see a pink-cheeked man dancing in place, holding out a gloved hand. His face was pleasant, Phineas thought, and round like a small boy's. "I'm Phineas, are you Larry?"

"Yep, nice to meet you." They shook hands and Phineas smiled at him. Larry jammed his hands back into his pockets and jerked his head toward the pub.

"Bitch of a problem here."

"What happened?" Phineas bent his knees and leaned back to peek through the door again. The men were nowhere to be seen.

"Friggin' water main breaks daan the bathroom. Damn thing blew this morning raand six."

"When did you get here?" Phineas made an O with his mouth and blew out the visible, cold air.

"Got here raand seven this morning." Larry shook his head with irritation. "Work here all damn night, have a few after work and get home to crash and my phone rings at six with this crap. You believe that shit?"

"Who called you?"

"Ah, one of the Mexicans I got cleaning the place after aarrs. I haven't had Spanish in twenty-some years, it took me forever to figure out what the hell was going on." He shook his head and snorted. "Anyway, you want a grab some lunch?"

"Sure, but I'm a bit, uh—"

Larry nodded, "A bit tight at the moment?"

"Yeah, well, maybe just some coffee or, um, bread?"

"Forget it, I know a place and plus, I can claim this kind of stuff."

The 1983 Duster that Larry Joy pushed into second gear, with Phineas' help, rolled across Forbes Avenue, up Oakland Avenue and farted a gray clump of smoke as it inched into progress along Fifth Avenue. Newspapers and various auto-parts, an empty pizza box and several home-made cassettes were scattered throughout the backseat. Phineas closed his eyes, shivered and mouthed the words, "Oh my God," as he exhaled. He bit his lower lip and Larry looked over at him as they crossed the Birmingham Bridge.

"Sorry about the windows, man." He shot forth two short giggles. "It ain't faar." The two front windows, the only two in the car, were frozen or jammed into place two inches above the window jambs. Phineas held onto his thighs and looked out the window, recalling the questioning twitch of fear that'd hit him moments before when Larry had pulled on a balaclava.

In this moment, for a reason Phineas couldn't understand, rolling across the Birmingham in 20-below weather in a windowless Duster, Phineas loved Pittsburgh. The pale sun hung over the skyline, smoke stacks produced their namesake and a few cars made their way along Carson Street. Despite his frozen state and his strange new comrade, Phineas smiled at this new, momentary adventure.

Larry turned toward the slopes then made a quick right, up past Jane and Sarah Streets and through an underpass, made a left at a transmission shop and up into the Southside Slopes. The row homes announced comfort and warmth, Phineas wanted to leap from his frozen seat, knock on a door and ask for a drink and a kielbasa. Smoke came from chimneys and neatly-lined garbage cans stood outside of most of the houses, waiting for the overwhelming influx that would occur later that day after the football game and then, ultimately, Monday morning pickup.

Just when Phineas had had enough and was seconds away from explaining an unexplainable medical or familial emergency, a dead pet or an incredibly recent stroke of luck that eradicated all need for dependent employment and, more importantly, this ride, Larry pulled over and stopped. They sat on a steep hill which overlooked the Monongahela River and Carson Street. Larry slipped the car into first, yanked the emergency brake back as far as possible and removed a brick from under his seat. After he propped the brick behind his back tire, they walked to the row homes across the street from the view of the river. One row home had broad, blacked-in windows and a wooden sign above the door that read: MAMA'S.

Phineas recognized the woman behind the bar as the telephone woman by her throaty voice and the great amount of laughter that she coughed through at his expense. When she had finished, she stuck her cigar back between her teeth and looked at Larry. "Gizmo?" she asked. Phineas' face grew red from both the temperature change and his escalating embarrassment.

"I don't know, Mum," Larry said, helping himself to a handful of cashews from a bowl on the bar. "Seemed like a good idea when I called in the ad."

And what time was that, sweetie?" She pulled another draft.

"Bout four a.m. last Tuesday."

"Sober?" She placed the beer onto the coaster in front of a fat man eating soup and slid 75 cents from the pile of money in front of him. He nodded and soup dribbled into his beard.

Phineas glanced around the room and, for the second time in ten minutes, mouthed a blasphemous expletive. A large black woman spun around on her stool with the concentrated assistance of a bearded man who resembled a down-on-his-luck mall Santa. A cigarette stuck out from his beard somewhere and his face was red with exertion.

"Whoo, whoo, whoo, he, he, he," the woman called.

"As a judge, mum," Larry said, popping a few cashews into his mouth.

"I love you, m'boy," she leaned across the bar and wiped his cheek. Phineas smiled at the sweetness of the gesture, it made him miss his own mom. "But you are a bigger bullshitter than your father was." She slapped his cheek, leaving a white imprint.

"Ouch," Larry lurched backwards, cashews jumping from his mouth.

Christmas lights had been hung around the room by, Phineas guessed, a drunken dwarf with depleted motor skills. The lights zigzagged, hung straight down at spots and shone dimly about three and a half feet from the floor. Another customer barked for a beer, literally barking like a seal; the barmaid poured it. A man with bushy eyebrows, surrounded by shopping bags filled with newspaper sat with the fidgety apprehension of a man who expected to receive a beer in his lap at any moment.

"Babe, you want something?" The barmaid looked at Phineas and Phineas looked at Larry.

"I'm having a beer, get what you want," Larry said.

"Light, babe?" she said to Larry.

"Yeah, thanks."

"May I please have a beer please too, ma'am?" Phineas asked. Larry and his mom laughed.

"Baby, you call me Mama, okay?"

"Yes, ma'am."

She poured him a beer as the other customers and Larry watched a Steelers' pre-game show on television.

"Phineas, this is my mum." Larry turned to them.

"I'm Phineas, nice to meet you."

"You too, babe." She put down his beer.

"Thank you, could you please show me where the bathroom is, please?" Phineas "double pleased" in moments of anxiety.

Mama pointed to a corner and Phineas nodded and stepped away from the bar. When he'd left, Mama leaned across the bar and turned Larry's face from the television by his chin. "This is the boy asking for a job?"

"Yep," Larry stretched his eyes as far as he could to see the television.

"You gonna haar him."

"I don't know yet."

"Larry Joycowski, that was not a question." She pulled his face until his eyes met hers and she leaned in more. "He's a good boy, he says please and thank you and yes ma'am. He's honest and he's got a heart. I can tell. Understand?"

"Yeah, I know. I think so too."

Phineas sat back down and sipped his beer. His face had begun to grow a mid-winter white again. Mama looked at him. "Good," she released Larry's face. "Now yinz two order some lunch and a few beers and it's all on Mama, okay? No questions asked, got it?"

"Yes ma'am, I mean, yes Mama," Phineas said and pulled open the menu. He hadn't eaten at a restaurant in four months.

"Good. Larry?"

"Okay mum," he said and turned to Phineas. "Okay, let's talk about this job before the game starts."

And so, Phineas heard the story for the first time. The story started with the ending of an infamous losing streak and involved a one-eyed bartender and a crocodile; it ended with a violent suicide and a phone call to the police.

Phineas, over a satisfying lunch of hamburgers and crinkle fries, told his own tale, though even he knew that his story paled in comparison. His tale told of his struggle to find a place and a path in his collegiate career. His story started in archaeology, ran through several humanities-based departments before landing in journalism. It told of a regrettable wild period, a gain weight of thirty-seven pounds and a sheepish visit to student health for insecticidal shampoo. Phineas talked about *The Rock Courier* and, after a few beers, admitted that while music journalism seemed a romantic occupation, it was, in fact, a disappointing and boring affair. The afternoon continued with drunken laughter and a football game won in the final play of the game which cost Larry $66. By the time Phineas caught a taxi back to Squirrel Hill (Larry's treat, as he was too drunk to drive); he'd been employed as a bartender and had made a friend.

The first six weeks of Phineas' employment as bartender at Larry's Pub and Grub were inventorial and medical nightmares. He broke three bottles of Stolichnaya vodka ($19 each), two bottles of Booker's bourbon ($48 each) at the same moment, a bottle of Bearitage red wine ($27), and a bottle of Early Times whiskey ($9). He broke pint glasses, shot glasses, and wine glasses. He forgot food and drink orders. He mistapped two kegs, one of which exploded all over Larry Joy, the other all over Phineas. Phineas had to clean the beer room after each incident. He handed in bar drawers $23 under, $29 under and $35 over, all of which Larry fixed after hours in his tiny office counting money, searching receipts, drinking vodkas with soda and smoking cigarettes.

Phineas received three stitches in his left thumb after a lime cutting accident. He sustained a huge gash in the back of his head due to a run-in with an open cooler door. He broke his little toe after dropping a keg on it, and his hands had cracked so badly from the sanitizer and cold water in the sinks that he needed to apply a special cream and Larry had to clean glasses during his shift for a week: doctor's orders.

In addition to this, *The Rock Courier* went under, dragging with it, of course, Phineas' job and any hopes of a respectable letter of reference. He was working four day shifts at the bar and Friday, Saturday and Sunday at the library. He was about to quit, about to admit that bartending was another one of those occupations that is romantic from the outside and crap from within, when the Monday night bartender, Lucy Franks, got pregnant and moved back to her parents' house in Baltimore.

Having nobody else available and no time to train anyone, Larry bit his cheek, rolled the dice again and gave Phineas the night shift, nearly doubling Phineas' weekly income. Phineas decided to stay for the time being.

One Tuesday, during the lunch rush, a woman approached the bar and sat down with a thump. She wasn't able to get a table, she explained, and then asked for a menu. She was large and black, with a monstrous bottom and wore massive, tinted glasses, which covered the entire top of her face. She was nice and she smiled at Phineas, so he treated her with his natural friendliness. She became his first and only regular customer, and he always had her diet cola ready and a fork and knife set for her. She began bringing friends with her, all women, all big, all friendly, all worked at the university, most of them in the Geology department. They had their meatball sandwiches, personal pizzas and diet colas. They made jokes, had fun and laughed, Phineas loved it.

After a little while they began coming for happy hour (4-6 p.m. $1 off all cocktails) and brought more girls from the university. Instead of their sandwiches and soft drinks, they drank cocktails and shots. They flirted with him, he flirted back. They ordered Gibsons because the pearl onions resided in a low cooler, requiring Phineas to bend over and give the girls an unwitting glimpse of his round rump. They giggled and whispered "mm, mm, girl" to each other, opened their eyes wide, sipped their Gibsons and vodka tonics and ate garlic bread.

They asked him on dates, he never accepted, they never expected him to accept. After he had refused so many times with credible excuses, he invented a phantom girlfriend named Julie Jones, who everyone knew was fake but they demanded as many details about her as possible. She was from a Mennonite family and studied Architecture at Loyola University in Chicago; she was tall and had brown hair. She enjoyed Robert Ludlum's spy novels and Hawaiian pizza.

Nevertheless, the Day-Bar Harpies (Larry's label for Phineas' cult) were good-natured, and loyal. When Phineas started working the Tuesday night shift, they showed up eager to drink, bringing dozens of portly friends and acquaintances. It was, as Larry had once coined the phrase, "A fat bar, for a fat man."

Then something interesting began to happen: Phineas began to get better. Then he began to get good. He remembered tabs, food and drink orders. He never broke anything and rarely hurt himself anymore. In the hectic onslaught that the Day-Bar Harpies had brought with them, they had forced him to become a better bartender. He was sociable and witty, people enjoyed sitting at his bar, and he made them feel welcomed and relaxed. He learned how to run a bar; he knew how to start conversations and then leave people to continue them. He didn't overwhelm.

He learned the subtle science of placement, where to put people so they'd stay for more than a drink or two. He cultivated an instinct for grouping people that might compliment each other's company. He enhanced his powers of observation, what did a customer want, and what did a customer need? They came to the bar to find a friend, a lay, a shot, a shoulder, a priest, a psychologist, or sometimes, simply, some food and a drink. No matter what, Phineas learned how to provide for them. And, in time, he became better than anyone else at it. He became the best.

More importantly to Phineas, he had begun gaining the respect of his co-workers. Gomez, the head waiter with a wispy beard and pants that were always too large, had stopped slapping his forehead when he saw Phin behind the bar. The waitresses seldom returned drinks and Larry's doctor allowed him to go off his blood pressure medication.

As his occupational situation improved, his social life got worse. He had two jobs and wrote articles as a freelancer for the city papers, which devoured much of his time. Moreover, as student loans began to pile up and everyday expenses grew, his financial situation too began to worsen. Trevor, a college acquaintance that had become his roommate, bought into a Peruvian llama farm during a hash-induced vision quest and disappeared overnight. In a very short time, Phineas found himself with nobody to share rent and very few friends.

He met Amy Lucas by accident. Her car had broken down at the end of his street and Phineas, eager to assist a pretty young woman in need, stopped to offer his help. She accepted. He called a tow truck and brought her to a bar up the road where they drank beer and ate cheeseburgers while they waited. She chain smoked, spoke in an exaggerated, excited manner and laughed like an Australian at a tuna tossing festival. She had wide, sleepy eyes and a crooked nose. Phineas found her irresistible. Afterwards, he took her food shopping where he taught her how to shake vegetables and poke red meat. It was there, over cantaloupes and Granny Smith apples that they kissed for the first time.

Their first kiss was also their last kiss. As first kisses sometimes do, this one had allowed them to glimpse their shared sexual future. An experience they both found to be utterly nauseating. And so, they swore off a physical relationship. Nevertheless, there was a strong personal connection and attraction so they became fast friends and were soon inseparable. As Amy was also dealing with an unpleasant roommate situation, she eventually agreed to move in with him. Things had started to come together for Phineas, but the battle continued between his journalistic efforts and the immediate money of bar work.

The first time Phineas gave up a reporting gig to work a night shift Larry almost refused to give it to him. Phineas convinced him that he needed the money to pay his rent and while the reporting job would pay him $50, the bar shift would put $200 in his pocket. Larry conceded.

That night Phineas made $312; there was a play at The Colgate Theater down the street. The following week Sally McDaniels, one of the night bartenders, was killed in a late night head-on collision on route 376. Phineas dropped his day shifts, picked up the night shifts that Sally's death had left vacant and quit his part-time job at the library.

His student loans were paid off fourteen months later.

3

Soon after Larry's story ended people began pouring through the front door of the pub.

It was a theater night.

Larry's Pub was surrounded by five highly exploitable customer bases: the university, the university medical center, the university basketball arena, the hotel district, which held three, four-star hotels, and The Colgate Theatre. These together made Larry very happy, his waitstaff busy and Phineas and Amy financially secure and experts on customer habits.

University kids came for cheap food and game night and made grinning, sloppy-faced appearances on their twenty first birthdays. Hotel people ate and left, often tipping well because many were paying on a company card. Sometimes hotel people slipped off their wedding rings and hung around in hopes of landing an out-of-town sex partner. Hospital people, in the form of a patient's family or hospital staff, were often morose or stressed, but occasionally introduced a great regular. It was how Dr. Gary Turner had found them. He'd started stopping down after his early shifts at the hospital, his attendance becoming more frequent as his addiction to the tomato, mozzarella and basil pizza grew. He eventually became a regular, enjoying a quiet, lateral involvement in bar action. Since he rarely drank more than one beer before switching to diet cola Amy dubbed him their "non-drinking barfly." A moniker at which he rolled his eyes, yet secretly adored.

Basketball people were in and out so fast that only the trail of destruction and a full tip jar served as proof of their presence. Some basketball people came back after the game.

Theater people were the actors, actresses and crew from the nearby Colgate Theatre who came in after late rehearsals and productions. They drank rum and cokes, gin and tonics and draft beer. On production nights, theater people included the audience who packed Larry's restaurant with cheap suits, horned-rimmed glasses and a tangible quilt of pseudo-intellectual theater terminology. Tonight was a special production night to put the cap on a successful play, which meant that Phineas was busy with a bar full of drunken, happy people and a service bar full of drink orders from the tables. Larry and Amy both offered to lend a hand but were told to keep drinking. Larry's eyes still gleamed from the shots he'd done after telling the story. A waitress approached and told him that there was a problem with the toilets, which resulted in a large swig of his bourbon and ginger ale and a doleful walk to the bathroom. "Back in a bit," he said over his shoulder.

"I gotta go, all." Gomez stood and put on his jacket. "Gotta open tomorrow and gotta date with Angela tonight."

Gary blushed. Angela was Gomez's bong, but for the first eight months that he came to Larry's, Gary thought it was Gomez's girlfriend. He learned the true extent of her torpidity only after extending an invitation to a dinner party. Every time he heard the name he blushed, thankful that his dark brown skin didn't betray his red cheeks.

After Gomez left Amy turned to Gary and lit another cigarette. "Just you and me, what do you think about that?"

"Could be worse."

"True."

Amy turned behind the bar and watched Phineas working and sweating as he made drinks. "Hey Phinny, when you get done I'll buy you a shot or three."

"Already there, my dear." Phineas winked and took a slug of peppermint schnapps from a blue coffee mug. "Hair of the old terrier."

Amy laughed and Gary shook his head. He unloosened his tie and looked at his watch.

"Well," said Gary, "am I driving both of you home tonight?"

"Nah, I'll be fine," Phineas said and cleared three pint glasses from the bar to their right, water dripping from the bottoms. "I have to drive in like five hours."

"That's what worries me," said Gary.

"Me too," Amy mumbled through her drink. "He's my designated driver."

Two hours later Larry returned and was soaked. He leaned a ragged-looking mop against the bar and sat down. It was after one o'clock and the bar had let out a bit. Amy sat with Gary and a short, wiry man with several facial piercings who was drinking a rum and cola and describing his piercings. Phineas listened in discomfort. His blue mug sat in front of him.

"I've got a Prince Albert," he looked at Phineas, "that's in the cock."

"Yeah, I know."

"Okay," the man continued, "a bar through each nipple, two in this ear and three in this one, right nostril and two studs in the tongue."

Phineas rubbed his groin and grimaced. "Ouch."

Upon Larry's approach, Phineas poured him a drink. Larry's arms were slick with water and the knees of his pants were dark brown, the right leg was torn.

Larry saw the bourbon bottle in Phineas' hand. "Better pour yourself one too, buddy," he called.

"Me? Why?" Phineas pulled his hand to his chest in mock surprise. His eyes opened wide and his mouth went agape.

"Amy Lucas, beautiful babe of the bar." Larry took a knee and held her hand. "How would you like to earn yourself a few shots of vodka?"

Amy rolled her eyes. "Oh God, what do I have to do?"

"Nothing really, just watch the bar for an hour or so while Phineas rolls around in shit with me. Frankly, I think you're getting the better end of the deal."

"Okay. But you have to make that man promise to stop talking about his penis." Amy pointed at the short man and Larry looked at him with such desperation that the man drank his rum and cola and walked out without another word.

Larry rubbed his hands together, "Let's go."

"Oh, crap."

"You couldn't possibly be more right, my friend." Larry grabbed the mop and motioned for Phineas to bring along his drink. "Come on."

They reached the basement and Larry covered his nose and mouth with a clean bar-towel, "Jeezus," he said. He threw a towel to Phineas who trailed behind and drank another sip of schnapps. Phineas put it to his nose, then took the last gulp of booze and put the mug on the wide railing post.

"Here, take this." Larry handed Phineas the mop and walked forward into water that was guarded by floating excrement. Phineas followed a few feet behind and reached out to grab the men's room door that Larry was holding open. Something moved along the wall. A large, black spider had moved from the floor in hopes of a drier home. Phineas screeched and dropped his hand from the door which then hit him in the forehead. He dropped the rag into the water and jumped back to the steps. The spider scurried through the darkness and was out of sight by the time Larry had come back out to see what the noise was about. He sneered at Phineas.

"Just shut up," Phineas said as he folded his pant legs up to his ankles. "It was huge."

"Let's go, dummy." Larry held the door again and Phineas held his breath and followed inside. The two men worked at the drains in the floor and took turns opening the tap to see if the water would stop overflowing.

On his next turn Phineas bent down to open the water pressure. He took in a deep breath through his mouth, held it and then began to open the pressure. The water began overflowing instantly and he turned it off. As he turned to stand again his shirt hooked to a small, thin pipe. He tried to remove it, but he struggled in his panic and was forced to breathe through his nose.

"Oh, my God." He thought he might vomit. He awaited the noxious fumes of defecation and waste. He readied himself for an overwhelming stench but it never came. He breathed again, wondering if his body had refused to recognize such a repugnant odor, but there was nothing. He unhooked his shirt and stood.

"I don't smell anything."

"Are you serious?" Larry asked, holding the bar rag over his face, which had grown a deep red that spread to the hair-free skin of his head.

He looked like a beet.

Phineas took a deep breath again. "Yeah, there's nothing. Are you sure it reeks down here?"

Larry took the towel from his face for a second and whiffed once. Phineas patted his back while he hacked and coughed.

Larry kept his elbows on his knees and breathed out through his mouth. "Let's call Al the plumber." He spit a strand of drool into the water.

"Let's go have a drink."

"Yes, let's do that."

As they ascended the steps to the bar, Gary and Amy began cheering a nameless collegiate fight song, but after seeing Larry's red, irritated face and Phineas' inquisitive looks and incessant sniffing, they stopped singing and Amy poured heavy shots of bourbon, Irish whiskey and peppermint schnapps.

4

The next day, at 2 p.m., Amy cracked open the door to Phineas' room and peered in. The room was as dark as his blinds would allow, with bright, dust-filled beams of light streaming in through small apertures, some strong enough to reach the bed. For the most part, the room remained dark and dank, stinking of dirty laundry soaked in various types of alcohol. The residual scent of chlorine from Amy's morning swim battled to be noticed, but soon lost out to the odor of old booze. Clothes were scattered on the floor and moldy plastic cups sat on his bureau, the windows were shut and the distant sound of street construction scraped at the walls. A clock ticked on the night table.

Phineas lay in the middle of it all, on a high-perched bed, half covered by a thick quilt and snoring into a pillow. Amy took off a flip-flop and threw it at him, striking him in the shoulder. He moaned, scratched his beard, dislodged a wedgie through an impressively graceful ballet-like move, and fell back to snoring.

Amy crept into the room, inching her way to the bed, she arched her back and curled her hands into a bullhorn around her mouth.

"Wakey, wakey little Phinny!" she yelled into the ceiling. She glanced down at him, but Phineas grumbled and pulled a pillow over his head.

She moved onto the bed and breathed a stroke of air into Phineas' face, to no avail. When he breathed, the almost liquid aroma of peppermint schnapps and beer singed her nose hairs. She laughed at him and sat up in the bed, wiping her hands on the quilt.

Amy reached over and pinched his pug nose between her thumb and forefinger. The snoring stopped, but after a moment he made several porcine noises through his mouth until the lack of air forced him to open his eyes and stare into Amy's.

"Ah, you're so cute," Amy said, mocking a mother's voice.

"What's happening?" Phineas asked. He moved his head and winced, shutting his eyes. "Head hurts."

"Do you need something?"

"Death. Please kill me." Phineas shut his eyes and lay back.

"Okay," Amy said and stuffed a pillow down on his face.

"Ah, stop, you shrew!" he pleaded for mercy. "Pills, pills are better."

"This is actually fun, can we do this every morning, um, afternoon?" Amy leaned on the pillow harder until Phineas loosened a hand and gripped her right nipple between his thumb and forefinger. He twisted until she squealed in pain.

She jumped off the bed. "Listen, jackass!"

"I got you good."

Amy laughed and started walking around the room, opening the blinds. "You need to get up and get yourself together so you can give me a ride." She gathered some of the clothing scattered on the floor and stuffed it into the already overflowing hamper.

"A ride—" Phineas sat upright in bed and his face showed terror. "Oh my God! Did I—"

"No, dummy, you didn't, *I* did." She opened the last blind and looked around, unsatisfied.

"Oh Jesus, thank God." He dropped onto his back and hid his face from the streams of light coming in through the now unobstructed windows. "Please, just let me hide for a while."

"No drunk-boy, I need a ride and you've got to give it to me."

"Take a bus."

"You're joking, right?"

"Of course I'm joking. Just—just give me a minute, okay?"

"All right. But first I'm going to air this place out a little." She pulled the window open and walked to the other one. "Then I'll leave you alone." She pulled the other window open and smiled at the sweet air that attacked the room. "See, doesn't that feel nice?" She grinned at his covered face. "See you in a few minutes," she said, patting the bed on her way out.

Thus began his morning detective routine. The mirror on the door betrayed his form: bloated and pale, squinting through a temporary, alcohol-induced blindness. His beard was a week old and his stomach protruded over his boxer shorts, back through which his penis had begun retreating from its morning vigil. Besides his boxers, he wore only socks, which had, through a centrifugal force that can only occur during sleep, rotated 180 degrees. The gray heel-patch protruded from the top of his foot.

He began the search for clues to the mythical end of his evening—the end of his intoxicated rainbow. His first course of action was in the clothes he had worn the night before. His shoes, laces still tied and covered in waste from his adventures in the flooded basement, were a foot apart and topped by his pants. It looked as if someone had evaporated and left his sad, empty clothing on the floor, waiting for him to return. His shirt, on the back of his armchair in the corner, was streaked in dirt and missing a button.

Fear struck him as he thought of tackling a stranger in the middle of a grassy knoll. Fear struck him worse as he imagined the man an undercover police officer. Worse still, as he imagined the man laying in that fictional patch of grass where nobody would find him and where he would die an innocent bystander to Phineas' moronic drunken activities. He broke a sweat.

Phineas stood in his trance, envisioning the worst that could have happened, then doubling it and tripling it and adding details until he was in immobile terror of his own unreal past. Amy poked her head in the room. "Are you taking me to work like that?"

"No, sorry Ame. Give me a sec." Phineas was startled into action.

He reached for his pants and relief hit him when he felt his wallet in the front pocket. He checked his funds. Two hundred and sixty dollars and one receipt from Goober's hotdog shop where he had, apparently, tipped an angel named Brenda seventeen dollars for bringing him two hotdogs at 5:18 a.m. After trying to deduce why he would use a credit card when he was carrying over $260 in cash, he unfolded the receipt to learn that Brenda had also brought him a ginger ale and, judging from the mustard stains on the crotch of his pants, no napkins. His signature looked as if it had been signed by someone with cerebral palsy.

In the right pocket of his pants he found two cocktail napkins, one had a phone number with no name and the other read: *not Tuesday, Friday bank, chili, check urine, peaches, important-bread.* Phineas frowned, more cryptic messages that would never be deciphered.

He pulled on a shirt, jeans and a pair of sandals and dropped his shoes on the back porch. Dabbing some toothpaste on his tongue, he checked his mouth for sores, his eyes for signs of jaundice and squeezed the lymph nodes behind his jaw. He knuckled the tiny hairs that pointed from the top of his nose and smiled at the Mohawk haircut that had formed in the night. He put on a Philadelphia Phillies cap and pulled a dark sweater over his shoulders and paunch. At least he had shoulders, he thought, arching them back, some chubby guys don't have shoulders and they look terrible. Also, if they can't grow a beard, they're screwed. At least he had facial hair and shoulders. He smiled, swallowed and walked out of the room.

"Oh, your dad called," Amy said as she rolled a lint brush across her chest.

"When?" He began to sweat again.

"Couple hours ago. He said to call him when you can. You ready?"

The cats were sniffing around empty hot dog cartons and Phineas glanced at the answering machine—no messages. Phineas looked at the cats. "Burt!" he yelled, "Ernie! Get out of there, you guys!" The cats scampered out of sight and Amy walked into the room.

"Don't yell at them." She looked hurt. "You're the one who left the cartons on the floor, drunk-boy."

"I know."

"Great, now they're going to take turns shitting next to the litter box all night. You happy?"

"Vindictive little monkeys." Phineas tightened his jaw. He grabbed his keys from the coffee table. "Okay, let's go."

They wandered to the car and Amy lit a cigarette, inhaled, turned her head away from Phineas and exhaled. She dug through her purse, the sound resonating through the cobbled back street in Squirrel Hill. They were the only two on the street.

"Gomez's at The Grub and wants to know if you want lunch."

"Do I?"

"Yeah," she scanned him up and down. "You could use some sustenance."

Amy found a hair-band in her maroon leather bag and slid the bag up her arm. She wrapped the hair-band around her wrist and pulled her shoulder length hair tightly with her right hand and then, like a cosmetics ninja, slid the hair-band down her left wrist and left her hair in a perfect ponytail. Phineas shook his head; it always amazed him.

"How do I look?" Amy said and turned toward him. She spread her arms out and rotated as if she was standing on a turntable. She had a swimmer's body; a flat stomach, long and lean muscular legs and broad feminine shoulders. Her crooked nose was the result of a collision with a low-lying branch during a drunken run from police. However, she would never ask Phineas about her looks. What she meant was cat hair.

A year before, Amy had convinced Phineas that it would be a good idea to adopt cats after she read an article about the growing number of homeless cats in Pittsburgh. Phineas, in a moment of weakness that he was never quite able to comprehend, agreed. As kittens they were cute and sweet and made squeaky purring sounds when they sat on his chest and pawed at his sweaters. However, they grew. And as they grew, so did their abilities to make noise and leave fur in unwanted locales. In an apartment with hardwood floors and high ceilings the hair gathered under chairs and tables, in corners and on beds. It was in food, drinking glasses, on the couch, in the refrigerator and microwave and in their clothes. Amy became obsessed with cat hair and bought several lint brushes, many of which had been dragged behind the couch and used as play things.

"You're fine."

"Thank God."

"Ame," he slipped his hands into his pockets.

"Yeah?"

"Please don't let Gomez make me drink."

"Oh, okay, I promise." She smirked; he made the same request at least three times a week and always ended up drunk.

Amy and Phineas arrived at Larry's pub twenty minutes later. They walked through the front door and Phineas let out a breath; a return to the scene of the crime. They passed the hostess stand and walked to the bar, which Amy got behind and started sorting through coolers and refrigerators. The restaurant was mid-afternoon empty, with a few tables of people in quiet conversation. Tom Waits sang about mornings after and the waitresses moved to the sad sounds, restocking and cleaning.

"Mr. Troy!" Gomez called from the corner of the bar. "Get your ass over here and order a drink!"

"I can't even think about alcohol."

"Who asked you to think?" Amy asked from behind the bar.

Phineas affected an expression of betrayal. "Et tu, Ame?"

Amy scanned each beer cooler and garnish bowl. She counted juice cans and sent the day bartender down the stairs with a restock list. Phineas shuffled toward Gomez and put his hands in his pockets.

"Yeah," Gomez finally added.

"Well, I guess I can't argue with that." Phineas sat on the stool next to his friend. He looked at Amy. "Why don't you drop those bottles and make yourself useful? I'll have a Bloody Mary, spicy, extra olive juice."

"That's more like it," Gomez said. "And two shots of Irish whiskey."

"Well, here we go."

Amy looked at Gomez. "Ducky, would you like another beverage?"

"Uh-huh," he pulled on the straw with his lips until the drink disappeared.

Gomez was one of the most highly educated waiters in Pittsburgh. After graduating at the top of his class from the university, he entered an MBA program with a dual master in computer science. After graduating at the top of that class, and with enough distinction to draw the attention of the most respected financial firms in the country, he went to work for Gardner Inc. in Pittsburgh. He continued to work part-time at Larry's to sustain both his cocaine and gambling habits, but after a year of falling asleep at his desk and colleague comments and complaints he decided things had to change. He had a sturdy talk with himself, renounced his lifestyle and made promises to shape up and get with the program. However, three hours and five Manhattans later he made another promise to never wake up before 10 a.m. again in his entire life. This one stuck. The very next day he quit Gardener Inc. by neglecting to show up. For the two years since then, Gomez had been the head waiter. He lived in the joyous state of perpetual college, sans classes.

"Heard you ended up getting shitty last night." Gomez made a face and opened his mouth wide.

"Oh, very good. Why aren't you still working?"

"Huh, oh Tara needs some extra cash so I let her take the second part of my double."

"That's nice of you. Is it really that you just needed a drink?"

"It sure is." Gomez nodded.

"And I might as well be on this boat as it goes down, huh?"

"Yep, speaking of which, here're the shots."

"Oh, dear God." Phineas shivered.

"What shall we drink to?" Gomez asked, holding his glass up.

"October 4?" Phineas picked up his glass as a look of disgust dressed his face.

"Sure, there it is." Gomez tapped his glass to Phineas'. "To October 4." They drank and Phineas regretted it. A wave of heat hit him and a load of excess saliva rushed to his mouth.

"Phinny, you okay?" Amy asked him.

"Yeah, I think I need to get some air. I'll be back." Phineas slid off the stool and started toward the door. Amy chased him down and handed him her cell phone.

"You can call your dad while you're out there."

"Thanks." The cool air filled his lungs and the sweat on his brow chilled. The traffic was light and the October sky was a brilliant, late afternoon blue. Leaves danced along the ground and two old black men sat on steps across the street and smoked cigarettes. A student walked by and Phineas looked to the sidewalk. The phone rang.

"Dr. Troy's office," a woman's voice whined.

"Hey Donna, it's Phin. Is Dad there?"

"Oh, hey hon. How you doing?" She sounded sympathetic.

"I'm okay. You?" The first alcohol of the day began to buzz through his system, he felt light-headed and euphoric.

"Doing okay," her voice rose in the fake-pleasant manner of a person who'd spent most of her life on the phone. "Let me get your dad for you."

"Thanks, Donna." Now he felt good, frisky.

"Phin?" His father's voice croaked into the receiver.

"Hey Dad, what's up?" He kicked a small rock down the sidewalk.

"Well, something bad."

He stopped. "What happened?"

"Grandmom died."

"Oh no. How? When?" He felt selfish.

"She had a heart attack last night."

"What?"

"She called an ambulance, but when they got there she was dead."

"Oh no." He was frozen in place.

"Yeah." His father sighed, and then it was quiet.

"Jesus, are you okay?"

"I'll be fine."

"Why are you working?" Now he began fidgeting and pacing.

"Oh, there was an emergency. Uh, Mrs. Trotter had an abscessed molar; nobody could cover it, so …"

"I'm sorry."

"Listen, the funeral's Friday, can you be here?"

"Uh, I think. Let me check, but it should be fine. How's Mom?"

"She's fine."

"How's Clay?"

"He's fine, too. She was my Goddamn mother for Christ's sake." His father's voice was old and dusty, like the inside of a chest in an attic.

"I know, I know, I'm sorry. Is there anything I can do?"

"No, just come home when you can."

"Yeah, I will. I'll talk to you soon."

"Okay. See you soon."

"Bye Dad. Love you."

"Love you too. Bye Phin."

Phineas switched the phone off and stood outside for a moment. The two black men laughed and rocked back and forth and the student was reading on a bench at the bus stop. The wind licked at Phineas' chin and he wiped a tear from the corner of his eye as he walked inside. The warmth hit him and he placed the phone on the bar. Amy was making a drink that involved a blender and, looking distressed, was searching for an open can of pineapple juice. She looked up to see Phineas.

"How's Dad?"

"Um, fine. He was with a patient, so we couldn't really chat."

"Busy dentists, I'll never figure it out," Gomez said. "Listen, we have a problem."

"Um," Phineas was dazed, he felt as though he was watching himself in a movie.

"Today is October 5, not October 4."

"Oh." Phineas' only thought was that his grandmother had died on the wrong day.

"Well, it'd be bad luck to drink to the wrong day." He pushed a shot toward Phineas and took his between his forefinger and thumb, "Happy October 5."

Phineas raised his glass, "Happy October 5."

5

Phineas' car was a 1993, two-door, blood red Dodge Neon that couldn't shift into first gear and sometimes fifth. Its grille wore a bra that hid a growing spread of rust beneath. The inside of the driver's-side door had been torn off in a laundry basket accident and the stereo had been removed by someone who must have thought they could exchange it for crack and then sobered up enough to realize that it was clearly worthless. The car, for no reason whatsoever, was named Samantha.

Phineas had found that Samantha's trunk was wide and deep enough to fit a sleeping man and the backseat was large enough in which to have sex almost comfortably, both depending on the size of the person involved. The various dents were well-placed and impressive, as if someone with great anger and large biceps had taken out a personal problem on its hood and fender. If the passenger picked up the floor mat at anytime, they would have an unobstructed view of the road beneath the car.

Phineas awoke in the backseat crusty-eyed and shook his head. He looked up through the back window and into the red and brown leaves that were hanging from a large oak tree. A leaf pinched itself from a branch and spiraled toward the car. Phineas watched it drift and blinked when it tapped against the rear windshield above his eyes.

His dream had been a memory. He'd dreamt about the summer between his sophomore and junior years in college. He sat up and felt his head, which pounded against his skin. His mouth tasted like the inside of an intestine and his shirt was sticky. In the dream he was riding his bike to Spiegler's Garage where he'd worked that summer cleaning cars, pumping gas, checking fluids and changing oil for $6.25 an hour, plus tips. The dream faded as he stretched his stiff neck and grimaced, but he kept thinking about that summer. He would rise every morning at six and drink black coffee while he made his lunch. Then he'd sit at the kitchen table and watch baseball highlights on TV while reading the comics in *The Lansford Observer*. He could still hear the buzzing of the cicadas and feel the hazy, suburban summer heat.

He opened the door and pushed the front seat until it touched the steering wheel, then slumped forward and placed his foot onto the ground with a victorious growl. The sky was gray and the air was moist. Phineas steadied himself with the door jam and pulled himself out of the car. A Jack Russell terrier stood a few feet from Samantha gripped at attention as if extraordinarily fascinated with what he saw. He seemed to frown when Phineas caught his eye.

"Boze," a man called. Phineas looked up at him. He wore a brown robe and had a rolled-up newspaper in his hand. "Jeezus, son," the man said. "Are you okay?"

Phineas sniffed and coughed to catch his breath. "Yeah, I'm fine. Rough night, you know."

The man made a crooked grin and raised his eyebrows. "Guess so."

"Okay, well," Phineas stood, shuffled and locked the door behind him. "What time is it?"

The man pulled a cell phone out of the front pocket of his robe. "Ten to eight." Then he sniffed twice, "Have a little party in your car?"

"No." Phineas shook his head. "Well, I don't think so, anyway." He straightened his shirt and dusted off his pants. He rubbed his head, tried to pat down his hair with a palm and scoured the back of his throat with his tongue, produced its desired ore and spat it to the grass next to the car. The dog went for it.

"Boze!" the man barked. "Come here, now!" The dog looked confused and hung his head in disappointment. He went toward the man but, having seen a squirrel in the tree behind him, ran off to introduce himself. Phineas stumbled toward the steps in front of his apartment building.

"Have a good one," he said.

"You too, young man," the man said.

The man's mouth was between a frown and a smirk and his brow was crinkled as if he was thinking about something. He nodded and started down the street. "Boze!" he called with his back to the dog, "Let's go!"

Phineas watched the man walk down the street and found the urge
to go with him. The cobbled street was lined with cars and two children
bounced a basketball off a wall. Trees crowded the sky above the street
and wet leaves lay everywhere. Smoke came from a chimney. He picked
up the morning paper and climbed the remaining steps to his apartment
building.

Again, he thought of that summer so many years before. It was
the summer that he'd found his interest in journalism. He'd start every
morning with the comics and then fold the paper into quarters and do
the crossword puzzle. The rest of the paper held little interest for him,
until an article prompted him to write a letter to the editor. The article
defended the destruction of a one-hundred-year-old theater to make
space for a gym. He'd written the letter in the late morning hours at the
garage, between the morning and the afternoon rushes. Two days after
sending the letter, the editor called him and asked permission to print
it. Phineas was stunned, but gave the editor the go ahead. The editor
changed a few words and corrected one grammatical blip (tense shift),
but Phineas liked it, thought that it read well and saw a glimmer of hope
in his otherwise pointless academic existence.

It had been a long road to that glimmer of hope. He'd started two
years earlier in archaeology. He decided, after a year of researching the
diameter and circumference of tombs and an alarming amount of scat,
that the salient details of archaeology were best left to those who had a
predilection for research and very little need for social interaction. He'd
come to this decision during Dr. Jeffrey Calingia's human skeletal analysis
lecture (with adjoining lab study). He was sitting in the back row of the
lecture hall staring at page two-hundred sixty one of his glossy, hopelessly
enormous textbook trying to construe the structural brain differences
between Australopithecus Robustus and Australopithecus Africanus
(greater frontal lobe breadth, expanded parietal cortex and non-projecting
cerebellar lobes, with robustus on the happy side of these advantages),
when he was overcome with the intense desire to beat Dr. Calingia to
death with the tome. Instead, he walked out, leaving all of archaeology's

unearthed mysteries behind him forever.

In the first semester of his sophomore year, a logic class and the relationship of C to D produced the same desire. And again, if only to avoid twenty-five years in prison for second-degree murder, he left the room and its philosophical conundrums. Nine months and another major later (political science) he felt lost and unhappy.

A week after his first letter was published, a short, seemingly hidden article spurred Phineas to write another letter. The article outlined the state game commission's campaign to change the state fish from the Brook Trout to the Largemouth Bass. Phineas wrote in defense of the Brook Trout and it was published the following week. Fewer words had been changed and Phineas' grammar and style (thanks to E.B White and William Strunk) were left essentially unmolested.

This had sparked an interest in him. He liked seeing his words in print and got a thrill thinking that other people were reading them too. His morning routine would start with the comics and crossword, but then he'd plunge through the front page, the region page, cultural section and the AP wire. He would then tuck the opinions and sports pages into his black lunchbox, curling them around the thermos that fit into the lid above the peanut butter and jelly sandwich and pretzel sticks, and walk out the door. Journalism had been his salvation.

The door was open and he went up the three floors to his apartment. He snuck in and, remembering that Amy would either be swimming or at home awake, shut the door with a heavy thud and went inside.

Phineas stripped off his clothes and threw them on the floor. He stood naked in front of the mirror sucking in his stomach before slipping into his blue robe. "Gorgeous, you're just gorgeous." He inched closer, and then checked his tongue, nose, eyes, throat and nodes. Everything looked okay.

He put on a pot of coffee as he walked through the kitchen, hearing it bubble and fume as he went in to the bathroom. His stomach rumbled and he sat down on the toilet, holding his bowels as he flipped through the sections of the paper. He chose the comics and let his lower body become one with the toilet.

Amy pressed a knee against the door to the apartment, juggling her gym bag and the two bags of groceries she had bought on the way home from the Jewish Community Center. Her keys mocked her as she tried to slip them out without dropping any of the bags, bending into a yoga-like position that sent searing pains up her spine. "Ouch, son of a—". She gave up and dropped the bags, then pressed the tips of her pruned fingers into her palms.

She had been swimming every morning for two decades. Her father had decided that she would be an Olympic swimmer and forced her out of bed every morning and into the pool in their backyard. In the cooler months she used to ride her bike to the local community college and swim there.

She realized the front door was unlocked and pushed it open. She grabbed the bags and kicked open her bedroom door just in time to catch Ernie chewing on a bra that was lying on her bed. They caught each other's eye, Ernie paused, stunned, and for a long moment they exchanged a sneer. When she tried an awkward move he scampered off the bed and spent the rest of the day lounging under her bed, like all cats, in the exact geographical position just impossible for human hands to reach. "Ernie!" She called under the bed and went to shut the door.

The running shower and the enticing aroma of brewing coffee piqued her interest. She looked at the clock on her night stand: 8:16 a.m. "Impossible." She danced around her room, stripping off her clothes and tossing them onto her bed. She kneeled on the floor and stared into the darkness under her bed. "You leave my bras alone, you hear me?" The cat's tapetum lucidum glowed back at her before he resumed cleaning himself with long, casual strokes of his tongue.

She stood and winced as her knee clicked.

Her father's plan had worked and Amy shattered records at St. Anne's High School for girls in the 100-yard breast-stroke, 200-yard individual medley and the 200-yard freestyle. She destroyed every competitor she had had in the Catholic League swimming finals for three straight years until her competitive swimming career was ended by an off-season motorcycle accident. She still loved to swim; it cleared her head.

She pulled a pair of flannel pajama bottoms on over her legs and a sweat shirt over her goose-pimpled shoulders. "Why do you do that?" she asked the room.

The gray morning light flopped in through the two large windows of the kitchen. It was her favorite time of day. She hooked her fingers into the plastic loops of her grocery bags and skipped into the kitchen.

"Finally," she called out. "Finally, you've made *me* coffee, Phinny!" She inhaled deeply as she passed the bathroom. Her face, split with a wide grin, twisted as she coughed in disgust. "My God!" she screamed into the bathroom. "What the hell are you doing in there?"

Phineas stood under the steady stream of hot water and let her words bounce off of him. Amy opened the door, knocking simultaneously. "Are you okay?"

"Yes! Why wouldn't I be?"

"Don't snap at me," her voice was nasally, as she had pinched her nose closed.

"Sorry," he spat out a bubble of water. "Why do you sound like a nerd?"

"Because I'm holding my nose."

"Oh. Why?"

Amy's eyes widened. "Are you serious?"

"Yeah, why?"

Amy released her nose and inhaled again. "Oh my-," she choked. "Phinny, are you telling me that you honestly don't smell that?"

Phineas opened the shower curtain, wiped the water from his face and jumped a bit at the sight of Amy crouched over. "What smell?" He sniffed. Then again, for irritated effect. "Yes, I am telling you that I don't smell a thing."

Amy closed the door and went through the kitchen, dropped her bags on the floor and went out the back door to the porch. She lit a cigarette and took a deep drag. She breathed therapeutically a few times and hugged the warmth of the sweatshirt to her body. The shower stopped and she heard Phineas dry himself off as he hummed something incoherent. His wet feet slapped against the floor as he stomped off to his room. Amy put away her groceries, then took two light green coffee mugs and filled Phineas' all the way to the top. She filled her own mug two-thirds and opened the fridge for milk. Inside the fridge there were two half-gallon cartons of milk, one dated October 8 and the other dated September 18. She then hid the good milk in the unused vegetable crisper.

Phineas was wearing his robe and had a towel around his neck, one end of which he was using to clean out an ear with a forefinger. He looked comfortable.

"Here Phinny," Amy said. "A nice cup of yummy coffee."

Phineas took a sip from the cup. "Ahh," he felt like an actor in a commercial. "Hey, what were you talking about? A bad smell or something?"

"Oh, nothing really. Can you grab me the milk from the fridge," she said as she busied herself with cat food. Phineas reached into the fridge and took out the milk. "Here."

"Oh," she said over her shoulder, "can you make sure it's okay?" Amy heard Phineas crease open the carton and sniff. She waited, staring at the overjoyed cat on the box of food.

"Yeah, it's fine."

"Are you sure?"

He sniffed again, "Yeah, it's fine."

Amy turned around just as he was lowering the carton toward her coffee. "No!"

Phineas jumped with a girlish yelp and dropped the milk onto the counter. "Good Lord, woman! What the hell is your problem?"

Amy took the carton and smelled it. "Oh God, Phineas, this milk," sniff, sniff, "smells so bad I might vomit. Can't you smell it?"

Phineas took the milk, he was beginning to feel warm. "No, I really don't. Come to think of it, I couldn't smell anything a couple nights ago when the bathroom overflowed." Phineas sniffed again at the milk, "That's weird." He smiled, "Hey, maybe I've built up an immunity to bad smells. You know, from the bar or something."

Amy took the coffee pot off the burner and stuck it in front of his face. "This smells wonderful; it's the coffee your mom sent us last month. Can you smell it?"

Phineas grinned and glanced toward the door to his bedroom, considering an escape attempt.

"Don't even think of it, you! Smell now!" Amy pushed the coffee closer to his face.

He leaned his nose over the urn and took a short whiff. "Nope. Nothing."

"Shit, Phin, maybe you should see a doctor."

He felt the uncomfortable tingle of sweat begin at the top of his head. "Or maybe not. I'm going back to bed to read." He picked up the newspaper from the counter. "Do you want to come down to Larry's when I head into work?"

"No, I'm meeting the guys in the afternoon. I'll see you later, though," Amy said and went toward her room. "You gonna air that car out?"

"Why should I? Can't smell it." He hesitated, frozen in the kitchen with his mouth open.

"Yes, honey, but Pittsburgh police officers can." Then she shut her bedroom door and turned on the television.

Gary Turner was dressed in a crisp white button-down Saddles shirt. His tie was red and black striped and his khakis were neatly pressed. His leather brown shoes had been buffed that morning and his sock garters stretched around his slim calf. Phineas liked the way Gary looked, together and classy. His wire-rimmed glasses perched near the tip of his nose. His head clean shaven. He ate his pizza methodically, stopping at timed intervals to take a calculated sip of diet cola.

"I can't smell anything," Phineas said.

Gary stored a chunk of pizza in his cheek. "What, you mean at the moment?"

"No, I mean at all. At least for the last few days, anyway."

"Are you stuffed up at all?"

"Nope," Phineas inhaled to prove the normal relegation of oxygen to lungs via nose.

"Do you have any allergies?"

"Not that I know of."

"Have you been sick lately, cold, flu, anything like that?"

"Not in ages. I feel totally fine, I just can't smell a thing."

Gary collected his brow and jostled his head. "Really? That's strange."

"Yeah," Phineas sniffed a few times. "I can't figure it out. But the other night when I helped Larry out in the bathroom, I couldn't smell a thing. Then this morning, I couldn't smell coffee or, well, anything else."

Gary took a sip of diet cola. "Do you feel okay?"

"I think."

"Really? No changes in any way?"

Phineas' cheeks grew red. "I, I don't think so."

Gary put his knife and fork against his plate and focused his gaze on the bar. "Hm, now that is really strange, my friend."

"Any idea what it could be?" Phineas poured a draft and dropped it off to a man who was whispering to a woman. The man nodded when Phineas approached.

"Well, it's not really my area of expertise."

"You ever hear of anything like this?"

"Sure—" Gary knew to be gentle with Phineas in these areas. "I mean, I know it happens, but—let me think about it." Gary sat back. "There's nothing, huh?"

Phineas put both hands on the bar and leaned in to Gary. "Gary, how shall I put this? If you painted my mustache with dog poop, I wouldn't know the damn difference."

"You, Mr. Troy, paint a beautifully descriptive picture."

Gary cut into his pizza with the dullest knife in the world and brought it to his mouth. With his knuckle he nudged his glasses back and watched as Phineas read a drink ticket that spat out of the squat machine near the register. He hooked the stem of a martini glass with his forefinger and put its cone-shaped bowl into a pitcher of ice water. Then he picked up a metal shaker and poured vodka into it for six seconds, before spraying vermouth over the shaker. "Just a touch," he smiled. "So, what do you think I should do?"

"Why are you asking me? You're the drink expert. Pour the son-of-a-bitch, I guess."

Phineas huffed. "What, no, I meant about the not smelling thing."

"Oh, I think you should see a doctor."

"You're my doctor, Gary."

"I'm a friend who happens to be a doctor."

"Yeah, but you're the only doctor I trust, so maybe I can come see you in the office sometime."

"I don't think that's a good idea, Phin."

"Because we're friends?"

"No, because I'm a gynecologist."

"Oh, oh yeah, that."

Phineas poured the freezing cold vodka into the shaker and tried to smell the martini without being noticed, poking his nose over the glass and taking in a silent breath. Gary ate another square piece of pizza.

"Nothing, huh?"

Phineas laughed. "Nothing."

It was shortly after 8 p.m. and the evening sky was dark in the spooky way only an October sky can be. Phineas cleaned one of the shelves that held pint glasses. He looked at his list:

Clean pint glass shelves

Cut limes and lemons

Stock juices

Sours mix

Stock cocktail napkins and bar towels

Eat cheeseburger and have iced-tea

Make To Do list

Phineas checked off number seven and smiled.

Gary was a creature of habit and his favorite habit was going to places that made him feel welcomed and relaxed. Larry's was his favorite place. Phineas was his favorite bartender. More than that, they had become good friends.

The restaurant bustled and waitresses stormed past with trays of dirty plates then past again with trays of stacked plates, full of food. Food orders spat out of a machine in the kitchen and someone called out orders riddled with modifications.

It was early, so the bar was nearly empty, only Gary and the couple lost in close conversation. It would fill up later, as it always did, people would pour in from the theater and the hotels. Regulars would drop by around midnight, often on the way home from other bars. For the moment, though, Gary had Phineas to himself.

"So, how's everything else?" he asked Phineas as he regained his hold on the cutlery.

"Eh," Phineas shrugged and poured a draft.

"Eh? Pray tell Troy, what does eh mean?"

"What? Eh means eh. Things are fine, okay…sort of." He dropped the beer on a ticket at the wait station and clicked through channels with the remote control.

Gary eyed Phineas. He stopped chewing, and then swallowed. "What's up, man?"

Phineas flipped through channels until he found a college football game and dropped the remote on the counter next to the register. "Nothing," he said as he wiped down a bottle with his bar towel.

"Phineas, look at me." Phineas looked at him. "What's up?"

"Uh, nothing, well, not nothing, I don't know, it's just, it doesn't really—"

"You're babbling."

"My grandmom died yesterday."

Gary stared at him. "I'm sorry."

"Thanks." Sadness hit him for the first time.

"Are you okay?"

"I thought I was, but I don't think it's quite hit me yet, you know?"

"Yes, I do know." Gary pyramided his hands above the bar.

"Natural causes?"

"Yeah, she had a heart attack two nights ago." Phineas felt as though he might cry, which surprised him.

"Phineas, I'm really sorry. If there is anything I can do, you know you only have to ask."

"Thanks, I'll be okay."

"When's the funeral?"

"What's today?"

Gary glanced to the left. "Wednesday."

"Oh, it's on Friday."

"I assume you're going," Gary said, regretting it.

Phineas' shot him a look, and then went quiet. "Well, I guess I should, but—"

"But," Gary paused, "what?"

"But I hate this stuff, man." He shook his head. "Family and death in one big knot of uncomfortable crapland."

"Again, beautifully eloquent words, my friend." Gary smiled and so did Phineas.

"You know what I mean, Gary."

"My friend, I completely understand. Why don't you go, though? It's your grandma. And I think it'll be nice to take a little time off and good for you to get away for a bit."

"Well," Phineas knew he was right. "What do you know?"

"I know a lot of stuff, lots of big words, but most of them are in Latin. Also, I'm your doctor."

Three waitresses stood at the end of the bar waiting for drinks, they spoke about a table that had been drinking too much. They shared a cigarette between the three of them and one of them coughed. Phineas poured a red drink into a pint glass and stuck a straw into it. He put his finger in the drink and poked his finger into his mouth. "Mm, yummy."

After Gary had resumed eating, Phineas wiped the bar and thought about the five-hour drive home to Lansford, Pa. He thought about his car and no stereo and he thought about his family. He shuddered and Gary laughed at him.

"Good Lord, what did you just think about?"

"My family."

"It's good to know that's a universal affliction." Both men laughed. "So, are you going?"

"You really think I should, huh?"

"I do. I think it'll be good for you to do this. Get your shifts covered and get out of here for a few days."

"Yeah, maybe you're right."

The door to the pub swung open with a loud clang and Amy Lucas, Larry and Gomez came in. Phineas dried his hands with a bar towel. They came to the bar and Amy wound up and smacked Gary on the rump with an open palm. Gary lifted off the stool and grimaced.

"Ow, the next time you wonder why I don't like women, call to mind this action."

"Let's do shots!" Gomez shouted and sank his tall frame onto a stool. His cigarette was topped with an ash two inches long and when he went for the ashtray his hand shook as if he'd recently had a stroke. "Hehehe," he knocked the ashtray over, covering the bar with ashes and cigarette butts.

Phineas cleaned up the mess, then observed as Gomez tried to light another cigarette but he had trouble connecting the flame with the tip. Phineas reached into his pocket, withdrew a lighter and held Gomez's face toward the flame. He looked into his eyes and saw that they had gone from their normal blue to a dark green, which meant that he'd been drinking tequila. Amy was talking nonsense to Gary.

"We should go out this weekend, okay, here's the deal. Here's the deal." She licked her lips and puckered them as if she had just put on ChapStick. "Here's the deal, okay, you and me are going to dinner Saturday, okay?"

Phineas watched Amy with a cocked head. Judging from the twitches of her head, the extravagant nature with which she smoked her cigarette, the size of her pupils and the number of times she uttered the same phrase in any given minute, Phineas guessed that she was eight, maybe nine drinks along.

Gary was laughing and eating. "Yes, of course. You can be my token girl. Yes, we'll go to dinner Saturday. Where do you want to go?" A muscle tightened in his jaw and a desperate glint covered his eye that only Phineas noticed, and he tried to find a way out for his friend. But he was trapped. They made eye contact and Phineas gave him a dire look, which Gary returned.

"Hm, okay I got an idea." Her eyes grew excited. "Ooh, yeah, let's go shopping first! Then we'll go to the Fish Market. Yeah, here's the deal, shopping then fish."

"That sounds good. What do you want to go shopping for?"

"Clothes, silly. Why else would I be bringing a gay man shopping, for power tools?"

"Oh come on! I thought I was precluded from these foolish stereotypes with you guys."

"Ducky, you're a black gay man," Amy said with wide eyes, as if this was information that Gary was learning for the first time. "You're blay!" She seemed delighted at this invented word and clapped her hands three times. "You help girls buy clothes."

"Amy," he looked into her massive drunken eyes, seeing but blind. "It should also be mentioned that I am renovating a house, my third, which means that in the last year and a half I have bought more power tools than anybody in this bar."

Amy stared at him, shook her head and then grabbed Gary's face. "Hey Ducky! When did you get here?" She looked at Phineas, "Shots! We need shots, Ducky just got here!"

Gary dropped his head and shook it. Phineas upped the number of drinks he had guessed by three and Amy looked around in total confusion. From two stools away, Larry, who had missed everything, thought it was time to take his shot and did so before the others.

"Larry!" Amy whined. "Rudeboy."

Larry looked dumbfounded, and he rubbed his bald head and face.

Phineas thought the shot might rejoin the bar in a second so he laid a towel on the bar in front of him, but instead Larry burped, held his breath and looked at Phineas through half-open eyes.

"There's, I…when did he go…I can't do this again…" Larry looked to the ground, defeated.

Phineas put a vodka and soda (97.5% soda) in front of him. "It's okay, buddy. Just have a drink and you'll be fine."

Gomez fell off his stool and lay on the ground laughing for two full minutes before Phineas and Gary could pull his giant frame off the ground. Gary looked into Gomez's face as if he were his cutman.

"You look fine. You okay?"

Gomez giggled and rubbed his head. "I think. It'll prolly hurt tomorrow."

"Nah, you'll be too hungover to notice," Gary said and went back to his pizza, which Amy had begun picking into. "You banshee!" He pointed with dramatic accusation. "You, my drunk dear, are buying *me* dinner Saturday night."

Amy chewed on a tomato. "You're a doctor."

"Okay, you're buying a doctor dinner Saturday."

"Fine, but then I can have another piece, okay?"

"Go ahead. I think I'm stuffed."

Phineas knew he was lying. Gary never stopped before finishing his pizza.

In the meantime, the restaurant had filled out and the waitresses were now moving about with the speed and grace of ballet dancers. Gary smiled at Amy and took a sip of his diet cola, then he caught Phineas' eyes and widened his own in pretend horror. "Go! Go man, run like the wind and escape this madhouse!"

"Maybe you're right. I'll talk to Larry tomorrow, or maybe now when he can't say no."

"Yes," Gary said. "But will he remember?"

It was too late. The restaurant had already turned its collective attention to Larry Joy, who had put two straws up his nostrils, perched on a stool flapping his arms like a seal and shouted into the restaurant. "I hate cocaine, but I love the way it smells!"

"I'll talk to him tomorrow morning."

6

The Blue Mountain Ridge cuts through Eastern Pennsylvania, flanked by the farmlands of the Cumberland Valley and the vast forests of striped maple and American Beech that made up the Allegheny Mountain forests. In October, Central Pennsylvania was a glorious representation of a Northeastern autumn, with magnificent colors Jackson Pollocking the forests. Through the lower half of Pennsylvania and this miracle of nature was a man-made catastrophe. It is the Pennsylvania Turnpike, and driving it was like making out with a sibling.

Phineas tried not to think about his lack of stereo. He drove through fog, three rain storms, two bumper-to-bumper traffic jams and the occasional patch of uneven pavement combined with four-foot concrete pylon walls that threatened Samantha's passenger side. He ate pizza with pepperoni and drank large quantities of coffee and defecated once at a rest stop, which he rued. His alcoholic antics had prompted painful diarrhea, which led to an unpleasant rectal condition. He winced as he leaned out of the driver's seat and shifted into gear at the same time.

After Bedford he made good progress and crossed his fingers in hopes of continuing his good luck. The windshield wipers did little against the constant, aggravating rain that dropped against the car. He squinted through the windshield. For a brief period in the late 1980s, Phineas tried his hand at the art of vulgarity, becoming proficient enough in that short time to dabble in planting curses into the middle of other curses. God-fucking-dammit was his expletive infixation of choice. Upon this sudden development in her son's language, Phineas' mom, Loni, explained that people who cursed didn't have a more intelligent way of expressing themselves. When this approach proved ineffective, she convinced him to clean up his language with a series of slaps to the cranium for the better part of a month. For this reason, he did not use vulgarity. Normally.

"Fuckin' God damn shit fucker ass fuckin' shit." He rattled the steering wheel in his hands as though he were trying to strangle two ducks at the same time. He apologized to Samantha and his mother and took a few deep breaths.

He snorted a blast of laughter at himself, happy that nobody was present to hear his childish rant.

As far as Phineas could tell, there were four stages a driver went through as he drove the Pennsylvania Turnpike. The first, paradoxically, was relief, happiness almost, as the anticipation of driving the turnpike was nearly as bad as the drive itself. Thus, the driver had begun the most unpleasant journey, and while that was a terrific tragedy, the driver took solace in the fact that at the very least the anticipation was over with.

The second stage of this dreaded condition was rage, an absurd rage that was an embarrassment to the driver and everyone within earshot. A fortunate driver was one who drove alone and could therefore forget his episodes of rage, discounting them later as ancient nightmares and swear himself to secrecy forever. Secrecy wasn't necessary, though, as anyone who had ever been on the Pennsylvania Turnpike fully commiserated and understood the ridiculous string of obscenities that sprang from one's mouth while in transit. The unwritten rule of ethics being that only a person who has driven on the turnpike could judge another turnpike driver.

The third stage of this damned road that was created by the Devil is one during which the driver begins to sing. He may even, to an observer (presumably also an afflicted Pennsylvania Turnpike driver), seem to be in a state of happiness. In reality, the driver is going through a delusional, demented episode in which his psyche is trying in a last ditch effort to trick him into believing that he is not the most miserable human being on the face of the planet. It never works. Symptoms include laughing, singing, drumming one's steering wheel and even being courteous and pleasant to other drivers. It must be noted that this stage often reverts back into stage two (rage), usually when the driver notices a mile marker informing him that he has more than a hundred miles remaining on the demon road. Thus, stage two and three often intermingle. It should also be noted that this stage transference is sometimes not limited to a single driver, but to several motorists who at once realize the depths of their anguish. The ricochet awakening effect (stage three to two) can be disastrous. Scientists at Juniata College hypothesize that a massive third to second stage exchange was the most probable culprit of the tragic three-hundred twenty nine-car pile-up of 1978.

Stage four is daydreaming, also known as the vision stage. The driver finds a small chamber in his brain where he can envision something nice, a good time in his life, or a fantastic imaginary situation that takes him from the road (noncommittal sexual intercourse, delivering an Oscar acceptance speech, rescuing Meg Ryan from a serial killer, sorority tickle fights). Essentially, it's what happens to those trying to escape the brutality of physical torture; the driver recedes into his happy place.

He had woken Larry Joy that morning with the news that there had been a death in the family and he was leaving for home. Larry wasn't happy, for several reasons, but he made a pot of coffee and called his bartenders. A death in the family was a death in the family. Ruth, the daytime bartender, would work a few shifts and a stupefied Amy Lucas would cover a few shifts. Amy was angry that Phineas hadn't told her first that his grandmother had died. However, as people who endure deaths in their family often did, he'd used the loss and grievance as a chess piece, citing sadness and confusion as partner emotions. He'd won.

Phineas got through the Blue Mountain pass and the weather broke, the rain stopped and threats of blue streaked in the distance. He sang to himself and when he forgot the lyrics, he hummed or made up verses that came to him at the moment. "Riding that train, high on cocaine, Casey Jones you better WATCH THAT SPEED. Trouble ahead, trouble behind, and you know that trucker better stay off my friggin' God-damn monkey-fuckin' ass. Doo, doo doot doot doot doo doo doo doo doo, Casey Jones is gonna eat that pizza, yep gonna eat the blah blah out of, ooh, hello madam in the blue Geo. Do you like Casey Jones? Uh, huh. Casey Jones."

Philadelphia: 145 miles. He stopped using his steering wheel as a drum and grabbed it hard with both hands and groaned. "Oh, my friggin' God! I hate this friggin' road!" He punched the top of his roof. "Fuck me!"

Finally, Phineas' body quieted and he sank back into his seat. He breathed evenly, drove automatically and allowed his thoughts to drift to his grandmother. She had been 70ish as long as he'd known her and she always had a smile on her face. She was a little white-haired Italian woman who never stopped moving around the kitchen.

He considered her qualities, as bartenders often do about laypeople, and decided that she would have been an outstanding bartender, she was aware and energetic. Christmas always meant ravioli and meatballs, very untraditional for an Italian household on Christmas, but nobody complained. Ever. Easter meant lasagna and homemade pizza. The absence of an Easter ham had never been mentioned; it had never been noticed. The Troy clan would sit around the table or watch television in the living room, waiting for the call to dinner. They were a close family, but when it came to food and who might get more than them, they regressed into territorial scavengers.

Phineas smiled as he thought about the old woman in the red apron, always transporting food from one place to another. She never ate, it occurred to him. She spoke in outdated terms, so long, was how she exited phone conversations and sore was how she described being angry. She was beautiful.

He remembered those nights clearly now, dark nights at the end of December when the family would come together and forget problems and work. Everyone ate and drank, the adults would talk around the kitchen table and the kids would run around in a state of utter joy.

It was a time when he enjoyed seeing his family, couldn't wait. Now, the thought of seeing his whole family sent a shudder down his spine. It was a simpler time, when he didn't worry about anything but waiting till the next morning to open his gifts. He remembered the tree in the living room and the piles of colorful presents and tinsel, his father and uncles sleeping in front of empty plates, Christmas music playing from a radio on the mantle. Neighbors dropping by to say hello, have a quick drink and deposit gifts.

It was six in the evening when Phineas came into Philadelphia and

he was sweating. Outside of Valley Forge he hit late rush hour traffic and
the back of his neck turned red and he started breathing in deep, low
breaths. The incessant honking bore into Phineas' brain and he squeezed
the steering wheel and twisted it through his palms. A man in an SUV
leaned out of his driver-side window and extended his middle finger to
a Bronco. "Fuck you, you fuckin' piece of shit!"

Phineas opened his eyes wide and braced himself for gunfire that
never came. More turnpike victims. An accident stopped traffic and
when people drove by they stared at a little girl who was crying, some
honked their horns to show their disdain. Windshield glass covered a
patch of highway and a cracked tail light sat on the side of the road. The
road cleared and Phineas got off the turnpike and made it to Lansford
without further incident.

Lansford, Pennsylvania, a town to the northeast of Philadelphia,
was home to 2,100 residents. About half of those were white, blue-collar
workers and their lower middle-class families, the other half were mainly
white-collar Jews. The remaining minority, to which Phineas' family
belonged, was a smattering of social classes, religions and ethnicities.
There were supposed to be somewhere between three and six black people
living in Lansford, but Phineas had never met any of them.

Lansford had a town center that consisted of a barber shop, chiro-
practor, gas station, two sandwich shops, dry cleaners, electronics store,
a dollar store, a pizza place called Sister's, a diner named Ron's, a dentist
and The Blue Duck Inn. Phineas' father was the dentist and his office
was the front portion of their large country home. The wide main street
was lined with trees of various sizes and species, the lawns were neatly
manicured. Phineas pulled up to the house and sat in the long driveway
that wound its way back behind the house. The house was tall and stone, it
looked solid and inviting. Glossy pictures of a white ghost and a pumpkin,
a cat and a smiling witch were taped to the inside of the front windows.
Leaves blew across the front lawn on which there stood a single-posted
shingle: Dr. Desmond Troy, DDS. A rectangular plaque next to the front
door read: Lansford Historical Society, Historical Site, Built 1801.

Phineas picked up his overnight bag from the passenger seat and got out of the car. He inspected for dog poop as he pranced on his toes across the lawn. A dog barked and a motorcycle drove down the small town street spreading smoke while irritating residents. Phineas walked up the steps to the front porch and looked into the window of the office. It was an antiseptic and white operatory, a single picture of a giant redwood hung on the wall over a table that held carefully placed objects. A CD player sat on the deep, low windowsill and a jar beaming with multi-colored toothbrushes sat on a long built-in table. The massive dental chair took up the middle of the room, surrounded by instruments of oral torture. The cushioned chair sat still, mountainous, a spit sink playing its sycophant. In the chair's shadow was a stool for the executioner, squat, simple. He could almost hear the whispered words, *is it safe?*

The porch wrapped around the side of the house and a picnic table and chairs stood in the corner of the bend. Phineas sat on one of the chairs and unwound. In the distance he heard an airplane defy gravity and logic and a car pull into a driveway a few houses away. Phineas didn't know them. His family had moved to the house after he had left for college. And, with the exceptions of his first two summers home from college, he had come home twice annually—for Christmas and Thanksgiving—over the last eleven years. Some of his family's neighbors had never met Phineas.

Phineas walked around the porch to the side door and opened it, heard a football game on the television and walked toward the kitchen. In the living room, his father's table was, as it had always been, a disaster area. It was covered with books, magazines, dental journals, notebooks, two pens (one red, one black), a crossword puzzle book, four half-empty coffee mugs (two with mold growing on the inside), two empty bowls that looked as though they had been used for chocolate ice cream, a wind-up radio, an unopened bonsai tree kit, two Snickers bar wrappers and approximately 600 pieces of mail, most of them unopened.

In the kitchen, his father was sitting with his back to him and smoking a cigarette, the television blared and he was reading a book while the game played. He rocked back and forth almost imperceptibly.

"Hey, Dad."

Desmond Troy turned around and saw his son. He was wearing large glasses with telescopic lenses set in the center of each lens. They made him look like a bug. "Hey," he marked a spot in the book with a pen, placed it on the table and stood up with a grunt. "Urhh, how was the drive?"

"Long and brutal, as usual." Phineas made spiraling movements with his finger around his father's glasses. "Um, new glasses?"

"Oh," he reached up and took them off. "They're my loupes, I lost my reading glasses, but these are fine. Jeet yet?"

"I had some pizza, but I could really use a beer."

"I think there's some in the fridge, take a look." Desmond took a step and grimaced in pain, rubbing his lower back. He walked toward his son. "Good to see you, pal."

"You too Dad." The men hugged, their bellies meeting in a bastardization of ancient sumo ritual. "How you doing?"

"Oh, I'm okay. You know—" He stopped short and Phineas noticed a tremor in his lip and a curl to his eyebrows.

Phineas patted him on the shoulder. "I know, Dad. How's Mom?"

"She's okay. She's staying out at the house getting some things together and trying to take care of a few things. I think she's going to stay there this week. She says to tell you she'll see you tomorrow at the funeral."

"How's Clay?"

"He's good. He's upstairs, I think he's waiting for you to go over to The Blue Duck."

"Good, thank God. I need a shot and a beer."

Desmond smiled and walked back into the kitchen. His beard and hair were gray and the middle of his mustache had turned yellow from years of nicotine. There was a light beer in the fridge and Desmond grabbed it. "Well, you'll see everyone tomorrow at the funeral." He picked up a bottle opener and popped the top off the beer. "Glass?"

Phineas took the beer and licked his lips. "Nah, thanks."

Desmond reached back into the fridge and removed a can of ginger ale. "Why don't you go say hello to your brother. I know he's been wanting to see you."

Phineas gulped at the beer and the Pennsylvania Turnpike drifted into a distant nightmare. He finished his pull and wiped the back of his shirt sleeve against his mouth. "Yeah, okay. You gonna be up for a while?"

"Yeah, probably. I want to watch the end of this game."

"Okay, well just in case, good night, and I'll see you bright and early tomorrow."

"Okay. Nice to see you, son."

"You too." Phineas slapped his father on the arm and walked off toward the upstairs bedrooms. He paused on the bottom step. "Dad, if you need anything, you know—" he called into the kitchen. The steps creaked and families of dust bunnies lay in every corner of the hardwood floor.

"I know," his miniature voice came from around the corner. "Thanks."

Halfway up the steps was a cove with dusty pictures of the family. A plastic light in the shape of a candle shone in the middle of the pictures and a spider had made home in the back corner of the cove.

Phineas drank more of his beer and walked up another set of steps to his brother's bedroom in the attic. Twelve beer cases sat at the top of the steps, all filled with empty bottles. A room on the left had a dart board and a glass-topped picnic table covered with more empty beer bottles. Many of them had been used as ashtrays and some had been used as spittoons and were filled with dark black spit and tobacco. Crushed, empty packs of cigarettes littered the floor and a poster of Jenna Jameson hung on the wall. She was nude and leered provocatively, her pubic hair was nonexistent and Phineas walked over to admire it.

"Who the fuck is this shithead?" Clay Troy walked in the room with a practiced swagger and opened his arms as he neared his brother. They hugged and Phineas felt the strong muscles in Clay's chest and arms. He held a cigarette and a bottle of beer in his right hand; he popped the cigarette back into his mouth and spoke through it. "How was the fuckin' drive?"

"It was terrible, just terrible."

"Yeah, I hate that fuckin' road. Fucking piece of shit." He pulled from his beer.

From behind Clay a larger figure appeared in the doorway. "Hey, Phin."

"Hey, Ben."

Ben Wagner knocked on the door frame twice as if testing its strength. "How are you?"

"You know how it goes." Phineas took a swig from his beer.

The large man stepped through the room with two easy and massive strides and pulled Phineas into his gigantic frame. "Good to see you, buddy. Sorry about your grandmom."

"Yeah, it's nice to see you guys, but the reason sucks."

Clay straightened his back and flared out his chest. Even still, Ben stood a solid five inches taller and was twice as thick in the chest. Phineas, short yet with a dense, stocky build, was the smallest man in the room. He tapped the poster with a knuckle.

"Nice girl. Secretary at the factory?"

Clay pulled his brow together and smirked, "You fuckin' moron, that's Jenna Jameson, she's a fuckin' porn star."

"I know, you dingbat. I'm joking."

"Ha ha," he pronounced deliberately. "You're a fuckin' hilarious douchebag." He slapped Phineas in the stomach with the back of his hand. "Let's go to The Duck."

"Yeah, let's go, I need a drink." Phineas turned to Ben, "You coming?"

"Yes."

The three walked down the steps and out through the side door, past Phineas' overnight bag and onto the porch. Ben pulled on a brown Carhartt jacket and Phineas called into his father. "Ok, Dad, see you later on."

"You guys going to The Duck?" His voice was small and quiet behind the commentator on the television.

"Yeah, don't wait up, huh." Clay flicked his cigarette onto the driveway and pulled on his sweatshirt.

They walked across the street, waiting a moment for a man passing on a motorcycle. Clay shook his head. "Fuckin' asshole."

"Who is that?" Ben asked.

Clay shrugged his shoulders, "How the fuck should I know?"

They walked to the corner, the crisp autumn air chilled their faces. While Clay peed against the side of a building Ben kicked at the dirt at the roots of a maple tree. Phineas yawned and stretched out his legs. "We're like eighteen seconds away from the bar," he called into the alley.

Clay reappeared zipping his fly and dancing on one leg. "Dammit, I swear I piss on myself more than I piss not on myself. Let's go, I need a shot."

The Blue Duck Inn sat at the corner of Maple Avenue and Edgewood Lane, its foundation had been built in 1786 and it was said to be the oldest pub in Lansford. A small parking lot and a balcony full of bright red azaleas were in the back. Statues of a black lawn jockey and a stoic pioneer guarded its doorstep. The lawn jockey had been stolen four times, the pioneer once. When the pioneer was returned it had been given a permanent makeover of ruby red lipstick, blue eye shadow and pink rouge. Jack Schorpp, the owner of both The Blue Duck Inn and a devious sense of humor, replaced the pioneer in his normal spot and said nothing about it. On Mothers' Day he dressed the pioneer in a blue dress and bonnet and, for Halloween, leather lingerie. He was so dressed now.

The inside of The Duck was a combination of dingy and quaint. The Duck had dark corners, a fireplace, cherry machine and jukebox. Its regulars ranged from college kids, toothless construction workers to Jewish real estate agents, shop owners, respected doctors to town drunks. The three men stepped inside and looked around the room through the haze of smoke and booze. The bar was full of regulars drinking and having loud conversations. They told stories that had been told a thousand times, changing them to fit the moment.

The barmaid defied physics by squeezing a massive behind into a not so massive pair of jeans. She also defied taste by squeezing an equally massive upper-body into a half shirt that read, Blondes Have More Fun. She was a brunette. She held a cigarette with a hand that pointed straight up and was supported by her other arm which was tucked under her bosom. She blew the smoke out expertly and nodded at the three men.

"What can I get ya guys?" Her voice was chalky, it fit perfectly.

"Gimme a Lager and three shots of, wait-" He looked at Phineas. "Phin, you still drinking schnapps?"

"Yep, sure am."

"Beer?"

"Whatever you're having."

"Okay, hon," Clay began, "gimme two shots of bourbon, a pepper-mint schnapps, two Lagers and a Grasshopper for the big faggot here." He jerked a thumb at Ben who giggled. Despite the clatter of the bar, the barmaid looked as though she could fall asleep from sheer boredom at any moment.

"Shame about Grandmom. Fuckin' sucks, man." Clay surveyed the room as he spoke and nodded at a few people who were sitting at a table near the fireplace. They were building a pyramid out of empty beer bottles. One of the women at the table was smoking a cigar.

"It's terrible, but I guess she lived a nice full life." The cherry machine reminded Phineas of Larry's Pub. The drinks arrived and a woman with four teeth and cracked glasses offered them each a Xanax. They all took one and handed the woman twelve dollars. She tucked it into her bra and sat back down next to a man wearing a suit and a cell phone clipped to his belt.

"To Grandmom," Clay said. He raised his shot glass and clinked it against the others. "A good fuckin' woman."

Ben's shot glass looked like a thimble in his gigantic hand. With his other paw he stirred his Grasshopper with care and precision. Phineas was jealous of his ever-present peaceful demeanor. Ben took a sip of the drink and smiled at Phineas, who reached out and put his hand on his friend's shoulder.

"I miss you guys." He said.

"Yeah," Clay said. "Let's get fucked up."

"Okay." Both Phineas and Ben nodded; it seemed like the right thing to do.

7

Phineas was sitting in a park and it was spring. Fresh-smelling green grass and leaves toiled around him. There was a slope in front of him that led to a creek that tinkled as it ran. The sounds relaxed him and his eyes drooped with pleasure. He heard a light splash in the creek and expected to see a fish. Another splash came and a hand reached out of the water, Phineas' face lost its pleasant countenance. Another hand and then the head of his grandmother came out of the water. Phineas held his breath, the flowers and trees grew distant as if down a long tunnel and his grandmother came out of the water with her apron and white sweater and she smiled at him.

"Relax," she said.

"Are you kidding?" he said back.

She reached out a hand. "Take it," she urged him.

He backed a step away. "I don't know."

"Come on, sweetie. Take a chance for once."

Phineas awoke with a start. The sun shone into the room and he had a pillow pulled against his erect penis. He stared into the closet opposite him and saw boxes of books, toys and old clothes; his mother never threw anything away. Absently, he rubbed his erection against the pillow, reviewing past and erotic situations in his head until he grasped one he liked and played it out in his mind. It involved a young lady who he'd met at a Super Bowl party three years before. They'd gone to her apartment and she masturbated for him before they had sex. After they'd finished having sex she poured oil on his back and gave him an hour-long massage. It was the happiest he had ever been; his eyes had glazed over and he fell into the deepest sleep of his life on that bed to the quiet sounds of slurping oil and a bossa nova band called Oh Campari whispering from a hidden stereo.

Phineas rolled onto his back. He peeked open an eye and searched for an old T-shirt or something that could be used in the situation without moving from his position. He found a pair of boxer shorts and laid them on his stomach; he pulled his boxers to his ankles. He began the subtle art of self-seduction, implanting entirely embarrassing dialogue where necessary, and barely noticed a light shuffling outside the door of his room. As Phineas' movements became more frantic so did the shuffling until a tiny Papa Smurf doll slid under his door from the hallway. The doll was missing a foot and an eye. Phineas kept his movement steady and the dog began to bark; it stood at the door and wailed. He heard footsteps approach and his father's voice.

"Oh, Ennio, whaddaya doin, eh?" His father affected an Italian accent. "Eh, paisano?"

Phineas pulled his sheets up around his chest and frowned in annoyance. The door swung open.

"Oh, hey Phin. Gotta get Ennio's doll. It's about nine, coffee's made."

"Yeah, I'll be down in a minute." The sheet resembled a small white hill.

His father left the door open.

"Dad!" Phineas called, "Close the door!" He shifted his hips, making the hill appear a bit grander and then he smiled.

His father hadn't heard and wandered down the hallway to his dingy study where he sat at the computer and lit a fresh cigarette. The dog came in the room with the Papa Smurf doll and barked through his teeth.

"Jerk," Phineas said and pulled his boxers to his waist. "You stupid dog."

Phineas' erection subsided as he stood over the toilet and urinated for a full minute. He tasted beer and peppermint. His father's television shrieked football analysis.

"Well, Bill, you're right about this football team for sure. They can't move the football inside their red zone and their kicker isn't strong enough to be solid outside their thirty."

"Sam, let me tell you something, if they can score ten points they'll win this football game. They're playing football against a football team that can't move the football inside their red zone, you're right, but the other guys can't hold onto the football when it's wet outside and rain is in the forecast."

Holding onto the door jambs, Phineas leaned into his father's study. Smoke sat in heavy levels throughout the room and his father squinted through one eye at the computer screen. In the corner, highlights of football games from the previous evening played on the television. Books lined the shelves and old photographs sat in frames with broken glass. Half-finished cups of coffee were scattered throughout the room (brewing with mold). The closed windows trapped the funk. On the desk with the computer was a cup of coffee and an overflowing ashtray. His father glanced at Phineas.

"Hi," he said, and then looked back at his computer. "I'm putting money down on some games tonight…" his voice, meant only for himself, trailed off. A moment later, "Checking out the scores and run down now…"

On the television screen a man was running a ball through the pouring rain. His uniform had once been white but had been dyed brown from the mud. Phineas' father picked up his cigarette and stuck it between his lips.

"Who're you taking?" Phineas said.

"I don't know." His eyes never left the screen. "I don't know."

"Okay, well I've gotta get some coffee in me so I'll see you in a bit."

"Okay, see you later."

His brother was sitting in the kitchen eating a ham and cheese sandwich. His eyes were glued to the television screen on which two men with bad haircuts were sitting at a desk talking about hockey.

"What's up?" Phineas pulled a mug from the cabinet. The kitchen counter ran along the wall in the shape of a horseshoe and was teeming with stuff. Pots, pans, boxes, bags of miscellaneous items, silverware, dog food, Tupperware, unopened packages, bags of Halloween candy and cans of soup took up every inch of space. On the refrigerator were pictures of people he had never seen and a Christmas card from an orthodontist.

"Nothing much, the Flyers are gonna kick ass this year. They've got Stanlinson back and Recchi's probably going to Pittsburgh."

Phineas nodded and feigned interest for five seconds. He sipped his coffee. "You driving to the funeral today?"

"Yeah, I think I gotta drive me and Dad."

"I'm going with Ben. He asked me if I wanted a ride, so I'll head out there with him."

"I think Dad's afraid of driving."

"What, really?"

"Yeah, actually, he doesn't leave the house at all."

"Since when?"

"I don't know. A while, I guess." Clay's eyes never left the television. "He gets me and Mom to do everything for him. Fuck!" Clay sat up straight and held an open hand to the television as if he were presenting it to Phineas on a showroom floor.

Having heard a French-Canadian name muttered along with a variety of curses, Phineas foresaw more hockey talk and fled the room. "I gotta hit the shower."

"Yeah," his brother called into the other room. "You stink."

"Rumor to me." Phineas stripped out of his T-shirt and carried his coffee into the bathroom. Lips, gums, teeth, tongue, throat, eyes, nostrils, nodes. Somewhat satisfied, he plopped onto the toilet and read through an *Entertainment Weekly*. When he'd finished, he kicked off his boxers and glared into the shower stall. "Damn you, elf spitter," he said.

Phineas and his brother had dubbed the shower 'the elf spitter' after comparing a shower in it to standing in a claustrophobic room while being spat on by several dehydrated elves. Any cleanliness attained while in the elf spitter was purely coincidental. Phineas stepped into the shower and let the few weak drops wet his hair and face. He pulled the detachable shower head off the wall and wetted the rest of his body. The soap stuck in his facial hair and stung his eyes.

Ben picked Phineas up a little after noon in his old orange Jeep Wrangler. Its bikini was torn in several places, beaten down with time and weather and the back of the jeep was full of tools. There was also a horseshoe and a small step ladder. Kenny Burrell played on the stereo.

The sky was blue and thin white clouds laced across it. People raked leaves in their yards, a postman walked from house to house and tipped his hat to a woman who walked a tiny dog down her driveway. The dog barked at everything it saw. Phineas was struck by the smallness of the town.

"So, how's Pittsburgh?"

"Good, the same."

"We didn't get much of a chance to talk about the bar last night. You still diggin' it?"

"The money's good. The place is doing well, and I like my schedule. Can't beat it, you know, working three nights a week and making tons of money."

"That's good to hear." He turned onto a side road that ran along the creek."

"Yeah. Plus I get to drink while I work. Can't argue with that. How're the mules?"

"They're great. Stubborn."

"You guys still busy, or is business slowed down at this point?"

"Well, the trips down the canal are still popular this time of year, you know with the leaves changing and everything. The weather's perfect for that."

"I'd kind of like to see that."

"You're here for a few days, right?"

"Yep, I took a few days off."

"Stop by tomorrow and I'll show you around. Plus you can see the mules, you know, say hi in person."

The road in front of them twisted through the woods and leaves danced in circles. Patches of the creek glimmered in the sunlight; the water looked deep and cold. Ben took a deep breath and rested his arm on the lowered window. "I love this weather."

In some way, the drive reminded Phineas of his ride with Larry Joy across the Birmingham Bridge. "What else you doing?"

"I'm still pet-sitting." He turned on his right turn signal.

"A lot?"

"Yeah, lots of people go out of town in the fall so I get busy this time of year. It's nice to make the extra money."

Phineas nodded, "So, what kind of pets you sitting?"

"Hm, I watch a few cats, several dogs, lots of hamsters, I feed fish, three boa constrictors, a llama, some frogs and turtles, oh, and a tarantula."

Phineas twitched and made a disgusted face. "Ugh, I hate those things."

"Frogs?"

"Frogs? No, dummy, tarantulas. You know I hate spiders."

"I figured you'd be over that by now."

"Negative." Phineas pulled his feet onto the seat and scanned the floor around him.

"She's not in the jeep."

"You can never be too careful, Benjamin."

Ben pulled into the parking lot of The Church of St. Charles. Dozens of people were meandering around the front door to the church. Phineas let out a sigh. Nothing, he thought, prepares someone to see his entire family in a good situation. When the situation is bad, it's astronomically worse. Like being stuck in a bad movie for three hours, it's inescapable.

"You ready for this?" Ben asked.

"As ready as I'll ever be."

"Hey, if you need to be, you know, saved—"

"What from family, you mean?"

"Yeah, just signal."

"The usual?"

"You know it."

Phineas saw his father and brother talking to some older men and smoking cigarettes. His mother talked to a priest he had never seen before.

Phineas walked up to his mother and smiled as she caught his eye.

"Phineas," his diminutive mother hugged him around his waist. "You look great. How was your trip?"

"Good, terrible, you know. Also, you're lying."

"Quit drinking so much beer and you'll look great." His mother's eyes sparkled and her cheeks and small nose were red, she fixed her glasses. "Oh, I'm sorry, Father Talbert this is my son Phineas."

Father Talbert reached out a bony hand and took Phineas' in it. He smiled and nodded his head. "Nice to meet you, Phineas. I'm terribly sorry for your loss."

"Nice to meet you Father and thank you."

Father Talbert released his hand and replaced a shock of white hair from his forehead that had tumbled away from his scalp. He was lean and ancient, his black outfit contrasted his white hair and his eyebrows danced from his eyes with wizard-like flair. Wrinkled skin on his neck hung over his collar. His eyes were dark brown, almost black.

Loni clicked her tongue on the roof of her mouth during the moment of silence. She wore a long black and green dress that hung close to the ground from her chubby form. "Did you get some dinner when you got in last night?"

Father Talbert excused himself and walked to greet other people.

"No, not really. Just went to The Duck and had a few beers with Clay. Did you get a lot done at Grandmom's?"

"Yeah, things needed to be taken care of. Oh, geez, Phin, this is terrible." The words rushed out, as if she had been holding them in all day and they finally escaped.

"I know, Mom, I'm sorry." Phineas looked over his shoulder, "Dad seems okay."

"Yeah, but I think he's hurting pretty bad."

"I would think so." He wanted this to end, now.

"She had a nice life, Phin. Remember that."

"I do." Phineas rubbed his belly. "Man, I should've eaten, I'm starved."

She eyed him, as if reviewing food that had gone bad. "Well, there's a reception at Grandmom's house after the funeral, so you can eat there."

The priest began telling people to go inside and Loni did the same. Phineas took a pew near the front. His brother and Ben sat next to him and his parents and Phineas' aunts and uncles sat in the two front rows.

The room began to fill and Phineas scanned the stained glass windows depicting the, apparently pugnacious, life and times of St. Charles. He looked at his watch, 12:57.

Father Talbert walked up to the podium and Phineas looked around him to see old neighbors, aunts and uncles he hadn't seen in years and a few unfamiliar faces. Father Talbert put on a sober face and began offering consolation to complete strangers. Phineas zoned out on the people in the front row. His mother and father sat next to each other, watching the priest and fixing their glasses. It was the closest they'd been to each other awake in two years. Next to his father sat his Uncle William who resembled a five-foot-ten pear with limbs. His hair had disappeared and he wore a close-cropped beard over his hanging face. He looked dignified, like a college professor. He wore a black pin-striped suit and thick glasses. Next to him, Aunt Janine was peering through her giant red glasses. She had cut her hair short and looked like a peach that had been dressed up for Halloween. Her nose was thin and sharp. Her cheeks were fat and pinched her eyes so that she looked almost asleep.

Phineas perked up when he saw his Uncle Robert, fresh from the farm he owned in Central Pennsylvania. His eyes were glazed over from that morning's joint and his suit was brown corduroy. He had shaved for the funeral of his mother so the lower part of his face was much whiter than the top. Even at forty-three years old, his hair was wild and black, without a hint of age. His face was tight and his chin was cleft. He looked inquisitive.

"…Let us pray…" Father Talbert held his hands out and called out prayers in a deep voice.

People were crying and other people had tears in their eyes that refused to drop. His mother was crying and his father frowned, but tears weren't in his eyes. He looked sadder than Phineas had ever seen him look and he wondered if it was because he couldn't be at home on his computer. He felt terrible for the thought.

Father Talbert finished his prayer and everyone said, "Amen."

"Now," Father Talbert said as he dropped his arms. "Now, William

Troy, oldest son of Emily Troy will say a few words. William?" Father Talbert nodded toward William and William stood and made his way out of the pew with difficulty. Desmond and his wife had to step into the aisle to let him out. William waddled to the podium and removed a piece of paper from his jacket breast pocket. He murmured as he scanned the paper, his voice cracking, and then paused to regain his composure. Phineas felt a pang of hurt in his chest and looked back at the stain glass and wiped a tear from his eye. He wanted to leave more than anything else in the world and felt angry that Catholics drag out pain for extended periods of time. It was one of several thousand times in his life that he wished his family had raised him atheist.

William looked out at the people, and then he took a deep breath. "First of all, I'd like to thank everyone for coming today to celebrate the life of my mom." He called her Mom, they all did. "Mother, grandmother, wife, teacher, friend. Everyone here who knew her, knows that she was a woman of tremendous strength and integrity. She always knew what to say, always knew what to do. I, along with my brothers and sisters, will always remember Mom as a wonderful and tough woman, but capable of such tenderness as would make your heart explode."

William shifted in his nice suit and parked his glasses with his forefinger when necessary. His eyes were watery and, at times, stared off into the distance. Desmond looked down into the pew in front of him. His eyes were gleaming and his mouth was tucked down into his chin. His back rose and fell with the weight of each breath. Phineas stared at the stained glass and traced the pictures with his mind.

William pursed his lips. "Now, I know I'm sad and I see a lot of sad people out there today too. I understand." He looked into the podium and swallowed, the knot in his throat almost visible. "But I want to ask you all to do something really brave, really tough." He brought his fist up and rocked it in the air. "I want you to be happy. Understand?" He took another deep breath. "You see, we aren't mourning the loss of a child today. We are celebrating a life well-lived, which follows here today with friends and family of all ages to carry on her memory. So, please, everyone, my mom raised seven children, who gave her sixteen grandchildren, she worked as a teacher and had hundreds and hundreds of friends and died with no regrets. Well, actually, maybe one I think, she'd probably be a little disappointed that she couldn't cater today." The room laughed and William nodded his head and put the papers back into his pocket. "Remember, friends, family, tell a nice story today about my mom and you will do her memory better justice than if you cry all day into a hankie. Thank you." William stepped from the podium.

Ben was crying with a smile on his face. His mind went from his mules to his friends' grandmother who'd made him dinner on hundreds of occasions. He wasn't sad about her death; he wasn't sad, but perhaps a little regretful that he hadn't been more thankful of her when she was alive. She had made incredible lasagna. Tears dripped down his chin until Clay put his arm around him and looked into his wet eyes and said, "You fucker, she was *my* fuckin' grandmom."

Emily Troy was cremated on a Thursday and on this Friday she was carried by her youngest son Robert, who carried her football-shaped urn and stared at the floor while weeping. Robert's forearms, ropy and tight from working his farm, shifted in his corduroy jacket and his crazy black hair flailed about him as he carried the urn down the aisle.

The priest stood in front of the crowd and leaned into the speaker. "Ahem, there will be a small reception at the home of Emily Troy at 3211 Dagers Road." Everyone followed Robert and people cried and twisted in their Sunday best. Phineas' mother zipped around the groups giving brief directions to Emily's house. St. Charles had been Emily's parish for 58 years, and she had walked to church every Sunday from her house, which was less than a five-minute walk.

Most of Phineas' immediate relatives, like Uncle William and Aunt Janine did the half-minute drive without a second thought. The pews in the church had made their backs ache. Phineas walked with Ben and Clay. His mother walked with Uncle Robert and many of the friends who had decided to take a walk and leave their cars at the church. Clay lit a cigarette and blew the smoke out; he loosened his tie and smeared a palm across his eye.

"Fuckin' hate these things, those douchebag priests never know what the fuck they're talking about." He hit the cigarette again and shook his head. "Fuckin' idiots."

They crossed the parking lot and stood at the edge of the street and watched cars pass. Uncle Robert and Phineas' mother approached them.

"Hey Phin, how you doing?" Uncle Robert shifted the urn under his right arm and hooked his left arm around Phineas' neck. He kissed him on the cheek and patted his back. "You look good."

"Thanks, Bob," Phineas said. "Nice of you to say."

Phineas' mother made a sound as if someone wearing a mask had just jumped out from behind a tree and shouted. "It's Uncle Robert to you, Phineas."

Phineas rolled his eyes.

Robert laughed, "Oh come on, Loni, he's a big boy."

"He should have more respect," Phineas' mother said and poked a finger into Phineas' chest.

"Mom, don't make me hold you down and fart in your face, okay?" He looked sideways at Robert, "Now, how's that for respecting your elders?"

Robert laughed again and looked across the road, "Jesus, where are all these cars coming from?"

A steady stream of cars continued down the small road from both directions. Robert handed his mother to Phineas and rooted through his pockets.

"Here, hold this." Robert padded his jacket pockets. "Aha." He removed several bright orange stickers that read FUNERAL in large block letters. "Here, take one."

Ben took one and handed another to Clay. A crowd of well-dressed mourners had gathered and Robert poked a foot into the street holding the orange placard well ahead of him like a police badge. Two cars passed but the third, a large black SUV, slowed and stopped. Robert straightened himself and gave the remaining placards to Phineas. He took back his mother, saluted the man in the vehicle and stepped across the road. In the other lane a woman with two children in the back of her Lexus stopped and began talking to the kids. Robert nodded and mouthed a thank you. Ben and Phineas handed orange FUNERAL placards to relatives and friends as they passed. Troys of all shapes and sizes crossed the street like a line of ducks following their mother for the last time, each one holding their orange FUNERAL placard in front of them as they walked. Some people applied the stickers to their jackets and dresses, displaying them as they crossed the street.

The people walked down a side street on the other side of the main street following Robert. A line of cars began to form behind the woman and man and some honked until they saw the orange placards. When all the Troys and friends had passed safely Ben and Phineas walked across with their placards and nodded thanks to the drivers. Clay walked ahead and swung his arm around Uncle Robert.

"It was a nice ceremony," Ben said, tucking his hands into his pockets.

"Yeah, I sort of zoned out when Father Talbert was speaking."

"That man did have a nice voice, it was relaxing."

"Yeah."

"Uncle William gave a great eulogy."

"He did, didn't he?"

"I haven't been to your grandmother's house in years. I think it was Christmas a few years ago."

"Yeah, I haven't been here since last Christmas. This is gonna be weird."

Dagers Road was a side street across from the church. It had six houses, no sidewalks and large oak trees lined the street. The third house from the corner was bought in 1947 by Salvatore Troy, two years after he had returned from the war in the Pacific. Like most men at the time, he was eager to start a family and settle back into civilian life. He bought the house on Dagers Road after he landed a job at Kaufman's Granite Inc. Phineas' uncle William was two and Emily and Sal Troy were awaiting the arrival of Desmond.

The ranch house was nestled in among a grove of oak and birch trees and a cement porch came off the front. Next to the porch were a small garden and a long gravel driveway. It had a wide yard in the back. From the driveway, Phineas could see people milling about through the kitchen window, between a glossy picture of a witch and a pumpkin. He remembered the holiday smell of meatballs and ravioli, lasagna and pizza and the busy woman buzzing through the house. They walked into the house and into the kitchen. Robert had put the urn on the kitchen table and Loni was putting out platters of cold cuts and bread. Ben wiped his shoes on the mat and came inside.

"Hey, Mrs. T, is there anything I can do to help?"

"Thank you Benjamin." She spoke as if she'd been expecting this question. "Can you bring some chairs in from the back bedrooms, please?"

"Sure thing. Phin, give me a hand."

Phineas was eyeing up the food platters and his gastronomical competition. "Yeah, sure." Several other Troys were doing the same.

Phineas and Ben walked into the back bedroom and started gathering wooden folding chairs that were leaning against the wall.

"Jesus, would you look at this stuff." Phineas said as he picked up a chair. "It's like walking through my past."

Ben put his chairs down and walked to where Phineas was looking at photographs tucked into the frame of the large mirror on the wall.

"Ha, oh my God, is that us?" Ben pointed at a worn picture of the two of them standing in Emily's driveway. Phineas was wearing a white suit and a wide grin. His eyes were squinted against the early morning sun that was behind the photographer. In the photo Ben was wearing a brown coat with a hood. One of his eyes was closed and his smile revealed a missing front tooth.

"I think that's my first communion." Phineas started perusing the other photographs.

Clay came in the room behind them and stopped at the door.

"Hey buddy," Phineas said, pulling one of the photographs from the mirror. "Who is this innocent looking kid, huh?"

Clay took the photograph and shook his head. "Wow, I haven't seen this in ages." Clay was five years old in the picture and wearing a Cookie Monster T-shirt. Pointing from his mouth was a large wooden spoon covered with cookie dough. His smile was the representation of pure, unmitigated joy.

"Clay, when was the last time you were that happy?" Ben asked.

"Oh," Clay's mouth opened but nothing came out. "Then," he finally said. Clay handed the photo back to Phineas and put his ginger ale on the dresser. "Hey, you guys need a hand?"

"Yeah, grab some chairs and bring them to the living room."

Clay took five chairs and Ben took four. Phineas picked up Clay's drink and followed them into the living room. They set them up and an old man walked up to Phineas. He was wearing a blue suit that hadn't been out of his closet since the last funeral he'd attended.

"Phineas, is that you?"

"Uncle Paul, how are you?"

"I'm good. I didn't recognize you with all that weight you put on in the last years."

"Thanks, Uncle Paul." Phineas moved his hand to his belly and studied the room for Ben, who had already made his way to the food.

"You still in Pittsburgh?"

"Yeah, Uncle Paul. I'm still there."

Clay stood ten feet behind the old man and, noticing Phineas' abject discomfort, began making faces and thumbing his nose at him. Phineas scowled at him and shook his head.

"What're you doing now?"

"I'm still working at the bar."

"Still bartending, huh? College graduate and you're still pulling drafts?"

"We serve cocktails, too," Phineas said.

"Is that right?" He was doing little to conceal his joy.

"Yeah Uncle Paul, well, I'm hoping to get into a few things soon. Will you excuse me?"

"Wait," he removed his glasses and stuck them into his breast pocket.

"You know your cousin Jimmy just finished medical school."

"You don't say." Phineas watched Clay go into the bathroom and scanned the room. He imagined setting the old man on fire.

"I've got a picture here somewhere, hold on." Paul pulled a wallet out of the hip-pocket of his jacket, murmuring to himself. "Taken after his first gall-bladder removal," he flipped through his wallet.

"It wasn't his, I assume."

The old man looked annoyed. "Don't be stupid."

Phineas shrugged, "I'm just saying, when he removes his own gall-bladder I'll be impressed."

Paul had stopped listening to him. "Hang on…"

Phineas considered running his head into the television to create a distraction. At that moment, Ben came into the room, hands and mouth full. Phineas stared at him with panic on his face and, placing his left hand on his right shoulder, he began to windmill his right arm.

"Yep, the old pitching shoulder keeps acting up on me." He stared at Ben and spoke in a loud, steady voice.

"He looks good, don't he?" He stuck a photo in Phineas' face. "Six one, two twenty, well he did have that football scholarship to Rutgers…"

"Yep, the old pitching shoulder keeps acting up on me," he said again.

Clay, drying his hands on his suit pants, noticed the distress signal. Ben, who was closer, heard the urgent call as well, used only in exceptional cases. Clay and Ben looked at each other.

"He's suffered enough." Clay laughed. "You got this?"

"Yeah, I got it," Ben answered.

"Then go!" Clay shoved him in the shoulder. "That's my Uncle Paul he's talking to, get him out of there!"

Ben ran across the room, wide-eyed and spitting bread and ham on his shirt and tie. He reached them just in time to hear about cousin Jimmy's thwarted NFL career, which had delighted the AMA. "Phin, your mom needs you…to water the flowers. Now."

"Oh sorry, Uncle Paul, please excuse me."

"Sure," he brought his highball to his lips, then paused and allowed a lascivious smile to spread across his face. "Good luck at the bar."

Phineas spoke with William about the eulogy, then had a few super-ficial conversations that all focused on his shortcomings as a person in one way or another. Three aunts and two uncles asked how his journalism career was going and offered sympathetic nods and patronizing smiles when he failed to tip toe around the fact that he was still working in a bar. A cousin he hadn't seen in a decade told him about his sky-rocketing business and hinted that Phineas could work there as a gofer. He also mentioned that Phineas looked "healthy," leaving Phineas to wonder how many more euphemistic terms for fat he was going to hear.

Phineas' pitching shoulder acted up on him three more times in seventeen minutes and after the final escape Phineas and Ben parked themselves at the living room window. They watched a line of Troy men move toward the kitchen.

"I am looking into my future here, aren't I?"

Ben regarded the room and chuckled. "Oh boy."

Phineas frowned at him. "It's not so funny from where I'm sitting."

"Phin, it's the same with everyone's family. Every family get-together I go to tells me just how bald, fat and unappealing I'm going to be in a few years."

Phineas shook his head. "Well, you really sugar-coated that one, didn't you?" He scratched his chin. "But look at these guys, they're like a herd." They moved in single-file to the kitchen. Some of them joked and others talked as they shuffled along in automatic steps.

"Yeah, so?" Ben shrugged his shoulders. "They're all Troys and there's a platter of lunch meats in the kitchen. You don't need to work for *National Geographic* to figure out why they're heading that way."

"I know. They just all look so…ordinary, is all."

"First of all, there's nothing wrong with ordinary and secondly, there's nothing ordinary about Robert." Ben pointed to Robert, who was tell-ing a story to an enraptured audience while rolling a joint on the piano. His sleeves were folded up to his forearms and his fingers moved with grace. He caught Ben's eye and waved, handed the joint to a woman at the piano, whispered to her conspiratorially and stepped across the room to meet them.

"Phineas, Benjamin, how goes life?" Uncle Robert shook their hands.

"Good, Bob. How's life on the farm?"

"Good. Great." He picked up a nearby plastic cup, sniffed it and took a sip. "Rum," he announced. "Incredible eulogy, huh? Look at this place." The room buzzed with smiling people. Some laughed out loud and others told stories, eyes gleaming, hands flailing.

"It's great."

"So, you still tending bar?"

"Yeah," Phineas said.

"Writing for anyone?"

"I've got, uh, I've got some—" Phineas tapped his knuckle on the window sill. "No, not at all."

"Why not?"

"I don't know." Phineas shook his head with a grin.

"Ah, so you have seen fit to make your living with your hands, perhaps following the lead of your late, great Uncle Robert of Carlisle."

Ben laughed. "Robert, you're not late, you're alive—"

"It rhymed."

Phineas folded his arms. "Thank you. But you're a scientist, so it's not exactly—"

"I work on a farm," Robert interjected.

"You *own* a farm and you work as an astrophysicist," Phineas said.

"Fair enough," he said, "not my point, however."

"And what was that?"

Robert looked at Phineas. "Are you happy doing what you're doing?"

The question caught Phineas off guard. "I don't know."

Ben and Robert didn't say anything and Robert nipped at the rum and cola again. Ben smiled. "So, Robert, anything gonna hit Earth anytime soon?"

"You watch too many movies," Robert winked. "But yes." Someone from the piano audience called to Robert and he put the empty cup on the window sill. "Boys, I'm off, there's cannabis afoot. Would either of you care to join?"

Phineas shook his head. "Enjoy. I'll stop over and say hi later."

Robert nodded and stepped away, in the middle of the room he stopped and turned around, his smile gone. "There isn't a bad job in this world, as long as it's what you want to be doing." With that he turned, did a solo waltz move and followed the group out to the back yard.

Clay came up to Phineas and Ben and sipped at his drink. "Remember what a screwed up family we have?"

"It's hard to forget, Clay."

"I guess we didn't fall far from the tree."

"Yeah, that much is true."

"You want to get a drink after this?"

"Yes, yes I do."

Clay looked through the living room and the hallway, both were carpeted thick brown and the walls were wooden, like the inside of a ski lodge. Clay sipped at his cola, "Where do you think we'll do Christmas Eve this year?"

"I don't know, man. You want to get something to eat?"

"Oh yeah. I forgot about the food."

They went into the kitchen where Desmond was standing in a line of people and peered over a man's shoulders to see what was left. He frowned at the slim pickings. Clay slid around the side of the line and approached an old woman wearing a pill-box hat and a fuzzy boa, whose fashion sense hadn't altered in forty years. Clay hugged her and she smiled the smile of the confused as he reached behind her and lifted some ham from the platter.

"Hey!" Desmond stomped his foot and pointed at his son's hand. "What the hell do you think you're doing?" A distressed frown smeared his face and his eyebrows arched as though he might cry.

"Dad!" Clay glared at his father. "If you shut up I'll share with you." He spoke without moving his lips, trying to hide the fact that he was the speaker.

"Okay, get me some ham, would you?"

The other Troy men in line began to boo and hiss. Murmurs and arguments began and non-relatives didn't say or do anything. Clay reached onto the plate and grabbed some more ham, pocketed it and ran into the living room. The Troy men grumbled in unison, knowing that the boy had ended further litigation by moving away from the line. Desmond shuffled closer to the table to ensure that he hadn't lost his spot during the incident.

Phineas tried to figure a way to get into line when his mother tugged on his sleeve.

"Hey," Phineas said and fixed his suit jacket. "The goods, old woman, don't damage the goods."

Loni smirked. "Did I kick you in the crotch, boy?"

"No. And please don't."

"Come with me."

Loni and Phineas walked past a large group of people eating and drinking in the living room and into the small bedroom in the back of the house. Loni closed the door behind her son. He grew nervous.

"Grandmom left something for you."

"Are you serious?"

"She left it for you and, actually, she told me about it last year. I found it the other day when I came to get some things in order."

"What is it?" Phineas was excited and began searching around the room for a hint of some sort.

"I honestly have no idea." Loni opened the closet door and reached into a bag. She produced a manila envelope that had something bulky inside. She handed it to Phineas. "Here you go."

Phineas held it in his hands. It was heavy and felt like cloth, but its core seemed metal. He racked his brain for what could be inside. Loni's green eyes narrowed at him. "Whatever it is, I hope you appreciate it."

Phineas shot her a look. "I will, Mom."

His mother left and Phineas sat down on the bed. He turned the envelope and squeezed it to get any hint of its contents. He put the package on the bed like a child enjoying the glorious agony of delayed gratification. He surveyed the room. A large window looked out onto a side porch and a huge, intricately-carved, wooden chest rested at the foot of the bed. The bed's headboard shelf was full of detective novels and books of ghost stories.

There was a picture of a six year old Phineas wearing a cowboy hat riding a distressed golden retriever. There was another picture of his grandmother at about thirty years of age. She was with a good looking man with dark eyes and hair. He wore suspenders and a crisp white shirt; the sleeves were rolled half way up his thick forearms. The picture had been taken in the early 1950s on the back porch of the house. His grandmother was smiling and sat on the lap of his grandfather. She wore a long summer dress dotted with tiny red roses. Phineas inspected the photograph, which was in color but somehow too bright. The window behind them was filled with flowers.

Phineas opened the package. He withdrew a tan piece of paper and opened it to reveal a recipe for meatballs. He laughed and his breath caught in his throat. A tear slipped down his cheek and he smashed it with a palm. Again, he reached into the bag and removed a black felt cloth, which he unraveled to produce a pistol. He held it in his hands and his jaw hung slack in shock. "Oh my—"

There was a knock on the door and Phineas rewrapped the pistol and replaced it with the recipe back in the bag. "Yeah, what's up?"

"Hey, I'm heading out of here. You want to come?" Clay called through the door.

"Open the door," Phineas said.

The door opened and Ben and Clay stood on the other side. "We need a drink, you coming?"

Phineas tucked the bag under his arm. "Yeah."

Clay and Phineas said goodbyes with as much efficiency as possible. Ben went out to the church parking lot and pulled around Clay's truck and then his jeep. When he pulled up Clay and Phineas were just step-ping outside.

"Is Dad coming?" Phineas asked.

"Nah, Mom's driving him home later. Thank fuckin' God."

"Okay, where to? Blue Duck?"

Clay looked confused. "Yeah, where the fuck-else we gonna go?"

"Nowhere, I guess."

They stepped to the vehicles and Phineas hopped into Ben's jeep and Clay got into his truck.

Clay leaned out of his window. "Last one there buys shots."

"Drive fast, Ben."

"You bet. Phin, you okay?"

"Yeah, I'm fine. Let's get a drink." Ben slipped the jeep into first and released the clutch; they moved onto the street, the turn signal clicked like a grandfather clock. Phineas clutched the bulk of the pistol through the bag and looked both ways for traffic.

8

In 1945 Salvatore Troy came home from the Pacific Theater of Operations. He brought with him some new idiosyncrasies—checking under the bed and tapping his sheets as if tuning a piano before getting in, closing cabinets, then closing them again moments later, then hours later, opening, and then closing them again, and then checking again the next morning. He refused to close the curtain when he showered, and when he sat on the toilet he kept his feet up on the tub across from him, all the while searching the floor for something unseen.

And, like most men returning from war, he brought home souvenirs. A Katana, a Japanese soldier's cap, a marble tiger doorstop bought in Tokyo after the war, and a pistol. The pistol was in no way magnificent, just a British standard issue Webley revolver entrusted to him by a friend who had been severely wounded at Peleliu and would later die of his wounds. Sal's three brothers, all of whom miraculously survived the war, had also brought back mementos from their time spent scattered all over the world.

Jenutz, usually called Jinx, wore a smashed bullet on a chain around his neck that had been pulled out of his right butt cheek. Vince, having fought in France and Belgium, brought home a Lugar, a flag with the Nazi insignia and a German Colonel's pin. Daniel, the oldest, brought nothing, but smiled through two deep scars on his cheeks. As he was storming Utah beach at Normandy in 1944 a bullet struck him in the cheek, travelled through his mouth without touching his tongue or a single tooth or tonsil, and went out through the other side. The last thing he needed or wanted was another memento. He wore his reminder of war on his face, and would never be able to tuck it into some forgotten corner of a basement closet. He smiled at his brothers around their mother's table, knowing he was the luckiest of the bunch; he had fought in the war the longest and knew he should have been killed. He had fought in North Africa, Belgium, France and Italy where, as far as he knew, he had killed relatives.

They were quiet and solemn for a while and then rejoiced as the wine flowed, the food made their bellies warm and they understood that the war was over and they were home safe. They toasted and drank and it was Jinx who spoke first.

"Vince, I want that Lugar when you pass away."

"For hell's sake, you kidding me?"

"No, I want it. Come on, you know I like pistols."

"I never seen you with a pistol once in your life, you bum." Vince was the biggest of them all, he rarely received arguments.

"Come on, Vin, you can get my bullet." He hung the chain over his finger and dangled the bullet in the air.

"I don't want nothing that's been in your ass, Jinx."

Jinx gave up on Vince, who was starting to look annoyed. "What do you say, Sal, can I get your pistol when you go?"

"I don't want a bullet that's been in your ass, either, Jinx."

The conversation became heated and their mother, a four-foot-six woman with a goatee, came to the table and yelled at them in Italian. They didn't quite understand what she was saying through the mouthful of tobacco, but they got the picture and settled down after she began slapping the backs of their heads and spitting on the floor.

For two hours the brothers Troy, sitting around half-finished plates of manicotti and bruschetta, discussed who would get what in the event of the others' deaths. They drafted a will of succession for all the items and by the end of the evening drunken Troy men were strewn all over the living room and throughout their mother's kitchen.

In April 1981, Phineas was six years old and curious and rambunctious enough to ask any question that happened to pop into his brain. He was sitting on his grandfather's lap, pulling at his curly white chest hair, when he pointed to the pistol on the table and asked, "Grandpop, what is that?"

Despite being weak from a stroke he had had nine months earlier, Salvatore had continued to take the pistol out for its monthly cleaning. "It's a pistol Grandpop got in the war."

"Oh, can I have it?"

His good judgment and decision-making abilities had been shaky since the stroke. "Sure, you can have it." Then, recalling some of the facilities, wit and foresight with which he used to decide important matters, he looked into the young boy's eyes and said, "But first you need a Bachelor's Degree."

"Okay," Phineas said, "I'll get one." Phineas had neither idea what a bachelor nor a degree was, but he wanted the pistol, so he agreed.

"Now Salvi," Emily said, "this boy cannot have that gun."

"It's not a gun, tootsie," he looked up from his rocking chair, "it's a pistol." Then he considered it for a few seconds more. "And he'll only get it if Jinx dies before Phin graduates from college, okay?"

"Okay," she said, "we'll see." She disliked the idea, but she disliked Jinx more. He was obnoxious and he ate with his mouth open and scratched his crotch at the dinner table. Besides, she thought, Sal might not be around too much longer and it might be nice for Phineas to have something to remember his grandfather by.

Four months later, Sal died of a heart attack at Einstein Medical Center, where his older brother Daniel would die in 1989 from complications of diabetes. Vincent had died in 1979 after a blood clot exploded in his brain following routine gall bladder surgery. All the Troys were gone, except Jinx.

After Sal's death, Jinx made a habit of coming to the house once a month to clean the pistol and get a homemade meal. In his old age, however, Jinx had lost interest in owning the pistol. He was lonely and sad; his brothers were all gone and he already possessed all the other war-loot by being the one to stay alive the longest. He knew of Sal's promise to Phineas and wanted the boy to have the pistol. Besides, he told himself, his eyesight was going anyway, he'd only hurt himself or someone he liked.

Jinx starting coming once every two months after he was diagnosed with stomach cancer and, after his death in 2001, his son John came once a month to clean the Webley. He never mentioned it or asked, but Emily suspected that he was trying to sneak himself in under the gun.

In 2003, Emily updated her will, leaving assets, money, bonds, the house, jewelry and odds and ends to various people. To Phineas she had left two things: her meatball recipe, which she had promised him years before, and the pistol that Sal had promised him on that April morning in 1981. Both of which she put in a large manila envelope, along with an unopened box of bullets that Sal had bought in 1949, and stashed it under some heavy sweaters in her hope chest. She told Loni about the package, but not about the pistol, avoiding an almost certain conniption.

After Emily died, Loni came across the package as she was cleaning and organizing belongings and details. She knew it was meant for Phineas, but she had no idea what was inside.

9

Overconfident Middle Manager chewed gum through his beer and watched as Clip-on Cell Phone balanced a beer bottle on his nose, resembling a six-foot-six drunken bald seal. Clip-on's wife sat next to him giggling as he did so, her upper ridge of teeth jutting out in Neolithic grandeur. The somnolent barmaid smoked and wondered how she'd ended up working in The Blue Duck for over a decade. Her shirt was too small and when she bent to reach a low cooler her stomach hung over her belt. The belt loops on her jeans stuck out like denim elbows.

Conversations buzzed through the smaller room next to the bar and a fire crackled in the corner. Phineas, Clay and Ben were sitting at a table next to the window. Phineas picked up empty beer bottles by poking his fingers into them and looked down at the table through a pleasant haze.

"Another round of shots?"

Clay looked at him through slits, "Did my head fall off?"

"Fair enough. Be back in a minute."

Phineas put the bottles down at the corner of the bar and waited for the barmaid, who was thwarting the advances of Toothless Landscaper. His large arms were covered with faded tattoos and his greasy hair hung around his thick neck. She blew smoke at him and Clip-on laughed and pointed.

"Betty ain't no dumb kid, she knows your game. Haha."

Toothless grimaced at him, the gaps where his teeth had once been showing in the dim bar light. "Fuck off."

Clip-on stopped laughing and looked back into his beer bottle. Toothless turned back to Betty who had begun her slow gait toward Phineas. The jukebox began playing a Grateful Dead song.

"You fuck off," Clip-on muttered into his beer when he was sure that he couldn't be heard.

Betty walked by him, shook her head and tossed her cigarette to the ground. She squashed the butt into the floor. Phineas raised his eyebrows and smiled at her.

"What do you need, babe?" She lit another cigarette.

"Two lagers, a Grasshopper, a peppermint schnapps and two shots of Irish whiskey."

"Coulda just said nother round."

"I guess that's true, but we hardly have quality time anymore," Phineas said with a smirk.

"Uh, huh. You're a cutie, aren't you?"

Phineas couldn't figure out if she was being serious or not. "Sure am."

Betty went to the cooler and returned with the beers and shots.

"Just throw those on the tab, okay?"

"What did you think I was going to do with them?"

"I don't know, just wanted to talk a little more. Remember, quality time."

"Go over there." She pointed to Phineas' table.

"Good idea." Phineas took a tray that lay nearby and placed the drinks on it. When he got to the table, Clay reached over and took his beer and shot. Ben stared into the fire and took a deep breath through his nose. Phineas handed him a shot and the Grasshopper.

"God, I love that smell."

"What smell?" Phineas asked, he'd forgotten.

Ben shrugged. "Cedar. I love it when Jack puts cedar in the fireplace, it smells great."

Clay took a deep breath and smiled. "It's nice, isn't it?" He loosened his tie with two short yanks.

Phineas inhaled and there was nothing. He sat down, shaking his head.

Clay and Ben exchanged a glance. "What the fuck is wrong with you?" Clay asked.

"I can't smell the cedar."

"What, you stuffed up or something?" Clay asked.

"No. Apparently I've lost my sense of smell."

Ben leaned forward, "Are you serious?"

"Yeah," Phineas inhaled noisily several times. "Nothing, there's abso-frickin-lutely nothing."

"Jesus," Ben said and sat back. "You seen a doctor about that?"

"I have a friend who's a doctor. He said it isn't anything too bad."

"Yeah, but maybe you should get some tests done or something, don't you think?" Clay asked.

"I don't know; let's just drop it, okay?"

"Yeah, okay," Clay said, though he didn't want to drop it. "Well boys, these shots ain't gonna do themselves."

They picked up their glasses and held them at chest level. Clay cleared his throat and leaned in over the table. "As a wise man once said, if it moves fuck it, if it doesn't move, fuck it 'til it does."

Ben and Phineas laughed and Phineas let his errant olfactory system drift away with the shot. Now, Eric Clapton played on the jukebox and sheets of smoke hung in the air. Phineas watched people at other tables, his finger stroked the bottle and his eyes floated. Toothless stood on his stool in the corner of the bar and spit beer through his brown gums. Betty slapped him.

At 1:30 a.m., the boys walked back to the house and linked arms and sang. Ben and Phineas each carried a six pack in a brown paper bag.

"You got me on my knees, Layla! Doo doo doo doo doo, you got me on my knees!" As if on cue, a dog whined in the dark autumn night.

They stumbled into the house and the Scottish terrier sat up in his cage. He stamped his leg into its metal floor and snorted. Clay gave him the finger. Ben took the six pack from Phineas and started up the steps.

"You hungry?" Clay asked as Phineas reached the bottom step.

"Hm, hungry, no I think I'm okay." Phineas patted his pockets. "Oh crap! Ben, Ben."

Ben peeked his head around the corner of the wall. "Yeah, what's up?"

"Can I have your keys? I need to grab that stuff."

"Oh yeah." He fished through his pockets and, seconds later, the keys went sailing through the air toward Phineas, who narrowed his eyes and held out his hand to snag them. In this nanosecond Ben remembered Phineas' trials and tribulations as the right fielder for the Lansford Redskins little league team. It had been said—behind Phineas' back, of course—that he couldn't catch a cold. The heavy keys missed his hand and scraped his ear on their way to the wall. They hit the wall with a rattle and slid down to the floor, residing with a clink. Phineas held his ear and winced.

Ben jumped down three steps with a frown on his face. "Jeez, are you okay?"

Clay started laughing and held his stomach. "What, you trying to kill my bro? Bastard! I'll kill you!" His face was red and he wiped away a tear.

Phineas looked at his hand for blood. "I think I'm okay. There's no blood. You're lucky I'm too drunk to feel anything."

"Would you two quit fucking around?" Clay looked serious. "Ben, you got a joint to roll and beers to throw in the fridge upstairs. Phin, I guess you gotta get something out of Ben's car. Me, I gotta make a sandwich. Ready, break!" Clay clapped his hands once and walked into the kitchen. "I'll be up in a minute."

Ben came closer to Phineas and turned his head to look into his ear.

"It looks okay, maybe a little red," Ben said as he held Phineas' chin. "Sorry about that."

"It's an accident. I'll be up in a sec." Phineas picked the keys off the floor and walked outside into the darkness. He removed the package from the jeep and shut the door again. The cool air surrounded the house and the cars, there were no lights or people. Phineas stood still and listened to nothing. He was reminded of late summer nights when he was young and would sneak out to walk around their old neighborhood in the lonely darkness. He recalled the absolute quiet of those nights, at times terrifying, but the world, in those long lost moments, belonged to him.

Phineas walked up the steps and went into the small middle bedroom where his bag sat on the bed. He tossed the package onto the bed and took the rolled-up neck tie from his pants pocket and threw it next to the package. He unbuttoned his shirt and unbuckled his belt, releasing his constricted belly and let out a deep, satisfying breath. He kicked off his shoes without untying them and pulled his pants to his ankles and kicked them off his feet. The dull buzz of the house joined the buzzing in his head and he could hear Clay lumbering around in the kitchen. He felt warm and his ear pulsed. He pulled on a pair of pajama pants and tucked his T-shirt into them. Sitting on the bed he held the package in his hands, running his fingers over the outline of the pistol. He allowed himself a peek inside.

He stuffed the package into his bag and brought his right foot to the bed and held it in his hands. He rubbed his cold foot and did the same to his left foot. Sitting Indian style, he looked in the open closet for a pair of thick socks. He stood and searched through drawers, then the chest that sat in the corner. He got to his knees and looked under the bed. A large pink rabbit's face on the front of a slipper stared back at him; he found the other after moving a box of baseball cards. They fit.

Phineas walked up the dark stairwell to his brother's room, his new-found slippers shuffling on the hardwood floors. He passed the empty cases of beer and Ms. Jameson in her available pose. He knocked at the door.

"Phin?" Ben asked from the other side of the door.

"Yeah."

"Come on in," Ben said.

Phineas pushed the door open and stepped into the room. It was large and had a slanted ceiling. An entertainment center was in the corner on which sat a giant television, a DVD/VCR player, large speakers and a huge selection of DVDs. A standing halogen lamp cast comfortable light along the ceiling and a computer sat along the wall. A blue fish was swimming around on its screen. Next to it was a dark-wood CD stand holding hundreds of CDs. Two armchairs and a long, cushioned couch sat in the middle of the room; they surrounded a coffee table that had an assortment of magazines fanned about it and coasters in a neat pile. There were large windows that looked out onto the front lawn and street. Ben sat in an armchair and was leaning over the coffee table. He took a pinch of marijuana that sat in a pile on a piece of loose-leaf and sprinkled it into a rolling paper.

He looked up at Phineas. "Beer's in the fridge," he said, motioning his head. "Grab me one, would ya?" Led Zeppelin came from the stereo near the computer. Posters of hockey players and musicians were trapped behind wooden frames and glass.

Phineas reached into the fridge and removed two lagers. The fridge was stocked with milk, eggs, cheese, ham, and a box of baking soda that sat in the back. Phineas walked into the sitting area and sat in the arm-chair across from Ben, who licked the paper and rolled it into a joint. Ben looked past the joint in Phineas' direction.

"Nice slippers."

Phineas looked down. "They're not mine."

"I know, they're mine."

Phineas cocked his head like a confused dog. "Do you want them back?"

"No, you can wear them." Ben finished with the joint and put it on the table, grabbed his beer and sipped it as he sat back.

"You serious?"

"Almost never."

In the corner where the ceiling slanted, Clay's futon lay snug to the ground. His bed had been made and the pillows were plush flannel. A low light shone in a terrarium that sat on the counter behind the bed and a turtle peered out through the glass, from behind a rock.

"Do you ever get the turtle stoned?" Phineas asked Ben.

"No, we wouldn't do that to Freddie." He shook his head.

"Aha, well what if Freddie wants to get stoned?"

"When he tells me he wants to get stoned, I'll roll him a joint. 'Til then, he stays sober."

Loud footsteps grew closer to the door until it swung open with a thud. Clay held a sandwich and a bag of chips. He put his plate on top of the fridge and reached inside for a beer.

"Let me sit there," he said, pointing at Phineas' chair. "I can't reach the table from the couch and I don't want to fuck up my new rug."

"Yeah, sure." Phineas moved to the couch and Clay sat with a groan and laid a napkin next to his plate. He set his chips on the table and ate with precision. Phineas plopped his feet onto the coffee table and Clay stared at them until they were removed. Ben waited until Clay had finished eating and lit the joint.

"Nice fuckin' slippers," Clay said to Phineas.

"They're Ben's, so if you want to borrow them you have to ask him."

"They're Mom's."

Phineas took the joint and inhaled in minor hits. He coughed hard and took another short hit. Clay took the joint and drew on it, allowing no smoke to escape the front or back. Ben hit the joint and spoke in a pneumatically constipated manner.

"Phin wans to get Fred high."

Clay glared at Phineas with a look that he hadn't seen since he'd given Clay his final wedgie. "You ain't smoking up my damn turtle." He sipped his beer. "If Ben won't let me get my damn turtle high, you definitely can't."

Phineas took another hit off the joint and his eyes drooped. He put his beer on the table and sat back. His head was light and he tried to keep his eyes open. The buzz in his head now sounded like a stereo blaring white noise. Ben and Clay were speaking and Phineas heard it as though he had his head against their chests; they were too clear and too loud. He heard them laughing and wanted to be a part of it, trying to pry his eyes open but was unable.

Through his fog there was a commotion, people walking around him and a dollop of pressure on his sternum. He opened his eyes to see Clay and Ben standing over him. Ben spoke to Phineas' chest and Phineas furrowed his brow in confusion.

"This is why you don't want to smoke pot, buddy."

Freddie the turtle sat on his chest and looked stoically into his face, elongating his neck as if trying to get a better look. Phineas raised his eyebrows and, picking the turtle up by his midsection, handed him to Ben. The turtle's limbs and head shot into the shell. Ben cradled the turtle in the crook of his giant arm and, as the turtle poked his head out again, gently rubbed his small, hard head.

Phineas stood, straightened himself and thought he said, "I believe it is time that I adjourn to my quarters. Hold my calls." He straightened his pajamas and nodded at Ben and Clay, then looked at the turtle.

"Good night, sweet Frederick."

But it didn't come out like that at all.

10

Desmond Troy had always been troubled by the lack of Italian in his life. His mother had named him Desmond after a poet she had liked, not to mention that it went better with Troy than any of the Italian names Sal had tried to throw into the ring. Sometimes Desmond would grumble and curse his bad luck, a full-blooded Italian man named after a minor British poet. It made him boil. The family's original surname, Torini, had been taken care of in 1911 by a nameless, faceless immigration officer who decided that Torini sounded too much like a variety of pasta to be of any good to the young man standing in front of him wearing an oversized newsboy's cap and two left shoes.

The young man in front of him, Desmond's grandfather, Rinaldo Torini (to be Troy in the extremely near future), took to it, finding it a strong, suitable name with which to begin a new life in the New World. And so, the Torini name was lost forever.

On December 14, 1974, a Friday, Desmond and Loni were celebrating six months as young, happily married newlyweds. Unfortunately, they were young, happily married newlyweds with serious car troubles. The 1961 Studebaker Lark that Sal had given them as a wedding gift had a bad starter and a faulty carburetor. So, instead of going to see *The Godfather Part II* in the theatre, they stayed home, ordered pizza, watched *Laverne and Shirley* and screwed like wild monkeys until the bed broke.

Nine months later, as Loni lay, sweating and breathing rhythmically through her intense pain with her legs perched up in the air making a femoral V, was when she laid it on Desmond. She told him, in a stern yet freakishly calm voice, that if she had to carry the thing around for nine months and thirteen days (Phineas was late), then she was damn well going to name it. Their previous discussions had elicited several names, as this was in the days before a couple could learn the sex of a baby and have it named and signed up for little league or ballet classes before it had developed limbs.

Loni liked Francis and Diane for a girl, Desmond liked Angela and Rose. For a boy, Loni was leaning toward Sam or Jack and Desmond had his heart set on either Angelo or Paul. The couple decided to wait until the child exited the uterus in order to name it based on looks and gut instincts. It was that moment that Desmond had planned to sway his wife with the story of his desperate struggle for Italian in his life. When Loni made her pronouncement on the delivery bed, she'd won. Desmond knew this and lost all hope. Phineas was named, on a whim so flippant as to surprise even Loni, after a Greek god featured in a film during a Saturday afternoon B-movie marathon. This information was never told to either Desmond or Phineas.

Two years and two months later, upon Clay's arrival, the same edict was made by Loni and Desmond was left with a vasectomy, a 100% Irish wife, the last name Troy and two sons with decidedly un-Italian names.

He tried to bolster his heritage through several artificial methods. He watched Italian movies, listened only to Italian opera; splurged on a $230 pair of Bruno Maglis, placed a miniature Italian flag on his bed-side table and ate Italian food until serious constipation and his doctor forced him to stop. Finally, he grew depressed and could only scratch his cultural itch once in a while, normally through the help of starchy pasta and mafia films.

In June 2001, the Troy family dog, Stuart (Clay's birthday gift from 1992, named in honor of a winsome storybook mouse), perished in an unfortunate kitchen accident involving a faulty toaster and a badly placed kitchen stool. With Stuart's rather fiery demise, Desmond saw a small, fusilli-shaped light at the end of his tunnel and decided soon after Stuart's death that he wanted another dog. Loni sensed his urgency and swore that he only wanted a dog so that he could name something, though Desmond would never admit to this. While his passion was concrete and his arguments eagerly voiced, they were also misguided. The other family members realized in a panicked frenzy that the only man who wanted another animal was the only person who had never walked, cleaned, nor fed their previous animal.

Clay, Loni and, to a lesser extent, Phineas took immediate action. In the months that followed, the family held several meetings, all of which centered on the delegation of duties and the strict appropriation of all canine affairs to Desmond. Phineas, who was working his internship at *The Rock Courier* in Pittsburgh at the time, would get late afternoon calls from Clay outlining the course of events, citing minutes and agreements reached amid a flurry of creatively negotiated curse words.

The culminating moment of these meetings came in early August 2001 when Dr. Desmond Troy was faced with the adverse reality of waking at 5 a.m. on January mornings to feed a dog, walk a dog and then pick up and carry the feces of a dog. He begrudgingly retired to his study where he played several hours of solitaire on the computer and smoked cigarettes at a rapid pace. He emerged in the very late evening to announce that not only had he decided to buy a dog, but that he had, in fact, just ordered the dog from Terrence's Dog Farm situated in southern Allentown. The dog would be a Scottish terrier; it hadn't been born yet. Desmond would go pick up the dog in early November. The family speculated on how much jail time canicide carried.

For the next months, Clay and Loni heard constant updates concerning the future walking habits, dietary habits, training schedule and possible names of a dog fetus that was drinking embryonic fluid inside the stomach of a larger dog about 68 miles northeast of their current location. Books were read, names were one-sidedly discussed between Desmond and whoever else had the misfortune of being in the same room.

The first name discussed was Alessandro, after a character in a book that Desmond loved. It proved too long and, since Desmond had had a falling out with an old friend named Al, he decided that it wouldn't work. Many other possibilities followed: Corleone, Gambini, Columbo, Boticelli, Boccaccio, Sorrento, Taranto, Palermo (which had the upside of the nickname Pal), DiMaggio, Loretti, Antonio and Amerigo.

When the dog finally arrived on November 8, 2001, Desmond ceremoniously promulgated the name of the animal was to be Ennio. He further explained that the dog was named after the famous Italian composer Ennio Morricone, to whom Desmond had built a simple altar in his upstairs study. Ennio Morricone was the name. Nobody asked why he had named a Scottish terrier an Italian name; it remained the most minor of the several questions and worries on everyone's mind at the time.

The dog showed up on a Saturday and Loni and Clay tried to remain as uninterested as possible. Loni washed dishes, Clay ate sandwiches and watched hockey in the kitchen. Ennio came to them with an endearing waddle, slipping on the hardwood floors and squeaking small, short barks. At one point, Loni and Clay exchanged a bitter glance of commiseration: this dog was cute, God damn him.

For a while, Ennio was good-natured and full of energy; he slid down hallways and yapped at the door when he needed to go outside. He chased flies and spiders and got his head stuck inside of shoes. Pictures were taken, laughs were had by all. Loni and Clay liked the dog and his slapstick antics, but remained steadfast against taking him outside. Desmond remained steadfast against going outside at all.

Against Loni's strict rules, Desmond fed the dog from the dinner table, turning Ennio Morricone into a troublesome and noisy fourth dinner companion. After a few weeks, he began to smack his thumb-like tail against the table leg if not fed from the table. The smacking became barking and the barking became growling. It bothered everyone but Desmond, who ignored it completely.

No matter, Ennio Morricone was around to fill a void in Desmond's life and that is just what he did. Desmond spoke to the dog in his limited Italian, calling him paisano and asking him if he capiched. Most of the time, he addressed the dog with an affected Italian accent. The dog would cock his head to the side and stare, as if listening to explicit instructions on how to disarm a bomb.

Soon, the Troy family began to hear less and less of the inner workings of the dog's life. Loni and Clay no longer heard about walking schedules, exercise, diet, or training. They began finding piles of defecation throughout the old country home's once-quaint hallways and under beds, inside of shoes and in doorways. The dog had given up on going outside, but rather stared at it through a cleared spot in a dirty kitchen window. He developed a taste for cloth and books, and growled if he was approached while indulging himself. Clay and Loni Troy pitied the dog, their pity eventually growing to hate. Desmond loved the dog because it had become exactly like him.

It was this dog that growled and ate a Papa Smurf doll in the hallway outside the middle bedroom on October 9, 2004 as Phineas lay in the bed and held his head to keep it from exploding. Phineas grunted and flipped onto his side, slapped a pillow onto his head and tried to ignore the sounds of the dog and the strong morning light that drove through the windows.

Outside the room, Ennio lay on his side and gnawed on the doll, his teeth gnashing the battery compartment inside the blue gnome's stomach. He was bored with the doll and was merely killing time until the need for a bowel movement hit him or Desmond dropped a pound of food into his bowl. He stared at the window in the study and the tree beyond it blowing in the wind. Phineas shuffled in the middle room, paused and then shuffled again. Still on his side, the dog stopped eating and used his back paws to stretch himself toward the door. Phineas moved again and Ennio knew what he was hearing. His eyes widened as he heard the rhythmic chafing of fabric and the low, metered breathing coming from the bed.

He scratched his back on the hardwood floor in a spastic twitching motion, then stood, stretched and moved himself into action. Pressing the doll next to the door, he heard the shuffling slow, and then speed up with desperation. Ennio Morricone then used both front paws to push the Smurf head-first through the small gap at the bottom of the door. He heard a grunt, a curse and the quickening of pace, met with faster breathing. Ennio shot a quick chortle through his snout and then began scratching the door and barking.

When Ennio heard the footsteps coming up the stairs, he sat on his back haunches and barked even louder, his knobby tail thumping into the ground. The woman approached with a laundry basket against her hip and whistled into the hallway. When she saw him she frowned. From inside the room was uttered a low, sharp spasm of verbose anger, and then it became as quiet as a forest in April.

"Ennio!" Loni screamed. "Get away from there, you'll wake him up!" Ennio stepped aside so Loni could open the door. She knocked it open with her hip and stood in the doorway clicking her tongue and breathing hard from her recent journey up the steps. "Good morning. Did the dog wake you up?"

"Sure, let's say that." Phineas' hands were folded over his crotch. Sweat beaded on his forehead. The dog chortled again at a job well done and then scampered down the hallway, barking at nothing as he neared a doorjamb beneath which to crap.

"I dropped back to grab a few things, then I'm back to Grandmom's. Get up and get your things together." She picked a T-shirt up off the floor. "What're you doing today?"

"I think I'm going to go see Ben and those mules of his."

"Oh, how nice. Well, tell him thanks for yesterday."

"Will do." He rapped his fingers against his thigh. "I'll see you later, Mom."

"Bye," Loni walked out of the doorway and shuffled down the hallway to the steps, Phineas raised his hand in hopes of asking her to close the door, but she had already disappeared. Phineas lay still and tried to re-remember what had been on his mind forty seconds before. Ennio Morricone walked by the room and barked at Phineas twice to gloat over his recent victory, he then picked up the Papa Smurf doll, walked down the hallway to the study and sat under the desk. Meanwhile, Phineas' erection deflated into a miniature exactness of its former self, adding insult to injury. The television in Desmond's study blared news and sports figures at nobody and every time Phineas tried to get himself back in the mood for self-love he was reminded that there were terrible storms in the south and that Miami quarterback Brett McManus couldn't handle the ball in the rain, among other sporting factoids.

Phineas tried to remember the woman from his past that he had been thinking about, her curly brown hair, her careful fingers, her smile and mischievous eyes. She had smelled of lavender and Phineas inhaled to remember her scent, drawing in his breath and shutting his eyes. He stopped, opened his eyes and inhaled again, this time in short bursts. His brow furrowed in a quest for answers. He smelled something. The unmistakable scent of his grandmother's meatballs wafted into his deranged nostrils and seduced him. He shot out of bed and pulled his pajamas from around his knees to his waist. He jammed his feet into the pink fuzzy bunny slippers and looked for something to give him cover. He searched the garment rack on the back of the door and found a baby-blue robe. He pulled the robe around him and stormed into the bathroom to rid his belly of its urinary swelling.

He stepped around a large pile of dog poop and, pulling his pajamas once again to his knees, peed as he sighed with relief. Everything left him and he shuddered with delight. He finished after a minute and stopped when he caught a glimpse of himself in the full-length mirror next to the towel cabinet. The pink bunny slippers matched his light blue, thigh-length robe. A logo of a book-toting duck decorated the left breast of the robe. His hair was flat against the top of his head and pointing straight up on the left side as if two faults had collided in the night. Throat, eyes, ears, nostrils, nodes, jaw, armpits. Phineas took another deep breath, his eyes bugged out, and he shot out of the room and down the steps.

He swung around Desmond's table of cluttered items and ran into the kitchen, expecting to see a pot of simmering pasta sauce packed with tasty meatballs bobbing around like mines off the shore of Tarawa. The kitchen table was covered by that morning's coffee cups, a pound of bread crumbs from a toast incident and a dinner plate littered with dozens of extinguished cigarette butts. Three weeks of newspapers were strewn on the bench that sat at the table and another hundred pieces of unopened mail were scattered among the table and floor. Ennio stepped out from under the table and looked up at Phineas, and then he pranced away and picked up the Papa Smurf doll from the corner.

Phineas frowned and searched near the stove and oven. Pots and pans, both used and clean, sat in toppling stacks on the wrap-around counter in the kitchen. Bags of dog food and pot lids, Tupperware containers, lids and boxes of canned soups, dried foods and cans of cola gave the kitchen the air of a fallout shelter. Phineas opened the oven to reveal a baking tray with two sad, burnt French fries. On the stove was a pan with dried egg remains and an opened jar of mayonnaise, a knife lay next to it. A bag of bread which had been cut open in obvious desperation sat behind them.

The smell of meatballs stuck in his head, he looked further along the counter only to be disappointed. On the television was an episode of *The Odd Couple*, and Felix Unger complained at Oscar about a spilt beer. Phineas laughed. He poked his head into the fridge and sniffed everything he saw. A bag of carrots, a pound of white American cheese, mysterious brown gravy in an opened Tupperware container and green beans in an opened can. His hands flipped through containers, jars and overturned lids at a frantic pace. Nothing.

Phineas took a bottle of water from the fridge and opened it, took a sip and sat in a chair at the table. He blew the ashes off of the remote and flipped through the stations, stopping at a cooking show in which a very energetic young man danced around a massive kitchen and told the giddy audience about his latest creation.

"Just smell that, would you! It's wonderful; there is nothing more appealing and provocative than the alluring scent of Italian cuisine adorning your kitchen! Am I wrong?"

"No!" the audience screamed with absurd enthusiasm. The man wore a red and white apron and jumped on a stool. He was smiling insanely.

"Screw you." Phineas switched off the television and threw the remote on the table.

He closed his eyes and enjoyed the comfortable silence until he heard a loud thumping coming from Desmond's office. He went through the bathroom that connected the house to the office. The room was immaculate, with neatly stacked paper towels and a soap dispenser on the sink, the toilet was pearl white and blue water sanitized the bowl. The thumping sound continued and he heard a woman's voice. He opened the bathroom door that led to the office.

On the floor in the office, Desmond was pounding his folded hands into the chest of an armless, legless mannequin. An unlit cigarette hung from his lips and his loupes were pinched onto the tip of his nose. A slim woman dressed in a red warm-up suit sat Indian-style on the floor next to him and shouted commands.

"That's it, doc! Now, remember the count!" She wore a blue ball cap and a blonde ponytail popped through the back of it. "Come on, again. Start it off. What do we start with, doc?"

Desmond didn't look up; he wiped the sweat off his forehead and pulled the cigarette from his lips. "Oh, uh, look, listen and feel?"

"You're close!"

"Uh, oh yeah, starting CPR."

"You got it!"

Desmond looked up as he placed his fingers below the dummy's imaginary carotid artery. "Hey Phin, good morning."

"Hey Dad, what the f-"

"Cindy, this is my son Phineas. Phineas, this is Cindy."

Cindy stuck out her hand and looked into Phineas' eyes with absolute confidence. "Morning Phineas, nice to meet you." She spoke with clarity and chewed gum like a high school football coach. When she gripped his hand there was an audible pop in his pinkie finger.

He winced. "Hi Cindy, nice to meet you, too. What are you guys doing?"

"Oh, medical professionals need to be CPR certified. So, once a year I gotta take the class." Desmond sat back and caught his breath. "Want to join?"

"No thanks, I'm gonna go see Ben."

"Hopefully, you'll change first." Desmond raised his eyebrows.

Phineas pulled his robe closed and stepped back into the bathroom to hide the bunny slippers. Cindy blew a chuckle through chomps on her gum.

"I'll probably slip into something less comfortable," Phineas said as he waved at them. "Nice to meet you, Cindy."

"You too, Phineas. Take care of yourself." Her eyes didn't release his until he turned around.

Phineas walked through the living room, stopping twice to sniff his surroundings. Paper, pens, books, knives, unopened bonsai tree kits, mail, everything smelled like meatballs. And not *just* meatballs, not store-bought meatballs. The odor tantalizing Phineas was the perfect combination of basil, beef, lamb, parmesan cheese, pork and oregano that his grandmother used for her meatballs. He stomped up the stairs and pushed his hands into the pockets of the robe, the fuzzy bunny slippers staring ahead with gentle indifference.

11

Phineas turned on the elf spitter, threw his towel and robe on the toilet and put his hand into the flimsy wisps of water, feeling the chill dance across his naked body. He looked into the mirror, the hair on his legs and arms standing at brisk attention, and began.

With a full-length bathroom mirror in front of him and a brain full of anxiety Phineas became the only guest on a twisted game show titled, *What Fatal Disease Do You Have Today?* Staring into a mirror, alone, is when a hemorrhoid became colorectal cancer and a pain in his stomach became gallstones. His sore back transformed into acute renal failure and a tingling knee became Multiple Sclerosis.

Phineas fingered his jaw, producing a clicking sound which made a discouraging mental note in his mind. He stuck out his tongue and broke into a chilled sweat when he saw a slight discoloration that ran along the sides like racing stripes. They're brown, he thought. Brown. What's brown? His mind shot through all possible intakes that could have left a brown residue and eventually recalled a late-night chocolate cookie that quelled his momentary fear.

The black circles around his eyes were an eerie indication of late-stage HIV or Phenol sulfotransferase deficiency. The small white lumps on his tongue and cheek resembled a picture of Leukoplakia he had seen in a book of his father's entitled, *Cancerous Diseases of the Mouth*. Rebel white blood cells attacked the weakening lymph nodes under in his arm pits. He rubbed them and felt the sore track of lumps press against his finger. He was falling apart, and at the end of it all, he could still get hit by a car. There was simply no hope.

Years before, when Phineas first began to notice every centimeter of his ailing body he deduced that there were two groups of hypochondriac. Group A hypochondriacs sneeze and sniffle and feel as bad as one could possibly feel with a simple ailment. He groans, complains and exacerbates the sickness twenty times its normally allotted damage until he has convinced himself that he is deathly ill. Hypochondriac A takes off three days from work, annoys significant others with his passive demands for sympathy and develops bedsores.

Group B hypochondriacs sneeze or sniffle and leap heroically over bed rest, green tea and sympathy squarely into pneumonia, Yellow fever and brain cancer. He doesn't complain, he questions. Hypochondriac B doesn't look for sympathy, he looks for blind confirmation. He seeks reassuring compliance. The Group B hypochondriac often has an intense fear of doctors and lacks the ability to sustain an authentic medical evaluation. He relies on selective conjecture and has become an expert in the art of casually mentioning symptoms to others hoping for nonchalant dismissal or well-intended, though unsubstantiated, words of comfort. Phineas belonged to Group B.

Since his junior year in college, when it all began, Phineas had had, yet never been diagnosed with, genital herpes (three times), liver cancer, diabetes, meningitis, pericarditis, hepatitis C, hemochromatosis, syphilis (two times), Crohn's disease, mouth cancer, the gout, fibromyalgia and Legionnaire's disease.

He opened his mouth wide and tried to look down his throat, turning his head so the dim light from the bathroom ceiling could catch his tonsils and uvula. His eyes were their morning bloodshot and he felt his throat for swollen lymph nodes. He held his breath when he felt a lump on one side of his throat that wasn't on the other side. Through extensive digital inspection he found the other lump, fondled both, decided they were normal and began to breathe again.

Phineas leaned closer to the mirror to further scrutinize small red bumps on his neck. He searched his stomach and chest for lumps and clumped cells; he felt his penis and testicles for lumps and searched for open sores and white spots that could represent the beginning of penile cancer or herpes. There was a disturbing constellation of moles along his stomach and he grimaced at the sight of more stretch marks around his waist. The water behind him dripped with loud clocks against the drain and steam poured out of the stall as he squatted to lightly finger his anus.

Phineas stood and pressed his nose toward the ceiling with his thumb, the wiry hairs tickling the inside of his nostrils. His inability to smell was one more cog in the wheel of his poor health; one more symptom of his slow and painful removal from Earth. The one idea that helps a Group B hypochondriac retain some sanity is that he is creating symptoms. This hope was gone for Phineas; you either had a sense of smell or you didn't. And he didn't.

He stepped into the shower, depressed at the sight of his discolored eyelids, the pale, vast chubbiness of his midsection and his hairy, surely cancer-ridden face and nose.

He stood in the elf spitter and pushed and prodded the top of the nose as if there were a secret scent-button somewhere that had been switched off. He rubbed the shampoo into his hair, the grease and gray liquid gathered at his feet. He longed to cleanse himself completely. Go back to start. Be better. He scraped the tiny piece of slimy soap against his torso and then his face and shoulders. The water trickled over him and he cupped it and splashed it against his face. The ends of his toenails were black and his feet were hairy, like a Hobbit's, he thought.

He scrubbed at his neck and face and chest and stomach, using his fingernails to dig the soap into his beard. Tears appeared in his eyes and his face met the water coming from the elf spitter. He spit water in spurts, like a stone merman in a fountain, and bent his neck to let the water run over his head and down his back.

Phineas wiped the steam off the mirror before he dried himself, his flab jiggled and water dripped off his beard. He erased a streak of soap that whitened his right eyebrow, put his face into the towel and moaned low into the brown paisleys and detergent stains.

12

Phineas wore brown pants, a navy-blue sweater and a green hunting jacket. The dog watched him while nosing around his doll. He heard his father in the kitchen banging plates and silverware as a reporter on the television talked about that afternoon's NFL football games. He poked his head in and saw his father lean over the mysterious brown gravy, smile and spoon it onto a piece of bread.

"Okay, Dad, I'll see you later," Phineas called in to his father.

Desmond looked up, surprised. "Alright," he said. "Oh, hey, look," he called before Phineas could turn to leave. He swung his CPR certificate in the air along with the mystery gravy-covered spoon. Mystery gravy smeared along the corner of the certificate.

"Hey, nice job. Armed and dangerous, huh, Dad?"

"Yeah, well, I need to do this once a year. Never had to use it once, though. Ha, knock on wood, I guess." Desmond knocked on his head twice, bouncing both the wallet-sized certificate and the spoon into his hair. A dab of mystery gravy stuck in his hair and the spoon dropped to the ground. Desmond looked at the spoon in shock, and then he frowned and looked at Phineas, who rolled his eyes and bent to pick up the spoon. Before he could get to the sink with the spoon his father reached out and took it.

"Dad, it's been on the ground."

"So, I can still use it. I'm told there's a general rule on these matters."

"Dad," Phineas slapped his palm against his forehead, "are you actually citing the five second rule?"

"Ha, I knew there was a rule!"

"Yeah, for college kids and 12 year-olds."

"Oh, come on," Desmond made a face and reached again for the spoon.

"Dad, you're a medical professional, CPR-certified and all. Why don't you just use another spoon?"

"Oh, fine. Grab me one, will you?"

Phineas dropped the spoon into the sink and took another one from the counter which Desmond took and stuck it into the gravy. On his way out, Phineas noticed a drop of brown gravy on his finger and wiped it onto a napkin he found on Desmond's table. Afterwards, he brought the napkin to his face and sniffed twice. Meatballs. He sighed, throwing the napkin into the overflowing garbage can and walked through the front door.

The early afternoon sky was crisp and refreshing. The sun hid behind the oak and cherry trees that lined the street and Phineas squinted against the glimmering windows in the houses. A breeze scattered dry leaves along the street and an old man raked wet leaves from the lawn on the side of The Blue Duck. The clear air made Phineas feel more awake. A boy with a red juice stain on his upper lip rode a tricycle on the sidewalk toward him and smiled. The boy stuck his tongue between a gap in his teeth and the hood of his coat bounced against his back with the motion of the bike. Phineas watched the boy ride past and got lost thinking that the boy reminded him of someone he used to know, but couldn't figure out who. The kid was out of sight before long.

Phineas walked along Maple until he reached The Blue Duck, then turned onto Edgewood Lane as a current of cool air blew through his jacket. Everything seemed clearer in the day; the trees, the leaves and the people moved with premeditated purpose. People raked leaves or tended to their gardens for one of the last times that season. Halloween decorations adorned every house and Phineas thought of that fantastic night. He became jealous as he tried to remember what it was like to be a kid on Halloween and not a young adult drinking abnormally-colored punch at a Halloween party in a dingy basement. He had vague memories of crowds of chaperoned children dressed as ghouls and witches, carrying pillowcases full of candy as they roamed the streets. The buzz of mystery that hung in the air, Jack-O-Lanterns and fake cobwebs, Halloween specials on TV. The excited scamper that would ensue when they saw the multicolored word SPECIAL rotate its way to the forefront of the TV screen and the 1970s music that accompanied it on the way. He remembered a sheep costume that Clay had been forced to wear as a toddler, pictorial evidence of which Desmond kept on his desk in the office. And how, at family gatherings, when Desmond had had one coffee liqueur too many, he'd bring the picture out and giggle as Clay's face reddened amidst the ohs and how cutes of his aunts and mother.

Phineas recalled that miniature Snickers bars were his favorite and that somehow he would end up with the occasional piece of hated fruit, no matter the extent of his scrutiny. Desmond had always handed out toothbrushes and plaque tablets which prompted many kids to skip the Troy house, leaving Desmond with dozens of toothbrushes and Clay and Phineas embarrassed at school the following week. In his moment of nostalgia, Phineas became aware that something was missing, something that made the memory not quite right. He paused and tried to put his finger on the reason, but couldn't. The memories weren't complete, though; they had no life, no depth. They lacked a crispness and color that would have otherwise made his reminiscence like watching a TV program. Phineas could feel the memories pass by him as they scuttled down the sidewalk with the leaves and around the corner like the little boy on the tricycle.

Two people dressed from head to toe in Philadelphia Eagles garb knocked on the front door of a house; one of them carried a bowl wrapped in aluminum foil. The trees in front of him created a tunnel over the road, with woods and houses on either side. Three young boys ran through the woods, one of them screaming about something Phineas couldn't make out. Their footfalls resounded through the woods as they stomped along to the tune of their imaginary world.

Phineas walked down the sidewalk and stuck his hands in his pockets. Looking around him and peeking over his collar to check that he was alone; he leaned into the breeze and shook his head.

"So, you smell meatballs all morning," he said aloud to himself. "What is that all about? I mean, here I am thinking of some chubby hairdresser and she makes me think of Grandmom's meatballs? Is that possible? Grandmom wasn't fat…was it a dream or something? Oh, who the hell knows? All I know is that I'm losing my mind. Meatballs, that's what I smell, meatballs?" Phineas inhaled and stopped walking. "That's not meatballs," he inhaled again and took his hands out of his pockets. "Meatloaf and-," he sniffed a couple more times. "-and, and," a quizzical look and a rapid series of sniffs, "-mashed potatoes! Oh for the love of…"

A man drove by in a Volvo as Phineas began jumping up and down yelling at himself. The man slowed, looking concerned, and watched as Phineas stopped and smiled at him. Phineas fixed the ruffled collar of his jacket and the man shook his head and drove off.

"Phineas Troy, you're smelling meatballs, and other meat products," he shot to himself, "and now you're talking to yourself. You're on a one way road to the nut house!" He grabbed his hair and kicked his legs out in a Tourette's-like spasm. "Okay, relax, relax." He picked up a handful of wet leaves and held them to his face, breathed in their scent and frowned when the overwhelming blast of meatloaf and buttery mashed potatoes hit him.

"Okay, here we go." He stomped off the sidewalk toward a cluster of trees and sized up a nice looking maple. He looked around again and, ensuring his solitude, leaned against it and inhaled. "Meatloaf! How can a tree smell like meatloaf?" He held the tree with both hands as if it was a woman's head and he was about to kiss her with great passion. He leaned in again, closed his eyes and concentrated on the tree. He thought of the cold bark, the dry leaves falling around him, the timeless smell of wood and dirt of an ancient tree. He thought of the sticky, sweet sap and the colonies of ants and armies of other animals and insects that called this tree home. He imagined a heart with initials carved into it and its branches becoming firewood and make-believe weapons in make-believe war games. He kept his eyes closed and hugged himself to the tree, pressed his nose against it and inhaled at a steady, slow pace for twenty-three seconds. He opened his eyes and stared into the tree.

"I can even smell the damn ketchup." He rested his forehead against the tree, snatched a piece of protruding bark and tossed it behind him. He then ripped off another hanging piece and strangled it as he screamed like a war-bound Comanche. Behind him the three boys who had been shouting and playing now watched him in awe. They were semi-hidden by trees, watching his breakdown. One of them held a long stick like a spear and the youngest switched his focus from Phineas to his cohorts every few seconds. Upon noticing them, Phineas stopped his flip out.

"This tree is sick." He brushed some bark from his sweater. "Don't take any branches from this tree, understand boys?"

The boys nodded and the tallest of them sprinted off into the woods, letting out a high-pitched screech. The two others followed, screaming as if they had just seen a monster. Phineas popped his hands back into his pockets and stepped off toward the river.

"Phineas, people are gonna start to talk." Mysterious origin notwithstanding, the smell was making him hungry. A dirt path on the right followed through a niche of woods to the canal that ran into the Neshaminy Creek. The path along the canal was muddy; the canal was murky and leaves and twigs floated on top. Occasionally, an eruption of bubbles disturbed the quiet surface. Phineas looked down from the small hill into the water for fish and frogs. There was nothing. He reached the stone bridge and crossed it.

On the other side of the canal there was a cabin for the mule tenders, a shack for the mule equipment and a low-ceilinged barn for the mules. The barn was thick and sturdy and made of crude wood. In front of the barn Ben was kneeling next to a massive mule, cleaning one of its hooves. The mule's face showed content and Ben worked slowly and carefully. He wore a pair of jeans, boots and a dark-brown sweater with holes in it. He wore a Phillies cap and glasses.

"Hey Ben."

Ben looked up from the mule's leg, "Hey, how you doing?"

"Good, you?"

"I'm fine, it's a gorgeous day." He patted a big paw against the mule's side haunch. "This is Miles."

"Hi Miles. What you doing to Miles there, Ben?"

"Well, we've got to clean their hooves every morning." Ben replaced the foot on the ground, stood, stretched his back then positioned himself to clean the back hoof.

"Seems like a pain," Phineas said.

"Actually it's relaxing. Besides, they like it a lot."

"Really?"

"Well," Ben said, "wouldn't you like someone cleaning your toes every morning?"

Phineas looked down at his shoes. "Depends who did it, I think."

"I guess. Hand me that bucket."

Phineas picked up a yellow bucket filled with brown water and went to put his nose in it, instead he handed it to Ben, who began scrubbing the inside of the hoof with a toothbrush. The mule made a low purring sound.

"I'm just about done, give me a sec."

Ben focused on the hoof, and Phineas' eyes glazed over watching him work. The mule looked at the ground.

Ben gently straightened the mule's leg, letting the hoof catch the ground, and then he picked up the bucket. He tossed the water into the canal and went to the barn. Phineas followed. Ben turned on a hose and filled the bucket with clean water. Inside the barn was another mule, bigger than the other.

"This is Sonny." Ben patted the mule on the back and stroked her hair.

"Hi Sonny," Phineas said and waved.

"Here, pat her head lightly, like this." Ben moved his hand between the mule's ears, and the mule showed its teeth in a smile. Phineas touched it and the mule reared its head and Phineas pulled back, wiping his hands against his pants.

"I don't think she likes me."

"Oh, she's just never met you. It takes them a while to trust someone."

"Really?"

"Yeah, they're pretty bright animals."

"I always thought mules were dumb."

They walked out of the barn and Ben placed the bucket of water in front of the mule and worked the brush north to south against the mule's coat. "Mules are much smarter than horses and donkeys. They have great memories; they remember people and actually hold a grudge if someone's nasty to them."

"Hm, I never knew that," Phineas said, trying to add to the conversation.

Phineas again grew comfortable watching Ben brush the mule, the unmistakable aroma of meatloaf pouring from everything in sight. Ben told him about the barn, the stables and the other mule tenders. He showed him the canal boat and the harness and ropes that were attached to the mules and allowed them to pull the boat during canal trips. Visitors sat in the boat as Ben gave a tour and sang traditional folk songs from 18th century Lansford. All the while, the mules pulled the boat down the canal that twisted through town, no doubt envisioning a meal and water at the end of the towpath. Phineas imagined the boat ride to be exquisitely relaxing.

"So wait." Phineas kicked at a root that bent out of the ground like a miniature whale breeching. "Mules are the offspring of a male horse and a female donkey, right?"

"Actually, it's the opposite," Ben said, cleaning the brush with his knuckle and forefinger. Phineas giggled and Ben rubbed Miles on his back while murmuring into his pointy ear. His giggle went to a chuckle and Ben waited for an explanation but knew he was out of luck when the chuckle turned into full-blown roaring laughter. The thought—in fact the only thought present in Phineas' mind at the moment—was of an undersized, self-conscious donkey sneaking up behind a large, muscular horse. His mind found morose, gooberish Eeyore sizing up valiant Shadowfax somewhere on a small farm in southern Jersey. He imagined the budding romance—in this case, homosexual—and then he thought, as he wept with laughter, about the early romantic sweet talk and the intense heat of forbidden barnyard love. He envisioned the first donkey that had been courageous, adventurous and horny enough to first take that cross-species plunge. He considered the brave donkey, the gallant relinquishment of self-preservation, the incredible self-sacrifice just to get laid and, secondarily, so that future generations of farm workers could get more efficient work from a large, crossbred animal. Phineas wiped a tear from his eye and mentally doffed his hat to him.

When his barnyard fantasy had ceased and after he promised himself that nobody would ever be privy to those thoughts, Phineas became aware that he was staring at Ben's huge back. His shoulders pressed against the sweater, the muscles rolling in waves against his skin and the thick neck coming out of the top of the sweater like a tree trunk. Past him, Miles stood relaxed, without a drop of fat showing under his smooth skin. Miles dwarfed Ben, Sonny back in her barn dwarfed Miles and Phineas, at that moment, felt like a lemur.

"Jeez, you sure take care of these big animals, huh?"

Ben turned, "Well, why not?"

"I don't know. It just seems a lot of attention to spend on animals, that's all."

"Well, what do you think we are?"

Phineas put his hands up. "I didn't mean anything by that. I'm just, feeling a little weird's all."

"What's going on?" Ben motioned him toward the cabin. He hooked Miles to a rope and walked him back to the barn, clicking his tongue to lead him on. Ben opened the gate in the barn and Miles grunted and stepped in next to Sonny. They looked at each other and hung their heads.

"I don't know, man. I think I'm losing my mind."

"More than usual?"

"Well, you know I told you guys the other night I can't smell, right?"

"Yeah," they stepped in to the cabin and Phineas sat at a basic wooden table. The chairs squeaked and the walls were covered with brochures, maps, charts and pictures of the mule tenders and the mules. Ben walked to the counter and turned on an electric kettle. "Coffee?"

"Sure," Phineas said as he looked around the room. Wooden shelves ran along the wall holding dusty knick knacks and framed pictures. The windows looked out onto the canal; between the trees in the distance he could see a slow river barge where the mouth of the canal let out into the Neshaminy Creek.

"So, what do you think the problem is?"

"Me, I'm pretty sure it's eleven different types of cancer mixed with hepatitis and four venereal diseases. Maybe even the gout."

The kettle steamed and bubbled. "Okay," Ben said, "what does a non-hypochondriac, paid professional think?"

"I don't know." He shrugged his shoulders.

"Don't you go to a doctor?" He jotted a note into a notebook and flipped it back onto the counter.

"I have a doctor." Phineas rubbed the cool from his hands.

"Oh, okay," Ben removed two mugs from a cabinet and spooned instant coffee into them. "Milk? Sugar?"

"Yeah, sure."

"So, what does he think?"

"Who?"

"Your doctor."

"Oh, he's not sure." He hoped the line of questioning would end there. "Beautiful view."

Ben looked out the window. "Yeah, sure is nice. Hasn't he done any tests?" He dropped the spoon into one of the mugs with a clink and swept some crumbs from the counter with the back of his hand.

"Who?"

Ben turned and curved his face into a smirk. "Your doctor." He put the coffee cups down after filling them with boiling water.

"No, no tests."

"Why?"

"Well, I haven't really asked for, you know—"

"Phineas, what the hell are you talking about?"

Phineas sipped at the hot coffee. "He's a friend and a specialist. And this isn't really his area of expertise. He basically just gives me free advice."

"What's his specialty?" Ben blew on his coffee then took a sip.

"Gynecology." Phineas looked out the window again, "That a river barge?"

"Yes. Um," Ben placed his cup on the table, "do you need me to tell you why this won't work?"

"No, I already know."

"Okay, because you know gynecologists typically look after—"

"I know, I know," Phineas scratched the back of his head.

"Okay, so why are you going crazy?"

"Well, since this morning I've been smelling things."

"That's good, isn't it?"

"Theoretically, yes."

"But?"

"But, not in this case."

"Oh," Ben dropped his smile and his coffee onto the table. "Why?"

"I'm smelling things that don't make sense."

"Kay…like what…?" Ben made a rolling motion with his hands, coaxing more from Phineas.

"Okay," Phineas looked over his shoulders and then leaned in. "This morning I smelled meatballs."

"Can I assume that nobody was cooking meatballs?" Ben whispered.

"Not a meatball in sight, and everything I smelled, smelled like meatballs. Everything!" He sat back, "And not just meatballs, but my grandmom's meatballs."

"Do you smell her meatballs right now?"

"No, now I smell meatloaf and mashed potatoes."

"Aha, of course." He rolled his knuckles against the edge of the table. "I mean is it a faint smell, like a memory or something?"

"Ben, I can smell the butter and garlic in the potatoes, I can smell the ketchup and tomato paste on the meatloaf and the salt and pepper. I can smell everything. It's, well, mouthwatering. But it's not a memory, I don't think." He wiped his lower lip with his sleeve.

"How does it make you feel?"

"Honestly, aside from the fact that it's freaking me out a bit, it's pleasant. Sort of…I don't know…comfortable."

Ben leaned against the wall in his chair. Phineas swore it was going to snap under his monstrous frame, but it held. He drank at his coffee and looked out the window. "What were you thinking about before you started smelling your grandmom's meatballs?"

Phineas laughed, "Having sex with a chubby hairdresser."

"Is this a good memory or a bad memory?"

"You kidding? It was fantastic. She brought me home, we drank this really sweet wine and had sex. Then she gave me a massage."

"So, maybe it's a nice memory and you related that to the comfort of meatballs."

"Are you telling me that getting off with some girl made me think of my grandmother? You're sick."

"Right, I'm the sick one in this conversation." For the first time since Phineas had mentioned his problem, Ben felt worried.

"Oh I don't know, man." He clapped his hands down on his thighs. "This is crazy."

"How about the meatloaf? What was happening when you started smelling that?"

"I was walking here. I was checking out the houses and Halloween decorations. There were little kids on bikes. It was like a Norman Rockwell painting."

"So, maybe it's a comfort thing."

"What do you mean?"

"You know, comfort food. Those foods you ate as a kid, they make you feel comfortable and safe again. Like how some people make chicken soup when they're sick and it makes them feel better cause it's what their moms made them when they were young and got sick."

"Really, you think it might be something like that?"

"Well, your grandmom just died and you smell her meatballs. You're walking here today and you smell meatloaf and mashed potatoes. Comfort and home and safety."

"You know, when you were brushing Miles I had the same feeling as when I was with that hairdresser, just comfortable and relaxed."

"Yes, but Phineas, you realize I rarely give Miles and Sonny handjobs. And never on Saturdays."

Phineas stared at him with his mouth open.

"I'm joking."

Phineas gave him the finger.

"Phin, joking aside, maybe something's going on inside and you need to figure it out."

"Like what?"

"Well, I'm afraid I can't help you with that one. It's on you, old friend."

"Thanks, buddy." Phineas put his hands over the coffee and let the steam warm them.

"No problem, that'll be fifty bucks, please."

Phineas sipped his coffee. Ben leaned forward and his smile disappeared.

"Oh crap, where the hell is Judy Garland?"

Phineas looked around his right and left shoulder. "What the hell are you talking about?"

"Judy Garland's gone; she's not in her terrarium." Ben walked to a table in the corner.

Phineas stood and turned. "Who is Judy Garland?"

"The tarantula I'm watching for Charlie."

Phineas turned white and leapt onto his chair with a high-pitched screech. He looked around him and clutched the back of the chair. "Tell me you're screwing with me!"

"What? No, I'm not. That little devil, she always gets out. Oh, man."

"Are you serious?"

"Yes."

"Ben, we discussed these things that have eight legs and my feelings about them."

"What, spiders?"

"Yes, spiders! How could you possibly forget? How on Earth can you forget every Boy Scout camping trip we ever went on?" Phineas' eyes moved across the room in a panicked frenzy.

"Oh yeah." Ben recalled a 12-year-old, towel-clad Phineas crying and standing on a cot in the middle of a tent as Ben carried a tiny spider outside in a mess-kit pan.

"I gotta get outta here!" He stomped on the chair.

"Ha, oh yeah, you do hate those little guys, don't you?" Ben lifted up his chair and peeked underneath.

"Yes!"

"Can you help me find her?"

"No!"

Even with Phineas' darting eyes and his fear-induced vigilance he didn't manage to glimpse the Mexican redknee tarantula on a dusty shelf amongst the aging knick-knacks and dark-wood framed pictures. Judy Garland, on the other hand, watched Phineas Troy with amazement and interest. He exuded such a sweet scent of terror that he was irresistible to her. She watched in fascination as he flailed his arms and patted his head, danced in circles on the chair and shivered. He was the most interesting person she'd ever seen. And when Phineas shot through the door that Ben had opened for him, moving with such speed as to impress even a tarantula, Judy Garland decided then and there that she would follow him and darted from her perch across the wall until she found a passage to the outside.

Crouching against the outside of the cabin wall, she watched as Phineas twitched and Ben laughed with his hands on his knees. She made her way to the ground, crossing in front of the mules, which gave her little notice, and waited for him at the side of the path that led to the bridge.

"I gotta go," Phineas called to Ben.

"Okay, hey, want to meet at The Duck in a couple hours? I got a canal trip at 2:30; should be out of here at four."

"Sure, I'll see you there."

"See ya, man, I hope you feel better."

"Thanks, see you at four."

Ben turned back into the cabin and Phineas shivered so hard that his back cracked. He straightened, the heebie-jeebies out of his system for the time being, and walked toward the bridge. He heard Miles and Sonny shuffle and nodded a goodbye in their direction. Ben's head poked out of the cabin.

"Hey, Phin?"

"Yeah?" Phineas turned to face him and walked backwards.

"What do you smell now?"

Phineas stopped and took two quick sniffs followed by a long inhale. "Rotten eggs." He stepped down the path, crossed the bridge and stuffed his hands in the pockets of his jacket as he headed back through the woods. Judy Garland stalked him from behind, stretching her eight hairy legs through the leaves and twigs as she kept low to avoid the white-nosed coati, her natural predator which resided only in Mexico and the southwestern United States.

13

By the time Ben arrived at The Blue Duck around 4:30 p.m., Phineas had been there for thirty minutes. He was sitting at the bar, leaning back against the stool with one hand on his stomach, an empty plate and a full beer in front of him. His smile was flat and serene, his eyes quiet and content. Ben sat down and Betty nodded to him, stuck her cigarette between her lips and pulled the crème de menthe out of the well. Ben waved his hand at her.

"Oh, no Bet, it's okay. Just a beer."

Betty smiled, "Thanks babe."

"So," Ben wiped a handkerchief across his forehead and stuffed it into his shirt pocket, "what did you get?"

"What do you think, old friend?"

"Well, let me guess. Yeah, I think I'm gonna go with meatloaf and mashed potatoes."

"Incredible. You must have ESP or something." He rubbed his stomach.

"I ain't seen no one eat like that in a while." Betty slid a lager in front of Ben. "He ain't even touched his beer."

"Oh my, you're right there, Miss Betty, aren't you?" Phineas leaned forward just enough to hook the beer in the crook between his finger and thumb and sat back to rest it on his belly. "This is the life." He slapped his gut with his open hand. "There's football on the television, I have a cold beer and I am fat with food. Benjamin, Bethany," he regarded them with casual formality, "this is what our forefathers had in mind when they kicked the crap out of the Brits. This exact moment is what our fathers and grandfathers had in mind when they landed at Inchon, and raised old Guts and Glory over Iwo Jima." His demeanor was confident. "Cheers to them." Phineas drew hard on the bottle then smacked his lips. His eyes shot open and he sat forward with a start, foam bubbling on his mustache.

"Oh God, Betty! What the hell?"

Betty examined him. "What's the matter?"

"It's this beer, oh my—" he dropped the beer on the bar and stood up. "Betty, I need a glass of water, please."

Betty poured a glass of water and held it out. Phineas grabbed it and began drinking, water dribbling down his chin. Ben took the beer from the bar and sniffed it.

"Smells fine," Ben took a small sip. "Tastes okay, too." He shrugged.

"You got to be joking me! That is the skunkiest beer I have ever tasted!" He pointed at the bottle, his finger shaking. "Good God!" Phineas sat down again and examined the bottle that sat in front of him.

Betty smirked and walked to the cooler, leaned into it, revealing too much as usual, and pulled a bottle of peppermint schnapps. She poured a shot and put it down. "Here babe, this one's on the house."

"Thanks Bet, that's nice of you." He nodded cheers to Ben and Betty. "Here's to swimming with bow-legged women." And put his head back with the kick of the shot.

Vomit moves fast. Fortunately, so did Betty. The customers at The Blue Duck Inn that day saw Betty the barmaid move faster than she had ever moved before. Also, she dropped her cigarette and for the briefest of moments her eyes snapped from their perma-cool droop to a wide-eyed horror only seen on bad guys before they take one in the gut in a Spaghetti Western.

As one customer put it, "She moved so fast, she was Betty Ali for a minute there."

In her defense, Jack Schorpp was heard to say during a Thursday night poker game, it's not every day that vomit is fired at you at approximately 197,000 miles an hour. After the infamous shot had been taken (and returned) and Phineas and Ben had cleaned up a great amount of peppermint-scented, undigested meatloaf and mashed potatoes from the bar, floor and floor behind the bar things got back to normal. Phineas sent Ben to the store to get flowers and two packs of cigarettes for Betty and cleaned the rest of the bar while he was gone. It was okay, he explained, he couldn't smell anything anyway.

After the bribes, Phineas still had his work cut out for him and had to promise drinks and one more surprise bouquet of flowers. Betty gave in and allowed him back in his seat and asked him what he wanted while she tapped her foot on the ground and cast furtive glances for escape routes.

"I'm not sure, Bet. I'll be back in a second." Phineas excused himself and stepped off to the bathroom. The gray door to the bathroom lacked a lock and a handle; large dents ran along at shin level. Two 40 watt light bulbs shone a dim light across the room from behind a white ceramic plate and cast shadows through the front of the stall in the corner. Phineas turned on the faucet and cupped water into his hands and sipped from them. He looked into the mirror, his eyes watery and his face red. He checked his tongue for spots and looked into his nose, hearing his breath and feeling the sweat of fear chisel a path down his scalp. He closed his mouth. "No, not a chance. You hear me? This isn't going to friggin' happen. Not this time." He pointed into the mirror at himself and curled his mouth into an enraged snarl. "You cowardly bastard! Get out there and get back to it! Not again, not now!" He seethed at himself in the mirror, the lights clicked behind him. A bearded face poked out from the stall and Phineas slid his eyes away from his reflection to look at the man. Toothless stood swaying in the doorway of the stall, most of his body lost in the shadows. "You tell em, bud!" He slurred through gaps. "Don't take no shit from that guy!" He burped and pulled the stall door closed behind him and then sent out two long snorts.

Ben was sitting at the bar when Phineas returned from the bathroom. He took the flowers and cigarettes and handed them over to a still skeptical Betty. He sat down. "Please, a shot of orange brandy, please." Phineas ordered then nodded at Ben who swigged his beer and watched.

Betty didn't move but stood watching Phineas.

"Bet, could I please have a shot of orange brandy. Please," he repeated.

Betty put her hands on the bar and opened her mouth. Phineas saw a rare emotion on her face. Concern, he guessed.

"You sure?" She asked.

"Yes, please. Orange brandy, please," he said again, biting his top lip and looking her straight in the eye.

Betty plopped the snifter in front of him and stepped back. "Hold on, let me get outta here first." She lit another cigarette, leaned against the bar with an eye on Phineas and chatted with Clip-on and Toothless, who were watching Phineas out of the corner of their eyes.

"Well, you gonna try it?" Ben asked him.

"Yeah, I guess." Phineas swallowed hard and closed his eyes.

"You okay?"

"We'll see." Phineas took a sip, allowing just enough alcohol in his mouth to form a puddle in the ditch under his tongue. The liquid seared at his mouth and throat like hot needles. Phineas grimaced and handed it to Ben, who tasted it.

"Tastes okay to me, buddy."

"Yeah, I know."

"What?" Ben asked.

"Well, you know if your smell is all screwed up then usually your taste is too."

"Oh yeah, I heard that also. But, well—"

"But well what?"

"Well," Ben shifted on his stool, "did your dinner taste bad?"

Phineas looked at the television. A truck-sized man ran over several smaller people in the pouring rain. The referee threw a yellow rag on a field of brown, and the television turned to a commercial. A man and woman stood in front of a washing machine while an orange ball was playing a guitar and singing to them. Phineas looked back at Ben.

"No, I guess the food was fine."

"So, it's just booze then?"

"Um, well, so far it's only orange brandy, peppermint schnapps and beer."

"What else do you drink?"

"Betty," Phineas turned toward the hiding barmaid, "could you come here please?"

Betty slinked over and stood in front of them with her arms crossed.

"Look, I gave you a damn shot, you ain't getting nothin' else for free. This stuff ain't all skunked."

"No, I know. Listen, could I get a rum and coke and a sex on the beach?"

"You're kidding, right?"

"No, come on, you know I'll tip you 'til your ears bleed."

"Well, if you're gonna sweet talk a girl, what choice do I got?" Betty smashed her cigarette into the ground.

"Interesting choices," Ben said.

"I figure we go sugary cola and sugary sweet. Does that make any sense?"

"I guess as much sense as this can make."

Betty placed the drinks in front of him and walked away. "Good luck," she said.

Phineas sipped at the rum and coke and it tasted like degreaser fluid. He tried the sex on the beach after several minutes of preparation, and its rotten taste stuck in Phineas' throat for five minutes. Phineas beckoned Betty. And again after that. By 7:49 p.m. He had tried, and passed along to Ben, nineteen different cocktails, beers, shots and, much to Betty's poorly-hidden dismay, blended drinks. Ben, on the other hand, was having a wonderful time drinking the rejects, though mentioned through a hiccup that with Phineas' Modus Operandi he was going to be home and in bed before 9 p.m. Nevertheless, he didn't complain.

At 8:12 p.m. Phineas paid his enormous tab, tipped Betty exceptionally well for her patience and patted Ben on his back. "Nothing for me to do here. Guess it's time to go."

Phineas stood as Clay walked into the bar and, upon seeing his brother, gestured to his seat. Clay sat, shaking his head, and pointed at Phineas. Before Clay could ask any questions, Phineas walked to the door and opened it, surprising a man on the other side whose hand was extended toward the handle. Phineas held the door for the man and his companion and presented the room with a sweep of his hand. They passed by him and nodded thanks. The man wore a red-and-blue checkered sweater.

Phineas stopped in the doorway then looked in at Clay, "Oh brother of mine, let me answer that question in your mind in terms that you'll understand." He paused, "I can't fuckin' drink, so I might as well go the fuck home."

Ben, who had been spinning himself around on his barstool, stopped himself with effort and fixed his crooked glasses. "Troy," Ben shouted into the din, "What do you smell now?"

Phineas balked in the doorway for so long that people began to watch him. "I smell bad teeth, Benjamin. I smell rotten, black teeth." He turned and walked out into the chilly night. Before the storm and main doors crashed closed behind him he heard Clay's voice above the bar clatter.

"What the fuck are you two talking about, and why the hell you so fucked up?"

When Phineas got home he brushed his teeth then dressed in his pajama bottoms, robe and bunny slippers. He could hear the television in the study throughout the house and peeked in to see his father using the computer. The ash on his cigarette was an inch long and his loupes glowed blue in the reflected light of the screen. Phineas pulled the robe close and tightened it, then sat on the bed staring at the toothbrush, which jutted north from his fist. He brought it to his nose and smelled it, then put the bristles into his nostrils and inhaled. "Cinderblocks?"

Phineas tossed the toothbrush on the bed and walked into the hallway. He heard the beginning of the evening football game as he began to pace back and forth through the hallway. He leaned against the wall and placed his nose against the peeling paper with its pattern of ships and whales. He sniffed. The unmistakable scent of new alarm clock pounded through his brain. Phineas folded his brow so hard in his confusion that he almost lost an eye.

Phineas stomped through the house and began his experiments. He smelled a scarf (old, dry wooden walls in a ski lodge), his fingernails (plastic army men) and a pizza delivery menu (flat Sprite, with a hint of orange-scented car deodorizer). Phineas smelled the walls in his bedroom (crab apples), his pillow (frog legs from Kim Chow's Korean restaurant in Chinatown, Philadelphia) and electric outlets (unsalted Planters peanuts).

A checkered tie smelled like the pink bathroom soap in his grade school and bananas smelled of woodchips covering vomit. He was disconcerted to find that his father's table smelled of KY jelly and mortified to learn that his mother's sweater smelled like his sperm; he let out a yelp that caused his father to raise his head from the computer upstairs.

Phineas licked a doorknob and the cloudy stench of mushrooms shot through his troubled mind, he stuck a finger in his nose farther than one should go and smelled pistachio ice cream. Throughout the course of the evening Phineas licked tables and chairs, fingers and (almost) toes. He sniffed cotton balls to find that they smelled of whipped cream and a bottle of Pepto Bismol reeked of toilet bowl cleaner and shoes. Phineas went to the kitchen and licked pots and pans (unwashed pillowcase) and the refrigerator stunk of body odor. The kitchen table smelled of birthday party hats and a spatula smelled of department store mannequin.

Upon secondary research the mystery gravy smelled of petting zoo and cheese smelled like light bulbs. The television in the kitchen smelled of ant farm, but when he turned the channel to the football game it smelled of freshly oiled baseball glove. He flipped through channels to find that cooking shows smelled like sin, all John Wayne movies (two different ones were on two different channels, creating an opportunity for comparison testing) smelled of chicken liver. Nick at Nite smelled good, like Hawaiian pizza and an early episode of *M*A*S*H* smelled like a comfortable couch. *The Judge Harold Jones Show* smelled of stupidity and the news smelled like rain.

Phineas smelled walls (Garner camping gear), beds (overall like dictionaries, but his father's smelled of bottled water) and floors (church). He licked lamps (a Godzilla doll he had had as a child), paperback books and hardback books (beer coasters and eyeglasses). He licked and smelled mirrors (LSD), a comb (Southern man) and plugs (burnt chicken). He rejoiced when he found that everything blue smelled of fresh blue paint on the wall of a 10-year-old boy's bedroom.

Phineas stood in the hallway upstairs, covered in its dim light and acknowledged the fact that he was nasally schizophrenic, completely out of his mind, as far as he knew the world's only olfactory and taste connoisseur of everyday household items and definitely the only person who could smell abstract nouns. He smiled to himself and listened to the television and the ticking sounds of his father typing, the fresh scent of rubber ducks dancing through his head. He bunched his hands into fists and stuck them to his hips, straightening his back and pushing out his chest. "I am Smellman!" he boomed into the hallway. The tapping stopped and Phineas imagined his father staring toward the hallway. The tapping started again.

"That's terrible," he muttered. His brain worked other possibilities. "I am Scentman," he said. He imagined himself standing on a high hill above Lansford, his robe flapping behind him in the wind, proclaiming, with super-heroic dignity, his intention to smell things for truth, justice and the American way.

"I am Noseman...I am Noseman?" he said, shaking his head and remaining dissatisfied. Maybe he could work for the FBI or the CIA as some sort of paranormal energy sensual expert. An alternate side of the situation, he thought, a new twist. The uniqueness of it invigorated him. "I am Nostrilzilla." It sounded better to him; he tried it again. "I am Nostrilzilla!" He could describe ancient objects to old people and scientists, calling forth an aura and a nostalgia that would make him in such demand that he would sell out theaters and antique shows. Maybe this was his calling.

The light from the television poured from his father's study into the dark hallway. He stepped toward it, the smell of pigeon-crap-covered statue burrowing its way through him and pushed the door open. His father stared into the computer screen and the television barked behind him. Ennio Morricone lay on the ground and raised his head when Nostrilzilla walked in. He tip-toed across the room and eyed the dog as he approached, he then squatted and pressed his nose against the confused dog's matted and black fur, which stunk of dirty jeans. The dog growled deep in his throat.

"Um, Phin, what the hell are you doing?" Desmond asked.

Phineas smiled at his father from behind the hind quarters of his dog. His robe hung open, revealing soft, white flesh and the bunny slippers gazed ahead. The dog, too frightened to move, played dead.

"Oh, nothing Dad. Sorry, I thought the dog could use a bath; I wasn't sure about it, though. I'm going downstairs. Who's winning the game, I hope it's the somethingorothers, I hate the other guys. Yep, screw those other people, that's what I say." Phineas walked to his father, who was staring at him through his loupes, leaned over and kissed him on the head, then stuck his nose into his scalp and took a quick sniff. "Huh, crazy glue. Never woulda thought."

"What?" Desmond asked.

"Nothing, good night, Dad."

"Yeah, good night buddy."

Before Phineas could leave his father grabbed his sleeve, "Hey, look what I found this morning while I was looking for a pen." Desmond searched a drawer, shifting papers and various objects around while he muttered to himself. "Aha," he said, producing a photograph which proclaimed the 1970s with its grainy color and rounded corners. The picture showed Phineas standing on a chair and eating soup in the nude. He took the photo and laughed, wondering what compelled parents to take such pictures. The house was his grandmother's and his Aunt Judy was behind him holding a full wine glass, her bright red cheeks supporting her glasses.

"Do you remember that?" Desmond asked.

"I don't think so. When was it?"

"Easter, 1978. There was a brutal snowstorm and we had to stay overnight at Grandmom's. I'm surprised you don't remember." Desmond rubbed the corner of the photograph with his thumb and smiled, his eyebrows arched. In this quiet moment Phineas saw Desmond not as the hermitic dentist in the loupes or the computer-obsessed gambler tapping away at the keys. He saw not the goofy slob who brought the idea of clutter to a new and impressive realm. He saw a man, his father, who missed being surrounded by the people who loved him, who watched more of them leave with each passing year, who missed his mother and his family and his youth. A man who had meandered so far down the tunnel of avoidance and denial that he didn't go out of his house anymore. A man whose hair, for that next short moment when Phineas brought his nose again into his scalp, smelled of regret and sadness and chunky peanut butter.

Phineas brought the photograph to his nose and smelled it. It smelled of Formica tabletop. He smelled it again, and the scent returned. He couldn't remember. He stared into the picture of his young self eating soup with absolute joy, his small penis protruding like a mushroom from under his boyish belly. The soup was in a low, wide brown bowl, a smiling Easter Bunny doll sat in the corner of the table. He concentrated. The memory was so close that he could reach out and touch it as if it were a person standing next to him on a bus, if only his arms weren't bound to his sides. He smelled it again, and again after that. His father, afraid that Phineas might start crying, went back to tapping at the keyboard.

He was no superhero. He was broken, unable to remember anything, and worse, smell things like a normal person, and worse still, drink alcohol. Phineas gave up and watched the memory round the corner down the street as the little boy had earlier in the day, with the leaves and wind.

"Goodnight Dad." Phineas dropped the photo. In his room Phineas sat on the bed and stared at the package from his grandmother that rested on the chair in the corner. He walked to it and picked it up. He then sat in the chair and held it in both hands. The adhesive flap had accrued tiny dots of lint and dark grains. He peeled open the flap and could make out the shape of the pistol's muzzle pointed at him through the cloth and pointed it away. He removed the cloth and pulled the weapon out by the muzzle and turned it in his hands, holding it by the butt and then the midsection.

He brought the gun to his face and pressed the girth of it against his cheek; he shut his eyes and let it cool him, turning the pistol around on his face and running his nose along the shaft of it, back and forth, inhaling and licking the butt as he did. A smell lingered, and Phineas took quick sniffs to place it. His eyes opened when he realized that he was smelling daisies. He looked into the chambers.

He cracked open the box of cartridges and tapped it against his palm, spilling a round into his hand. He rolled it between his fingers, cupped it in his palm and squeezed it until his fingertips turned white then brought it to his face for a closer look. Its brass shell was stocky and squat numbers circled the bottom. Phineas put it to his nose and inhaled, then put it in his nose and let it clog his nostril. He whiffed again and then again before putting it in his mouth. He rolled and swirled it around, pushing it with his tongue. Phineas put it between his teeth and tasted it, swallowing hard. "Hmph," he spit it into his palm and washed the taste from the back of his teeth with the tip of his tongue.

The telephone rang in the study and after four rings his father gave in with a curse and picked it up. Phineas heard murmurs and his father opened the study door and called his name.

"Yeah," he called back.

"Phone's for you. It's Amy."

"Okay," he said, "be there in a sec."

The study door closed and Phineas dropped the pistol and bullets back into the bag and tossed the bag into the chair. "So, daffodils it is."

Phineas took the phone call in the kitchen and called to his father to hang up. After some grumblings about having to stand again, Desmond made the two step journey to the phone and replaced it in its cradle.

"Hello," Phineas said.

"Hey Phinny, how you doing?"

"Hey!" Phineas was happy to be speaking to Amy. He smelled pepperoni.

"We miss you so much."

"I miss you, too. Things are pretty screwed up here."

"Here too, you wouldn't believe what happened. Gomez got a DUI."

"Really?" Phineas smelled steel and paused to wonder why. "Well I guess it was only a matter of time."

"Yeah, he's real bummed out about it."

"I'm sorry to hear that." He opened his mouth to say something.

Anything. He wanted to unload everything onto Amy, but there was too much. He felt overwhelmed. He changed the subject. "How's the bar?"

"Great, everyone asks for you." There was a moment of silence that drove Amy nuts. "We all miss you. We just did a shot for you and I told them I'd call you. Hold on." Amy held the phone in the air and a group of drunken people called out babblings to Phineas. Since they all did so at the same time, Phineas couldn't understand any of it.

"That's nice of them," Phineas said.

"When you think you're coming back?"

"I don't know. There's some things I need to sort out here. Is everything under control?"

"Everything's fine. We just want you to get back here so we can get you drunk as a skunk again."

"Don't worry; I've been doing that out here. Well, trying anyway."

"Huh?"

"Oh, nothing."

"Well, we miss you."

"Me too, Ame." He switched the phone to his other ear. "Ame, could you please put Larry on, please?"

Amy blinked. "Yeah, sure."

Larry took the phone, and Phineas knew he was drunk by the number of syllables he put into different words. "Hey schamookems, when youuu getting your butt back here?"

"Hi Lar, I need a little more time. Is it possible to take another few days?"

"It's no problem, we've got your shifts covered and you're all set. You take aaalll the time you need, okay?"

"Thanks, pal. I'll call you in a few days."

"Sounds good. Now, go get drunk somewhere!"

"Okay," Phineas frowned, "put Amy back on the phone, would you?"

"Phin," Amy said, "you okay?"

"It's a little rough at the moment, to be honest. I got some things going on. You know...."

"Listen, if you need to talk, you can always call me. I have unlimited calling on my cell on the weekends, I can call you back for free."

"Thank you. Listen you tell all those guys I said hi and I'll call you this week sometime."

"Okay, be good, Phinnycakes."

"Thanks. Do another shot for me."

"Already ordered. Bye, sweetie."

"Bye." Phineas hung up the phone and took a mug out of the cabinet and poured a glass of water from the kitchen sink. In the corner of the counter, partially obscured by a mountain of pots and pans, was a bottle of orange brandy. He opened it and smelled it. The almost visible odor of mud came out. He took a sip and spit it into the sink, gagging. A bottle of crème de menthe that Ben had brought over for his Grasshoppers sat under two paper bags and Phineas took it up. Its contents smelled of chicken pot pie. With interest, he took a sip and smiled. It tasted like chicken pot pie. Another swig produced the same taste. "The drink that eats like a meal." He had two more.

The package with the gun and the bullets sat on the chair in his room. He opened it and looked inside; the recipe was folded into a square at the bottom. Phineas reached in and rubbed it between his fingers. Then opened it and stared at the instructions in his grandmother's neat handwriting. He smiled and brought the paper to his nose and inhaled with his eyes closed, his nostrils suction-cupping the paper to his face.

"Whoa." He sniffed again. The paper smelled of a crisp spring morning. He smelled it and tried again to remember the Easter morning in the picture. Snippets of memories came back to him, like vague pictures from a drunken evening. He put the paper in the pocket of his robe and shut out the lights. He climbed into bed at 10:58 p.m. and went to sleep thinking of a quiet spring morning, the perfect heat of an April sun on his cheeks, the cool dampness of reawakening nature surrounding his form and the birds' chirping resonant in his mind.

In his dream, he awoke on a wide field that was being tinted gray by the blue moon. The high grass rustled in the cold breeze that carried across the field like the wave at a baseball game. Phineas sat up, his ears tickled in the wind and his vision passed from eye to eye. He heard the light, eerie ringing of wind chimes. Phineas looked to his right at the side of a house. The house was white and stucco that was peeling and dirty.

An apple tree stood to his left, surrounded by small green crab apples that were rotting in the grass. A shabby fence ran from the tree to twenty feet in front of Phineas. Phineas followed the fence toward himself with his eyes; his vision got blurry and then better. He pulled his fisted hands to his eyes and rubbed them with his forefinger knuckle. When he opened them again his sight was perfect, and he looked up at the enormous blue moon and the millions of twinkling stars that hung around her. Everything was blue and gray and with the next cold breeze that hit him he felt calm and relaxed. He took a deep breath into his lungs. He noticed that there stood a house in front of him as well; it was his grandmother's house. He stood to see it better; his shoes glistened in the moonlight. He wore a white suit and dark shoes, the laces tied across the top, tucked under the perfect cuff in his pants.

His grandmother's house was also old and dirty, with peeling stucco and an overgrown garden. There was a light in the front kitchen window.

14

Amy hung up the phone with Phineas, stared into the mirror and listened to the people at her bar. She didn't like the way Phineas had sounded on the phone, and she didn't feel like dealing with anyone, let alone The Colada Pins. The Colada Pins were the university bowling team comprised of university professors and medical doctors, ranging anywhere from paleobotanists to orthopedic surgeons.

The doctors drank gin martinis in various forms: Gimlets and Gibsons, smoky and dirty. Their first martinis were always accompanied by a discussion of the evening's bowling match. If they had lost the match, there were subtle and indirect comments of blame. If they had won, subtly was forgotten and the doctors laid on thick, wordy compliments. As the second martini approached, the match was analyzed from a scientific point of view and the physics of bowling often made its first appearance. Diagrams were drawn on cocktail napkins and the evening's first arguments brewed. The second martini prompted scientific and medical shop talk.

After the second martini, the doctors began speaking in the exaggerated manner peculiar to animated Disney professors. Their terminology became more academic and their references became more obscure.

The third martini *was* the conversation.

"Storch, now the martini is a delicate thing. Look at the way the gin dews the glass, the way the vermouth and the olive juice fogs it just the minutest bit and the olives reside against the side of the glass as if they were green links packed with beautiful red berets throughout a heavenly chain anchored to the sphere at the bottom of the glass. This, Storch, is a *martini*." Dr. Jolsen's face had gone red with effort.

Amy rolled her eyes to her mirrored self and turned around. "Okay, Dr. Ducky, what have I told you about metaphor and philosophy at the bar?"

Dr. Storch retreated into the collar of his blue and white Hawaiian shirt with a playful grin on his chubby face. Only his deformed nose—a 40-year-old gift from an anxious Rottweiler—stuck out from the field of white and blue flowers. Dr. Jolsen, with mock indignation, tightened his jowls and thread his eyebrows together over his wire-rimmed glasses. He placed the martini glass on the bar and lowered his head as though he were an intellectual bull challenging. Amy could see his eyes peering at her from between the rounded tops of his glasses and the lowered brim of his Panama hat. She readied herself.

"My love, sweet Amadilla, there was no such metaphor in my statement, simile, yes of course, but no metaphor. And how can you ask a man who's had three vials of this near-perfect nectar not to philosophize? It is, after all, in man's nature to pine for heaven once he's had a taste, is it not? Just ask any of your former loves, my dear." Dr. Jolsen took her hand and doffed his hat, leaned forward and kissed the air with a quiet pop a half inch above her hand. Amy looked down at the white hair, matted from the hat and thinning from age, and let out a dramatic sigh.

"Oh, all right. Philosophize you crazy botanist."

"Thank you, darling Helen, however, I'm a horticulturalist." Dr. Jolsen turned again to the glass and raised it to the light. Dr. Storch smiled a smile that betrayed his alcohol-induced quietude, wrinkled his nose in half and flung a backhand against Dr. Leibowitz, who scanned the bar around him. Their bowling bags were stacked in the corner behind them and the smoky air of the bar hung above the men in great slits of fog.

"Doc, that's the greatest thing I ever heard." Gomez pointed with his cigarette at Dr. Jolsen and nodded, his lower lip bulging and curled.

"My dear lad, you turn back to your gang and allow us old fogies the pleasure of a vicarious thrill at your joyous expense, will you not?"

"Sure thing, doc." Gomez turned around and Larry, trying with all his power to understand Dr. Jolsen, was suspended in a state of lexical confusion. Gomez tapped him on the shoulder, winked and turned him back to the priority at hand.

"You'll explain later," Larry said as he moved back to his stool.

"Sure thing, Lar. Hey ladies, what are you whispering about over there?"

Larry and Gomez sat on either side of two drunken girls. One was blonde with an inch-long scar on her cheek that resembled a check mark. Larry was making circles on her forearm with his index finger. Gomez was standing and holding his arms out wide, he wore a Pittsburgh Pirates baseball cap and a blue T-shirt with a yellow penguin on the left breast. His eyes were bloodshot and he was slurring; his fingers held a cigarette.

Amy watched them, pulled the green coffee cup from under the bar and took a sip. Larry leaned in close and whispered something to the girl with the scar. The brunette stared up at Gomez as he began another story.

"It wasn't that big!" she yelled at him, touching his stomach.

Gomez sat down. His face was red and a smile stretched across it. The music of Elmore James played background to Amy's bar and the restaurant. It was busy, people shuffling from the hostess stand to the bar or to a table. People stood everywhere, many of them dressed in sweaters and jackets to thwart the evening cool. The doctors were in the corner of Amy's bar, as they had been every Saturday night for the last year and Larry and Gomez ran the rest of the bar with stories of drunken revelry and situations gone so badly that they were now glorious.

But Amy was thinking about Phineas, sitting alone in the big wreck of a house on Maple Avenue, she wondered what the hell was happening to him. She monitored her bar.

Gary ate his pizza from his perch on the other corner of the bar. To his left were three University secretaries playing Go Fish, one was from Phineas' old lunch gang, "The Day Bar Harpies." They drank Cape Cods and Gimlets and chatted about the man they worked for, who was a flamboyant dresser and evidently had a thing for raisin-skinned nannies. The commotion of the restaurant was at Gary's back, which Amy had joked with him about, saying that he liked to avoid the world when he came into Larry's Pub. He was seated bolt upright and she could see the muscles in his jaw work against the skin. He stared at the television with an expression of dedicated concentration. She giggled into her collar, understanding the source of his tension. He brought the fork to his mouth, holding the knife in his right hand parallel to the bar. He placed the knife down and sipped his diet cola. Amy looked into the sinks to hide her smirk.

The girls between Larry and Gomez squealed and the one with the scar leaned in and whispered to the brunette. "We have to go to the bathroom," the brunette said and they picked up their purses and walked down the steps arm in arm.

Larry wrapped an arm around Gomez's neck. "You and I are going to have some fun tonight, my friend."

Gomez placed his hand on the bar in front of Amy and spread his fingers out wide. "Ame, can we get some shots, please? Whenever you're done washing glasses."

"Sure." She dried her hands on the bar towel that sat next to the sink. "Usual?"

Gomez thought for a moment. "Larry'n me'll take bourbon, and how about a couple B-52s for the chicks?"

"Ooh, doink a little carpet bombinkk are we?" Larry said, affecting his best German accent. Gomez's eyes widened, "Lar, you wanna head downstairs and hit the rest of that blow?"

"Yep, but here's the thingy, if we hit that blow we won't be able to hit the girls."

Gomez stroked the few straggly hairs that constituted his goatee. "True, I guess it's one or the other. Blow or girls, blow or girls." He held his hands before him, palms up and weighed them as Larry watched him, hitting his cigarette while awaiting the decision. His face and head were red and Amy put the shots in front of them, then she reached over and pinched his ears, turning them white. She shook her head as she felt the warmth radiate off his head.

"You're hammered," she said and poked a finger through the ear on her coffee mug.

"mmmmm not, I'mmm Larry."

Gomez straightened his cap. "Okay, we do the shots annn then I'll meet you in the bathroom in a minute or so, cool?"

"Good plan," Larry said. With his blue-collared shirt and red head he looked like an Oompa Loompa. The girls returned, and the one with the scar pointed at the bar.

"Uh oh, we got shots!"

"Yes'm, we surely did!" Gomez picked up his shot glass and held it in the air and took a deep breath. "If it moves, fuck it. If it doesn't move, fuck it til it does."

Everyone laughed. The blonde with the scar spilled her shot and the brunette, who had already begun sipping her B-52 when Gomez started his toast, spat most of the coffee liqueur onto the bar. Gary snorted once and Amy took a sip off her coffee mug; they'd both heard the toast thousands of times. Larry rubbed his head after the shot and breathed in stuttered blasts. Amy stared at nothing, she washed glasses and when she blinked her eyelashes flopped off each other.

Game night at Larry's had been popular since its inception the previous November. Any group playing a board or card game got a free round of soft drinks, beers or cocktails under five dollars and two half-price pizzas. The buzzing room was alive with rambunctious card players, too-serious poker players, ostracized Dungeons and Dragons gamers (all male), chatty gin players, a few meditative grad students playing chess and even a group of middle-aged housewives playing Mahjong in the corner. The clicks of rolling dice on tables and calls of trump filled the gaps between songs.

"Third martini for the docs?" Gary asked between decisive bites.

Amy flashed a gummy smile. "Yep. How'd you guess?"

"Just a hunch." He rolled his eyes. "So, how is he?"

"Who?"

"Phineas Troy. The guy you just talked to on the phone."

"Oh," she said, looking at Gary, "I don't know."

"Really?"

"Yeah, something's going on. I don't know what, though."

Gary took a moment to sip at his diet cola. He knuckled his glasses higher on his nose and chewed in slow chomps. "How did he sound?"

Amy stopped washing glasses and dried her hands on a towel. The girls spoke to each other in whispers; the one with the check mark-scar sipped her drink and closed one eye as she spoke. Larry looked over the girls' heads and tapped his nose twice with his finger. Gomez nodded and stepped behind the girls. "We gots to goze to the bathroom now." The girls giggled. Larry wrapped his arm around Gomez's waist and they stepped down the stairs together, like a mismatched pair in a three-legged race.

A man from one of the card playing tables stood on his chair and cleared his throat. His great belly hung over his belt and he tugged it up to drop his corduroy pants to his ankles. "Night and day, you are the one…" he sung in a cracking baritone and held onto his beer. The zebras on his boxer shorts stared at the group of people they had just been abruptly introduced to. The others at the table held their playing cards over their faces and snickered.

Amy hooked a finger into the coffee mug. "I don't know. He sounds weird. Something's not right."

"You sound almost concerned."

Drink tickets rolled out of the machine, and Amy ripped them off and read them as waitresses gathered at the wait-station and bitched about customers. She reached for a pint glass and filled it to the brim with ice, then pulled the rum and vodka from the well and poured a shot from each into the pint glass. "I am a little concerned, I guess," she called over her shoulder to Gary. She poured a glass of Chardonnay and pulled a pint before finishing the drink. Gary watched her work, arms moving as if she were an octopus trained in ninjitsu. "You'd have made a great ER doctor."

"What?" she asked.

"Oh, nothing. I mean, what is the extent of your worry?"

"I don't know, he double-pleased." She snatched the triple sec between her forefinger and thumb.

"Ah, the double-please," Gary said, "his anxiety-tick. I haven't heard him double please since…" He shook his head. "You think something's seriously wrong?"

Amy shrugged.

Gary watched her pour the remainders of the Long Island Iced Tea, splashing in tequila and hitting the drink with a quick blast of cola from the soda gun. She capped the pint glass with a large metal shaker and shook the drink for ten seconds, her ponytail bobbed around behind her. She stuck a lemon wedge onto the rim of the glass and slid a straw into the drink, then placed it on top of the ticket which sat on top of the rubber mats in the wait station.

Elmore James sang about a crying sky, and Amy couldn't help but think about Phineas being alone and sad. The more she thought about it, the sadder and more alone her mind made him. She thought about his smile, his charming penchant for late night hot dogs and how he always helped people at Larry's when they needed it. He'd helped people move, he'd lent them money and never asked for it back and had spent hours writing resumes and letters for people and unwillingly accepted a single drink in payment. He'd sat up with people all night in the emergency room and often, after his shift, drove around the city until the wee hours picking up friends who were too drunk or stoned or coked up to drive. He did this so often that the guys in the kitchen called him The Bus. And now he was sitting at home, by himself, with his own problems and the only thing they could do for him was send him a drunken hello over the phone, and promises of a shot that would've been drunk anyway.

"Amy," Gary said, shooting a glance toward the doctors, "what are you thinking about?"

Amy sipped at a large plastic cup of water. "I don't know. I feel like we should be doing something."

"Okay," Gary said, "like what?"

"I'm not sure, but I can't help but thinking that he might be going crazy and we're just sitting here doing nothing."

"Do you think he needs us to do something?"

"Yeah," Amy said, "I do."

"So, what can we do?" Gary refolded his napkin and wiped a smudge of grease off his drink glass. "I mean, do you need to talk to him again?"

"Yeah," Amy stared at nothing again. Two waitresses stood at the wait station counting money. One fixed her bra and coughed. The other smoked a cigarette while three men dressed like loggers walked out the door, two of them sending a friendly wave as they went. A woman from the table of card players began clucking like a chicken and ran around the dining room, her arms tucked into her armpits and flapping against her ribs as she ran. The others pointed and laughed.

"I need to see him," Amy said.

"How, though? You gonna go to Philly?"

"I'd love to but I need a car that'll make the trip." She smirked at Gary, who had begun to attack another smudge of grease at the bottom of his fork. He hadn't noticed the quiet until he looked up into Amy Lucas' remarkably beautiful eyes and her fluttering eyelashes and her hooked nose and the brown hair that hung across her forehead into her face. He saw her sly grin and her finger hooked in the coffee mug and knew what she had meant.

"But I do." He reopened his napkin to clean under a fingernail. "Amy, I'm a doctor, I can't just take off and have someone cover my shift. I have patients and women who are nearly ready to dilate. I can't just go gallivanting about the state of Pennsylvania to see a buddy who's lost his sense of smell and grandmother in the same week. I just can't do it, it's unrealistic. It's absolutely out of the question." Gary planted his forefinger onto the bar and held it there. He stared at her as she sipped at her coffee mug. "I'm sorry."

"So, you'll try at least?" she said, arching an eyebrow and flashing him her sexiest look.

"Well, first off, you know that the sexy gaze thing tends not to work on gay guys, right?"

"And..."

"And you should find a new sexy look as this one makes you look a bit constipated."

She grinned and looked into the corner at Dr. Leibowitz. "Go on."

"Oh, you harpie." He hung his head. "Give me ten minutes to see if there's something I can do. When would you want to go?"

"Great," Amy clapped her hands and jumped up and down twice.

"I'll ask Larry if he can cover my shift tomorrow night, then we can go tomorrow morning and come back really early the next day."

"Okay, I'll be back. Don't throw away the rest of my pizza." Gary stepped to the corner of the bar occupied by the doctors and interrupted, holding up a hand in apology to Dr. Jolsen and led Dr. Leibowitz past the hostess, through the crowds and out the front door.

Larry and Gomez had come back to the bar and were sniffling in counterpoint. The girls giggled and the one with the scar moved forward to talk to Amy. "Could I get a beer?"

"Sure, Ducky." She poured the beer and nudged closer to her. "Hey, listen," Amy said, "Larry's a little, um, distracted at the moment, would you tell him to meet me at the wait station?"

"You're the girl with the beer; your wish is my command." She pushed away from the bar, which she had leaned against to hear Amy speak. It had taken all her strength not to slur.

Amy handed her the beer. "That's on me."

"Thanks. You're the best bartender ever. I swear, you're the best. I love you."

"Thanks," Amy said and pointed at Larry. "Remember."

"Oh, yeah," the girl with the scar whispered, "no problem."

Amy, after reminding the girl three times over a period of eight minutes, gave up and met Larry's glance and pointed to the wait station. Larry, having consumed several drinks and taken a great amount of abuse to the septum, was not quick on the uptake. He pointed at his chest, ruffling the blue shirt, and raised his eyebrows in a questioning manner. Amy nodded her head and pointed again at the wait station. Larry looked at the wait station and looked at the girl with the scar who shook her head with genuine ignorance and drank at her beer. The brunette's cell phone rang and she answered it, shouting. She looked dazed and then walked out the front door with her phone, past the hostess who was dumb but sexy and wiping menus with a white rag and Windex while trying to figure out why people were leaving the bar in droves.

"Oh, my God," Amy said. She hoisted herself upon the bar and leaned across it, pinched Larry Joy's ear and brought it to her mouth. "Larry Joykowski, I need to talk to you about something, but it is of a personal nature and I would appreciate it if you would step over to the wait station to talk to me. Do you understand?"

"Yes." He was lying.

Amy walked to the wait station and cupped her hands around her mouth. "Larry Joykowski, come here now!" It was moments like these that Amy thanked God that Larry never got behind the bar, or the wheel of a car, when he'd been drinking.

"Okay, geez, that's all you had to say." He shuffled toward her like a little boy in trouble, staring at the floor, and balanced himself against the bar as discreetly as he could manage. Amy had taken a pen out of her pocket and had begun scribbling something onto a cocktail napkin.

"What's that?" Larry plopped down on the barstool nearest Amy.

"Proof."

"Proofff. Of what?"

"Okay, Larry, we've got a little problemo."

"Uuuh ohhh. Did I do somedink bad? Are you gonnna yell at me?" His eyes grew wide, his pronunciation of consonants worsened.

"No," Amy rubbed his head, creating streaks of white that disappeared into pink, and then back to red. "Listen, I think I need to go visit Phin. I need to make sure he's okay. Can you cover my shift tomorrow if Dr. Gary can get off call?"

Larry focused all of his attention on Amy. "Is he in trouble?"

"I don't know," she sat down on the barstool next to him, "but I need to see him to figure that out. Can you work tomorrow night so I can head to Philly?"

Larry frowned and seemed to be thinking in depth. He looked at Amy, "Okay, but you know I'm gonna forget this entire conversation, right?"

"My dear, lovable Larry Joykowski, that is why we have this." She held up the cocktail napkin that she had scribbled on.

"What's that?" Larry held a hand over his left eye in an attempt to gain optometric composure and focus. It didn't work.

"This is a contract and a reminder for you to sign and put in your pocket and read tomorrow so that you don't forget you need to be here."

"Can you readdd it to me?" Larry dropped his hand and then slouched, his blue shirt shining with the magenta of the bar top and the deep red of his head.

Amy stood and cleared her throat. "Ahem, this contract is to signify that I, Larry Joykowski have agreed to work the evening of Sunday, October 10, 2004 at my own pub, Larry's Pub and Grub. I shall arrive at 6 p.m. sharp and not complain or claim that I was taken advantage of in a moment of total drunkenness. Amy Lucas owes Larry Joykowski a dinner of whatever the hell he wants, whenever and wherever the hell he wants it. Okay, does that sound good?"

"Dinner sounds great!" He rubbed his hands together. "What did I order?"

Amy dropped her face in her hand and handed him the pen. "Sign this."

"Okay." Larry took the pen and looked at the cocktail napkin. "Amy."

"Yeah?"

"Are my eyes open?"

"Here." She put her hand over Larry's and scrawled his name on the line that Amy had drawn under the words she had written.

Gary returned with Dr. Leibowitz and watched as Amy helped Larry write and sign his name. She patted Larry on the head and called to Gomez, who had been holding the scarred girl's breasts in his hands calling them names of cartoon characters. He had reached Rocky and Bullwinkle when Amy motioned him to come over to them.

"Excuse me, all of you," he said, speaking to her, and then her breasts. "Duty calls, I believe." He stepped around the bar and put his arm around Larry's shoulders.

"Get him back to his seat, for the love of God," Amy said and ducked back behind the bar.

"Sure thing, cap'n." He saluted and turned Larry toward him. "Hey buddy, come with me, okay?"

Gomez wrapped him in his long arm and walked him back to the other end of the bar. He sat him in a stool and turned him toward the bar. "You okay?" he asked.

"epp."

"Okay, good." Gomez turned back to the girl and regripped her breasts. "Where were we?"

"Rocky and Bullwinkle," she said with a giggle and a sip of her beer.

"Yes, we were, weren't we?" He looked at her breasts, as a mall Santa would two little children. "What do you think about that, Grape Ape and Captain Caveman?" He shook them as if he were testing the freshness of cantaloupe at a grocery store.

Gary stared at them as he walked by. He stood behind Larry, pointed down at him and mouthed, "Is he okay?"

Amy nodded yes and looked at the both of them, then leaned across the bar and pulled Gary forward until his head was next to Larry's. "Geez, you guys look like a coupla multicolored tits."

Gary pulled away. "Be quiet, I don't want Gomez to start naming our heads cartoon characters." He made a face at Amy. "Do you want me to tell you what happened or what?"

"Yes, yes, I'm sorry. Tell me."

"In a super-galactic turn of events and coincidences—" he spoke in a hushed voice.

"Oh, my God, you can go!"

Gary straightened his tie and extended a forefinger to tap his glasses back in place. "Shh, in a super-galactic turn of events—"

"This is great," Amy said and clapped her hands together.

"Excuse me, but I've rehearsed a short monologue concerning this matter and if you don't mind I'd like to continue."

"I'm sorry," Amy sat on a cooler and folded her hands in her lap.

"In a super-galactic turn of events and coincidences, Dr. Bartholomew Leibowitz has agreed to take over two of my appointments for tomorrow. The other two had already been rescheduled by the patient. And my fifth, well, she died today in her sleep."

"No," Amy put a hand on her chest and grimaced, "that's terrible."

"She was 97 years old and to be honest the idea of missing that particular gynecological exam isn't exactly ruining my day."

"So, we're going to Philly?"

"I suppose so. But we have to leave early and we have to get back here by noon the next day. I basically had to sell my soul to do this, so let's do it. And before I forget, could you please put three martinis on my tab for the doctors." Gary placed his napkin on his lap and cut into his pizza again.

The Doctors' fourth martini brought about the recital of odes and lyric poems in unusual, often unwanted, locales. Amy jotted a mental note to cut Dr. Jolsen's martini to avoid another bathroom incident.

"Do you know how to get there?" Gary asked.

"I was there about a year ago in the summer; we stopped off on our way back from the Jersey Shore. I think I remember."

"Good. I'll pick you up at 6 a.m. Are you going to be ready?"

"I guess so."

"Amy. Do I need to remind you about my recent soul-selling?"

"No, I'll be ready. I promise."

Elmore James had been replaced by Keller Williams and a woman playing Trivial Pursuit laughed so hard that it triggered a coughing attack that sounded as though she were dying. Even the card players stopped their shouting. She apologized to the room and pulled a menu in front of her reddened face, the man next to her smiled and kissed her on the forehead. It made Amy feel better.

The waitresses waited for Amy to hear the sputter of the drink tickets as they were spat out of the machine. They smoked and muttered about Gomez and the girl with the scar. One of them tried to hide her seething jealousy, biting down as Gomez blurted out names of cartoon characters. She and the other waitresses blew great clouds of smoke into the air. They called the scarred girl dirty names while she rested her hands on his thighs and he held her breasts.

The brunette walked back into the bar, her cell phone closed in her hand, and walked past the hostess who had put on glasses and manipulated a few strands of curly blonde hair to dangle in front of her eyes. An Asian man wearing a Pittsburgh Steelers jersey, one of the card players, stood to the cheers of his comrades and maneuvered to a table of three young ladies who were playing Parcheesi and began chuckling when they realized they were his target. He turned back once to his friends, pleading to be let out of his punishment, then turned back to the girls and got on one knee, the name Thigpen stretched across his shoulders.

At the bar, the reception of the free round of martinis, courtesy of Dr. Gary Turner, spurred Doctors Jolsen and Storch to stand and recite (more Jolsen than Storch) a mild Persian ode to geese. Gomez turned to them and freed a breasted hand to slap Storch on the back, whose eyes shot open as if the girl's right breast itself had touched his shoulder blade. Larry Joykowski stared at football highlights on the television and held a ruby-red hand over his left eye. In his right hand was his signed contract, looking as though it had been signed by a poorly-trained chicken at a roadside show.

In the dining room a woman who was three beers along screamed "Yahtzee!" and a man wearing shorts, though it was October, mooned the hostess while offering his sincere apologies.

15

At 8:50 the next morning, Gary and Amy sped out of the morning fog on the winding mountain road in Midwestern Pennsylvania and were passing the Bedford exit on the Pennsylvania turnpike. The mountains and the great clumps of trees that had surrounded the road gave way to large intersections of highways and overpasses. Weather-beaten signs craned and twisted everywhere.

Once past the exit, the serenity of the countryside returned. The trees with their dying, brown leaves reappeared and the mountains were replaced by low-lying hillsides. Though the road was not as winding as it had been in the mountains, it was still uneven and demanded constant single-minded attention. Potholes remained unseen until the last, unavoidable moment and the fog was complimented by a steady, pelting rain. A deranged sign informed them: *No shoulder next 4000 feet*. After a moment, the shoulder on the right side of the road became a dense, gray wall. Dark streaks ran along it at handle level and pieces of colored plastic were scattered on the pavement. After the wall, a dead deer lay on the side of the road, its torso partially torn apart, but held together by strands of muscle and tattered innards.

"The turnpike is like having syphilis," Gary said after propping his paper coffee cup back into the holder.

"What?" Amy was looking at the deer carcass.

"Syphilis. The turnpike's like having syphilis, believe me, I know these things, I've seen some syphilis in my line of work."

"We're talking about syphilis now?"

"I've been trying to think about how I could describe this road to people who've never been on it. The closest approximation I can come to is that it's like having syphilis. A bad case, too."

Gary clenched his jaw and pursed his lips. He shifted in his seat and frowned.

"Do you want me to drive for a while?" Amy asked.

Gary hadn't heard her. "I mean, I'm talking brain-swelling syphilis. Like, never-recover-from-syphilis, syphilis. It's unbelievable."

"Let's play a game."

"I always wondered why Phineas never wanted to go home. I sometimes thought he hated his family, or something weird like that. But—"

"Why don't we talk about something else?"

Gary spoke through her as he leaned over the steering wheel. "It's this road."

"Yeah, this road is horrible," Amy chimed in. "If I lived in Philly or Lansford, or wherever, I would fly home."

"I would fly a plane into turnpike headquarters," Gary said.

"Hey," Amy said, tapping his shoulder, "let's stop for lunch."

"It's nine a.m." He didn't look at his watch or her, just stared ahead at the road.

"Brunch then," Amy said.

Shortly thereafter, Gary and Amy pulled into the Blue Mountain rest stop and each ate a slice of pizza. A gray governmental building squatted in the center of a huge parking lot, an American flag flapped in the wind on a gray pole out front. A gas station stood near the building, closer to the turnpike. Gary walked around the building with his hands in the pockets of his pleated khakis; his dark green sweater hitched up over the backs of his hands. Amy went to the bathroom and bought a bottle of water. She smoked a cigarette in front of the car while she waited for Gary, who came around the corner of the building smiling.

"Sorry, this road takes it out of me."

"I know. You want me to drive for a while? You can take a nap."

"No, it's okay, I'm fine. Let's get to it."

They stepped into the white Cherokee and pulled to the gas station, parking in front of a tank. Amy went to pay for the gas and Gary cleaned the windshield of kamikaze bugs while he waited. He pumped the gas and checked his watch. Amy came out holding up a five dollar bill.

"I won five bucks!"

"No way! That's great! What're you going to buy with it?"

"Ooh, I don't know. I'll have to think about it."

Gary finished pumping the gas and stepped into the jeep. Amy gulped at her water and then tucked her lottery ticket into her jeans. They put on their seatbelts and Gary handed her a book of CDs. "Here, choose one," he said.

Amy flipped through the CD book as Gary pulled back onto the turnpike with a sigh. With a finger she slid a CD out of its compartment and eased it into the stereo.

"Miles Davis. You like him, right?" she asked.

"I do. Thank you."

The baseline of "So What" began and they passed an oversized pick-up truck with a bumper sticker that read: *If I had known it was going to be like this, I would've picked my own cotton.* They sped past and had cleared the truck by several hundred yards before Gary moved back into the right lane. The rain continued but the sun showed itself in intervals throughout the morning and the wind blew against the jeep with such force that Gary had to hold the steering wheel tightly to keep from swerving into the guard rail and the Lancaster County fields. Amy released a deep breath with a sigh.

"So, what do you think is wrong with Phineas?"

"How much time do you have?" Gary slapped his knee.

"About another three hours."

"What exactly do you mean?"

"With the smelling thing. I mean, I don't think I ever heard of that, have you"

"Oh, it happens more than you think."

"But, why?"

"That's a good question." Gary turned the windshield wipers on to a higher setting as the rain became stronger.

"Well, what do you think it is?"

"I don't know. It could be lots of different things."

"Such as?"

"Such as an allergic reaction to something, a neurological disorder, a head injury, a nose injury, a reaction to cocaine use."

"Okay, but Phineas only did cocaine a few times."

"It affects everyone differently. Some people die the first time they use cocaine. Some people vomit, it totally depends on the person."

"Do you think it's cocaine?"

"No, I don't."

"What do you think's going on?"

The wipers streaked back and forth across the windshield and the rain tinned against the roof and hood. Amy waited for what Gary was going to say next. The rain and wind had herded branches and leaves onto the road and the trees swayed like athletes doing pre-workout stretches.

"Sometimes," Gary paused, trying to word his answer with concision. "Sometimes our bodies know things are not right in some way and try to get our attention somehow."

"What does that even mean?" Though, in some way, she understood.

"I used to have a patient, a woman who was about thirty or so years old. Relatively healthy woman, worked out, ate well, sexually responsible, all that stuff. Anyway, one day she came in for a routine exam and didn't really seem herself, she seemed a bit stressed, down or something." A line of 18-wheelers passed by on the left and sprayed the jeep with water. "When I did the exam I noticed a rash on her thighs, in between her legs, and I asked her about it. She said it'd popped up a few days before and she had no idea what it was. I asked her all the questions I needed to ask about sexual partners, allergies, other problems and everything's a no go. For a few weeks we did tests, tried creams, medicines, steroids, it was aggravating. I sent her out to a great dermatologist I know, nothing. Then one day after she left my office one of the nurses mentioned how she felt bad for the girl, how the girl had a real jerk of a boyfriend. I guess he really treated her badly. The next time she came in, I asked her about her personal life, how things were going and such. After a little while she told me that this guy was pushing her around, apparently terrible verbal abuse. So I recommended she break up with the guy, that maybe this was the cause of the rash. I didn't see her for a while after that, but when I finally did, about two months later, the boyfriend and the rash were gone.

"That's a great story."

"Thank you."

"What's the point?"

"It means that I don't necessarily think that Phineas' problem is physical."

"You think it's psychological?"

"Yes, well, maybe. Amy, the first step Phineas should take is to have every test that a qualified ENT or neurologist would order. And that would be blood tests, MRI, CAT scan and full physical. After the physiological possibilities are exhausted and if this remains unresolved, then he should see a psychologist."

"So, if this girl's body was trying to tell her about her jerk boyfriend via crotch then what is Phin's body trying to tell him about by cutting off his smell-o-meter?"

"I don't know, and I don't think anyone but he knows about that. But it could be anything."

"For example?"

"The possibilities are honestly unlimited. It could be anything from his choice of pet to his lifestyle, from his sexuality to what he's doing with his life—"

"I think he's a pretty happy guy, don't you?"

"I think he can keep his act together long enough to make people think he's okay."

"Hm," Amy sat back in her seat and watched a Volvo pass on the left. "What do you think he needs to do to figure it out?"

"That's not up to me."

Four hours and twenty two minutes later, at 1:32 p.m., Gary and Amy sat in the long driveway at the Troy house. Their late arrival was due to morning rush hour outside of Gettysburg and a two-car accident, in which a woman putting on make-up clipped a man who was chatting to his brother on a cell phone. A misdirected turn at Amy's navigation resulted in the relinquishment of her $5 booty to Gary as compensation.

"Yep, this is the place." Amy stowed the water bottle in the middle compartment and undid her seatbelt.

"You're sure, right?" Gary asked.

"I'm positive. I've been here before."

Gary stepped out of the jeep and stretched his arms high in the air. Amy hoisted her orange overnight bag over her shoulder and slid a cigarette into her mouth. Gary removed a black bag and a light, blue jacket. The engine clicked and wheezed with relief and a thin wisp of steam rose from the hood in the chilly afternoon. A car drove by, disrupting dry leaves and spraying them in an air trail behind it.

"Let's get in there," Amy said. She looked in the front window and saw a heavy man moving behind the half-cinched blinds and plastic Halloween decorations. They walked down the driveway, along the house and around to the side entrance.

"Why aren't we going to the front door?" Gary asked.

"That's for the office. Last time I was here, we came in this way." She glanced at him. "Trust me."

"I did," he said, "that's what got me a tour of beautiful downtown Cranesville."

"Oh, shush."

"Well, if I ever get a Trivial Pursuit question about the main manufactured export of Cranesville I'll know it's plywood."

"Hey look," Amy said, pointing. "See, I told you this was his house, there's his car."

"Even a broken clock is right twice a day, my dear."

"Shush."

They walked on broken twigs and gravel to the side door and onto the porch.

"Wait a sec," Amy said, "let me finish this." She took a drag off her cigarette and Gary stepped off the porch back onto the driveway. Phineas' dilapidated car was parked in front of the crusty old garage and covered with leaves. Tall cedars and oaks stood around the house and above the garage. It reminded Gary of the cottage in upstate New York that his grandfather used to bring him to in summer. A thought occurred to him.

"So, what's our tactic?" he asked.

"What?" She blew out a plume of smoke that got lost in the breeze.

"I mean, we never discussed what we were going to do when we got here." Gary looked around him, then he whispered. "Do we pin him to the ground and force him to tell us how he's feeling?"

Amy coughed out a laugh. "No." She crushed the butt with her shoe. "No. We'll get a few drinks into him. He'll be more willing to talk then."

"OK," Gary said.

Amy rang the doorbell; the sound resonated through the living room. Through the dirty window on the door Gary saw a couch and a chair and heard the clicking of a dog's uncut nails on a hard wood floor. Amy rang the bell again.

"I hear a TV," she said.

"Me too."

They heard heavy footsteps. A shadowy figure came into view behind the door and hesitated. The door opened and Clay stood there, his mouth hung open in an almost question.

"Amy?"

"Hey, Ducky," she sang and raised her arms in the air.

"What the-, I mean, what the hell are you doin' here?"

"Came to see that crazy brother of yours."

"He is crazy, that's for sure," he said. "Come on in. You guys eat?"

"Oh, yeah, about an hour and a half ago, in Cranesville," Gary said.

"Cranesville, why the fuck'd you go to Cranesville for? And who are you?"

"Ah, yes, Clay, this is Gary. Gary, this is Clay, Phineas' brother."

Clay extended his hand and Gary shook it with a smile.

"Pleasure to meet you, Clay, and we went to Cranesville to see what all the talk was about."

"What, fuckin' plywood or something, huh?"

"Yes sir, plywood indeed. And bad pizza, too."

The dog growled and then barked as they stepped inside; his stout body trying to vault itself off the floor. "Hey, shut up, Ennio. Get the hell outta here." Clay shooed the dog with his foot and Ennio Morricone waddled into the dining room and sat under the table. He plopped himself down next to a hardback book and checked his progress. He turned his head sideways, steadied the book with a paw and stretched his mouth over a corner. His teeth made ticking sounds as he chewed.

"I think I heard of you," Clay said to Gary. "You're a buddy of Phin's, right?"

Amy laughed, "He's Phin's gynecologist."

Clay's face stuck in a sneer. "You're Phin's gynecologist? Amy, why does Phineas have a gynecologist?"

"Oh, she's joking. I'm a gynecologist, but more importantly, I'm a doctor and your brother's a hypochondriac. He likes to ask me for advice. By the way, I'm really sorry to hear about your grandmother."

"Oh, thanks. Yeah, she was a good woman. It's a shame, but she led a good life." Clay spoke with the practiced cadence that comes with saying a sentence a thousand times in a week.

"Oh yeah, Clay, I'm so sorry," Amy said.

"It's okay, thanks. Things are just getting back to normal around here."

"Good."

"Anyway," Clay said as he shut the door, "Where'd you guys eat?"

"A crappy little joint, I don't even know what it was called. Actually, I'm starving," Gary said. "Let's grab Phin and get some food. Clay, please tell me there is a good pizzeria around here."

"No problem, about a five-minute walk. Let me get Phineas. Make yourselves at home." Clay walked them into the dining room and jogged up the steps to the second floor. Gary looked down at Desmond's table and flinched.

"*That* is a cluttered table."

"Try," Amy tapped her fingers on the table, "just try to hide that obsessive-compulsive-meets-neat-freak-meets-anal-gay-guy side of yourself today, okay? If you don't, this is going to be a rough day for you. The Troys are a cluttered family; they excel in this area."

"I'll try, Mother." Gary looked over his shoulders, "Clay's kinda cute, isn't he?"

"Yeah, in a blue-collar, tough-guy kind of way, I guess." Amy shrugged.

"Rugged. I like that." Gary made fists and held them out for Amy to inspect. "Great handshake, hands of stone."

"Oh, stop it, Mary Poppins."

"Oh, you stop it, Magellan." Gary laughed and the dog growled, his teeth cutting against the book. The sound of shuffling came from upstairs, and then someone running up steps. Moments later, Phineas appeared at the top of the stairs and did a double-take worthy of video footage.

"Holy crap, what are you guys doing here?" He started down the steps and outstretched his arms. "How are you?"

"Great, man. How're you doing?" Gary walked toward him and Ennio Morricone barked once, but stayed at his book.

Phineas grabbed Gary and hugged him. "I'm great, I'm fine, fine. Man, I miss you guys." He let go of Gary and grabbed Amy, who had been waiting behind Gary dancing in place.

"Hey, how the heck are you?" Phineas said, still wearing a stunned expression.

"I'm fine. Surprise!"

"You're damn right, surprise! I can't believe you guys are here!"

"Well, we missed you so much, we thought we'd come out and make you get drunk with us. What do you say?"

"Thanks?" he said, scratching his chin in mock wonderment.

"Where's Doctor Des?" Amy asked.

"Oh, the old man. I think he's with a patient. We'll catch up with him later."

"Yeah, I've heard a lot about him, can't wait to meet him," Gary said.

"I can't believe you guys are here. You eat yet?"

"In Cranesville. Two hours ago," Gary said, kicking Amy's shoe.

"Phineas, would you please get some pizza into this man ASAP? I'm sick of hearing him bitch," Amy said.

"Oh dear, you got bad pizza in Cranesville?"

"Yes, we did," Gary said.

"What, was it made of plywood or something?"

"Ha, it might well have been," Gary said.

"Come on, there's a great place around the corner."

"Is Clay gonna join us?" Amy asked.

"Nah, he's gotta work this afternoon, but he'll meet up with us later."

They walked down the street to the tune of passing cars and the occasional sharp breeze that advocated the buttoning of jackets. Phineas pointed out The Blue Duck and they ate lunch at Sister's. The turnpike had drained them and the lunch was filled with yawn-laced conversation.

When they arrived back at the Troy house, Phineas put Gary on the couch in the living room and Amy in his bedroom so they could take a nap. Phineas watched television until he dozed at the kitchen table, then moved to the armchair in the living room and slept for a few hours. When he awoke, around 5:30 p.m., Clay was standing above him holding a brown paper bag as if it were a football. Drool was dripping down Phineas' chin and had settled in a small pool on his right shoulder.

"Yo, what the fuck'd you guys do?" Using his finger as director, Clay helped guide Phineas toward the drool on his left shoulder.

"Wha-who, how, wait, I don't know. How do you mean, things, I can't to you." Phineas wiped the drool from his face and beard. He blinked and sat up and shook his head. "Leave me alone."

"Ha, you guys going out tonight?"

"Yeah, I think so. I'm gonna wait 'til they get up then we'll head to The Duck."

"Hey," Clay checked his watch, "it's after five, why don't you get them up now?"

"Fair enough."

"You know Dad wants to come out, too. Unbelievable. I can't remember the last time he went out for a beer. I can't remember the last time he went outside when there wasn't a funeral. Also, Ben's coming. So, let's go hit it."

"Yeah, okay, give me a minute."

Clay walked into the kitchen and opened a beer. He flipped the television to ESPN, grew serene and opened the bag which held his sandwich. Phineas woke Gary, who yawned, stretched and sat up.

"We're going drinking, Troy style," Phineas said.

"Jesus, what does that mean?"

"My dad and Clay are coming."

"Can I go to the bathroom first?"

"Yes." Phineas walked upstairs and woke Amy, informed her of the same news and allowed her to use the facilities as well.

Twenty-six minutes later, the group convened in the living room. Clay held back the growling and confused Ennio Morricone and Dr. Desmond Troy made his appearance. He had removed his loupes. Ben came from out of the darkness of the front door and removed his hat; Amy and Gary fell in love with him. They went to The Blue Duck Inn and found it inhabited by lawyers and gapped-tooth landscapers, coked-up real estate agents and pediatricians. Amy slid to the bar and handed her credit card to Betty, who smoked at her own pace and raised an eyebrow.

"Hello, could you start me a tab?" Amy said in her Pittsburgh drawl. "What you guys drinking?" Amy asked without turning her head or waiting for Betty's reply.

"I would love a Grasshopper," Ben said.

"I'll take a light beer," Gary said.

"Usual Bet," said Clay.

"A coffee liqueur on the rocks, please," Desmond said.

"I'll take a crème de menthe on the rocks," Phineas said. Everyone looked at him.

"Are you serious?" Amy asked.

"Look, don't give me any lip. It's the only thing that doesn't taste awful to me, OK?"

"Crème de menthe is disgusting," Amy said.

"Well, it doesn't taste like crème de menthe," Phineas said.

"What does it taste like?"

"Chicken pot pie."

"Oh, of course," she said.

"Well, it's official: You're a fuckin' faggot," Clay said.

"Aren't we all?" Gary asked. Everyone else stared at the ground.

"Well, let's have a toast, shall we?" Desmond said.

"Absolutely. To what?" Amy pulled the quickly-poured drinks from the bar and her own into the air. "Service is quick here." She and Gary were the only ones who didn't realize that this was unusual.

"She must like you," Clay said.

"Here's to a great woman, Emily Troy. How about that?" Desmond said and raised his glass. Everyone raised their glasses and touched them in the middle. Betty blew out a stream of smoke like a 747 taking off out of O'Hare and raised her eyebrow, again. Some regulars drank in the corner and waxed philosophical about beer. Bob Dylan played on the jukebox.

Some of the group had moved to a table and the fireplace roared with cedar. Ben and Clay stood at the jukebox choosing music and Gary talked with Desmond. Amy took Phineas by the hand and led him to the bar.

"Shots, Phinny. You're doing a shot with me."

"Amy, I can't drink anything that isn't crème de menthe."

"You're serious, aren't you?"

"I swear to God."

"Damn. Okay, you can have crème de menthe and I'll have bourbon."

"Torture. You're absolutely torturing me. You love this, don't you?"

"No, I really don't." She shook her head. "Are you okay?"

"I don't know." He stared at his glass.

"What the hell is happening with you? You seemed weird when I talked to you on the phone. Is this about your grandmom?"

A man at the bar began playing his fingers like drum sticks on the bar until Betty gave him a dirty look.

"I don't think so. I've just been thinking about some things, you know?"

"Such as?"

"I don't know. Crap. Lots of crap. I can't smell anything real like steak or this drink, but I can smell blue, John Wayne and the 1930s. I can't drink alcohol, except for crème de menthe because it tastes like chicken pot pie, which is nauseating but better than the hot needles and turpentine that other alcohol tastes like. That damn dog of my father's has it in for me in a weird way. I mean weird. This dog knows when and where I… do things and it's freaking me out. I'm having weird dreams, I'm having weird thoughts, I'm afraid of what's gonna go next, it's my smell and now my taste so next my hearing? My sight? And I don't know what the hell is going on. Is that enough?"

"Okay. So, crème de menthe it is." She had shrunken back on the stool.

"I'm sorry, I didn't mean to rant." He leaned over and rubbed her thigh. "Tell me something fun. What's happening at Larry's?"

"Nothing, same shit, different day. Listen, maybe you should see someone."

"About what?"

"Everything. Maybe you should see a doctor about your taste and smell and maybe you should talk to someone about your feelings. I'm here. Gary's here for you. Big Ducky over there seems like a guy you could talk to."

"Ben? Yeah, he's a great friend."

"Is he single?"

"Oh my, you want to take on the Ben?"

"Maybe I do. Is he single?"

"Amy, he's like nobody else. I don't know what to tell you. He's like something out of a Greek legend. All I can say is good luck." They both smiled. "Tell me about Larry's."

"Larry's is good. Larry is good, hitting the blow a bit lately, but he's alright. Gomez got a DUI, but I told you that."

"What happened?"

"He was booty called at 3 a.m. by some girl from Kazanski's and he went, big dummy. Anyway, cops pull him over and he blows a .23 or something like that. It was awful. I had to bail his ass out in the morning, and he was still wrecked."

"The rest of the gang?"

"Same old, same old. You know how it is. We hit Dee's Café a few times this past week, I love that joint. The docs say hi, everyone just wants their favorite bartender back."

"They've got you."

"Their other favorite."

"The martinis are poured with the same gin as when I make them. The bottled beer tastes the same, too, I assume."

"You, of all people, know that doesn't make a good bartender."

Amy and Phineas sipped their drinks and Amy looked over at Ben and Clay. Ben turned and raised his Grasshopper to them, his green teeth glowing in the light. "Lay, Lady, Lay" played on the jukebox. From the corner of the bar, someone made an incoherent comment showing his agreement with the song. Ben joined Amy and Phineas and Clay joined Desmond and Gary.

"What you two talking about?" Clay asked.

"I am learning about online football gambling," Gary said.

"Aha, Dad's favorite topic. Wait 'til he gets to overs and unders. Then you're really fucked."

"Ah, my eloquent son. Clay, shut up and get your old man a coffee liqueur on the rocks, would you please?"

"Alright, old man. Gary, you need anything?"

"No, I'm fine."

"Wait, Gary, have a little sip of the orange brandy I was telling you about," Desmond smiled. "What do you say?"

"Sure, why not?"

"Oh, goodie." Desmond's face was red and he giggled at the warm feeling that was spreading through his stomach. Clay laughed, too, but at his father and not with him; he hadn't seen Desmond this happy in a long time.

Clay leaned against the bar when he talked to Betty, the barmaid, his thick back stretched against his shirt. Gary tried to look, secretly. He slid his chair alongside the table so that he could survey the bar and Clay. Desmond's belly poked the table from the booth. He squinted his right eye and smirked.

"You know when the Miami Dolphins are really done?"

"No, Dr. Troy, I don't," Gary said. He leaned into the table.

"When that bastard McManus grows a beard. I swear all I have to do is bet against that guy at the end of the month when he's got a beard, he's screwed and I'm sitting pretty."

"Really?" Gary peeked out of the corner of his eye to see Clay shift on his right leg.

Clay took a drag off his cigarette and blew it out of the side of his mouth. Phineas peered at him, blowing the smoke away.

"You can't smell anyhow," Clay said.

"It burns my eyes."

Betty slid a shot of crème de menthe, an orange brandy, three Irish whiskeys and a coffee liqueur on the rocks toward Clay. Clay passed them around and Ben, Phineas and Amy stepped toward the table. The fire roared and three men who were covered with soil from a day of working outside ate sandwiches at a table in the corner.

"Everybody got their shot?" Clay asked and looked for order errors. "Cool? Everything's cool? Okay, let's do this thing."

"May I propose a toast?" Desmond asked.

"Another one?" Clay asked.

"Here's to my boys and their friends, it's nice to meet you, Gary, nice to see you again, Amy. And my mom, who was a great woman." Desmond looked into the table and everyone's eyes got misty and they brought their glasses toward their mouths. Desmond started speaking again. "And here's to Brett McManus botching a fourteen-point lead going into the fourth quarter which led to an upset and a sweet parlay that found me $200. Cheers."

Everyone drank and made post-shot sucking and blowing sounds, some coughs and *whoos*. Desmond excused himself to the bathroom and Phineas and Amy brought the empty glasses to the bar. Clay looked around at the others.

"I'm gonna head back for a little and smoke a joint. Any takers?"

"I'll come with you," Gary said, "I'd like to get out of this smoky bar for a few minutes."

"Ben, you in?"

"No, I'm okay, I'm gonna stay here."

Phineas and Amy stepped back to the group.

"Hey, me and Gary are headed back to hit a joint, you guys want in?"

"Gary, you're going to smoke a joint?" Amy asked, her enormous eyes gleaming.

"I'm just going for the walk." He winked at Amy, but he wasn't sure why.

"Aha, well, be safe. We'll see you in a little bit?" Amy asked.

"Thirty minutes. There's a college game on I want to see. It starts at eight, I want to be back for that." He tapped Gary in the ribs. "Let's move."

As Clay opened the door into the cold October evening, Gary had the feeling that he was doing something different for the first time in years. A rush of cold air blew into the room and Amy shivered. Desmond returned to the table and looked around.

"Where'd Gary go?" he asked.

"Oh, he and Clay went to get a quick sandwich at Sister's. I think they were hungry."

"Oh, well let's get another drink," Desmond said. "There's a game on soon, I want to be home for that, so let's have one more." Two pens stood like soldiers in his shirt pocket.

"Why don't you watch it here with us, Dad?"

"No, it's okay. I want to get back and relax. I've got an early day tomorrow."

Ben sat across from Desmond and Phineas went to the bar to get his father another drink. Amy sat at the table diagonally from Desmond, sipped on a beer and smoked, blowing the smoke away from people at the table. Toothless and Clip-on eyed her from their corner and Betty glared at them. The wood in the fireplace popped and seethed and Frank Sinatra sang about his way from the jukebox.

Clay and Gary passed the second floor and stomped up the narrow steps to the attic-bedroom. Gary walked behind Clay, catching some of the murmured dialogues and stories that Clay was telling about his job. He stifled his disgust at the outer room of Clay's compound. Jenna Jameson leered at him, bottles of chewing tobacco spit, old beer and cigarette butts stood at attention. It smelled of dank pub and a number of viable excuses for leaving were processing themselves with compulsive order in Gary's head when Clay opened the door to his room.

Gary filed his excuses for a later emergency and stepped inside. The slanted ceiling wore a comfortable light and the quiet was interrupted only by Frederick's gentle tapping on the aquarium near Clay's bed. Clay stepped to the stereo and pushed buttons. Johnny Hartman began crooning into the quiet room.

"Nice choice," Gary said.

"Thanks. Phin likes it, so I threw it on yesterday." Clay sat on the couch and pointed to the armchair. "Make yourself at home; let me roll this thing." He pinched the marijuana and slipped into a robotic coma. Gary walked around the room and looked at the CDs and posters. He stepped over to the tapping sound and stood above Frederick.

"That's Frederick. Don't piss him off; he's a killer."

"Really?" Gary asked, moving back a step.

"No, it's a fucking turtle, I could make soup out of him if I wanted." Clay licked the paper of the joint and then held his lit lighter under it for a few seconds. He flicked the top of the joint and lit it. "You sure you don't want any of this?"

"Yeah, I'm fine. I can't with my job, you know." Above Frederick's tank was a poster of Eric Clapton wearing a bandana and playing the guitar with his eyes closed. "I love Clapton," Gary said.

"Yeah, he's awesome. I saw him a couple years back with B.B King. Great show."

"I saw him about ten years ago with Jimmy Page."

"No way! You went to that?" Clay stopped fiddling with his joint and looked up at Gary.

"Great show," Gary said. "You should've seen those two together, they're really incredible."

"I bet they were." Clay pulled some flecks of marijuana off of the end of his tongue. "Huh, strange."

Gary smirked, "What's strange?"

"Well, you just don't seem the type."

"The type for what?"

"You know, rock 'n' roll. I figured you for a jazz and classical guy."

He shrugged. "I am, but I love rock, too."

"I don't mean anything by it, just I see you as a white-collar guy. Jazz and classical music, Mercedes Benz, J Crew shirts, squash and tennis on the weekends, you know, that sort of stuff."

"I love jazz, tennis, squash and wish I had the money for a Mercedes. But I also drive a jeep, love rock 'n' roll, play the guitar and like buying houses and renovating them."

"No shit?" Clay asked, dropping the joint to the table. "You renovate houses?"

"Yes, I do. It relaxes me. No people and no vaginas and that's a welcome change.

"So," he let out a giggle, "no vaginas, that's a good thing?"

"Yes, it is."

"So," Clay smirked, "Do you like your job?"

"It's alright, I guess."

"I just figured with all that cooter around you'd be in heaven."

"Nah, you'd be surprised. First of all, they're not always healthy vaginas and even when they are the women aren't always very attractive."

"Yeah, that would suck," Clay said. "What's the worst thing you ever seen?"

"Hm." Gary was still looking at posters and the technological fish swimming around the computer screen. "You know, first outbreak herpes is pretty damn awful. No matter how many times you see it."

"Fuckin' A, let's change the subject. What about J. Crew shirts?"

"If it were possible I'd have my internal organs made by J. Crew. However, and don't tell this to Amy, I have a weekend flannel fetish. Call it a guilty pleasure."

Clay inhaled and kept the smoke in his lungs, his chest out and barreled. "Hmp hmp." Clay smoked the joint and Gary wandered around the room. Johnny Hartman sang for them and Frederick clicked on the aquarium as if he were asking for a hit off the joint. Clay asked Gary about property tax and cost of living in Pittsburgh. Gary answered his questions and, once or twice, breathed in the sweet smelling air with his eyes closed.

"You sure you don't want a hit?"

"No thanks, it's the smell. I love the smell of marijuana."

"Did you ever smoke?" Clay asked.

"I tried it in college a couple times and I didn't like it to be honest with you. It's just the smell that I love."

"Yeah, it smells great, don't it?"

"Another guilty pleasure of mine. I'm chock full of them, I guess."

Clay sat forward and held his breath, staring at Gary, interrogating him with his eyes. He released a long breath, filling the air over the coffee table with smoke. "Go to the DVD player."

Gary walked to the DVD player and the rack of movies next to it.

"What do you see in the collection?"

Gary scanned the collection.

"Read them out loud," Clay commanded in a quiet voice.

"Um, *The Terminator, Heat, The Dirty Dozen, A Bridge Too Far, Jaws.* OK, what am I looking for? It seems pretty standard for a guy."

"Remove any three DVDs."

Gary removed three boxes and held them with his middle finger and thumb; he leaned in closer and squinted. "What the—." Gary stooped over the rack and slid DVD cases aside to look behind them. He replaced the DVDs and returned to the couch. "Animal movies?"

Clay flinched as though a bee had stung him. "Yeah, I know."

"What's wrong with that?"

"I don't know. It's embarrassing."

"Clay, there could be a lot worse, you know."

"I guess." He sat back again after pressing the remainder of the joint into the ashtray.

"No, I mean, a *lot* worse. A friend of mine from college was just arrested for child pornography."

"Yeah, I know some guy that got caught jackin' off to animal porn. It could be a lot worse."

"Yeah, it could be."

"You probably don't even watch porn anymore with your job."

"That's a loaded statement."

"Oh yeah, why's that?"

"Well, I'm not really into women that much." Gary braced himself as though he were awaiting an overhand right from a world class heavyweight. He waited, the muscles in his legs and back had tightened.

Clay's mouth opened. "You're gay?"

"Is that what the kids are calling it these days?"

"Wow. You seem pretty normal." Clay sat back.

"I am pretty normal," Gary said.

Clay put a hand up. "That's not what I meant." His face was red. "I just wouldn't think it."

Gary sat on the chair and crossed his legs. "I guess I don't fit into some of the stereotypes out there."

"Right."

"But then, neither do you." Gary grinned.

"Me?" Clay's heart rate stepped up a notch.

"Yeah. You don't seem like the animal-movie-fetish type."

Clay laughed and his pulse settled. "So, was it the, uh, overload at work that sent you to the other side?"

"No!" Gary laughed. "I've been gay a lot longer than I've been a gynecologist." His laughs came out like machine gun fire. "And what about you?" he asked. "What started your animal fetish?"

Clay stood and folded his arms. "You are now Dr. Homo."

No more detail was offered by Clay and his dry mouth soon caused a serious thirst for beer, so they went back to the bar. Frederick clicked on the glass of his aquarium as they stepped out of the room.

As they crossed the street Desmond came toward them from The Blue Duck Inn. He held a bag of potato chips; a lit cigarette hung from his lips.

"How were your sandwiches, guys?" he asked them.

"Uh, I—" Gary muttered, looking at Clay.

"Good. Why you leaving, Dad?"

"Tired and I want to watch this game at home. See you tomorrow, Gary?"

"No, sir, I'm sorry but I've got to get back to work tomorrow evening."

"Well," Desmond shifted the bag of chips to his left hand and held out his right. "It was a pleasure meeting you. If you're ever in town, stop by and we'll have a drink."

"I'd like that. It was my pleasure Dr. Troy. Good luck with the game."

"See you later, Clay," Desmond said, and then he waddled down the sidewalk.

"Sandwiches?"

"Yeah, it's what Ben and me call smoking weed."

"Code. I like that. Very counterintelligence of you guys."

When they got back to the bar more people were there. A group of young ladies sat at a table near the bar chatting and smoking cigarettes. Beer bottles covered the table and lipstick-smeared cigarette butts sat in the ashtray like tombstones. One of the girls waved to Clay; in return he jerked his head back in a reverse-nod and stuck a finger in the air to Betty. The football game had started and Clay watched the screen.

Amy drank and smoked more rapidly now, her eyelids drooped, Phineas sat with his arm hitched onto the back of the booth, his face carved into a wide grin like the bottom rung of a totem pole. In front of him sat a half empty martini glass of crème de menthe. Ben walked across the bar room with several shots in his large hands, he placed them on the table and nodded at Clay.

"How was your sandwich?"

"Good. You got more shots?"

"Of course."

"Thanks. What did we get?"

"Crème de menthe for Phineas and Irish whiskey for everyone else. Is that okay, Gary?" Ben asked.

"Oh sure, I should probably call it quits after this, though, I have to drive tomorrow."

They tapped the glasses in the middle and Amy cleared her throat. "OK, this one's mine. This is to Phineas Troy, the best bartender at Larry's Pub and in the whole damn city of Pittsburgh. May he get his big butt back to us soon, so we can pick up where we left off, Cheers." They drank. They made sounds. They watched football through glistening, heavy eyes.

"Amy," Phineas called from across the table, "Where, exactly, did we leave off?"

"Everyday life in Pittsburgh. You being a great bartender, being near your regulars and rampant boozing and partying that won't end 'til our livers and kidneys go. That's where we left off and everyone misses you."

"Life seems to be going on," Phineas said, sipping his crème de menthe.

"Yeah, but we miss you. You're a huge part of the group and we miss you." She exhaled smoke.

"I know. But I've got to make some decisions."

"Decisions about what?" Amy asked.

"I don't know, everything." He watched the football game. Gary and Clay had moved to a table closer to the television and talked about remodeling kitchens. They had pulled two cocktail napkins from the bar and had begun scribbling notes on them. Ben ran his finger around the rim off his glass and listened to Amy and Phineas' conversation. He sipped his Grasshopper and picked his nose as music spilled into the room and the clutter of the pub hummed in the background.

"Phin, are you coming back?" Amy put her beer down and leaned across the table.

Ben watched Phineas and waited for his answer. Phineas sipped his drink and breathed out through his nose.

"I don't know. I need to do some thinking."

"Well, when are you gonna know?" she asked.

"I got a few extra days covered from Larry, so I got a little time. But soon, I hope."

"Well, you better," she said.

"Don't you think I want to? You think I like this? You think I like that fact that my grandmom just died and it's making me think of weird stuff and now I'm freaking out about everything. You think I like this? You don't think I want this to be finished and over with?" Phineas sat back and Ben was staring at him, Amy had sat back and wore a hurt expression, like a small child whose hand had just been slapped away from cookies.

"It's just, the cats miss you, is all," she said.

Phineas frowned. "I'm sorry. I just have a lot on my mind and I don't know what it's all about. I'm changing, physically, mentally. I can't smell, I can't drink. I don't know what to think right now and I miss the hell out of you and the cats. I don't miss them pooping next to the litter box, though."

Amy laughed.

"What?" Ben asked. "What do they do?"

"They poop next to the litter box," Phineas said.

"You're joking me, right?" Ben asked.

"Ducky, they don't just poop next to the litter box," Amy said, lighting a cigarette. "They stand in the litter box and poop outside it."

"That's hilarious," Ben said. "Cats are amazing animals." Ben nodded his head and then looked at Amy. "Did you just call me Ducky?"

Phineas leaned forward. "Ben, don't" He shook his head. "Amy calls everyone Ducky?"

"Oh, of course," Ben said. "Why?"

"Because she couldn't remember a name if you held a steak knife to her windpipe." Phineas laughed. "I lived with her for seven months before I was upgraded to Phillip."

Gary had overhead the conversation and turned around from the other table. "I sat at her bar for four months before I was Gil."

Clay didn't remove his eyes from the cocktail napkin he was doodling on. "I was Cloris for a while." A pause. "Then Carey, then Corey, then Cliff."

"Therefore," Phineas said, "everyone is Ducky, except in very special cases. It keeps life simple for our young barmaid here."

"Sounds like life in Pittsburgh is pretty interesting," Ben said.

Phineas rolled his eyes. "Nicknames, Cats pooping on the floor, drinking, friends getting DUIs. Wild stuff, huh?"

"Sounds like it."

Phineas knuckled the bar once. "It's not. It's like that all the time. Nothing ever changes in Pittsburgh. Ever."

Gary and Clay's sketch book had graduated to a placemat, which they had flipped over and were using as a blueprint, drawing sketches of kitchens, decks and living rooms. The football game played on the television and the ladies at the large table had moved from light beer to red drinks in cocktail glasses, filling Amy and Betty with disgust.

Two hours later, drunk and happy, the group walked to the Troy house. Ben said his goodnights in front of the pub, then staggered into the night toward the mule cabin to sleep. Gary and Amy linked arms and skipped across the road and Phineas and Clay walked behind them. When they reached the house, Amy sat on the couch and pulled off a shoe; the momentum throwing her back onto the couch. Gary took her other foot in his hand, untied her shoe and slid if off.

"Listen folks, I gotta hit the hay," Clay said sticking his hand out to Gary. "I got your email. I'll use it."

"Please do," Gary said. He took Clay's hand.

"Have a safe trip tomorrow. Oh, just come in whenever and grab that couch in my room tonight. I'll leave some sheets and a pillow out."

"Thanks for the hospitality," Gary said, still holding Amy's shoe.

Clay leaned down and tapped Amy's head. "Hello, Amy, have a nice trip tomorrow."

"Bad road," she slurred without opening her eyes.

Clay walked out of the room and up the stairs. Phineas grabbed Gary from the side and kissed him on the cheek. Gary looked amused.

"Uh oh, it's kissy drunk Phineas."

"Uhh ohhh." Amy moaned.

"What, I miss you guys. So, what's a little kiss?"

"Listen Phin, we've got to leave tomorrow at 4 a.m. or something terrible like that. Why don't we say our goodbyes tonight?"

"Yeah, maybe that's best," Phineas said. "I wouldn't want to be forced to kill a good friend for waking me up at 4 a.m."

"Good to see you, buddy. Come back soon, we do miss you." Gary hugged him and kissed him on both cheeks.

"So good to see you, Gary." He sat next to Amy. "I'm going to bed."

"Okay," she opened her eyes and kissed him on the lips. "I love you."

"I love you, too. Have a safe trip tomorrow. Can you call me when you get there, so I know you got in okay?"

"Sure thing. Good luck, Phin, if you need anything or just to chat give a ring, okay?" Gary swung Amy's legs onto the couch. They walked up the steps, Phineas saying one final farewell to Gary as he stepped into his bedroom. Gary made his way up the narrow dank steps and into Clay's room. He pulled off his shoes and listened to the soft snoring that came from the direction of the bed. Frederick tapped his glass and Gary lay down in his clothes, set the alarm clock on his cell phone and drifted off to sleep with his phone on his chest.

Downstairs, Amy snored, her nose stuck into the air as though she were sniffing for a lead. The television in the kitchen played on mute and Ennio Morricone slept in his cage, twitching occasionally. Phineas wore his robe and pajamas; he crept into bed and slid the covers over himself. Outside, winds pounded the windows and a half moon hung in the air, peeking at the house through scantily dressed trees. Down the hall Desmond clicked at his computer and stared into it through his loupes. He listened to sports news on ESPN. A cigarette dangled from his lips. A commentator joked that McManus had begun to look like a mountain man again. Desmond smiled and went to his online gambling website, his eyes glistening behind his glasses.

16

Loni Troy returned home the next morning too late to meet Gary and see
Amy, who had left at quarter past five in the morning. She pulled into the
driveway as dawn's gray blanket unwrapped itself from the Troy house
and the neighborhood. She dragged the errant trashcans up the driveway
and stood them next to the house. Scott Johnson, the optometrist who
lived next door, pulled down his driveway with his headlights on and
Loni waved as he went by. It was 6:52 a.m., the birds wished Loni a good
morning through a melody of chirps and whistles and she responded
with her own absent-minded repertoire.

A few scattered lights dotted the homes on Maple Avenue. The early
quiet was disturbed only by a bread truck making its morning deliveries.
Loni stepped into the house. The blue light from the kitchen television
covered a section of the table and the fridge clicked and groaned. A dent
and swirl of blankets on the couch marked the spot where Amy had slept,
but Loni didn't notice this. She hummed like a bee and moved like one
too, dashing from room to room.

She'd spent the better part of the previous week at Emily's house,
organizing and sorting through boxes and papers. She'd handled accounts,
settled bills and tended to Emily's affairs. She'd also cleaned the basement,
garage and both bathrooms, and had spent the evenings on the couch,
grimy and exhausted, watching reruns of *Wheel of Fortune* until she
dozed under a homemade afghan. Her own morning routine had long
been set and staying at Emily's house did nothing more than set it back
by half an hour.

She opened the door, allowing some fresh morning air to sneak in.
She folded a kitchen towel into a neat rectangle and dropped it in the
sink as she ran the water. Then she pulled the trash can to the table and
flipped on the radio. Her morning sports talk show spilled into the room
behind the sound of the running water.

She hummed, whistled, clicked her tongue and da-da-da'd her way

around the kitchen. She walked into the den, leaned over Ennio Morricone's cage and placed her wet hands on her thighs. *"Good morning,
sunshine!"* Loni sang to the dog. *"Your mom says hello, you're sleeping so
peacefully, now it's time to poop."*

The dog's ears twitched and he raised his head to acknowledge the
singing woman above him.

Loni smiled at the dog. *"Hello, you little piece of crap,"* now she sang
to the tune of "Twinkle Twinkle Little Star", which had been stuck in her
head all the night before. *"Are you ready for another day of ruining my
carpets and eating books?"*

Ennio Morricone yawned and whined his agreement. He stood, his
legs popping open under him like rusty legs on an old card table.

"Ugh." Loni flipped the latch to let him out of the cage. Ennio Morricone waited dazed for a moment then trotted up the steps. Loni watched
him, then stretched and walked back into the kitchen. The room had filled
with more light and sparse raindrops began tapping at the windows. She
emptied overflowing ashtrays and threw away plastic cups, sandwich
wrappers, coffee-soaked newspapers, a dried-out pen, six empty cigarette
packs, a broken hairbrush with thick black hair entwined in its teeth and
several damp, browned napkins.

She opened the dishwasher and, in a Zen-like manner, began putting
the cups into cupboards and dishes into the pantry overhead. Her eyes
glazed over like those of a submerged frog. Her meditation ended with
a startle when a robin flew into the closed window above the table and
dropped in front of the garbage cans, where it sat with a confused look.

"Oh!" Loni rushed to the window, which was caked with dirt. She
searched the window at table level, finally spotting the clean portal that
Ennio Morricone had licked into the dirt (through which he viewed the
outside world) and hunched over to peep through. "Mrs. Robin, are you
okay?"

The bird answered by pecking at nothing and taking off sideways into
the still morning air. "Goodbye," she squeaked in a little girl's voice and
pulled the rug from the floor. She slid out onto the cement porch and

snapped the rug in the air, humming and listening to a discussion about quarterback Brett McManus.

Before the snapping began, Judy Garland had been stalking down the steps of the porch toward the stunned robin. As the barrage of flaps and snaps began above her, she clinched herself into a terrified ball of hair, eyes and legs. When the rug was dustless, Loni went inside and Judy Garland remained a hairy, dust-covered fist for several minutes.

Loni opened the windows above the sink and allowed more air to pour in and the stale cloud of the Troy men to seep out. After emptying the dishwasher and putting the coffee pot on, she began loading the dishwasher, dumping the occasional cigarette butt from a plate or cup. She recalled the thought that had leapt upon her the evening before in the haze of near-sleep wakefulness. Around the time a septuagenarian was buying a vowel she'd realized that she'd spent her entire adult life cleaning up after Troys. On the cleared kitchen table sat a new pen—a Razor Writer, Desmond's favorite brand—waiting to be used. It had been removed from the package, tested once for grip and tendency to smudge, and left on the table to be used later that day. Surely, Loni thought, it would be initiated in one of Desmond's asinine sacred pen ceremonies. She picked it up and threw it in the trash among the cigarette butts and plastic cups. She pushed it down into the rubbish, through the potato skins, sandwich wrappers and egg shells, stopping when her hand couldn't move any further south. "Ahhh," she released.

She closed the dishwasher and switched it on. The machine growled to life and thumped to a start, then settled to a low, steady purr. Then she walked into the basement and down the steps to the laundry room.

At 7:36 a.m. Phineas woke and found a note taped to his forehead.

Phin- See you soon! Thanks for the hospitality. Love, Gary and Amy

Phineas recognized Gary's medical scratch and dropped the note to the floor. He lay on his back and squinted into the morning light. The skewed taste of chicken pot pie tingled on his tongue and lips, both of which had been tinted dark green.

The morning was both eerily still and pleasantly unusual for the Troy household. Phineas stretched his arms and adjusted his boxer shorts. With this action, his erect penis popped its swollen head through the urinary slot. He raised the blanket and looked down at his member, which stared back with a depressed, denied look in its closed eye. He slipped his boxers off and pulled the old pair of boxers from the floor beneath his bed. He grasped his penis in his right hand, fitted the dirty boxers onto his lower abdomen in the receptacle position and listened for the dog. Nothing. It was early, the perfect storm in the Troy house when neither dog nor human was roaming around and Phineas could be alone with his depraved thoughts.

He began manipulating himself while scouring his backlogged sexual rolodex. It came down to Fantasy 1392G: An after-school scolding from a licentious older teacher. She wore black, half-rim glasses and a dark suit. Then, as the routine went, he would switch at the crucial moment to Memory 24176B: After hours sex on the bar at Gilda's restaurant with a sun-dress clad 19-year old. His toes wiggled as he worked toward his goal; his face reddened and a merry vein bulged in his forehead.

Ennio Morricone had been having a wonderful morning. He'd been set free from the cage and ascended the stairs. After sniffing around the hall and study for a few minutes, he found a neglected niche between a low dresser and the wall and backed himself in. He viewed the quiet room with utter serenity and then urinated and defecated until completely sated. Afterwards, he sauntered to the study and began chewing on a mislaid Leon Uris novel. It wasn't until he heard a commotion from Phineas' room and sensed libidinous urgency that he decided to torture Papa Smurf.

Ennio Morricone found Papa Smurf in the study and carried him to Phineas' bedroom door. He dropped him, squatted, and then took the amiable Smurf into an artificially vicious death roll. While he chewed, the slowed-but-determined footsteps of Loni approached as she neared the top of the stairs.

Meanwhile, Phineas had made the integral switch from Fantasy 1392G to Memory 24176B and was thumping away with joyous abandon. His toes had gone from wiggling to clenching to a condition he referred to esoterically as "tiny fists of fury." The house remained quiet, even the birds outside couldn't interrupt his self-seduction. Amidst this maelstrom of pleasure, something caught his attention at the door. Papa Smurf was staring at him with his good eye, his hat and most of his head had been torn out, but remained attached.

Phineas stopped and eyed the decimated patriarch and the groping paw snatching about him. Nanoseconds before he could react, the door swung open and Loni stood before him scolding the dog, a laundry basket wedged against her hip. Phineas pulled the blanket over himself with great flourish; the dog looked about with an air of success, and then walked away. Loni pulled the door shut then explained that she was off to work and staying at Emily's house that evening, so Phineas would have to fend for himself, dinner-wise. She buzzed around upstairs collecting scattered clothing, dropped the basket at the top of the basement steps, and went to work.

"Oh, for the love of Paul!" Phineas sat up in bed. He shifted his jaw and popped his ears, he couldn't hear a thing.

"Hello, Oh my—what the hell?" Nothing. He stood and went into the bathroom. Phineas looked in the mirror and shook his head. He splashed water on his face and gargled. He sang, plugged his nose, held his breath and puffed his cheeks out like Dizzy Gillespie. Nothing worked.

"Oh my God," he said through teary eyes. "This is a nightmare." He turned on the elf spitter and stripped. He toyed his jaw and stepped in without checking the water temperature. Soft, useless water dribbled over his body as he worked his index fingers into his ears.

"Come on, come on!" He grabbed a slimy, minute piece of soap and lathered it in his hands. The murmurs of his own breathing came to him in wet rumors; as though he were under the ocean, drowning.

Clay walked down the hallway yawning and scratching his testicles through his boxer shorts. He stood outside the bathroom and Desmond appeared at the door of his bedroom smoking a cigarette, his torn briefs revealing far too much for an early morning.

"Morning Dad, you're looking lovely," Clay said.

"You're one to talk." Desmond puffed at his cigarette, "Do you know where my pants are?"

"Dad, what kind of fuckin' question is that? Why the hell would I know where your pants are?"

"Do you smell something?" Desmond asked, glancing around him.

"It's dog shit," Clay said.

"You know, every stench in this house is not dog shit."

"Yeah, it is."

How the hell do you know?" Desmond began fingering an itch that mercifully rested under a gaping hole in his briefs.

"Look," Clay pointed at Ennio Morricone's latest installment, steaming in the intentionally well-hidden corner.

"I have to find my pants. Who's in the shower?"

"Who the fuck do you think?"

Desmond ignored this comment and stepped to the bathroom door, opened it and scanned the floor.

"I'm next," Clay said, "Go find pants."

"Okay, fine." Desmond walked back into his room and Clay rapped on the door of the bathroom.

"Yo, you almost done?"

No response came, and Clay fondled his genitals, rolling them between thumb and forefinger. He knocked again. "Phin, hurry up, I gotta go to work."

Clay knocked again and cracked open the door, calling in with his deep voice and knocking. "Phin, you okay?" Clay flipped the light switch off and on a few times.

Phineas kicked and slapped at the dirty shower curtain. "Ah! What is that?" he shouted. He felt the water thumping off the top of his nose.

"It's me, dumbass! Why the hell didn't you answer?"

Phineas peeked around the shower curtain and saw Clay's yawning, scruffy face. "Clay, Clay, I can't hear!"

"What the fuck you talking about?"

"Clay, I can't hear!"

"Are you insane?"

"What?"

"Jeezus, what the fuck is it with you? You're a friggin' wreck."

"Hold on, I'm getting out." Phineas ducked back into the shower, rinsed off the soap and shut off the water. He stepped out and hung a towel around his neck. He stuck fingers in his ears and used the towel to dry his hair and beard. Ennio Morricone looked up from his book when Phineas ran into the hallway. Clay stood there looking at him with a grin on his face.

"What the hell you griping about now?"

"Clay, I swear to God, I can't hear a thing!"

"Okay, okay, quiet down," Clay said, backing away as Phineas dripped on him.

Desmond stepped out of his bedroom wearing a pair of tight, pink sweatpants and a concerned look on his face. "What the hell is all the screaming about out here?"

Clay was holding Phineas' head, looking into his eyes. "Phin says he can't hear anything."

"Really?"

"Yeah, I don't think he's kidding either."

"Oh, he'll be fine. I've gotta find my pants." Desmond lit another cigarette and stumbled down the hallway, plumes of smoke snapping back toward his kids as he rumbled out of sight.

"Phin, look at me. Look at me!" Clay pulled Phineas' head toward him and looked into his excited and wild eyes. "Can you hear me?" he asked, slowly and loudly.

"What?"

"Hold on," Clay ran down the steps to his father's table. Phineas waited in soundless agony until Clay returned carrying a pen and a pink pad of paper. He clicked the button on the pen and wrote on the pad.

Can you hear anything at all?

Phineas took the pad and wrote: *Not a thing, I swear*. "Hnak, Hnak!" he sounded off like a deranged goose. He wrote again: *Nothing*.

Clay took the pad and wrote: *How about I bring you to the hospital?*
Phineas was sweating, his hands were shaking. *No.*
What the fuck? Why not?
I want to talk to Gary first.
Why?
*I HATE DOCTORS! I'M TERRIFIED OF THEM! GARY'S THE ONLY
ONE I TRUST!*
He's a pussy doctor!
So?
*You might be a pussy, but your ears aren't! You ain't that motherfucker
from Nantucket.*
This is no time for jokes.
Phineas, why are you writing?
???
I can hear fine. Why you writing to me?
I don—"I don't know. Is this better?"
It's fine but you need to quiet down.
"Okay, is this better?"
As good as it will get I guess.
"What should I do? Oh my God, what do I do?"
Let me bring you to the hospital.
"Please Clay, please, not yet. Please let me see if this works itself out."
What if this is a serious problem?
Phineas hesitated before speaking. "I don't know."
Clay took the pen and the pad; he turned the page to a clean one and
started writing.
*I have to be at work in an hour, I can bring you to the emergency
room now or I can leave you here and we can call Gary later. He's not even
in Pittsburgh yet. If you want to sit around here deaf and noseless, be my
guest, MAN!* The impression the pen made on the paper got deeper and
brighter with every word Clay wrote, as he grew angrier at his own words
and at Phineas' actions, and at this absurd situation. *But let me know now,
because I'm not coming back for about 7 hours. It's your call .*He threw the

pen down and a drop of mucus jumped from his nostril to his lip. He wiped it away with his wrist.

Phineas took a deep breath, held it and released in shaky, broken sections. "A little while," he spat out. "Maybe it'll stop soon." He nodded his head. "Go to work, if it doesn't clear up then we'll talk about the emergency room."

Clay shook his head. *Okay.* He wrote and stepped into the bathroom. Phineas rooted through his bag until he found a pair of boxer shorts and put them on. Then he put on a sweater and pants. He felt through the pockets, pulled out a receipt and opened it: four hotdogs and a pack of cigarettes. Amy. He felt as though he might hyperventilate.

He met Ennio Morricone in the hallway; they observed each other and Phineas saw his snout snap and his body jolt in what must have been a terrible bark. For the first time that morning, Phineas smiled. Then he raised his middle finger to the dog and screamed, though he couldn't hear it, "Screw you!" The dog stepped back and frowned. Phineas bounced along the rail as he walked down the stairs, his legs lurching forward like clumpy extensions of his beleaguered body. His brain swam in the stillness surrounding him. He held onto everything he passed.

The world moved in slow motion. A house fly zipped around his face and Phineas missed it with an oafish swat. He reached the bottom of the steps and wandered into the kitchen, hoping to see his mother. The table had already been recoated in a new layer of muck. Newspapers, toilet paper, donuts, cream, two coffee mugs and a knife pasted in strawberry jam circled a makeshift ashtray that had once served as a dinner plate. The pretty morning moved in through the windows and birds flew through the air outside.

Phineas yelped, then he barked like a dog and there was nothing. A murmur in his head told him that the sounds had actually been produced and the appearance of his brother solidified this conviction. Clay's hair was wet and slicked back, he had shaved and small red burn marks dotted his neck.

Clay handed him the pad. *You okay?* It read.

Phineas shook his head.

What are you going to do today?

"Going to see Ben," he said

I'll be back at 5. We can call Gary when I get back.

"Fine."

Why are you making dog sounds?

"I don't know."

Well, stop it.

Phineas looked at the note and then at Clay. His blue shirt was unbuttoned revealing a patch of curly black hair. Clay's deep brown eyes looked into his as he took the pad. Clay was whole, he was strong and unrelenting and unbending. He wouldn't give in to this, Phineas thought. He'd fight whatever it was and win. In the second it took Phineas to respond to Clay, he envied everything about him, his looks and his swagger, his confidence in everything he did and said. And for that reason, he responded in a manner that confused even him.

"Can I sing?" he asked.

Clay reared back and shut an eye; he fixed the pen in his hand. *Yeah, but wait 'til I'm gone.*

"Please leave then."

See you at 5, dickhead.

Clay handed the pad and pen to Phineas and walked out the door. Phineas went into the living room and sat on the couch, his head resting against the blanket that Amy had slept under hours before, when he'd still been the owner and proprietor of three and a half senses. He smelled linoleum tiles. He growled like a lion until his throat burned and his eyes felt tight against their membranes. There was nothing.

Phineas hummed at a steady tone for one minute and heard it from a distant place somewhere inside him. Then he placed his hands over his ears and hummed again, this time the inward sound was intensified. He hummed "Fly Me to the Moon," and then sang the opening lines, since it was all he could remember. He heard himself as if he were a deep-voiced didgeridoo, moaning his plaint to the Australian outback. He walked through the front door, stopping in the cool morning and allowing the breeze to travel around him and through his ears, as it would a hollow tin can in a vast trash dump. He walked down the street, past The Blue Duck where Jack Schorpp waved at him from the balcony and called to him. Jack was holding a pot of bright azaleas. Phineas waved and crossed Maple Avenue and turned at The Blue Duck Inn, on to Edgewood Lane. Jack Schorpp watched after him with a disquieted look on his face, the reflection of the azaleas tinting his squinted eyelids red.

Phineas walked toward the canal that ran into the Neshaminy Creek and the mule tender's cabin. The leaves fell from the tunnel of trees that surrounded him. Wind pushed into him and tears rolled down his cheeks; he felt as if he were in a cave. He hummed "I've Got You under My Skin" and heard a tiny voice inside him. He then imagined a tiny man standing in his sternum singing for his collective *organum*. The little man wore a tuxedo and was clean-shaven and had slicked back hair. He sang into a microphone and was surrounded by organs and miniscule organisms, all of whom wore dresses and suits and cheered for him. His heart held a baton and conducted this little man with self-propelled ecstasy.

Phineas yearned to understand the source of this deranged fantasy, but soon gave up and instead decided to keep it secret forever. He reached the path that ran through the woods to the canal and started along it.

"Phineas," he said aloud to himself, "what you got yourself into here, bud? I don't know, man, this ain't good. This ain't good."

Two young women wearing matching warm-up suits and pushing identical strollers eyed him. He smiled at them and trotted down the path.

"Jeezus!" Phineas laughed. "People are gonna start to talk!"

Fishermen were scattered along the canal on both sides. Some of them were old and others were dressed in camouflage and Phineas wondered why. A pair of middle-aged joggers came toward him and said good morning. Across the canal were the mule tender's cabin and Miles and Sonny in the crude barn. He jogged across the bridge and went to the cabin and looked in the windows. On the door was a note:

Charlie, be back later. Ran into Cranesville to get a load of plywood and run a few errands. Mules are fed and cleaned. Be back for the 2:30 run. See you then, Ben.

"Damn!" He went to the window again and looked in. The coffee pot was on the table and Ben's Phillies hat was on the hook. He opened the door and almost walked in until he remembered Judy Garland, then he shut the door and walked to the mules. He ducked his head into the barn and waved at them.

"Hi guys. How are you? I can't hear at the moment, so if you're saying something for the first time ever, I'm missing it."

Miles grinned and swatted Sonny with his tail, who then also grinned. They beheld him in silence and Miles winked his right eye.

"Well, I hope you guys are getting a real kick out of this, cause I sure am." He walked out from under the awning of the barn and back across the bridge. The little man sang to him and his voice jiggled a bit. Phineas walked along the canal, away from the fishermen. A pair of young, professional-looking men in taut running shorts jogged by and looked at him as they passed. Phineas felt a rush of fear and embarrassment, as though he were about to be addressed in a language he couldn't speak. He inspected his shoes and the men jogged in place and looked over his head. Phineas followed their gaze until it reached a fisherman wrangling with a fish. The man had stood and the rod was bent into the dark water. Every man along the canal—jogger, fisherman, deaf bartender—had stopped to watch this man battle the fish. He pulled a large bass onto the bank with a slippery yank and his friends approached and slapped his back. The man wore a look of indescribable joy.

For a moment, Phineas forgot his ears, nose and palate. He forgot his grandmother, and hemorrhoids and the little man singing inside his sternum to a visceral audience. He walked along the canal, the little man serenading him with a Bob Dylan tune whose name he couldn't recall, and sat in the grass. He laid back and spread out his arms and legs and fell asleep. From a nearby thicket, Judy Garland observed Phineas as she swooned and scraped at the dust and dirt that irritated her eyes and stuck in her hair.

17

As Ben drove down the dirt road that led to the mule tender's cabin he noted a round clump of body and clothing in the grass across the canal. He didn't give much thought to the chest rising in rhythmic breathing, assuming it was one of The Blue Duck's barflies drying out before the evening's shenanigans. He wandered into the cabin and pulled his baseball cap from its hook, then opened the tailgate of the truck and put on a pair of old work gloves. It wasn't until he had started unloading the plywood and took another glance at the resting body that he recognized the scruffy face, dark hair and the mound of belly that rose from the grass. Not to mention the gentle throat-based snoring which echoed into the trees.

Ben walked across the bridge, watching the fishermen sip coffee from their metal thermoses and talk about the day's catches. Wondering what they had in the bucket, he squinted into the sun and tipped his baseball cap away from his brow. When he reached the other bank his boots sunk into the mud and he paused a few feet from the outstretched man sleeping in the grass. Two joggers shuffled by; one of whom was wheezing, his chin attached to his chest. The other's face was red and he looked down at Phineas.

"He okay?" the jogger called to Ben, turning and jogging backwards as he spoke. A breeze followed the man and cooled Ben's neck, which had been baking in the sun all morning. The coolness of the air drew a smile out of Ben.

"Sure," Ben said. He pulled his gloves off and stuffed them in his back pocket, then tipped his hat and the man turned to join his miserable friend.

Ben walked up to Phineas and looked at his face as he slept. The rounded end of his nose sported a small divot which Phineas had created many years before by scratching off a chicken pock. The line of his double chin creased beneath the dark hairs on his face. He snored in timed breaths through his open mouth. His arms and legs were stretched wide and his open palms faced the sky. Ben squatted next to him and brushed a beetle off his sweater.

Ben considered letting him sleep for a while until he noticed a colony of black ants stirring nearby and feared they might become overzealous and attack. He imagined, with some joy, a thousand black ants carrying Phineas off to their hill, euphoric with their booty. The ants seemed to halt their bustling actions when Ben leaned in to start Phineas.

"Phin," he whispered. "Phineas Troy," he said in a sing-speak voice. "Oh, sweet Phinny baby," he said a little louder and waved above his head. He nudged him on the side and again when he still didn't rouse. The beetle returned and Ben placed his finger in its path and allowed it access. When the beetle had boarded his digit, Ben called through an imaginary loudspeaker. "Kssht, this is the final boarding call for Beetle Air, Flight 1109 at Neshaminy Airport. Please, stow all carry-on luggage in the overhead compartments or under the seat in front of you. That is all. Kssht"

He carried the beetle to a nearby tree and spun around in circles, made engine sounds and carefully raised and dropped his hand to appear more like a roller coaster than an airplane ride. The beetle hung on to his forefinger with its six black legs and wings whirring about. Ben announced the landing, found a dry spot on the ground near the roots of the tree and left it there. He returned just as Phineas stirred, opened his eyes and squinted into the sun. Ben squatted down above him.

"Hey buddy, taking a little nap?"

Phineas stared at Ben, shading his eyes with his hand, unable to see anything other than a wide, dark shadow mantling the sun. Ben moved his head forward, blocking the sun so that his friend could see his face and repeated his question. Phineas could only hear his own breathing, which ran through him like the dead, whispering draft in a deep cave. He blinked and started, then bolted upright and grabbed Ben's pant leg.

"Ben!" He had gripped Ben's calf now. "I can't hear!"

Ben watched Phineas tug at his leg. "Phineas, what the hell are you talking about?"

The world remained quiet around Phineas. "Ben, I can't hear anything! I woke up this morning and couldn't hear!" He scrambled to his feet.

"Okay, buddy." Ben held him by the shoulders. "First, let's quiet you down a little bit."

"What?!"

"It's okay." Ben grabbed Phineas' shaking head and forced him to look at his mouth. "Come with me."

"What?" Phineas struggled, but Ben's strength held him in place until he calmed.

The fishermen had quieted and were staring at them and Ben hooked a large arm around Phineas and took him across the bridge. Phineas' screaming had turned to a low murmuring. Dark clouds threatened the sky and Ben took notice. He leaned in close to Phineas to discover that Phineas was humming "The Star Spangled Banner" in his throat, like a patriotic frog sitting on a hidden pad in a pond.

Ben brought him to the cabin and stood ducked beneath the door. Phineas stopped in front of the door. Ben latched onto the door frame with his huge hands and waited for an explanation.

"Spider." Phineas' voice came out small. Ben collared his shoulder gently and led him away from the cabin. Ben knew that the tarantula could be anywhere and that the safest place to be in terms of spider-avoidance was probably the cabin. Either Judy Garland wasn't in there or she was and had been killing off the nasty wolf spiders that had been seeking warmth in the cabin since the cooler autumn nights had begun. However, he resisted the urge to convey this message.

Judy Garland was perched in a clutch of roots at the base of a poplar tree some thirty feet away. Like an obsessed teenager, she kept Phineas in her periphery at all times, her eyes too weak to watch him, she sensed his presence and remained near him, out of sight, but aware. At that moment, she was pretending to be interested in a few wasps that were buzzing about. To Judy Garland, Phineas was playing the part of the popular and aloof football star, oblivious of her presence and preoccupied with greater matters at hand. Phineas' ignorance was genuine and this exacerbated her desire for him. With her two back legs she slipped a batch of urticating hairs off her abdomen, at once marking her territory and dissuading the wasps from coming in for a closer look, crouched and settled into the cluster of roots.

They went to the barn where Ben turned Phineas' head to him by his chin and pointed to the ground with both hands. Then he opened his palms to Phineas in a wait motion. Phineas turned to the mules and Ben jogged to the cabin and pulled a green notebook he kept for the accounting from a drawer.

Sonny licked her lips and stamped a hoof into the dirt, a mild vibration of which Phineas felt and then mimicked. Miles jerked his head and Phineas petted him on the nose. A look of understanding and compassion overtook his long face. Phineas rubbed up and down the nose, feeling the smoothness of Miles' coat as he stroked down and the bristly resistance as he stroked up, against the coat. They looked each other in the eye and Phineas felt Sonny pound another hoof into the ground.

"Don't worry, Sonny, my intentions are pure!" His voice rang out across the quiet canal.

Phineas took his hand away from the mule's snout to take the notebook that Ben handed him, already open to a page with a note written into it.

"Am I really being that loud?" Phineas cast glances around him.

Ben nodded and took the book and scribbled into it with his pencil, which was less than two inches long. It looked like a sewing needle in Ben's hand. He handed the notebook to Phineas.

"Like this?" he asked a little quieter.

One of the fishermen filled a metal pail with water and rinsed it out, then dumped the water back into the canal. The other one hooked a mealworm and switched a chaw from his right to left cheek, then worked his tongue against his teeth to rake out the dry flecks of tobacco. Ben motioned his hands down toward the ground and Phineas lowered his voice.

"Like this?"

Ben continued and Phineas kept lowering his voice and began bending his knees, as if physically lowering his body would help him lower his voice.

"Like this?"

Ben cracked a smile and scribbled in the notebook.

"Well, I am definitely *not* trying to talk dirty to you!"

The fishermen looked back above the hill with curious and confused faces. One took a nip off a silver flask, giggled like a drunken Spaniard and handed the flask over.

Again, Ben moved his hands toward the ground and Phineas moved his body closer to the ground. "Like this?" he asked again and was at a volume level normal enough for Ben to give up the game. He jotted something in his notebook.

"Okay," Phineas said and handed the book back.

Ben wrote again.

"I told Clay earlier that I wanted to talk to Gary first."

Ben's tongue peeked out of the corner of his mouth as he wrote.

"Yeah, I'm pretty sure. I want to give it a day or two."

Ben took the book again, his giant hand working in easy, fluid motions. The back of the pencil was like new; no bite marks, the eraser almost perfect. He handed the book to Phineas.

"Yeah, I'm sure. I just want two days."

Though Phineas stared, he couldn't hear the sound of the pencil scribbling on the page, the curt snap of Ben's t or the smooth glide of his s or the tap as he dotted the i. "I smell a Phonics book, Ben."

Ben smiled at that and continued writing.

"Exactly. See Dick Run," he said. "See Ben write. See Phineas not smell or hear…" he shook his head.

Ben handed him the book.

"I am absolutely terrified," Phineas said without hesitation.

Ben scribbled again and handed it to Phineas.

"Okay, I'll wait here."

Ben went to the cabin and picked up the phone. Phineas looked out at the fishermen and scratched his back. They bantered with each other animatedly, seemingly stuck in a film of perpetual movement. One of them spooled up his line and sat on a green director's chair with the name Lester printed into the back of it. The bottom of the s had worn away and resembled a snake readying attack on the t. The standing fisherman was crouched and his thick, dirty hands were spread wide in front of him. The wind had picked up and the sky was changing from blue to gray. Out on the Neshaminy Creek, a few fishing boats specked the water. The colorful trees on the opposite bank swayed in the breeze. Ben returned and followed Phineas' gaze to them and wondered if he was longing to hear them rustle against one another, the vibrantly colored leaves clicking from branches and hurtling to the dry ground.

Ben tapped Phineas on the shoulder and handed him the notebook. "Are you sure?"

Ben nodded, took the book back and wrote again.

"When do you think he'll be here?"

Ben wrote again and Phineas took it.

"He's at work 'til five. We'll call Gary then."

They walked back to the mules. Sonny reared her snout in the air and snorted, blowing mucus all over Phineas' face. Phineas frowned.

"Oh, crap," he said and Ben stifled his laughter. Instead, he handed Phineas the handkerchief that had been in his back pocket. Miles grumbled a mild epithet toward Sonny, one that Ben seemed to understand.

"Hey, relax guys," Ben said. He rubbed Sonny's ear and blew a short breath onto her nose. He talked to them, telling them that Charlie would be there soon and that he had to go help out a friend. He then unloaded the remainder of the plywood and some 2x4s that rested along the inside panel of the truck bed. When he walked out of the cabin he was holding a naked Snickers bar, which he tore in half and held out in front of the mules. Miles opened his mouth and panted. Sonny's tail swung and her ear twitched to redirect a pesky fly.

"Are you gonna be good for Charlie?" Ben asked and waved the pieces past their eyes. "Hm?"

The mules stamped their back hooves into the ground and Ben put a half in each of his palms and presented the chocolates. The mules turned their heads and ate them, shaking their snouts to gain control of the chocolate, like Ennio Morricone laying into a book of haiku.

A blue Hyundai pulled toward the truck and Ben waved.

"Can I have a Snickers bar, please?" Phineas asked.

Ben wrote into the pad and handed it to Phineas as Charlie stepped out of the car with a smile on his face.

"They like Snickers?" Phineas asked and Charlie came to them and shook Ben's hand.

"Heya buddy, thanks so much for covering me this afternoon," Ben said and wrote in the notebook.

"Really, well, that's interesting," Phineas murmured. Charlie extended his hand to Phineas.

"Hi, I'm Charlie. Nice to meet you."

Phineas shook his hand and smiled, then watched Ben talking to Charlie. He guessed that Ben was explaining his predicament. Charlie's face was tight and freshly shaven, his bright eyes sang out as Ben spoke to him. Dark hairs grew out of the top of his nose like tiny slivers of wood. He was dressed in denim overalls, a blue and yellow flannel shirt that matched Ben's and a straw hat that made him look like Huck Finn. Phineas found himself attached to Charlie, whose expressions traded between stunned and piteous.

Charlie clasped his fingers in front of his stomach with the casual and sturdy strength of a man who'd worked with his hands his whole life. His build was strong and trustworthy and his boots were worn and muddy. Charlie regarded Phineas with shy sympathy and took the pencil and notebook from Ben. He smiled and began to write. Ben observed that Phineas seemed calmer near the mule tenders.

"Is there anything you need done before I split?" Ben asked and looked around.

"Do we have any Snickers?" Charlie asked.

"Yep, there's a few on the table in there. I just gave 'em one, so give it a while."

"Okay, go on, get out of here," Charlie handed the notebook to Phineas.

"Thank you, Charlie. Me too." Phineas stumbled when Ben turned him toward the bridge. Charlie watched them cross the path and start through the patch of woods. Then he waved to the fishermen and walked back to the mules. He slid the notebook into the front pocket of his overalls.

Phineas and Ben walked along the path and storm clouds began filling the sky. Two squirrels dashed around a tall cedar tree, their fluffy tails bobbed behind them and they clucked at each other. Phineas stepped toward the tree to get a closer look at the squirrels.

Ben watched him inch through the forest. He reminisced about Phineas, or as he sometimes secretly referred to him, Young Phineas. Young Phineas was a renegade, a boy with a constant source of energy who put on football helmets and ran headfirst into trees. Young Phineas ate glue with a knife and fork and once painted his cat orange to convince his neighbors that pigmy tigers roamed the neighborhood. Ben wondered about the change, when it had started.

Phineas crept toward the tree and Ben considered the transformation as he watched after him. When had he begun to worry about things more, the way that all Troy men did, it seemed, except maybe Clay. Ben wondered when the fuse had blown. And what had caused it? He supposed that in some way Phineas was only guilty of ordinary growing up, with the everyday worries that barnacle to getting a job, having quasi-regular sex and your own apartment.

The squirrels froze in place, their natural mohawks pointing from their little heads. Phineas also stopped in his tracks. He remained crouched in an attack position and waited for a signal.

Ben surmised, there was still a twinkle, a glimmer of some part of Young Phineas. The part of him that used to stage ghost-story marathons in his basement on rainy days, or the Phineas who once led day-long adventures to the deep sections of the forest. After which he'd come home much too late, covered in ticks and poison ivy and grime. His neck and cheeks baked from the sun, his nose sore and raw, but his eyes gleaming euphorically, and a wide, pure smile as if to tell all of Lansford that he was expecting a severe spanking for his infractions and that, and only that, would make this day complete. Desmond would always comply with enraged fervor and Phineas' bottom would match his face, cheeks and nose by the time he dropped into bed that evening, completely satisfied.

The squirrels snapped into action and scurried up the tree. Phineas let out a war cry that rang through the forest and scattered birds that were resting in the trees. He wrapped his arms around the tree and barked up at them. Ben bent over and laughed until his stomach hurt. Yes, he thought, that part of him is still in there somewhere. He watched Phineas rummage around the ground and thought about the process.

For the most part the Troy men were settlers. They aimed short, got there, landed an anchor and never moved again. Ben had always known this. Some of the Troy men broke free from this pattern, Uncle Robert had, for sure. Mostly, though, any promise they'd shown as boys dissolved and left a man who could step through his daily routine if he were blindfolded and hogtied. Any diversion from this routine was met with irritation and panic. He tried to pinpoint what Phineas needed to break that pattern and couldn't. Maybe a nudge, he thought, just a nudge to get him moving again. Something to knock that kid with no fear loose from this overgrown boy stuck in whatever he's stuck in.

Phineas approached in a toddle, his hair was spiky with dry leaves. His sweater covered with twigs and dirt. He regarded Ben with a half smile, as if he knew what Ben had been thinking about.

"Let's go, Ben," he said.

"OK." Ben brushed the leaves from his sweater, then he licked his thumb and wiped a smudge of dirt from Phineas' forehead. Ben turned Phineas around and blew a short blast of air onto his back to clear some dirt and slapped his back clean. "It'll be all right, old buddy," Ben said to Phineas' back. "But I got a bad feeling it's gonna get a lot worse before it gets any better." He turned Phineas' face to him and slapped him soundly on the cheek.

Outside The Blue Duck Jack Schorpp was reviewing an inventory list as other men were carrying kegs and cases of beer in through the back door. Upon seeing them, he stretched and waved.

"Hey Ben," Jack said.

"Hey Mr. Schorpp. How are you?"

"Good, you?" Jack took a clipboard from a short fat man who was sweating in waterfalls, scanned it and signed at the bottom. "See you next week, Ralph," he said.

"See you Jack." Ralph got in a truck and left.

"I'm good," Ben said, when Jack's attention was back on him. "Beauty of a day, huh?"

"Yeah," Jack said and looked at Phineas. "Hey Phin, how you doing?"

Phineas had been doing everything he could to act natural. He rubbed his hands together and glanced around him, keeping his eyes as frantic-free as possible. He felt like a high-school student who had just smoked marijuana in the school parking lot and was now being confronted by the principal. Jack was tan and gray haired, he wore a green T-shirt and blue work gloves poked out of his back pocket. Phineas looked at his face trying to avoid eye contact.

At the moment Jack Schorpp asked Phineas how he was doing Phineas had been staring at Jack's mouth. He took a stab at it.

"Fine, Mr. Schorpp, how are you?"

"Good, beautiful day. Your friends have a good time last night?"

Phineas stared at Jack with huge eyes. He then looked at Ben for help, who only stared back at him. He had decided to see where this would go, purely for the sake of entertainment.

"I don't feel well," Phineas said. "I must go now..." his voice got louder with each syllable. "To my home..." He couldn't move his legs. "Which is where I live and where I am now going to go to now." Phineas began sweating and Ben took Phineas by the arm and started to move him down the sidewalk, stiff step by stiff step, toward his house.

"Please excuse him, Mr. Schorpp, he's pretty sick," Ben called back to Jack and waved. "I was just bringing him home to bed, actually."

Jack had gone back to his inventory. "That nasty flu that's been going around?" Jack asked, his eyes scanning the paper.

"It might be, we're not sure yet. Bye, Mr. Schorpp."

"Bye, bye," Phineas called ahead of him. He moved like an old man who had been confined to a wheelchair for decades. "Bye, bye."

"See you, Ben. Take care of yourself, Phin. Oh, by the way," he looked up from the paper, "just got in another three bottles of crème de menthe. You boys drank me out of it last night."

"Thank you," Ben said and held Phineas in place at the edge of the street. He looked both ways twice, then walked him to the house. There were three cars in the driveway and Desmond was sitting on the porch with two men, all of them were eating pizza. Ben walked up the driveway with Phineas and Desmond stood and waved with a slice of pepperoni pizza.

"Hey guys," he called. "Come on over, I want you to meet some people."

Ben stared at Desmond and then at Phineas, who shot him a desperate look of panic. Ben giggled and looked toward the side door, which was only a few yards away.

"Um, well, Dr. Troy, um—" Ben stammered and stepped in place.

"Come on, come here." Desmond sat back down and Ben could hear his voice over the traffic on Maple Avenue. "It's my son and his friend," he said to the other men.

Ben started toward the porch and Phineas grabbed his shirt with both hands and pulled him back. "What are you doing?" he tried to whisper but it came out as a raspy grunt.

Ben had no notebook. "It's cool. It's fine. Trust me." He reached through his pockets and found no pen, no pencil. He turned Phineas' face toward his own. "Phineas, look at me," he put his finger to his lips. "Shh, shh, relax, buddy. Shh, Okay?"

Phineas nodded and they walked up the porch to where Desmond and two men sat in wicker chairs and ate pizza. On the table, surrounded by bees, was a closed box of pizza and a half empty bottle of cola. The men had on matching brown pants. The older man wore a yellow and brown shirt that was buttoned all the way to the top. Gray suspenders stretched over his belly. The younger man wore thick-rimmed glasses. His shirt was blue and his suspenders were red. They laughed at each other between enormous bites of pizza. Phineas could tell by their sloped cheeks and deep-set eyes that they both had Down's syndrome.

Desmond patted Ben on the back. "Hey guys, this is Ben, Ben this is William and Steve." Desmond's eyes were gleaming slits and a smile reached across his chubby face. His cheeks propped his loupes above his eyebrows.

William and Steve stood and extended marinara sauce-covered hands. "Hi Ben," they said at the same time.

"Hi guys, nice to meet you." He shook their hands and left the marinara on his palm.

"This is my son, Phineas," Desmond said as he touched Phineas on the back, leaving a stain of tomato sauce on his sweater. Desmond brushed at it but only rubbed it in deeper. "Oh well," he said.

"Hello," Phineas said, and shook their hands. Desmond went back to the pizza and cola. William held Phineas' hand for a moment. His sunken features were pocked, red rashes speckled his temples and small sores ringed his neck. His smile was genuine, his eyes showed innocent friendliness.

"Do you want some pizza?" William asked him.

Ben stood behind William and Steve and nodded his head with surreptitious vigor. Phineas followed Ben's motions. William walked to the pizza box, shooed the bees with gentle swipes of his hand and removed a piece. He handed it to Phineas who then stuffed it into his mouth. He ate in loud chomps and left the slice in his mouth when he paused for a breath between chews. Ben was laughing with the men as he ate a slice that Steve had given him.

Desmond handed Phineas a plastic cup of cola and winked at him through his loupes. He went to work on a new piece of pizza and Steve clicked his teeth together several times. His hair was in a flat top and his eyes were dark and inset.

"Do you like the pizza?" Steve asked Phineas

Ben stood behind Steve and again nodded. Phineas nodded, "mhmmff," he mumbled through his pizza, "Grrt." He widened his eyes to show that he truly meant this.

"Why are you guys having pizza?" Ben asked Steve.

"Dr. Troy told us that when we got our bridges all done we could come back for a pizza party."

"Really?" Ben asked. "That's nice," he looked at Desmond, who was swirling a long piece of cheese around his finger. His telescopic lenses focused on it with surgical intensity. Ben turned back to Steve. "Well, I think that's great." He meant it.

"Thank you," said Steve.

"Thank you," William said, reaching out his hand, still covered in sauce. Ben took the hand and shook it, complying with William's explosive pumps. After the excitement of the handshake, William twitched and snapped his hands up and down.

"Dr. Troy, we have a little work to do. I'm sorry to leave the party so quickly, but we have to go in."

"No problem. I'm sure I'll see you tonight," Desmond said and smiled.

"It was a pleasure to meet you guys." Ben shook their hands.

"Goodbye," Phineas said, shaking their hands. "Goodbye." He took off toward the end of the porch with Ben. They went around the house to the side door and Phineas ran through it and up the stairs. His hands and back were covered with tomato sauce and dirt; his mustache tinged with the flavor of marinara. He ran into the bathroom and washed his face and hands. He looked into the mirror and fingered the rings under his eyes. Eyes, tongue, nodes, ears, nostrils, throat. Ben stood in the doorway, watching him.

Phineas gargled water and spit it into the sink. He gargled again and sang through the water. While gargling, he opened his mouth into a large

O and then closed it, the difference in sound echoed off the walls in the small bathroom. He leaned back, staring at the ceiling with his arms out wide. He looked, for this moment, like Christ, Ben thought. He laughed when he realized that Phineas was gargling to the tune of "The Gambler." He pursed his lips to reach the low notes and spread his mouth wide to hit the high notes. He looked like a cartoon opera singer. He spit again, then refilled his mouth with a suitable amount of water and leaned back into his position, this time gargling "Yankee Doodle Dandee." The vibrations seconded through his neck and chest, it rang through his entire body.

Spit sprayed Phineas' face like great fireworks exploding in the night sky on the Fourth of July. One glob hit him in the eye and he wiped it away with his hand. His back was arched and his face parallel to the ceiling. Ben moved above him to see what the water was doing in his mouth. When Phineas opened his eyes to see Ben above him, he jolted and choked on the water, most of which stuck in his throat, some of which sprayed Ben in the face. Phineas fell to the floor and Ben stepped back.

"Don't sneak up on me like that!" He stood, his eyes red and his face flushed. "What are you trying to do, kill me?" He was flinging his hands in wild gestures. Phineas saw Clay standing behind Ben in the doorway. The front of his blue shirt was streaked with dirt. Ben handed him a notebook.

"I am? Now?"

Ben nodded and so did Clay.

"Well, why didn't you say something sooner?"

In the excitement, Phineas' voice had risen to a steady shout. Ben and Clay both placed their hands in front of them palms down and motioned toward the ground.

"Like this?" Phineas said.

They shook their heads and continued their downward gestures.

"Like this?" Phineas almost whispered.

Ben nodded and Clay stuck his thumbs up.

"Motherfucker sounds like a demented Barry White," Clay said.

Ben took the notebook back and wrote on it.

"Okay, I'll try to keep it like this," he croaked through the back of his throat and stepped past them out of the bathroom. "Where's the phone?"

Clay and Ben pointed in the direction of Clay's room and Phineas walked in front of them. He guided himself down the hallway and sprinted up the steps, past the beer cans and posters. He went through the dark hallway and pushed the door to Clay's room open with force then paced around the couch while he waited for the others. They came in and Clay took the phone off the coffee table. A football game played on the television. Clay took out a piece of paper, surveyed it and began dialing the number.

"Gary?" Clay asked into the receiver.

"Yep," Gary responded.

"Gary, this is Clay, Phin's brother." He smacked himself in the head with an open palm.

"Hey, Clay, how are you?"

"Good, well, okay, I guess. Listen, we got a problem here."

"Oh God, is everything okay?"

"Phineas can't hear anything."

The other line was quiet. "What do you mean?" Gary asked finally.

"No joke, man. Motherfucker can't hear a God damn thing."

"Is he okay?" Gary asked.

"He's been off and on. Okay for a while, then a freak out."

Phineas alternated between trying to read Clay's lips and monitoring Ben's face for some reaction. Neither technique was enlightening him, so he tapped his foot with impatience.

He tapped Ben on the arm. "What is he saying?"

Ben wrote a note and handed it to Phineas.

"Oh, for the love of Pete." He shook his head.

He tugged at his arm again. "Ask him if there's anything I can do."

Ben spoke to Clay and Clay spoke into the receiver. He watched Phineas and listened to Gary. Clay spoke to Ben and Ben wrote in the notebook and handed it to Phineas.

"Go to a doctor, that's the advice I get?" Phineas moaned.

Clay pulled a finger to his lips and frowned at him. Phineas tugged at Ben's shirt again. "Ask him if there's a chance it'll get better by itself."

Ben spoke to Clay, who then spoke into the phone and listened to Gary's response. Clay then spoke to Ben, pinching the phone between his shoulder and neck and Ben wrote in the notebook. Phineas took it.

"Well, that's not too depressing."

Clay took the notebook, wrote in it and handed it to Phineas. Phineas read the note and turned his jaw in a clockwise motion, then plugged an index finger into each of his ears and shook his head.

"Nothing," Phineas said to Clay, who in turn said it to Gary. Clay listened and took the notebook back from Phineas. He started writing and stopped to ask Gary a question, then he continued writing and handed Phineas the notebook.

"Nope, not at all. Doesn't hurt a lick," he said and handed over the notebook.

Clay talked and listened to Gary. He wrote again in the notebook and handed it to Phineas. Phineas read it and handed it back.

"Is that exactly what he said?" asked Phineas. Clay nodded.

"Ask him if I can wait a day or two."

Clay spoke into the receiver and shrugged his shoulders. He wrote in the notebook and handed it to Phineas.

"Fine, then tell him I'll go if it's not better in two days."

Clay shook his head in frustration and spoke again to Gary. He walked away from Ben and Phineas.

Phineas frowned. "Where the hell is he going?" he asked Ben.

Ben shook his head and shrugged his shoulders. Clay hung up the phone and turned around a moment later. He was smiling.

"Well, what did he say?" Phineas asked.

Clay wrote in the notebook for a minute and handed it back to Phineas, who read it and dropped it on the table. He looked at Clay and Ben and Frederick the Turtle in the corner, tapping his beak against the glass.

"Just give me a God damn day, okay?" he walked from the room, down the steps to his room. He sat on the bed, dropped his head in his hands and took a deep breath. "Jesus, Phin, what are you gonna do?" He watched the inside of his fingers.

Ennio Morricone waddled into the room like a sumo wrestler and stood at the foot of Phineas' bed. He stared up at him, his jaw set, and started grunting in his throat though Phineas couldn't hear it. Phineas smiled at the dog and stuck out his tongue.

Ben and Clay sat around the coffee table in Clay's room. Clay rolled a joint and Ben sat back with a beer and watched him work. They were quiet. Ben was exhausted. Clay wouldn't look anywhere but at the paper and his fingers working their magic with the cannabis. From downstairs came a raucous sound, like a metal baseball bat connecting squarely with a wooden table. Ben looked up, but didn't stand. The sound came again. It was angry, harsh. Looking to the ceiling, Clay exhaled. The sound came again. This time they recognized the dog barking. They didn't move, Ben sat back and swallowed. The bark was followed by another and then another.

The barking was interrupted by another sound, once, twice and then three times. It was another set of barks. Now, Clay looked at Ben with concern and paused his doobie rolling. The barks continued and they realized that it was Phineas barking back at the dog. Then the dog's barks joined Phineas'. Ben laughed out loud, though he wasn't sure why. He wondered what was happening, but couldn't make himself go find out. They both leaned over the table, as if doing so was going to help them better hear the exchange from the floor below. The other sets of barks started again and were interspersed with screams and a high-pitched giggle that could only be described as maniacal. Ben winced at the sound.

Clay finished rolling the joint and when Ben reached for it, Clay handed it over. Ben slumped back into the couch and listened. The terrible barks had stopped, and it was quiet until a moment later Phineas roared and it bounced off every wall in the large house.

"I don't have to hear your damn barking or smell your Goddamn crap anymore, you miserable mutt!"

Ben handed the joint back to Clay who had downed most of a beer

sky was a blackish blue and he heard crickets and the soft breeze swaying through the high grass. His white suit appeared light gray in the moonlight and his shoes were hidden in the deep grass. The grass shuffled against his pants as he stepped toward the house and the light in the kitchen window. He could hear movement coming from inside and the click of his shoes as he stepped onto the cement patio.

He felt pleasantly intoxicated and wore a smile which implied that he knew something he shouldn't. There was movement in the window. As he crossed the patio to the front steps it seemed to get younger and less derelict. The garden became less overgrown, transforming from a weed-infested patch to a trim, neatly-lined assortment of planted herbs and vegetables. The faraway sound of music came from within.

Phineas walked up the steps to the house and leaned against the front door. He pressed his face to it and heard a piano playing and people talking. He looked both ways, as if he were going to walk across a street, and raised his hand to knock. From inside came the unmistakable scent of homemade Italian food, which teased his palate with horrendous delight.

In the morning, Phineas woke to his father standing in the doorway with his lips moving. He stared at Desmond, his somnolent befuddlement augmented by his deafness. His father stopped speaking, waited and then walked down the hallway, a cigarette dangled from his lips. During the night his shirt had rolled up to resemble a training bra. He acknowledged his white stomach spreading out beneath the shirt, let out a low grunt and pulled the robe over its pasty expanse.

He dressed and went to the kitchen, which was bright with late morning sunshine. He removed a frozen pizza from the freezer and turned on the oven. As the oven heated up he sat down to watch television. Sports commentators were seated around a large, semi-circular table. Behind them were blown up photos of various football players. Phineas spotted the remote control under a half-eaten jelly doughnut, picked it up, flung a glob of jelly across the table and hit the closed captioning button. He put his pizza in the oven and sat down to watch the show.

"McManus never does well against Philadelphia. Even when he

played for the Steelers, he wasn't able to bri@g the goods in Philly, what do you think Bob?"

"I think that McManus is a great athlete and h* is due. If you look at this young man's record as a coll-#** athlete and as a professional athlete, you will see that he is a competitor—"

"Well, Bob, no matter what, he's got an enemy worse than the Philadelphia Eagles."

"Oh yeah? What's that, Jim?"

"Rain. The man can't play in the rain, he's constantly, excuse the p%n, but, dropping the ball. I take Philly over Miami, 21-7."

"Okay, Jim, I take Miami over Philly in the upset 14-10. You can take that one to the bank."

Laughter…Laughter…La##@ter…Laughter.

For one fleeting moment, as Phineas read the idiotic statements and watched the overly-made-up faces of the commentators jiggle with emoted guffaws, he was happy that he'd gone deaf. He checked on the still frozen pizza and slammed the door shut then went back to the refrigerator. Now he was thankful for his crippled sense of smell. A brown sludge crept across a blackened ham and a furry red mustache grew on guacamole that Desmond had opened earlier that week. In an untracked crisper at the bottom of the fridge a hot dog peeked its head from a slew of rotten vegetables. Phineas pulled the crisper further open to reveal more; it was a Nathan's hot dog and the lone survivor of the pack. Beheld in the light, it was supreme. Its golden skin glimmered in the light of the refrigerator. It arched with slick intelligence and its knotted end ogled Phineas' chin. He loved this hot dog. He smiled and, though he didn't know it, moaned with joy.

And then, cruel tragedy struck. In his celebratory elation, he dropped the hot dog which then rolled under the table and rested beneath the chair. Though he couldn't understand what had happened, he knew that things had gone terribly awry. This glorious hot dog, once glistening with a perfect brown skin, was now covered in dog fur and mouse droppings. Phineas gasped and reached under the chair to retrieve it.

Ennio Morricone had been sitting around all day eating books. When the heavenly hot dog presented itself, he dropped the ratty copy of *The Mysteries of Pittsburgh* and extended his snout to relieve his peckish urges. When Phineas' hand came in after it, Ennio Morricone growled to show that his territory was being invaded and warned that the encroaching hand should be removed under fear of mauling. Having been unable to hear the growl or see Ennio Morricone, Phineas continued to paw the ground in search of his lost treat. Singing loudly, his face began turning red.

"Where are you, my little doggie?" he sang into the back of the chair. *"Five second rule, five second rule, five second rule, six second rule."*

When Ennio Morricone sunk his teeth into Phineas' hand, he again had no idea what was happening. He smacked his head on the underside of the table, yelped and fought to free his hand from the mysterious, but all too recognizable, assailant.

"I'm going to kill you, you little sonnavabitch!"

Ennio Morricone, having masterly flung the hot dog under the radiator for later consumption, scampered out of the kitchen, his overgrown nails scratching on the floor. Phineas started after the dog but stopped when he saw that his hand was bleeding. "Morricone! I'll get you!"

Desmond came out of the office wearing his scrubs and loupes. "Phin, what the hell is the matter with you?" he asked.

"What? Dad, I can't hear."

Desmond stepped over to Phineas and looked at his hand. "Geez, how'd that happen?"

"Dad, I can't hear you!" Phineas ran water over his hand. Bright red blood dripped into the sink, over dishes and cigarette butts.

"What are you talking about?"

Phineas shook his head and let out a sigh. He thought he might cry.

"Let me get my first aid kit." Desmond wandered back into his office

The blood rolled down his fingers and into the water. He made a fist and smelled flashlights. "Dammit," he said. "Just God damn it all."

Desmond sat Phineas in a chair and cleaned his hand with a white towel. He applied pressure, checked that the flow had been slowed and then sprayed antibiotic ointment on it. He raised Phineas' hand while he wrapped it in a bandage. He spoke and a cigarette jutted from the corner of his mouth. Phineas took the pen from Desmond's pocket and saw fear shoot through his eyes. He wrote on a piece of paper, which his blood stained dark red.

I can't hear anything. I've gone deaf.

Desmond read it. "What do you mean you can't hear anything?"

Phineas shook his head and wrote again.

I can't hear anything. I can't hear you when you speak. You have to write things down so I can read them.

Desmond read it again and started to speak but in one motion Phineas reached behind Desmond's head and grabbed a handful of his hair. Terrified, Desmond reciprocated the action. They stared at each other for a long, intense moment, their heads shaking with adrenalin.

"Phineas, what are you doing?" Desmond's already wide eyes were magnified by the loupes.

"Look at me!" Phineas' eyes were filled with tears. "Look at me! I am deaf, you moron!"

"Deaf?"

Phineas let go of his hair and put his face in his hands. Desmond took off the telescopic lenses and blinked several times, then he picked up the paper and wrote on it. He held it out and let it touch the back of Phineas' hand.

When did this start?

"Yesterday."

Have you gone to the doctor?

Phineas shook his head. "If it hasn't cleared itself up by tomorrow."

Desmond frowned. *Why haven't you gone to a doctor yet?*

He hesitated. "I am afraid." Then he put his face back into his hands and breathed in heavy shanks.

Desmond's lips moved but made no sound. He would have offered anybody anything to be anywhere but in that room at that moment. He looked at the swirl of Phineas' cowlick bounce as his head shook. He inched his hand out and tried to pat his head, but instead he reached for the pen. He wrote on the paper.

Everything's going to be okay. If it hasn't cleared up by tomorrow I'll bring you to my doctor, he's a good friend and a great doctor. I'm sure it'll be okay.

He handed it to Phineas who read the note and nodded. Desmond wrote again.

I have to go. Mr. Crothers is waiting for me with a dam in his mouth. "Thank you, Dad."

Desmond gave Phineas' head a quick pat and rushed to the office with an awkward smile.

Phineas washed his face and squeezed his hand into a fist. He took an aspirin and sat in his bed thinking about his diminishing system and throbbing hand. He thought about Amy and his grandmother and his phantom, psyche-ruled sense of smell. He imagined the style of revenge he was going to exact on Ennio Morricone and he thought about his belly, which was groaning for sustenance in the wake of the lost hot dog. Somewhere in this thought process he decided to do some ill-advised research on the Internet.

As he pushed open the door to his father's study his nose filled with the scents of pigeon crap and metal statue, which in turn filled him with the overwhelming urges to kill pigeons and read Auguste Rodin's biography. He gazed around at the book shelves and the computer. There were three dinner plates on the desk which were covered in cigarette butts. The remnants of a Lo Mien dinner were decorating the keyboard, just below a blackening slice of pineapple. Phineas sat on the chair in front of the computer and stared at the mess. He clicked the "P" key on the keyboard and picked up the pineapple slice with the tips of two fingers. He deposited it on one of the plates, producing a brown sludge which added the smell of clamato juice to those of the pigeon crap and metal statue. A blue light took over the dark of the screen and Phineas tapped away at the keys, wishing he could hear the satisfying clicks.

This is what they always said, he thought; if you're a hypochondriac don't look on the Internet for symptomatic research. He laughed at himself. He had been strong about the Internet, knowing it was a place where hypochondriacs perused the diseases of their lives and found new and exotic ways to die. He had fallen into a similar trap once before with a physician's reference book. In four minutes, he had developed all the late-stage symptoms for hemochromatosis and ALS and didn't sleep for six days. Nevertheless, seconds after typing "loss of smell" into the search engine there were 28,397,387 directly related hits. My God, he thought, I don't stand a chance.

On the first website, he learned that his condition, well, one of them, was called anosmia. And before he clapped a sticky palm over his eyes, he also learned that it could be caused by several different factors. When he dared peek through his fingers, the phrase he locked onto was "some forms of cancer." He clicked on the "x" in the top right-hand corner and stood. Pacing the room, he convinced himself that he could handle another search and against his better judgment, went back to the computer. This time he typed "loss of hearing" into a search engine and stared at the safe, information-free bottom left corner of the screen while the computer tallied its responses. When it had finished, he shut both of his eyes and opened them in miniature stages until he read "tinnitus" and "loud music" through the dark fence of his eyelashes. "Dah!" He perched over the keyboard again, this time refining his search.

"Sudden loss of hearing," he typed. There were thousands upon thousands of hits and Phineas let out a long, controlled breath. The only words he saw were "see a doctor immediately." He shut off the computer and felt his heart thumping in his chest at a disturbing pace. He frowned and felt tears well up in his eyes. "Dammit!" In a fit of rage that surprised him, he vaulted one of the plates against the wall. Shards of ceramic scattered around the room and cigarette butts settled on the wooden floor. A wet circle of black began dripping in trails down the torn wallpaper, diverting and forking along seams.

Phineas wiped his eyes dry and locked his jaw. His hand throbbed and he closed it, straining against the bandage. He knelt next to the broken plate and cigarette butts and took a whiff. Paradoxically, the floor smelled of creamed spinach roasted with onion and garlic and Phineas smelled it again, drawing in a long breath. He touched a piece of ceramic and for some reason thought of the famous trout sandwich at Larry's Pub and Grub, battered in Guinness and deep fried until golden brown, best served with onion rings (also battered in Guinness). His mouth watered with his thoughts.

His gastronomically pornographic thoughts eventually led him back to the pizza that he had put in the oven before the Ennio Morricone fiasco. When he got to the kitchen black smoke was spewing from the oven. When the smoke had cleared and the pizza was pulled to safety it resembled a charcoaled Frisbee. Phineas scanned the surface for an ingestible portion but ultimately gave up and threw it in the trash. His mouth still watered, however and his belly still ached, so he put on shoes and walked to the corner store to find food.

In front of the convenience store, which stood at the corner of Maple Avenue and Crane Road, three young boys played cards on the ice cooler. At the pumps, a beautiful young woman clothed in workout gear and sporting perfectly maintained make-up filled her Nissan Stanza with premium ultra. Phineas sucked in his stomach and puffed out his chest and one of the boys grinned at him. The day was gray and sinister clouds threatened. Phineas squinted into the sky and pushed through the door as a bell jingled his arrival. From behind the register a round butt wearing a thong as a headband greeted him, their owner was buried in a warehouse box of menthol cigarettes. She turned her head and nodded hello to him. Phineas looked along the shelves through slits for eyes and picked up and carried several assorted snacks. Pretzel barrels, salt and vinegar chips, sunflower seeds, Oreo cookies, two hot dogs with mustard and sauerkraut, which were in plastic containers, a soft pretzel, a Chipwich and a Choco Taco. He stared into the freezers through burning eyes, his lids trying to protect them from the blazing lights in the freezers. Hovering above a pepperoni pie like a starving vulture he realized that he had no free hands. He searched his body, hoping to find a new appendage that could be used in this troubling situation.

"Hm, I see. Well, that is a problem," he said.

A pink hat appeared through the mist that plumed from the freezer. As the mist evaporated in the warm air of the store, a pair of bright pink glasses emerged. Two very sober blue eyes stared at him from the center of the frames. The woman's lips were moving and she was hoisting two cans of cola in front of her. The woman, who by Phineas' guess was no younger than 97 and no taller than 4'5", spoke into his nose and vocally weighed the pros and cons of buying a root beer. She wore a pink-pastel polyester track suit to match the frames of her glasses and in the steam that surrounded her, seemed to be an apparition. Phineas feigned normality.

"Excuse me, ma'am, but I have no free hands, can you please hand me that pizza straight ahead? The pepperoni one, please?"

The woman extended a sad smile.

"This one?" She opened the door.

Phineas cleared his throat and blinked his sore eyes at her as he formulated his next plan of attack. "I'm sorry, but I am deaf. I can't hear you. Can you please point at a pizza and I will tell you if it is the correct one, please?"

The woman stared at Phineas and her smile got lost in the cold smoke that billowed about her. She pointed at a pizza and questioned him with her eyes.

"The one to the left of that one, please." He spoke with clarity and formality. He thought about the order of dining. Pizza, hot dogs, pretzels. French fries were then considered. The woman pointed to the desired pizza and looked at Phineas with an expectant grin.

"Yes, that's the one. Thank you very much."

The woman pulled the pizza from its ranks and turned to hand it to Phineas. She stopped and searched him for a free hand. Then she searched for a free finger. Phineas joined in her quest for an unused appendage or digit. She moved his arm and tucked the pizza under it, wedging it in his armpit and walked away with a satisfied nod.

"Thank you, ma'am," he called after her. A young girl stared at Phineas as she pretended to read a teen magazine.

Phineas dropped the contents on the counter and the girl regarded him with conspicuous boredom. She chewed gum and her ordinary brown eyes were surrounded by what appeared to be thirty-six gallons of green eye make-up. She began running his items under a price gun while Phineas rubbed at his eyes and squinted at her through them.

"Do you have any sunglasses?" he shouted at her.

The girl stopped scanning his items and wore a hurt expression. "Why—"

"I'm deaf, I can't hear and it's a recent condition so I can't figure out the volume thing yet. Okay? I'm sorry, I'm not shouting at you, but I really need some sunglasses. Can you just ring up a pair and hand them to me and I'll get the heck out of here and never bother you ever again. Deal?"

The girl's look went from wounded to disgust. She stepped over to a large rack and spun it until she found a suitable pair. She finished ringing the items and dropped the sunglasses on the counter, then pointed to the total on the register. Phineas handed her a credit card. She threw two bags on the counter and stood waiting for the tape to spit out of the machine.

Phineas bagged everything but the hot dogs and the sunglasses. He stepped outside and put them on his irritated eyes. He started in on the first of the hot dogs and stopped only to stare at his reflection in the window of Sister's pizza.

Mustard stained his mustache and a piece of sauerkraut rested on his sweater. His bandaged right hand held a half-eaten hot dog and a boxed hot dog. His left hand strained with the weight of the shopping bag.

"That little jerk!" His sunglasses were immense, nearly covering the entirety of his forehead and extending well below his cheekbones. They were rectangular and gave him the appearance of an intergalactic super-hero from a 1950s B-movie. He pulled them off and winced at the bright light. After replacing them the world turned a bearable gray again. He took them off again and couldn't open his eyes.

The pink-clad woman from the store walked up to Phineas and

tapped him on the shoulder. He turned and she held his face with both of her hands, then she lowered his face to hers and spoke with a gleeful friendliness that showed in her face. "Those are some real sharp sunglasses, young man."

"Oh, for the—" Phineas fit the sunglasses on more snug and looked up and down the street. Two girls walked toward him, neither of them wearing sunglasses. They wore light jackets and smoked cigarettes. A man stood on a ladder and worked to re-shingle an eave. He wasn't wearing sunglasses either; he didn't seem to be bothered by the light at all.

He shuffled down the street, into his home and dropped the snacks on the kitchen table. Phineas looked outside through the kitchen window. People walked with their dogs and a mailman walked toward the center of town. Phineas sat at the table, his chest rose with each heavy breathe and his heart raced.

Clay's truck pulled down the street and turned into the driveway as great spears of rain started hitting the ground. Phineas went out on the porch to meet him and pulled the gigantic sunglasses down over his nose and peered into the street. He couldn't do it and he had to reposition the sunglasses. Winds started picking up and leaves sailed down the road. Clay came up the steps of the porch.

"Hey, how you—what the fuck you wearing those for?" Clay shook his head and scribbled on the pad and handed it to Phineas.

What the fuck are you wearing those fogie glasses for?

"It's a long story. Want to hear something funny?"

Yes I do. Clay lit a cigarette.

"I'm losing my sight."

How is that funny? He looked confused and looked into the lenses of the sunglasses, as if the answer to his question was written in them.

"I was being facetious."

Clay's mouth worked the word facetious and his face bunched into a fist. *What does facetious mean?*

"I was being sarcastic."

You're going to go to the doctor now? The cigarette bobbed in his lips, sending snatches of smoke into the air like a smoke signal. The wind picked up more and Clay squinted an eye in defense.

"No."

This is ridiculous.

"You're telling me?"

He yanked the pad away from him, writing fast and sloppy words. *I mean that you won't go to the doctor.*

"I don't know what's happening to me, but I don't think a doctor can help me."

Why not?

"I don't know. But either way, nobody's making me do anything."

Clay watched him. *What happened to your hand?*

"Ennio Morricone bit me."

Want me to kill him?

"No," Phineas answered, knowing full well that Clay was making a serious offer, "I got something brewing."

Do you want a crème de menthe?

Phineas thought for a moment. "Not today."

Clay wrote again.

I've got to take a nap. If you need anything I'll be in my room, okay?

"Good night."

Clay went off to his bedroom and Phineas went in and sat at the kitchen table to watch the storm gain strength. He looked at his watch: 2:17 p.m. Dark clouds squatted over the small town of Lansford, Pa and dropped water onto its inhabitants. Piles of leaves on various lawns disassembled and scattered through the streets and driveways. Cars inched along the road with headlights on and windshield wipers hurrying to keep up.

Phineas sat at the table, his unopened pizza thawing in a bag in front of him, dampening the other snacks. As the darkness moved in he watched the world move by without him, soaked by the rain and covered in wet leaves.

19

That evening rain fell on Lansford. It filled the gutters and enveloped the streets, leaving tiny islands of land between expanses of rain water. Thunder cracked and lightning creased across the sky. Inside the Troy house, Phineas had been experimenting with his sight all day. With the night dark and rainy, Phineas learned that while any normal light blinded him, he could see clearly in the dark. So, he walked around the large house and shut off all the lights. Desmond was in his study placing bets on the computer while Clay watched television in his room.

Meanwhile, Phineas was like the Phantom of the Opera, lurking in the shadows and nooks of the cavernous house. His heightened vision enabling him to pick up the grimy details of Desmond's table in the living room and the mounds of acrimonious waste that Ennio Morricone lay strategically throughout the house. In the pitch black of the windowless basement, he stood in perfect silence and watched mice dart around corners and cockroaches step out into the darkness. Phineas took off up the basement stairs when he noticed a few large spiders watching him, waiting for him in their webs.

Phineas walked from room to room unable to hear or smell, but with his new, Cimmerian vision he felt the mildest resurgence of confidence and strength, dancing through the rooms around tables and chairs like a demented ballerina. He went to the side door and watched the trees swing in the wind until his eyes began to burn from the ambient light, forcing him to retreat to the core of the house.

He went up the stairs and into his room, drew the curtains and sat on the bed. The house moved around him. A mosquito, the last survivor from the summer, flew in confused circles about the corners of the room. Lying back on his bed, Phineas watched it bounce off a corner and into another. The door to his bedroom was open and he winced and covered his eyes when his father opened the study door to go to the hall bathroom. He cowered beneath his pillow and waited until he was reasonably sure his father had gone back to his computer. He stared at the inner-weaving of the pillow, wishing he could climb within. Slowly, he raised his head and looked into the hall; the darkness looked back at him.

Into the doorway stepped a squat frame. Ennio Morricone, who'd slipped out of the study, stopped as he caught a glimpse of the figure sitting on the bed. He had smelled Phineas before he'd seen him, Phineas, in turn, saw Ennio Morricone and smelled plastic chairs and newly spayed cat.

"You," Phineas whispered. Ennio Morricone locked his legs to present himself in a more offensive stance. He stood still but trembled in the drafty hallway.

Ennio Morricone growled with the thick voice of a well-lubed motorcycle. Phineas squeezed his hands into balls and felt the sharp pain in his right hand where the hound's teeth had punctured. Ennio Morricone reared his head and took in Phineas' scent. Phineas went to the edge of the bed and glared at the Scottish terrier.

The showdown had begun.

"You ain't gonna smell fear on me, boy," he breathed in a whisper.

Ennio Morricone let out a snarl as if he were trying to speak, then stepped into the room and cocked his head. Phineas badly wanted revenge on the lowly animal walking toward his bed. He waited on his knees and hands as Ennio Morricone strode toward him like a short bear.

With wide, sensitive eyes, Phineas hung over the edge of the bed now, clutching his fists as the dog came to a standstill. He felt behind him and found his pillow, the weight of which hung down as he raised it. The dog let out a bark that Phineas could see and he took action. He launched the pillow and it pounded against the dog's face with a thump, and then he jumped to his feet on the bed, recocking the pillow for further assault.

Ennio Morricone was stunned by the blow, and crashed to his side. He flopped around on the floor and then got to his feet, he was baring his teeth. Phineas swung the pillow from north to south and it landed on the dog's back with a solid and satisfying smack. Ennio Morricone looked upset now, as though he knew he was in no position to attack the man and that he was losing the battle. Phineas readied the pillow again, laughing giddily as he did so. He swung. This time it glanced off the dog's right side, and in the odd light of Phineas' vision, he saw the dog grimace.

The dog staggered at first, but then settled himself and sat; Phineas raised his pillow one more time. One more dose of blunt head trauma would do it, he thought. But then Ennio Morricone looked up into Phineas' face. The dog didn't look angry; he looked sad. Phineas dropped the pillow and sat on the bed. Ennio Morricone licked his lips and the bits of book and doll that remained attached. Phineas saw this lonely dog, this dog that hadn't been out of the giant house in years. The dog who'd come to this house five years earlier hadn't come in the hopes of becoming an angry recluse. He didn't like scrounging for play things to destroy or crapping in corners like a caged ferret. It was what he'd been forced to get by on. Phineas hated to understand the dog, hated to commiserate with him, but he had no choice. The dog had lost the lottery, he was a pure-bred terrier, and in another household he'd be winning dog shows, fetching papers or saving families from house fires.

If Ennio Morricone had lost the lottery, Phineas thought, then so had he. In the hands of another soul, his body would be traveling the world, captaining a yacht in the America's Cup race, or enjoying his life as an Olympic fencer/underwear model. But here he was, similarly stuck in this house getting by on what he could, clinging to a flimsy and ebbing bastion of hope. And before this unusual sensual affair, had it been much different? Not really, he thought. It hadn't been much different at all. He didn't like these thoughts, but it was true. He'd been deaf and blind for far longer than the last day. His body had just finally caught up.

They were both trapped. They were both long past hope. They were both Troys. At this, Ennio Morricone seemed to hear Phineas' thought and bowed his head toward the floor in shame.

Phineas brought his hand down to the dog, who flattened his ears against his head expecting the death blow, and petted him on the head. Ennio Morricone leaned into Phineas' strokes, the gritty fur leaving streaks of grease on Phineas' hand.

"I understand," Phineas whispered to the dog. Ennio Morricone sat on his back haunches and began to eagerly lick the spot that had once been inhabited by his genitals.

"You're welcome."

When Clay turned on the light Phineas fell backwards on the bed and Ennio Morricone disappeared through Clay's legs and skittered down the hallway.

"What the fuck you doing in here?" Clay asked.

"Turn out the lights, for the love of God!" Phineas pleaded.

Clay turned the lights out and walked over to the bed. In the dark, Phineas clasped his face and rolled on his back. Clay couldn't see him clearly and pressed his hands against his shoulders. Phineas stopped moving.

"Yeah, what is it?" Phineas asked. "Clay, can you get my sunglasses?"

Clay left the room to search for the sunglasses. Phineas lay on the bed and opened his eyes in the darkness.

"I'm a freak," he said to himself. "I'm a mole man."

Clay stormed through the house, turning on lights, looking for the massive sunglasses that he'd seen advertised on television in between afternoon reruns of *Hogan's Heroes* and *Gomer Pyle USMC*.

Desmond left the computer and went to the kitchen to watch a football game he'd bet on. He opened an orange cola and began rummaging through the refrigerator to find a game-time snack. After shutting the fridge with a pout and becoming aware of the adverse conditions outside, he was delighted to find a pizza, pretzels and Oreo cookies sitting in a soggy bag on the table. He cackled like a lunatic and flipped to the station showing the game.

Clay went through every room in the house, with the exclusion of his own. He turned on every light, overturned every pillow and paper and looked under beds. He went back to Phineas' room and went inside, shutting the door behind him. Phineas lay on the bed and moaned.

"Phineas, what the fuck is wrong with you!" Clay pounded on the wall.

Phineas continued to moan and Clay ran to his room and found a lighter, grabbed a piece of paper and a pen and went back to Phineas' room. Outside the room, Clay slammed the paper against the wall and wrote on it. Phineas stared at the bed, his neck was hot. Clay took Phineas' hand and pressed it against the paper. Phineas looked at the paper and then at Clay, who then flicked on the lighter. Phineas shielded his eyes from it and then tried to peer at the paper but the light was too strong and he crammed his eyes shut. Phineas took the paper and looked into it, squinting and turning the paper in different directions, holding it away from him like an old woman reading a prescription without reading glasses attached to a chain. He threw the paper down on the bed.

"My superhuman powers are denying me," he said.

Clay held up his finger, turned and ran out of the room, letting in a thin slice of piercing light as he went.

As the pain seared his eyes, Phineas cried out. "Damn, Damn, Dammit!"

"Oh fuck me, fuck me." Clay ran around the house looking for something he could use to communicate with his brother. He rooted through drawers in the living room. He found crayons and pencils, lighters and creased yarmulkes, old driver's licenses and credit cards. Clay walked into the kitchen where Desmond sat dipping an Oreo cookie into a glass of orange cola. A football game was blasting from the television. Everyone on the screen was covered in mud and grass, when they breathed thick clouds of cold air fumed from their facemasks.

"Jesus Dad, can I turn this down a little?" Clay reached for the remote. He hit the volume button.

"Wait! Ah come on! I can't hear it now…" Desmond held his Oreo above the glass, dripping with orange liquid.

"What, you kidding me? Dad, that is so friggin' loud the fuckin' neighbors can hear it."

"Well, why don't you go to your room, huh? Leave me alone." Desmond chewed on the Oreo, a half pack sat in front of him, circled with crumbs.

"Dad, why don't you get your hearing ch—", something on the table had caught his eye. Among the wrappers, cola bottles and cigarette butts sat the solution to his problem.

"Dad, what the hell is that?" Clay pointed behind his father.

"Where?" he began to turn and stopped. "Oh no, not again you don't." Desmond laughed and with his finger persuaded another Oreo out of the pack. He moved the remote away from Clay.

"Ha, you're too quick for me this time." Clay watched the television and they sat without speaking for a moment. A referee's whistle blew.

"Want a cookie?"

"No thanks. Hey, so who's playing here?"

"Western Michigan and Ball State." Orange cola was everywhere.

"Who you got?"

"I've got Ball State getting seven and the over at sixty-six."

"What's the score?"

Desmond shuffled in his seat and dipped his Oreo; orange cola ran down his chin. "ten to seven, Ball State *and, and* they've got the ball inside the twenty."

"Sounds pretty good. Who else you got this weekend?"

Desmond finished off the Oreo and wiped his hands on his sweater. He reached into his pocket and fumbled around, his breathing sounded as though it was coming from a coffee machine. "Let's see here," he said and looked down at what he had drawn out of his pants pocket. When he did, Clay took his chance. He quickly and covertly snatched the loupes from the table. Desmond found the paper and started reading off his bets. Clay held the lenses behind his right hip and, opening the refrigerator, slipped them into his pocket.

"Hey, I'll stop down in a minute. I gotta see Phin about something." He ran up the stairs and knocked on the door, laughed at himself for doing so and entered the room.

Phineas was sitting in the chair in the corner. His arms were along the arm rests and his feet were planted on the floor. Clay waved his hand at him.

"Hello Clay, I see you," Phineas said.

Clay wrote on the paper and handed the telescopic lenses to Phineas.

"Oh thank Go--, Clay these are...Oh my God! Do you think it'll work?"

Clay shrugged and Phineas put on the lenses. He closed his eyes and then opened them one at a time. What he saw was remarkable.

Phineas didn't see things, he saw prepositions. He saw in. He saw above. He saw through pillows and into electrical sockets. He saw below the floor and under paint. He smelled an old person's cane as he looked around the room at what had been there a moment before. It had changed. Armies of mites stormed every article of clothing and bedding. Rats and spiders danced around piles of Ennio Morricone's crap as though they were campfires, and commenced meetings on how to attack Phineas. His kindred cockroaches mocked him for escaping rooms that were suddenly lit. The paint and wood and stone of over a hundred years called out to Phineas, with dreadful voices.

Phineas gasped and recoiled. In himself, he saw the fibers of his skin, the diseases in cahoots, the singing man and his adjoining happy-go-lucky, well-dressed viscera. And then, in his hands, he saw his disease. While his mind pleaded with him to look away, his macabre sense of curiosity forced him to look closer. The disease was ugly and black and green, it was scaly and blistered and festering. Phineas whimpered, but couldn't stop watching. It was the disease of cowardice and of the sedentary, of inaction and fear and paranoia.

At last, Phineas thought, it had come for him. He bit his lower lip as the disease took form, building itself up like disgusting, viral Legos. It came together in fast-motion, collecting the splashes of dark green and chunks of black that had been dispersed throughout the room moments earlier. Phineas drew a soft breath, then he saw a leg and then another leg and then another. His teeth drew blood from his lower lip. Great streams of sweat poured from under his hair. He fell back on the chair.

It was a spider. On Phineas' chest, looking into his eyes, was a spider. The spider was black and green, with eight beady, demonic eyes. Beneath its eyes, pedipalps curled inward, beckoning him. Its disgustingly slick and smooth cephalothorax undulated, coming ever closer to Phineas' chest. An enormous hornet-like stinger came from the rear of its opisthosoma menacingly aimed at Phineas' stomach. Its legs were black and twisted and smooth, exact, green stripes wrapped around them. The sharp points at the bottom of its legs were digging into Phineas' trunk.

Phineas' mouth and face shook in terror as every fear he'd ever had in his life sat on his chest looking him in the eye, daring him to do something about it, daring him into action it knew he wouldn't take. Finally, Clay pulled the lenses off Phineas and threw them across the room.

Phineas curled into a ball on the chair and Clay made sure the loupes weren't broken. Phineas was shaking and he wouldn't move. After ten minutes, Clay stretched Phineas' legs back to the floor and rested his arms on the chair. He took him by the arm and leaned him forward. With his index finger he traced a large A on Phineas' back, followed by a large B and then a C. Phineas looked up at Clay.

"ABC?" Phineas' voice was weak.

Clay tapped him on the head twice and traced a large D and T and R. "DTR?"

Clay tapped him twice again.

"Ah, Clayton, you're a genius."

"Don't call me that, you fucker."

It was a rainy Saturday afternoon in May 1986 when they'd invented the game. The Troys were living in their first house, an unassuming Cape Cod in a development tucked within the McGinly Forest in West Lansford. Phineas had spent the bulk of his allowance money on a pack of rub-on-tattoos. He'd waited all week for Saturday to become a tattooed biker, maybe even a sailor, and gallivant around the neighborhood scaring the adults and ravishing the ladies. He'd related his plan of rascality to Clay who, dying to be just like his brother, decided that he too would become a scallywag tattooed biker.

Clay got to the tattoos first, which had been hidden in between *Tom Sawyer* and an *Encyclopedia Brown Mystery* on Phineas' bookshelf, and adjourned to the bathroom to start the transformation. Upon his return from a Friday night sleepover party, Phineas was unable to find the tattoos and panic rippled through him. Seconds later, he was rampaging through the house, smelling the blood of a nine-year old tattooed biker. After fifteen minutes of Phineas wailing on the bathroom door, and promising physical asylum, Clay, shaking, finally opened the door.

What first struck Phineas was not Clay's watering eyes nor was it the near-empty pack of tattoos on the bathroom counter. What first caught his attention was the "Born to Ride" tattoo in the center of Clay's forehead. Phineas' mouth hung open. As Clay's sweatshirt and jeans were in a heap in the corner, it was not difficult to inspect his body. Yosemite Sam on his belly, and a snake wrapped around a sword on his right arm was being courted by a smiling cherub-like devil on his chest. On his right thigh was a howling wolf silhouetted against a full moon. On Clay's left thigh there was a white piece of paper; a tattoo in development. Phineas brusquely stripped it off to reveal the bottom half of Kermit the Frog. Bringing the sheet to his face he was confronted with the top part of the amicable Muppet's torso, banjo spread across his stomach.

"I-I l-left some for you," Clay stammered, pointing to a sheet of paper on which only two tattoos remained; one presented a bouquet of pink flowers and the other a glorious unicorn with a shimmering golden mane.

Phineas was enraged. "I wanted to be a biker, you idiot!" A slap fight ensued and Desmond, who'd been watching a baseball game and doing a crossword puzzle, shouted up the steps at them. They fell out pathetically, Clay naked but for his Fruit of the Looms and covered with tattoos and red hand prints, Phineas with a red face and tears of anger in his eyes. Desmond ordered them to the kitchen and muttered staple phrases of scolding while trying to glimpse the game on the kitchen television.

It was Loni who administered the punishments; Desmond just tried to stay out of the way and keep quiet, early on practicing his trademark technique of familial *laissez faire*. Loni, however, was at her sister's and the game was heading into extra innings. To boot, he'd just remembered a six-letter word for intoxicated and had lost it due to his impromptu refereeing duties. This needed a swift solution.

He sat them at the dining room table, each with a *National Geographic*, and demanded silence and a full oral report on their respective cover stories. This didn't work. As soon as he'd left the room Phineas began underarm-farting and burping the "National Anthem," which sent Clay into loud, sustained, mucus-filled, otter-sounding laughter. Within seconds Desmond was at wit's end. He was tempted to send the boys to their rooms and be done with it, but a tattooing and a slap fight had to be disciplined and Loni had been lecturing Desmond about his passive role as patriarch. So he brought them into the kitchen and sat them down across from him at the table. He turned the volume up a notch and set about trying to remember the six-letter word for drunk.

Whenever the slightest peep came from either Phineas or Clay, Desmond would glare at them with such intensity that they would look back at the television and try not to burst into laughter or tears. Sometime in the 10th inning Phineas slid his hand to Clay's thigh and made a small shape. Clay was confused so Phineas made it larger. A and then B and then C. Clay nodded and then mouthed, "ABC."

Phineas nodded back.

Clay reached over, his eyes peeled to the game on the television, and traced, *DAD IS FAT.* They dammed their laughter. Desmond knew something was going on but settled for the quiet and didn't disrupt. By the time Gary Carter popped out in the bottom of the 13th to end the game, Phineas and Clay had traced epic descriptions of Desmond's physical features, lacking personal hygiene and overall bad character. From that day forward, the game became their fallback mode of communication during car trips, church and at dinner tables when silence had been demanded.

Phineas leaned forward again as Clay traced large slow, forceful letters into his back.

"W...A...I...T....Wait?" Phineas asked. Clay tapped his head twice.

"I...B...R...I...N...G...I bring?" Phineas had stripped off his shirt and was fingering his chest and stomach in search of spider bites.

Clay used only upper case letters and concentrated on the slow steady motion of his index finger.

"Y…O…U…You?" he felt for enflamed liver, spleen and any abdominal pain due to metabolic acidosis.

"T…O…To. D…A…D…S…Dad's, R…O…O…M…to Dad's room. Wait, why?"

Clay exhaled. "I…L…O…O…K F…O…R G…L…A…S…S…E…S I…N…H…E…R…E. Oh, you'll look for the glasses in here."

Clay pointed Phineas' face at him and nodded. Phineas shut his eyes and let Clay slide the robe over his bare back and his goose-pimpled arms down into the sleeves. Clay shut off all the upstairs lights and walked Phineas by the arm down the hallway. Phineas shuffled along next to him like a sick old man. His pajama pants were damp with sweat and he was muttering to himself. Clay tried his best to guide Phineas in the dark, however, Phineas stubbed his toe and fell on the floor. His pinkie squished into a recently deposited pile of Ennio Morricone. Clay used toilet paper to clean the bulk but didn't have time to bring Phineas to the bathroom.

Phineas felt the uncomfortably cool draughts run across his bare chest and stomach. He relished it, his only sense, and enjoyed its bittersweet enticements. He listened for the little man singing and the minute orchestra playing, but they were silent. Perhaps, he thought, the spider had gotten them. A cold shiver ran up his neck.

Clay sat Phineas on the bed in his father's room and turned off the lights. Then he walked around the house searching for the sunglasses, flipping on lights in each room and cursing. He got to his room and set the halogen lamp to full blast.

From behind him Clay heard a step and turned to see Ben pushing through the door with a smile on his face. He was eating a cupcake, some of the icing had attached itself to his upper lip.

"Ben, we got fuckin' troubles."

"Phineas?"

"He can't fuckin' see now."

"He's totally blind?"

"I think he can see some things, but he needs his glasses."

Ben spotted the loupes on the bed, "Those?" He licked his fingers clean of icing.

Clay shook his head. "No fuckin' way. I don't know what the fuck happened when he put those things on, but it was no good."

"So, what are you looking for?"

"His stupid sunglasses. Help me, would ya?"

Ben kneeled on the ground and looked under the bed. "What do they look like?"

"They're fuckin' huge. Huge, like those old fuckin' fogie glasses you see on old people." Clay reached his hands out as if he were lying about a fish he had caught.

Ben squinted at the ceiling as if he were trying to conjure a picture of the sunglasses. "I don't know…"

"You know, they always show them old fuckers wearing them in commercials in the middle of the day. After *People's Court*, or *Murder, She Wrote* or something."

"Oh, yeah," Ben said, "I always liked those."

"You fuckin' jokin' me?" Clay padded his comforter and lifted his pillows. He was lost in his search.

"Yep," Ben smiled. "Is he okay?"

"I think he'll be alright for a little while."

"Where is he?"

"He's in my dad's room." Clay opened the lid of his laundry basket and began sifting through the contents.

"Are you okay?"

Clay stopped searching through his laundry basket. "What do you mean?"

"Nothing, you just seem a little stressed out."

Clay sat back and pushed himself against the bed. "This man is…" he shook his head. "This man is falling apart."

"I think Phineas has got some things to work out."

Clay stood up, "No shit. Fuckin' guy losing all his fuckin' senses, like this. What the fuck's gonna happen next, man?"

Ben shrugged. "What can I do to help?"

"You been drinkin'?"

"No."

"You got your jeep here?"

"Yeah."

"Is it still pouring outside?"

"Big time."

"Then you can give me a ride to the store so I can buy him some more sunglasses."

"Okay, let's go."

"We gotta be quick."

Phineas sat on the bed in his father's room and smelled socks, which, for once, wasn't out of the realm of possibility. Next he smelled an old lamp. He thought about the last week. Amy laughing behind the bar, smoking in her elegant way. Gary eating pizza at that very moment, enjoying the company of friends and the thunderstorm, as he would have been. Larry telling stories, half true, half fiction, to a captive audience. Gomez drinking, laughing and flirting with a couple beautiful young ladies.

He considered his grandmother, who had escaped the week before and his mother, who was buzzing about his grandmother's house at that moment. He thought of his father gleefully ignored, watching a football game, left alone. The cats would be eating Amy's take-out scrambled eggs or soiling a hardwood floor and Ennio Morricone was chewing on a Penguin Classic somewhere in the house. He thought about Clay and Ben, happy to be workers and players in this life. The mules, who were outside observers of the world, tenderly loved by Ben and Charlie, pulling a boat down a canal for weekend tourists and leaf peepers. He thought of the chubby hairdresser, mesmerizing some young man with her manipulative powers of manual sex somewhere in Pittsburgh.

And then his thoughts led to himself. Sitting alone in the dark and unable to escape his own screaming silence. He smelled verbs, abstract nouns and ideas. His taste had destroyed his relationship with one of his true joys: alcohol. He could hear only a visceral lounge singer within himself. He only saw in darkness and had clear, disturbing visions. And now, he huddled in a dark corner like Gollum.

"Yeah, fuck this." Phineas stood and opened the door. The light from the hallway pierced his eyes so he shut them and fumbled forward like a drunkard. His shin slammed into the corner of the chest that sat against the wall.

"Shit! Clay! Clay!"

He continued down the hall and Ennio Morricone watched him. Phineas felt his way along the walls and into his bedroom, where he tripped on a shoe and fell to the ground. He tried to peek open an eye but couldn't and crawled his way to the chair. He swept his hands on the floor next to the chair until he found it.

The envelope was under his overnight bag, wedged against the chair and the wall. He groped it to him, it tore and the box of rounds fell with a thunk onto the wooden floor. He reached into the torn bag and pulled out his grandfather's gun, still wrapped in cloth. He unwrapped it and struggled with the cylinder until it slid open. He couldn't find the box of rounds in the envelope, so he slid his left hand over the floor with his face close. Against the frame of the armchair he felt a protuberance and flipped the chair out of his way. He wrestled with the flaps of the box until it ripped open, rounds hit the floor around him. He reached into the box and removed a bullet, the familiar smell of daisies rushed at him.

He put the round in the pistol, stammering, his hands shaking. He snapped the cylinder closed and stood up, put the barrel into his mouth and cocked the hammer with his other hand. Random scents and thoughts attacked his brain. Bert and Ernie. Larry's Pub and Grub. Purple Thong. The Pennsylvania Turnpike was created by the Devil. Crème de menthe. Tattooed Biker. Ennio Morricone is a Scottish terrier. The Scottish terrier who won't let me get off. John Wayne is Chicken Liver. Oh Campari! Peppermint Schnapps. Mama's. Brett McManus. Meatballs. There is a tarantula at large in Lansford, Pennsylvania and her name is Judy Garland. Blue coffee Mug. Prince Albert, that's in the cock. Who's cock? My cock. The Demon Road. At last, and for reasons that would forever remain inexplicable to him, he recalled Sister Redempta, the 4'1", Sisters of the Holy Family of Nazareth nun who ruled his world in the third grade with an iron fist and a 12 inch, wooden Dober ruler. And then he squeezed the trigger.

The blast knocked Phineas to his knees, a trickle of warm blood dribbled out of his mouth, over his chin. He held the pistol and opened his eyes to look at it, eyes watering and seething in the intense light. The hammer was still cocked. It was at that moment that Phineas realized that the blast had come from the opposite direction.

Clay kicked Phineas in the back and Phineas hit the ground with a groan and dropped the gun. Clay hooked his foot around the weapon and slid it across the room, and then he kicked Phineas again, having wound up to do so. He began punching him in the ribs and face, Phineas curled into a ball on the floor.

"You fuckin' faggot! You fuckin' pussy! Faggot! Cunt! Coward! You fuckin' coward! You fuckin' piece of cunt shit!" Clay's handsome face was twisted and red. "You motherfucking piece of faggot fucking shit!" Clay kicked Phineas and beat him with stony fists, "You wanna fuckin' die, you fuckin' pussy? Here, I'll fuckin' help you out! Here's how you're gonna die!" He worked on him until he heard symphonic music and then a high buzz in his ears. He shook and wailed on his brother until he was physically unable to any longer. Out of breath, he dropped and kneeled over Phineas' body, slapping him with the little strength he had left. Ben arrived at the door of the room in time to watch Clay place his fingers to Phineas' wrist, stand up and walk out of the room. Ben picked up the gun and, after uncocking the hammer and removing the bullet, hid it on the top shelf in the hall closet. Phineas' body was curled into a ball, a large welt growing on his forehead and blood coming from his mouth. Ben squatted and laid his massive hands on Phineas' ribs.

"Ben," Phineas coughed, "I have to go to the bathroom." His head hit the floor.

20

Phineas stood outside his grandmother's house with a white suit and the darkness faded into light. Music and voices came from inside; he leaned against the door and pressed his ear up to it. He could just make out the sounds of people talking. When he knocked on the door nobody answered. The kitchen window was too high to look through and some spider plants on the window sill blocked his view.

Phineas pushed against the door. It was locked so he walked down the steps and a cool breeze passed through him, rustling his suit. There was snow on the ground. The kitchen light cast a beam onto the snow on the garden and a car turned down the driveway. A man, woman and child got out of the car, talking and collecting bags of presents and food. They ran up the steps, past Phineas, and rang the doorbell.

Emily Troy answered the door, drying her hands on her red and white apron. She hugged the child and the man and woman kissed her on the cheek, Phineas walked in behind them. The door opened to the kitchen and Phineas smelled, heard and saw everything. It was Christmas Eve and his grandmother's house was filled with the smell of cooking Italian food. Aunts and uncles sat around the large kitchen table, drinking wine and smoking cigarettes. They leaned out of their seats when they spoke; their faces were red and merry. At the counter the cooking food drove everyone insane with hunger. The meatballs, swimming in sauce, stewed in a huge pot. Peppers and spicy sausage sizzled in the crock pot in the corner, taunting Phineas and the guests. Ravioli were boiling in another pot, bobbing up and down like sea-taken sailors. He jammed his face into the steam of the sauce pot, allowing the rich flavor of the sauce to attack his famished nasal passages.

Phineas walked past the screaming children, one of whom was him wearing a hideous sweater that his Aunt Carol had bought him in a flea market, and went into the living room where Loni was chatting with his Aunt Judy. Desmond and William Troy slept in armchairs in front of a television showing a football game. Uncle Robert watched the game with a smile on his face; he finished off a beer and bribed a passing child to get him another one.

The Christmas tree was immense, as it had always been. It stood to the right of the television and filled the front windows, with sparkling lights and old-fashioned decorations. Mountains of presents surrounded it. Phineas surveyed the scene with mouth agape. The child returned with Robert's beer. He cracked it open, flipped the child a quarter and winked at the same time.

"OK," a woman called from the kitchen, "dinner's ready." The children charged into the kitchen and Robert nudged Desmond awake. William snorted himself awake. "Is it ready?" he asked. His eyes alert with ravenous hunger.

Phineas sat in the bathtub with his eyes closed; the hot water stung his body. Ben washed his shoulders and back with a sponge. He dipped the sponge into the water and squeezed it over Phineas' head. Soapy water ran down his back.

"How you feeling, buddy? Everything's gonna be okay now." Ben said. He squeezed the sponge over Phineas' cut face and he winced as the hot, soapy water ran over his gashes. Two large bruises had appeared on his face, one above his eye and the other circled a large cut next to his mouth.

Clay opened the door, "He okay?"

"He'll be fine." Ben answered without turning around.

"Alright," Clay shifted in the doorway, "I'll be upstairs." He shut the door.

Ben rubbed the sponge over Phineas' back and the bruises that swelled over his ribcage and arm. He dropped the sponge in the water and placed his hands on Phineas' shoulders and pressed downwards. At first Phineas resisted, but eventually slid his knees up and his back down so that his head went under the water. His hips poked up and his penis and thighs came out of the water. His pubic hair swayed in the soapy water like reeds in a pond. Ben held him under for a moment and then released his shoulders. Phineas stayed under, holding his breath and keeping his eyes closed. Light bubbles travelled in neat rows to the surface. Ben watched.

Inside, Phineas slipped into a strange coma of comfort. He felt the water invade him and he let it take him over. There was no sound and then the sounds of a flowing river, which gradually turned to waves crashing into him. He swayed with the gentle water.

When he came out of the water he released his breath and spat out the water that had gathered around his mouth and beard. He sat back. "So, anything interesting happen today, Ben?"

"Nothing at all, just lay back, would ya?"

"Okay, don't get pushy." Phineas shifted and then stopped. "Ben, I heard you! Say something else, say something else!"

"I had sex with Denise Zelinski when we were in high school."

"Really? You prick! Wait, I heard you! Haha!"

"Can you see?" Ben asked.

Phineas peered through half shut eyelids and shut them again. "Ouch, ouch. Did you find my sunglasses?"

"We couldn't find them, so we got you new ones. You want 'em?"

"Please."

Ben left the bathroom; Phineas sat back into the water and felt the pressure slide from his ears and down his neck. He splashed water onto his cheeks and listened to the light buzz coming from the overhead light. The sounds were intense. He submerged all but his head in the water; he felt like a frog.

Ben slid the sunglasses on Phineas' face and then removed the price tag. They were smaller than the others and let in light.

"Dammit, these won't be any good."

"Why's that?" Ben asked.

"They're not big enough. Did you see the bigger ones there?"

"No, I looked, too. These were the best ones we could find." Ben tended to his friend's feet and legs and wore a grin like that of the Mona Lisa, eyes flat and level. Afterward, he dropped the sponge in the tub and walked to the door.

"Here's a towel."

"Wait, you're leaving?"

"Yeah, why not?" Ben said, holding a large green towel.

"Well, I just tried to kill myself."

"Do you feel like killing yourself now?"

"No..."

"If I walk out this door are you going to kill yourself?"

"No, but..."

"Then we have now become a man washing a naked man with a sponge. Please let me go make myself a Grasshopper, okay? It's been a hell of a day."

"Mine with no cream, please." He became very aware of his nudity.

"Oh, by the way, Clay checked on you a few minutes ago, before you could hear again."

"Guess we have to have a chat, huh?"

"You think?"

"Go make Grasshoppers."

Ben left and Phineas reclined in the tub. Small ripples circled his protruding knees.

Nail-like bolts of rain pelted the house and the windows. Phineas was calm and he let his mind drift. He thought about baseball cards, Brett McManus, and, ultimately, how many lost Frisbees were currently residing on the rooftops of the world. He rose, squinting and shivering in the chilly room until his nipples hardened and his penis recoiled. He shut off the light, closed the door and looked in the mirror. He fingered the bruises covering his ribs and spotting his face. The large cuts near his eye and mouth tingled with pain and when he touched the swollen areas, he flinched.

Phineas dragged the towel over his body, happy to feel it, happier to hear the cotton scraping his skin. Cherishing each sound, he drank them in. He opened the door and heard Desmond rattling around in the kitchen, the television filling him with information. He wondered if his father had the slightest inkling of how different his night had almost been. The rain rattled the old window in the bathroom and Phineas walked to it, wrapped in the towel, and smiled at the annoying pelting.

The steam rising off the water in the tub reminded him of fishing on an early April morning with his father, years before. They had gone to Tawicki Park and drove down a small road that led to a parking lot near the creek. As they found a place to fish, Desmond sipped on the coffee he had bought at a 7-11. Phineas was drinking chocolate milk and carrying a Styrofoam container of night crawlers, which had been the source of most of his excitement.

He stood draped in his large green towel, his hair frayed and damp, and remembered the singing of birds and the occasional mysterious splash in the river. He remembered his father pinning his fishing license on his red and black flannel shirt and impaling a worm with the hook. He could clearly see the green backdrop which sat a thousand years away, on the other side of the river. The forest was alive with trees coming back to life, the animals returning and the early morning sounds of fathers and sons coming to fulfill something they couldn't quite understand, but couldn't live without.

Phineas remembered the damp morning and the trees and the first fish that he ever caught. It had an unconcerned look on its face and flipped its tail in weak desperation. He remembered the feel of the slimy scales and the thud it made after Desmond had unscrewed the hook from its cheek and tossed it back in the water, giving him yet another chance to defy his appetite.

Phineas lay in bed that evening and listened to the trees swing dancing in the wind and the storm slap the face of Lansford. He gazed in the direction of the storm through wide eyes hidden behind a silk sleeping mask that Ben had borrowed from his mother. He lifted his head, slipped the mask above his eyes and squinted at the almost empty envelope in the corner. He snorted like an angry bull staring down a chubby matador. He had looked into the other side and lived to tell the tale. His worry had gone away.

In the morning, the rain had ceded and Phineas' face and ribs were terribly sore. He sat up, forgetting for a moment his bruised ribs, and let out a pained whimper. He held his ribs and poked at his mouth wound with the tip of his tongue. Despite the rain, it was bright outside and light penetrated the borders of his sleeping mask. He took it off and felt around the window sill until he found the sunglasses.

The light came in and Phineas was forced to squint and even cup his hands around the lenses to prevent light from sneaking in from the sides and top. He wandered around the house looking for his old sunglasses and testing the range of his seeing abilities in comparison to his squinting necessities. They were such that he needed to guide his way through the house with one hand up to his sunglasses acting as a roof and the other sidling along furniture and wall panels.

It seemed hopeless until a figure scattered across the living room and came to rest under Desmond's table. Phineas bent over, holding his knee for support. Ennio Morricone sat under the table eating a plastic fork and pawing a rubber hamburger that had been a Christmas gift. Phineas smiled.

"Hello there."

Ennio Morricone sat up and eyed Phineas, dropping the plastic fork but constricting pressure on the hamburger so that it made a whistling sound from beneath his paws.

"Don't you move, I'll be back," Phineas said and walked into the kitchen. Desmond stood at the counter eating a donut and drinking a cup of coffee. His light blue scrubs were already, at 9:45 a.m., covered in coffee stains and jelly smeared across his stomach.

"Hi," Desmond said, "Oh wait," he stuck the donut into his mouth and reached for the new Razor Writer in his chest pocket.

Phineas sifted through drawers and bins, "No Dad, I can hear, but I'm blind now." He framed the right side of his sunglasses with his hand as though he were holding a telescope. He had shut his left eye and squinted through his right. It made him sore.

"Oh drrr," Desmond mumbled through his donut, a shot of jelly popped out through a small hole in the back. He reached out his finger to scoop it off the counter, but stopped when he felt Phineas watching him.

"Dad, do you know where Ennio Morricone's leash is?"

"His what?"

"His leash, it's the thing you attach to a dog when you want to walk outside with him."

He had sudden, vague recollections of Loni shouting at him to walk the dog. "Ah, I think your mother keeps it near the front door."

"Thanks," Phineas poked his hand into a box in a cabinet and pulled an object out from it.

"I haven't seen that hat in years," Desmond said. "It looks brand new."

"Yeah, it does." The hat was a little league baseball cap from the early 1980s. The face was white, the word REDSKINS was printed across it. The back was dark blue mesh with a plastic clasp across the middle bottom. The brim was flat and broad. Altogether, the cap was enormous and Phineas brought it up to his head and tried it on over his sunglasses. It stretched out above his face like the roof of a deck. Phineas manipulated the polyester into an appropriate shape, the mesh squeaked against his hair.

"How did we ever fit into these things?" He asked.

Desmond looked around, "What?"

"How did we ever fit into these things, I asked."

"Oh, you didn't. None of you ever did. You were never meant to. In fact, that was one of the best things about little league, watching you guys all dressed up and looking ridiculous. We all got a kick out of it, drinking beer, watching you guys trip over your stockings. Lots of fun."

"Get the hell out of here."

"Have you ever seen a good little league picture?"

Phineas closed his eyes as he searched his mind. The white baseball pants always three inches too long or short and baggy or tight, the shirt with his misspelled name and scratchy rayon-polyester blend and stockings so long that they could have doubled as garter belts for a transvestite basketball player. He opened his eyes and his mouth hung open.

"Let me answer that for you, no," Desmond said. "Come to think of it, what about the boy scouts—I mean, shorts *and* a kerchief? We wanted you to look like a band of miniature Aunt Jemimas. Jesus, do you remember how we dressed you for school?"

"Why?" Phineas pulled the hat closer to his sunglasses. It blocked out enough light that he could see without holding his hands over them.

"Because *we* did. We did, so you did, and when—sorry, *if*, you have kids, they will. It's a tradition that will never end, I hope."

"Well, thank you." Phineas said and backed out of the room.

"You're welcome. You'll thank me one day," Desmond said. He scooped up the jelly with his finger and plucked it into his mouth with joy and stepped through the bathroom into his office.

Phineas found the leash and lay on the ground near Ennio Morricone, who watched Phineas with one eye as he tore apart the remainder of the plastic fork.

"Ennio Morricone, you dirty bastard." He slid closer and reached forward with a bandaged hand. Ennio Morricone stopped eating and stared at it. Phineas pet Ennio Morricone and attached the clasp on the leash into the loop on his collar. Confusion overtook Ennio Morricone.

"Come on buddy, come here. Tch tch tch tch tch," he clicked his tongue against the roof of his mouth and Ennio Morricone stood, as though an inherited evolutionary trait forced him to comply. He followed Phineas to the side door with hesitation on the threshold. In the driveway, the rain spattered about Phineas while he opened a golf umbrella and called to Ennio Morricone. "Tch tch tch tch tch."

Ennio Morricone stepped under the umbrella with Phineas and through the puddles and out onto the sidewalk. They walked through the driving rain. After his initial agoraphobic anxiety Ennio Morricone starting barking at cars and people. They walked to the store where Phineas peered through the window for another pair of sunglasses. The cashier from before shot him a dirty look and they ran away. They walked past The Blue Duck and Ennio Morricone chased a beetle in the doorway. He lost him.

Ennio Morricone had spent the first few minutes behind Phineas, who stepped into puddles and cursed into his giant hat. By the time

Phineas had reached The Blue Duck, Ennio Morricone was walking alongside him, stopping to examine everything: flowers, cars, trees, bushes, grass, sticks, plastic bicycles that were far too large to be eaten. He sniffed and urinated on everything he could, in the end audibly pushing with his breath, willing the urine out.

Phineas imbibed the music of the day. Cars passing and horns honking, people chatting outside and a man singing along to a Stevie Wonder tune while waiting for the light to change. He could hear everything. Phineas listened to himself; the sounds of the day took to the background as he concentrated on his breathing. From deep within came the double pounding of a piano, as if to say "Ta Da!" at the end of a magnificent orchestral crescendo. Before his concentration was lost to two men shouting at each other on the street, he heard the quiet voice inside say to his well-dressed audience, "Thank you and good night, it's been a pleasure playing for you, thanks for coming out for our last show." Then, just before Phineas came back to the world, barely audible as the voice slipped away forever, "Don't forget to tip your waitress." And that was the last he ever heard of the conductor and his visceral audience. He laughed.

On the path to the canal, Ennio Morricone pulled Phineas through the trees and inspected everything along the way. He barked at the birds and joggers and when they reached the canal he stared at it with fascination. The water was high; the river was spilling over the levee into it. The mules stood in the barn which had been covered with large sections of plastic tarp. Phineas waved and Miles grumbled.

Ennio Morricone's nose was busy on the ground when he jerked his head up and his entire body grew stiff.

"What is it, E.M?" Phineas asked. "Jesus, I feel like Timmy." He looked back at the dog, "You don't get that joke, do you Lassie?"

Ennio Morricone growled and pulled Phineas toward the patch of woods. Phineas slipped along with him as Ennio Morricone sniffed and stuck his snout in the base of an oak tree. The dog fought and barked until Phineas had yanked him out of the woods and dragged him back into the town center.

Judy Garland spread out on the inside of the tree, three feet from the ground. She had been stalking Phineas when the dog stuck his snout in the tree. She had just escaped up the bark until the dog couldn't reach her. She rotated and viewed the aperture at the base of the tree, a puddle served as a moat for the tree and the gray day shone in the water. She crept toward the hole, stopped and waited for dark.

The elated dog led Phineas through the strengthening rain and around houses and through yards, soaking his feet and splashing his pants with mud. The dog pulled him through a playground and a basketball court. People watched from their homes at the sunglassed, hat-wearing weirdo who darted through their yards with a golf umbrella and a dominant Scottish terrier. Twice, the dog ran him into things. The first time it was a trashcan that had been uprooted by the waters near the Jackson's house, which Phineas tripped over and landed on his elbows. The second time Ennio Morricone ran past a telephone pole and quick-stepped to the right after passing it, causing Phineas to crash brim-first into the pole, flattening his protective sanctuary.

Phineas let the dog run and listened to the rain and the few cars as they drove by, spraying great waves of brown water onto the sidewalks. He squinted through his sunglasses and kept his hat low. Ennio Morricone tugged him along and he felt as if he were the man with the bass on his line, fighting with joy against an almost unseen foe. The umbrella couldn't protect his legs and feet and he was soaked from the knees down.

They approached the house and Clay stepped out on the porch with Ben. They watched as Ennio Morricone ran through the yard with Phineas in tow.

"Morricone!" Clay yelled.

The dog stopped and looked at them. Then he led Phineas to the porch.

"What the fuck you doing?" Clay asked.

"What, I needed to get out of the house. I was going batty," Phineas said.

"Gotta go, guys. See you later." Ben flipped his collar up around his neck and stepped into the rain and down the street toward the canal.

"I hear you can fuckin' hear now," Clay said.

"Yeah, I guess it happened last night after you beat my ass." Phineas dropped the umbrella upside-down near the door and sat on the small couch with a sigh.

"You think I didn't have good reason to do that?"

"That's not what I'm saying." The rain got stronger and louder, as if someone had turned up the volume on a relaxation CD of a rain storm.

"What the fuck were you thinking?" Clay sat on a wicker chair, the remains of Desmond's pizza picnic with William and Steve still present. He raised his voice to be heard over the rain.

"I really don't know, Clay."

"Twenty hours ago, you had a gun in your mouth and you're gonna fuckin' say you don't know why?"

"I guess so."

"That's fuckin' great." He slapped his knees and looked around the porch as if searching for agreement. "Great." He could see through the sunglasses that Phineas' eyes were closed.

"Clay, I can't explain it to you."

"Explain what?"

"I've been afraid for a long time. Afraid to take a chance." He opened his eyes halfway. "Afraid of everything."

"So, what does that mean?"

"It means that this day, today, right now, is the first time in about fifteen years that I don't feel afraid of something."

Clay started to stand. "You ever fuckin' do-"

Phineas grabbed him by the thigh and sat him back in his seat. "Clayton. Enough."

"Yeah, fine." Clay wanted to storm off, annoyed that Phineas had snubbed his final attempt to vent. But he knew Phineas was right, it was enough. He settled back into his chair and they watched the storm in silence for a few minutes. "Don't fuckin' ever call me Clayton again, got it?"

"Yeah, I got it."

The rain was so thick that they couldn't see the houses on the other side of the street. The asphalt wasn't visible beneath the streams of water and cars pulled over and waited along the side of the road. Steam rose from their hoods and their windshield wipers squeaked in chorus.

It was unusually dark for 12:30 p.m., and Phineas and Clay watched from the porch, stunned by the Biblical quantity of rain that fell from the sky. Ennio Morricone lounged at their feet, exhausted by his morning and his first workout, licking the mud off of his paws. More mud was caked behind his ears and under his snout.

In the upstairs study, Desmond sat at his computer having just placed $100 on the upcoming game between the Miami Dolphins and the Philadelphia Eagles. He took the Eagles by six for $50 and took the over at 44 points for another $50. A cigarette stuck out from the middle of his giant grin as he hit the keys and listened to the news on the television behind him. All of his late morning and afternoon patients had cancelled due to the rain, leaving him the rest of the day to play solitaire, check scores and make bets. Desmond's eyes shone behind the loupes, the flicker of the computer screen reflected in them. He smiled. The rain pounded the house and leaked in through the window, water logging books and drenching papers that were scattered around the floor.

21

As Brett McManus tied his laces at Miami's Pro Player Stadium he felt electricity in the air. It was unique electricity different from the usual intense feelings before a big game. It was something he couldn't understand, but he knew that this night was oddly magical and that extraordinary circumstances would soon be taking place. He scratched at his ten-day beard and tucked his helmet under his arm, and then he ran out on the field to the shouts and cheers of 75,783 fans all the while unknowingly and telepathically thinking of a fat man, a couple mules and a Mexican red-knee tarantula.

Roughly 1,043 miles to the north, in Lansford, Clay and Phineas were sitting on the porch watching Lansford get a pounding from Mother Nature. Ennio Morricone dozed and then slept at their feet. He pawed at the air in front of him as memories of the physically demanding day attacked his dreams of tasty books and luscious dolls. Desmond sat at his computer smoking and typing every conceivable word from the term coitus interruptus: tore, tour, tours, trip, trips, step, steps, rupture, ruptures, topic, topics, etc…

The two mules whined into the downfall. Ben backed the truck up to the trailer used to transport the mules and stepped out to latch them together. The trailer was an old milk wagon that he and Charlie had rebuilt by reinforcing the wood with white oak. The roof of the trailer was an extended bikini top from a 1978 CJ-5. It just barely covered the mules and was only used in cases of short transport and emergencies. This was an emergency. He hooked the latch to the tow-hook and locked them into place. The rain beat against him relentlessly so that even the mules watched with worry from behind the tarp. Ben put the truck into second gear and pulled past the mule barn and angled it so the mules would have to spend a minimal amount of time in the downpour. The woods were totally dark and the running path around him was becoming a mudslide into the canal.

Ben stepped out of the truck and dropped the tailgate of the trailer to the ground. He held onto the gate to the barn and lifted the tarp to the roof. Waterfalls of rainwater abseiled from the bill of his Phillies cap.

"Hello, my friends," Ben smiled at them, "I'm here to get you out of here."

The mules snorted as if to say, "Well, that's all well and good, Mr. Wagner, but who's going to get you out of here?"

Ben pulled the leads and harnesses out of the equipment shed and stood under the roof while he organized the harnesses. He threw one over his shoulder, the other one he held in his hand. He opened the latch to the barn, swung the door out and stepped inside. He attached the harness to Sonny, patting her thick coat and the dense muscles in her neck as he pulled the harness tight and snug against the skin.

Miles waited. The dark sky lit up with lightening and resounded with tooth-shattering crashes of thunder. His leg stamped into the soggy ground and he chortled as Ben led Sonny out of the barn and situated her in the trailer. He then led Miles to the gate and was easing him in when his cell phone rang. He picked it up, hoping that it was Charlie. They would put the mules in his garage for the night.

"Hello," Ben said into the phone.

"Hey Ben," Clay said into the other line, "You doing okay over there?"

As Ben looked around him at the angry Neshaminy Creek, the ground from around his feet disappeared and slid with great speed into the canal, bringing with it Ben, Sonny, and the back part of the trailer, which had snapped in half.

Clay heard a large snapping sound. Then he heard nothing.

The front part of the trailer remained attached to the truck on the path. Sonny had flipped into the canal, her immense weight bringing her to the bottom immediately. The back part of the trailer hit her in the head with a crack that Ben could hear over the horrendous storm. And then the trailer landed on Ben's leg.

The trailer pinned him against the slope that had been created by the mudslide. Its weight pushed his hips and legs down into the mud. Searing pain travelled through his left leg and he watched his favorite hat swim down the canal. Miles reared and bolted toward the canal. He peeked down the slope at Ben and shuffled back as the ground dissipated beneath him. He stormed back to the relative safety of the barn area and stamped his feet as he tried to figure a way down to Ben and Sonny.

Sonny stood in the canal, agitated and she looked around, confused. Ben pulled at a thick root that jutted out over his head to keep anymore of his body from going under the bitter cold water. Blood was staining the jeans covering his thigh. He felt the rocks and stones that had been hidden for hundreds of years prodding his back and buttocks. Sonny looked at him and at the trailer holding him down and nodded.

She took a hesitant step in the rushing waters and Ben could see that she was not fully coherent. Her head hung down and she shook it back and forth above the surface of the water.

"Sonny, hey baby, come over here!" It was lost in the storm. Sonny took a step and stopped, her legs sinking in the water and into the mud. Ben tried to pull himself out from under the wagon, but his left leg was completely pinned and, he was certain, broken. Badly. Miles bolted to the bridge and then back past Ben and Sonny. He tried to find a way down the bank. The water carried lawn ornaments, patio chairs, tricycles, pizza boxes, trashcans lids, a plastic flamingo and a half-load of plywood that Charlie had forgotten to put away before his trip. Ben laughed and then frowned.

"Come here, baby!" Ben couldn't budge. Sonny was snorting against the surface of the water. Though her legs were planted, they were shaking in the cold water. Ben's temperature was dropping and his fingertips were turning blue. The pain in his leg was gone, which he knew wasn't a good thing. Again, he shouted and yelled to get Sonny's attention. He screamed words and songs and barked high pitched sounds and whistles that were deafening him. Her head remained down and her nose was coming close to the water. His songs and words weren't enough to get her misplaced attention.

"Sonny! Baby!" Ben called to her, crying through his own fear. His leg split and bleeding, the creek draining his energy and life. "I'm here, I'll do anything you want, just look at me!"

Miles had backed himself away from the ledge of the slope due to the crumbling rocks and dirt that threatened to bring him down into the creek. He thumped up the path to where Ben was and watched in desperation at Sonny sinking into the mud and water. He looked at the car. An onlooker might have thought he was trying to remember how to drive stick.

The day, at 2:00 p.m. had become so apocalyptically dark that anyone looking from their house would not have seen Ben or the torn-in-half trailer. They wouldn't have seen the open barn or the giant mule sinking in the middle of the canal. The dark sky was so dense that nobody would have noticed that a monstrous, muscular mule was sprinting back and forth along the path. It was so dark that when Clay and Phineas and Ennio Morricone ran across the old stone bridge, Ben almost couldn't make out the figures.

Clay peered over the side of the bridge at the disappearing gap between water and bridge. "Fuck."

"Jesus Christ, Clay, what's going on?" Phineas was stunned. He reached the other side and Miles stopped in his tracks as the boys fell backward to avoid getting stomped. Even the neo-rambunctious Ennio Morricone scattered in the tremendous presence of Miles. The gargantuan mule relinquished his ground and allowed them to walk to Ben, half submerged and under the trailer. Clay poked his face over the ledge and saw Ben, who looked back at him.

"Hi Clay, how are you?"

"You fuckin' kidding me?"

"I'm in a bit of a pinch here; could you guys help me out?" Ben dropped his freezing hands from the root and they splashed in the water.

Phineas' round face poked in from behind Clay, "Hi Ben, need some help?"

"That would be swell." He wore a pleasant expression and then it changed. "My leg's broken pretty badly," he motioned toward the trailer with his chin.

Clay and Phineas slid down the embankment until they were standing next to Ben, water to their thighs. Clay squatted into the water and felt for the bottom ridge of the dense trailer. It was deep in the mud and pinching Ben's leg to the bottom.

"Phin, get on this side," Clay said. Phineas leapt over Ben and squatted next to the trailer opposite Clay, he also felt the wood for the edge. Clay and Phineas planted their legs into the side of the embankment, which was under water, and gripped the bottom of the trailer. They pushed off with their legs as they tried to lift it off of Ben. The trailer rose, but when a wave of brown water hit them, they dropped it and fell into the water.

"Ah, God!" Ben bit his fist.

"Shit!" Clay had half fallen in the canal and half on the wagon. Phineas had dropped backward into the water and his sunglasses slipped away with the current.

"Crap," he said to himself.

Phineas opened his eyes in the darkness and could perfectly observe the terrible scene. Ennio Morricone had retreated to the stone bridge to avoid Miles and was watching the men struggle in the water. Clay nodded at Phineas, "One, two, three, Go!" They pushed, using their legs again and pressing in a great upward heave. The trailer lifted out of the water and Ennio Morricone barked at them in the rain. Their veins strained against their necks, their teeth rode against each other and threatened to turn to powder. The strain reopened the bite on Phineas' hand and felt like daggers pumping into his bruised rib cage. He couldn't breathe.

With effort, the trailer lifted away from Ben and toward the sky. When they had the trailer vertical, Ben pulled himself out from under it, using his elbows, his leg dragging uselessly. Clay and Phineas flipped it over into the canal and it sunk beneath the brown waters. Phineas crept to Ben and Clay grabbed him by the shoulder.

"Now, that is a broken leg," Ben pointed.

"Phineas looked down at his leg and took hold of Ben hips. "Okay, big boy, we've got to get you out of here."

Clay scampered up the slope and reached down with both hands to clasp Ben. Phineas tried to maneuver him up the slope, but even with Ben's help, he wasn't moving anywhere. Phineas called to Clay, who was in the equipment shed searching for something that could help them. He found tools and a few saddles, but no rope. In the barn he noticed the lead folded over the barn door. He grabbed it and brought it to the truck with him.

Clay pulled the truck forward and into the trees where he disconnected the front-half of the trailer and pulled it to one side. He then pulled the truck back and attached the loop of the lead to the hitch and sent the other side over the embankment to Phineas and Ben. Phineas hugged Ben to his chest and slipped the lead around his back and across his chest, under his arms. He fumbled with a knot until Ben took the lead from him and finished it. Rain pounded all three of them.

"We'll have a class on knot tying when we get through this," Ben said.

"You got it, pal." Phineas motioned to Clay who got back in the truck. "Ben," Phineas said, "this is gonna hurt, but it's got to happen."

Clay slipped it into first and released the clutch; Phineas guided Ben up the slope by his arms and then hips. Phineas quailed at the sight of his thigh bone, jutting out of his jeans like a downed tree in a shallow lake. The tip of the broken bone was black and a leaf had wrapped itself around its length.

"You were right," Ben called over the storm, "this hurts an awful lot."

"Oh, shit," Phineas turned away.

"That doesn't look good, does it?" Ben backed across the ledge and onto land again. Clay leaned out of the window and watched Ben come back onto land, he pulled the truck up to the woods and got out, kicking the emergency break into place. He stood above Ben and saw his leg.

"Jesus Christ," he said. "I'm gonna call 911, is the phone in your cabin working?"

"I hope so."

Clay went to the cabin and dialed the phone. Phineas poked his head above the ledge and called to Ben.

"Ben, who's in the river?"

"It's Sonny!"

"Why won't she get out of the water?"

"I think she has a concussion. The trailer hit her in the head."

"Is there anything we can do?"

"Just try to get her attention and get her out of there!" He was barely audible above the wind and the rain. Everything was so dark that nobody else in the world existed. They were completely isolated.

Phineas stepped back down the slope and into the water again. His legs were shivering and his steps were clumsy. He faced the animal. "Hey there, Sonny? Remember me?"

The mule made no move, steam was coming from her hanging snout as she panted. "Hey Sonny, look at me! I've got something you want! You can eat my shoe if you want!"

Sonny shook her head and Phineas kept calling to her. The sky, dark as night, was but an early morning fog for Phineas' troubled vision. "Sonny, look at me! I've got rhythm, I've got something, blah blah blah blah, who can ask for anything more!"

Clay had returned to Ben and placed his fingers on the leg. "How does the leg feel, Ben?"

"I can't feel it and I'm cold."

"I called 911 and they said they'd be here ASAP but they got a ton of shit going on right now."

"What'd they tell you to do?"

"The fuckin' line cut out. But they know where we are and I caught something about keeping you warm and not moving the leg at all. I found this." He threw the tarp over Ben, who fitted it into place under his neck. Clay lifted it a little and handed him a wool blanket he had found in the cabin. "Try to keep warm, they'll be here soon. The freezing river had occluded the flow of blood, but in the warmer air it had begun again. Clay stripped off his shirt and pressed it against the gaping wound, touching the bone as a wave of nausea hit him. "Hold this on there tight." Clay looked around him as he stood up, "What the fuck is Phineas doing?"

He couldn't see him in the dark and rain.

Phineas had moved in front of Sonny and was patting her head with downward strokes ending at her nose. Her breathing was labored. The red, blinking emergency light of a river barge moved down the river and Phineas waved, realizing seconds later that there was no way that they could see him in the dark.

"Phineas!" Clay called to him.

"Get a Snickers bar from the cabin!" Phineas called back.

"What?"

"A Snickers bar!" Phineas turned around to face Clay.

"Ben, did he tell me to get a Snickers bar?"

"There're some in the cabinet above the sink."

Clay returned a moment later. "Phineas! Here, catch!" He tossed the candy bar through the dying rain. Phineas dropped it and dove into the water to find it again, snagging it before it disappeared in the bed.

"Okay, Sonny, here you go. I've got a nice treat for you here. How about a Snickers bar!" He held the mule's ear as he yelled into it. Her head lifted. "Aha! Yeah, that's right you sonnovabitch, you! You want this now don't you!" Phineas stepped away from Sonny and toward the bank without turning his head. His outstretched hand waving the Snickers bar in the mule's face. Another step backwards and Sonny blinked and moved her head toward the candy bar, which Phineas pulled just out of reach. She struggled with her front legs, seeming almost confused as to why she was suddenly in this predicament. The river had risen such that half of the mule was under water and Phineas was up to his shoulders in water. The moving water forced Phineas to plant his feet and hold on to a root on the bank to prevent himself from being carried away.

"Here you go, come and get it!" Phineas stepped again and dangled the Snickers in front of her, three feet away. Sonny pulled a leg out of the mud and the sound of the broken suction farted across the river, breaking the storm. She stepped out with her other front leg and staggered toward Phineas and her prize. She eyed Ben, Clay and Miles on the path and the small man in front of her with the loud voice and squinty eyes.

"Come on, here it is, all yours!" Phineas backed up to the slope, grabbed hold of a root with his left hand and held the Snickers with his right. Sonny walked toward him, opening and closing her mouth, already tasting her snack.

"Hand it up." Clay reached down for the Snickers.

"Yeah, good," Phineas said, handing the soggy candy over. He was perched on the side of the bank as if levitating.

Sonny stomped up the slope with such speed that Phineas had to duck to the left and cover his head. "Jesus Christ, I need health insurance."

Ben laughed from his position on the ground, covered with plastic and wool and Clay dropped the Snickers to the ground in an attempt to get out of the way.

The rain slowed further, and Clay reached out a hand to help Phineas up. Phineas took it and looked back into the canal to survey of the scene. Ennio Morricone stood on the stone bridge and barked, giddy with over-excitement, the water rushed muddily along with debris scattered along the surface. A piece of plywood was dancing in circles with the eddying current against the front of the bridge. A salad plate sized blur of dark rested in the middle, its legs spread.

"What the—" Phineas said, holding onto Clay's wrist.

"What? What is it?" Clay asked.

"Ben, I found Judy Garland!"

"Really?"

"Well, unless there's another tarantula in this canal, then yes, really."

Clay blinked. "Are you telling me there is a tarantula in that river?"

"Yes, her name is Judy Garland."

"Well then," Clay said. He had no idea how to respond to this information. "Well then."

"Oh, fuck me." Phineas crawled out of the canal and ran to the bridge.

"Where the—" Clay was stunned.

Judy Garland's legs were spread wide, all eight of her eyes peeled to the rampaging waters around her. In her petrified state, she could neither move nor react; she stayed low and hoped for the best. When Phineas appeared above her, staring down at her, she could have cried with joy. Her ploy had worked and now her hero had come to her rescue.

Phineas gripped the plywood between two fingers and almost fainted when the large, hairy spider moved a leg in his direction. But he kept his hold and pulled the plywood toward him onto the bridge. The plywood scraped against the stones and Phineas squatted over it, inching it to safety. He pulled the makeshift surfboard onto the bridge in one shaky, yet determined final heave. When he did so, primordial instinct took precedence over love and Judy Garland jigged forward and bit Phineas in the soft flesh between his forefinger and thumb.

Phineas clasped his hand, which had now been attacked by two surnamed animals in less than forty-eight hours, and stumbled forward into the water. He went down to the bottom and gulped in a lungful of silty canal water.

After Ennio Morricone watched Phineas fall into the water he dropped his head, with this move complaining that it had been such a lovely day and was now ruined. He then sighed, knowing exactly what had to happen, watched the idiot bob to the surface of the water and looked around as if to find an audience for his thoughts. He then barked twice and took off through the woods toward the Troy house.

Phineas kicked so hard that his shoes were lost in the current and his socks followed suit. He felt frozen and was seeing double. His breathing became labored at the cold water ensnaring his chest. He neared the bank and watched Clay and Ben watching him, Clay from the ledge and Ben arching his neck up as far as he could manage.

"Fine, fine," Phineas tried to say, but couldn't. He then laughed sound-lessly, commenting to himself that he had always known that a spider would bring about the end of him. He caught one more view of Judy Garland on the bridge and slipped beneath the brown waters without another sound.

22

Before Ennio Morricone reached the house, the water had puddled in Desmond's study and was creeping toward his massive concoction of plugs, outlets and modem wires. The mobile pool gathered strength in the final minutes of the storm and made a strong push along the wall to the center of Desmond's electronic universe. When the circuits blew and sparked in Desmond's face he could do nothing but let the cigarette drop from his mouth. He went downstairs to microwave a hot dog and consider his position.

When he heard the scratching and barking at the door he was walking from the kitchen back upstairs with an uncooked hot dog tucked neatly inside a bun. The electricity had been knocked out in the entire house and Desmond hadn't noticed that the microwave timer hadn't dinged. The aggravating sounds didn't subside so he peeped outside and was surprised to see Ennio Morricone on the porch with a leash around his neck.

"Heya, how'dya getta outta, paisano?" he asked, opening the door for him. Ennio Morricone planted his paws to the ground and stood fast. He continued his barking and Desmond stepped out the door and peered up and down his driveway. Ennio Morricone ran down the driveway, barking, and stopped halfway. After a deep sigh, Desmond wobbled toward the dog in the middle of the driveway amid a succession of deep barks. A neighbor hidden behind lace curtains looked through the window to see what the racket was about. Desmond waved at her with his hot-dogged hand and winked. A gesture she would have appreciated, had she been able to see his eyes behind the loupes. The sky was still dark and Desmond picked up the looped end of the leash and turned to bring Ennio Morricone back into the house, the dog resisted and Desmond was jerked back around and almost fumbled his snack. He grunted under his breath.

"You listen to me, dog, get over here."

Ennio Morricone pulled and growled and darted down the driveway with Desmond in tow, trying to nibble his hot dog with each step down the soaked gravel and smile at his observing neighbors.

"What, Timmy trapped in a well or something?" he laughed through a chunk of cold hot dog, bread and mustard. He clenched his jaw, "Timmy better be trapped in a God damn well, you little mutt."

Phineas floated above the bed of the canal and beneath the surface of the water. He floated in a dark brown void and slipped deeper and quieter along the water. His arms were outstretched and his naked feet glided with the water. His eyes were closed and his mouth was open. He felt nothing. There was nothing. Everything was black and calm; a deep warm buzz crawled over his form as he drifted away from everything. He was, for this one perfect moment in time, completely senseless.

There was a total sense of nothing, a complete sense of freedom and calm. It was so quiet that it was deafening, so black that it was bright. His fingers nearly grazed the bed of the three-hundred-year old canal. He floated above arrow heads, stones, skulls, rocks, an eighty-year-old tug boat, bones and fossils. He disappeared within the water; conscious of nothing. He became a part of the canal; a part of history.

When Phineas opened his eyes he was warm and staring at a painting on a wall. The painting was of two old men, both fat and wearing belts, drinking beer out of dark steins. They had beards with no mustaches and smiled through their rosy cheeks. The background was earthy and reminiscent of a medieval pub, a plate of meat sat in front of one of the men. Phineas understood the painting.

His attention was taken from the painting by the slow influx of conversation. He hadn't heard it before; it had come from nowhere. From a cicada-like buzz it grew tighter until it was crisp. He looked around him at the kitchen table in his grandmother's house. People were eating, dead relatives were chatting about politics from fifty years before and there were several empty bottles on the table.

Phineas' plate was empty and there was no wine glass before him. His uncles and aunts laughed and talked, his grandfather wore a suit and smoked a cigarette in the corner, eyes cool. He winked at Phineas. The familiar paisley wallpaper and the red bells and green mistletoe on the table linen were vibrant. Phineas sat back into absolute content and relaxed his tongue in his mouth.

The kitchen smelled indescribably good; a feast with meat and chicken and fresh-baked bread. Ricotta cheese was drenched in home-made sauce. He smelled the ravioli and the slow-cooked meatballs and his mouth watered. An assortment of cakes sat in the corner waiting for the brave.

"How you doing?" a voice asked from behind him.

"Oh, I'm great, how are you?" He turned around.

"Well, what do you think?" She was probably thirty five years old, with sharp brown eyes and dark hair that spilled out of barrettes and curled around her eyes and cheeks. She smiled at him again, "You're not fooling me. You're doing lousy."

"You're dead"

She nodded. "So are you."

"Well that's just great," he said. "I guess it's been that kind of week."

"How's that?"

"I don't know..."

"Really?"

Phineas rested his elbow on the table, his face poised in thought. "Well, about a week ago, you died. Then, just to make things more inter-esting I lost all my senses. That was fun. Then I tried to kill myself." He pulled his elbow off the table and smiled.

"Yeah," she sighed.

He nodded a few times.

"Why'd you do that?"

"I'm a fuck up."

"Why do you say that?"

"I haven't done anything with my life."

"You haven't even started your life yet."

"Yeah, but I'm stuck in the mud."

"Do you think you can get out?"

"How?" He felt so tired.

"That's not for me to answer, but I think you know."

"Yeah," and he did.

"You staying?"

"No," Phineas said looking at the empty plate in front of him. "I think I've got to go."

"Yes, you do. We'll see each other soon enough," She kissed him on the forehead and followed it with a light slap on the cheek.

Phineas stood with the weight of a dozen moons on his back and moved toward the door. He waved his goodbyes and so did the rest of the relatives at the table.

"So long," his grandmother said.

Phineas waved again, unable to open his mouth and barely able to keep his eyes open. He stepped out the door and into nothing in particular. They all watched him go.

Clay hadn't seen Miles gallop down the path; he only heard him and felt a breeze as the distressed mule passed behind him. The mule leapt down the slope into the water and stepped around the brown mess. He galloped a little further down the canal and Clay matched his movement along the path. Miles poked his nose under the debris and the waves and stepped to his right with two legs like telephone poles. Debris passed through the mule's legs and around his frame.

When something hit Miles with enough speed to make him buckle, Clay jumped into the water and struggled toward him. As Clay stepped through the waves he saw a hand and the back pocket of Phineas' pants. He saw a pale face and brown hair gathering around his ear. When he reached the mule, he turned his brother to him and stared into his face.

"Oh no." He pulled him to the bank by his shirt. Clay grunted with each step and Ben raised himself on his elbows to watch what was happening. When Clay reached the bank he dipped his shoulder and pulled Phineas' arm across his back. He then hoisted Phineas over the ledge and onto the bank. He climbed up behind him.

About a minute after Phineas Troy died, the sun came out. It spread its light long against the sky and painted the clouds red and orange. The dark shadows recessed and beams of light spotted the town.

"Clay," Ben called, "is he breathing?" Ben's breathing had slowed and the words came out in gasps.

"No!" Clay yelled back, trying to find a pulse on his brother's wrist. "Where the fuck is that ambulance?" Clay caressed the wrinkles on Phineas' face and tried to push down on his chest.

They heard Ennio Morricone before they saw him. They saw Desmond and then heard him. Desmond walked onto the scene confused, with wet shoes and a mouth full of hot dog.

He stood on the stony bridge. "What the heck is going on here?"

"Phineas isn't breathing, Dad!" Clay was hunched over the body on the bank.

"What happened?"

"There's no time to ask stupid fucking questions!" Clay screamed at him.

Desmond walked across the bridge and past a hulking mule, which he didn't notice. He passed the barn and the cabin and Ben. He kicked Ennio Morricone once by accident as he neared them on the bank of the canal. Desmond walked with determination, his hands sliding along his pant legs as if he were a marine corporal.

"He's not breathing." Clay was squatting above Phineas.

"Move," Desmond commanded.

"What?" Clay asked.

"Move now, boy!"

Clay stepped aside. He said nothing more. Desmond sat next to Phineas and felt his wrist and then the carotid artery in the neck; there was nothing. He leaned over his mouth and nose and looked at his chest; there was no wind or movement.

Desmond folded his hands over one another and looking up at Clay, said, "Starting CPR."

"Well," Clay said, "get started, motherfucker."

He pressed down on Phineas' chest. He pumped several times and then held Phineas' nose and blew into his mouth. Clay watched Phineas' chest rise and fall with each breath. Desmond went back to Phineas' chest and pumped again, working his fat hands over his son's chest with rhythmic power. He chanted along with his mantra, imagining Cindy's rhythmic gum-chewing. Desmond's face turned red and his chin disappeared into the pillows of fat that surrounded it. His sweat dripped on Phineas' face and Clay ran to try the phone again, stopping at the door when he heard hacking. An ambulance pulled out of the woods and two EMTs jogged across the bridge.

Phineas coughed and choked, and so did Desmond who sat back and wiped his mouth with the back of his sleeve. They both vomited. Phineas took a deep, painful breath that filled his lungs and opened his eyes wider than they had been opened before. Ennio Morricone watched Judy Garland creep along the outer wall of the cabin. She'd had enough excitement and had decided to go home.

"Did I just eat a hotdog?" Phineas asked, after he had caught his breath. The EMTs worked on Ben and Clay stood frozen in place. Desmond stood to watch.

Phineas giggled, "Sure, go to the guy with the broken leg. I just died and had a conversation with my dead grandmother." His smile evaporated.

Desmond approached the EMTs, one of whom was pulling the tarp over Ben's head. Through the adrenalin and confusion of the most spectacular day of his entire life, Phineas heard the EMT whisper to Desmond. "I'm sorry, he just lost too much blood." And then Phineas passed out.

23

January 1. Phineas sat in the lounge and watched the last few months move past him like a parade. Amy and Gary had come from Pittsburgh for Ben's funeral, which had been on a Thursday. The mules, driven by Charlie, carried his broken body down the canal. Lansfordians and Pittsburghers alike had watched from the banks in stunned misery.

The weather had been beautiful but nature raged. Fish leapt out of the canal causing massive slaps to crack across the valley. Bees and wasps roared dangerously close to viewers and robins crapped on Jack Schorpp's shoe.

For Loni, Desmond, Phineas and Clay it had been two funerals in under two weeks. This one was more difficult than the first. Amy and Gary were devastated, for both Ben and Phineas. They stayed for three days; The Blue Duck made $2,400.

After Amy and Gary had returned to Pittsburgh, Phineas and Clay sat at The Blue Duck for an entire night without saying a word. Betty put drinks down in front of them and the regulars spoke in hushed voices. Football played on the television. The next day, Clay got in his truck and drove to Pittsburgh. He had taken Ben's death harder than anyone. Ben had been his best friend since Phineas had left for college and was the only part of Lansford life that had given him any enjoyment. He went to Pittsburgh to take a short vacation and to help Gary with his latest house renovation. After a week, though, he returned to Lansford, quit his job and moved himself and Frederick to Pittsburgh.

By that point Phineas had decided that something needed to change. So as Clay headed west on the Pennsylvania Turnpike, Phineas headed east. Around the same time, Ennio Morricone decided that the outdoors suited him and nagged Desmond until, exasperated, the dentist in the loupes stepped from the house with leash in hand. Loni returned home and settled back into her daily routine, which was aided by a newly acquired Xanax prescription. She cleaned the house, sang a Barry

Manilow tune to the dog and fed him some linguini that was leftover from the day before.

Phineas sat at an absurd angle in his seat sniffing the woman next to him, as had become his habit in the previous months. The young woman was smeared in black make-up and built like a gelatinous casserole. Great stains of sweat spread from her armpits. Phineas drank in her muggy scent with disgusted fascination. People crowded past him.

"…This is flight 2807…Boarding…"

Phineas waited.

The paramedics who'd come to the canal that afternoon demanded that Phineas accompany them to the hospital. He refused, but after they'd cited death as a condition necessary to check up on, they coaxed him into the ambulance. He was unconscious most of the way but aware of Ben's body lying next to him.

"Now calling first class, gold class, and exclusive club travelers…"

The doctors at the hospital were dubious of his fantastic story of disabled senses, especially since all of his senses were then intact. Clay, Desmond and Gary verified his story and the doctors ran every existing hematological and neurological test with negative results. They called it a "spectacular case of psychosomatic symptomatology." Phineas didn't know what it meant, but didn't care. He lay in his single bed, stared at reruns and thought about Ben. He thought about his grandmother and water and tarantulas and death. Being alive amazed him. It was inconceivable. He'd gazed across the hedgerow once; he'd gone across the hedgerow once, and yet, he had somehow survived. He was unable to comprehend how he was alive. Nevertheless, his fear had stayed on the other side.

"Now boarding rows forty through twenty-nine…"

Phineas stood, people passed by him but he didn't really notice. After the hospital and the funeral Phineas moved his things from Pittsburgh and worked with Charlie and the mules for a couple months while he decided on what to do.

"Now welcoming passengers for rows twenty eight to fourteen…"

As he shuffled down the aisle, stale cool air spilling into his ears and sides, thoughts sped through his mind. He thought about Amy, Bert and Ernie and their new roommate, Clay Troy. He pictured Gary at his pizza and diet cola, and Larry working on a post-work cocktail.

In this moment, his mind found Larry's Pub and Grub, the place where it had all started, the customers, the mirror behind the bar holding a thong, a liquor license and a postcard of an elephant and a fat woman, neither of which discernable without squinting.

He thought about the little man inside of him and his body, which had physiologically brought him out behind the tool shed. Clay, who'd beat his ass to save his ass and the loupe-wearing dentist who'd saved the day. And he thought of Ben.

And so, at the end of this whole thing, nothing happened. There was no grand gesture. Phineas' part in the story simply ended. Like any good pub tale his story would be told and retold to a captive audience, the imaginary parlayed with the truth, until it, like all others, ended, and in doing so became the beginning of another story. Phineas left this story for the next, the ambiguity of which was exhilarating.

He arrived at his seat and reviewed his current position. The row was 22, the seat C, the kosher meal, unintentional.

The End